PENGUIN BOOKS
THE LAKE OF DREAMS

Kim Edwards is the author of *The Memory Keeper's Daughter* and a collection of short stories, *The Secrets of a Fire King*. Her honours include the Whiting Award and the Nelson Algren Award, as well as the Kentucky Literary Award and a National Magazine Award. She is Associate Professor of English at the University of Kentucky.

The Lake of Dreams

Kim Edwards

PENGUIN BOOKS

PENGUIN BOOKS

Published by the Penguin Group

Penguin Books Ltd, 80 Strand, London WC2R ORL, England

Penguin Group (USA) Inc., 375 Hudson Street, New York, New York 10014, USA

Penguin Group (Canada), 90 Eglinton Avenue East, Suite 700, Toronto, Ontario, Canada M4P 2Y3
(a division of Pearson Penguin Canada Inc.)

Penguin Ireland, 25 St Stephen's Green, Dublin 2, Ireland (a division of Penguin Books Ltd)

Penguin Group (Australia), 250 Camberwell Road, Camberwell, Victoria 3124, Australia
(a division of Pearson Australia Group Pty Ltd)

Penguin Books India Pvt Ltd, 11 Community Centre,
Panchsheel Park, New Delhi – 110 017, India

Penguin Group (NZ), 67 Apollo Drive, Rosedale, Auckland 0632, New Zealand
(a division of Pearson New Zealand Ltd)

Penguin Books (South Africa) (Pty) Ltd, 24 Sturdee Avenue, Rosebank, Johannesburg 2196, South Africa

Penguin Books Ltd, Registered Offices: 80 Strand, London WC2R ORL, England

www.penguin.com

First published in the USA by Viking Penguin,
a member of Penguin Group (USA) Inc., 2011
First published in Great Britain by Viking 2011
Published in Penguin Books 2011

1

Illustrations by Laura Hartman Maestro
Family tree by Jeffrey L. Ward

Printed in Great Britain by Clays Ltd, St Ives plc

ISBN: 978-0-241-25351-9

www.greenpenguin.co.uk

For my family, especially my parents, John and Shirley

I learned both what is secret and what is manifest,
for Wisdom, the fashioner of all things, taught me.

—The Book of Wisdom, 7:21–22

Distance in a straight line has no mystery.
The mystery is in the sphere.

—Thomas Mann, *Joseph and His Brothers*

The Lake of Dreams

Prologue
1910

ALTHOUGH IT IS NEARLY MIDNIGHT, AN UNUSUAL LIGHT SLIPS through a crack in the wool, brushing her arm like the feathers of a wing. In the next room her parents sleep, and the darkened village is silent, but she has lain awake all these hours and now she climbs out of bed, the floorboards rough against her feet. For weeks people have talked of nothing but the comet, how the earth will pass through clouds of poison vapors in its tail, how the world could end. She is fifteen, and all day she and her brother helped seal the house—windows, doors, even the chimney—with thick black wool, hammers tapping everywhere as their neighbors did the same.

The narrow triangle of strange light touches her here, then there, as she crosses the room. She is wearing her blue dress, almost outgrown, the worn cotton soft against her skin. In this room, a low space over the shop that is hers alone, the wool is only loosely fastened to the window, and when she yanks a corner the cloth falls away, pale comet light swimming all around. She pushes the window open and takes a breath: one, and then another, deeper. Nothing happens. No poison gas, no searing lungs—only the watery spring, the scents of growing things and, distantly, the sea.

And this odd light. The constellations are as familiar as the lines on her own palms, so she does not have to search to find the comet. It soars high, a streaming jewel, circling the years, thrilling and portentous. Distantly a dog barks, and the chickens rustle and complain in their coops. Soft voices rise, mingling, her brother's and another, one she knows; her heart quickens with anger and yearning both. She hesitates. She has not planned this moment—the turning point of her life it will become. Yet it is also no impulse that pulls her onto the window ledge, her bare feet dangling a few yards above the garden. She is dressed, after all. She left the wool loose on purpose. All day she has been dreaming of the comet, its wild and fiery beauty, what it might mean, how her life might change.

The voices rise, and then she leaps.

Chapter 1
2006

MY NAME IS LUCY JARRETT, AND BEFORE I KNEW ABOUT THE girl in the window, before I went home and stumbled on the fragments and began to piece the story back together, I found myself living in a village near the sea in Japan. It had been a spring of little earthquakes, and that night I woke abruptly, jarred from a dream. Footsteps faded in the cobblestone lane and distant trains rumbled; I listened harder until I could make out the surge of the sea. But that was all. Yoshi's hand rested on my hip lightly, as if we were still dancing, which we'd been doing earlier in the evening, music from the radio soft in the dark kitchen, our steps slowing until we stopped altogether and stood kissing in the jasmine air.

I lay back down, curving toward his warmth. In the dream I'd gone back to the lake where I'd grown up. I didn't want to go, but I did. The sky was overcast, the faded green cabin—which I'd seen before, but only in dreams—musty and overhung with trees. Its windows were cracked, opaque with dust and snow. I walked past it to the shore, walked out onto the thick, translucent ice. I walked until I came to them. So many people, living their lives just beneath the surface. I caught them in glimpses, fell to my knees, pressed my palms against the glassy surface— so thick, so clear, so cold. I'd put them here, somehow, I knew that. I'd left them for so long. Their hair stirred in underwater currents, and their eyes, when they met mine, were full of a longing that matched my own.

The window shades were trembling. I tensed, caught between the earthquakes and the dream, but it was just a distant train, fading into the mountains. Every night for a week I'd had this same dream, stirred up by the shifting earth, stirring up the past. It took me back to a night when I was seventeen, wild and restless, sliding off the back of Keegan Fall's motorcycle, apple blossoms as pale as stars above us. I fanned my fingers against his chest before he left, the engine ripping through the night. My father was in the garden when I turned toward the house. Moonlight caught the gray in his short hair; the tip of his cigarette burned, rising, falling. Lilacs and early roses floated in the darkness. *Nice of you to show up,* my father said. *I'm sorry you worried,* I told him. A silence, the scents of lake water and compost and green shoots splitting open the dark earth, and then he said, *Want to go fishing with me, Lucy? How about it? It's been a long time.* His words were wistful, and I remembered getting up before dawn to meet him, struggling to carry the tackle box as we crossed the lawn to the boat. I wanted to go fishing, to accept my father's invitation, but I wanted more to go upstairs to think about Keegan Fall. So I turned away, and in a tone as sharp as broken shells I said, *Dad. Really. I'm hardly little anymore.*

Those were the last words I ever spoke to him. Hours later, waking to sunlight and urgent voices, I ran downstairs and across the dew-struck lawn to the shore, where they had pulled my father from the lake. My mother was kneeling in the shallow water, touching his cheek with her fingertips. His lips and skin were bluish. There were traces of foam in the corner of his mouth, and his eyelids were oddly iridescent. *Like a fish,* I thought, a crazy thought, but at least it silenced the other thoughts, which were worse, and which have never left me: *If I'd gone. If I'd been there. If only I'd said yes.*

Beside me on the tatami Yoshi sighed and stirred, his hand slipping from my hip. Moonlight fell in a rectangle across the floor, and the shades rustled faintly with the distant pounding surf, the breeze. Gradually, almost imperceptibly, the shaking grew stronger. It was subtle at first, as soft as the rumble from the train a moment before. Then my Tibetan singing bowls, arranged on the floor, began to hum all by themselves. My collection of small stones began to fall from the bookshelf, hitting the mats with a sound like rain. Downstairs, something crashed, shattered. I held my breath, as if by being still I could still the world, but the trembling grew stronger, and stronger still. The shelves lurched sharply, heaving several books to the floor. Then, in one fluid convulsion, the walls swayed and the floor seemed to roll, as if some great animal had roused and turned, as if the earth itself were alive, the ground mere skin, and volatile.

Abruptly, it stopped. Everything was strangely quiet. Distantly, water dripped into a pool. Yoshi's breathing was calm and even.

I turned and shook his shoulder. He opened his eyes slowly. These little earthquakes left him unfazed, though that season there had been hundreds of tremors, sometimes several dozen in a day, many so tiny they were noted only by seismic machines; others, like this one, strong enough to wake us.

"Earthquake?" he murmured.

"Yes, a big one. Something broke downstairs."

"Really? Well, it is over now. It's quiet, no? Let's go back to sleep."

He closed his eyes and pulled me close. His breathing quickly grew deep and regular again. Through the half-open window, beyond the roof of the house across the street, I glimpsed the scattered stars. "Yoshi?" I said. When he didn't answer, I slid out of bed and went downstairs.

The aloe plant had fallen from the kitchen windowsill, and its pot had shattered. I put water on to boil and swept up the scattered dirt and glass and broken stems. Probably Japanese housewives were doing the same thing all up and down the street, which made me feel uncomfortable and faintly bitter—clearly, I'd been without a job for far too long. I didn't like being dependent on Yoshi, having no income or meaningful work outside the house. I'm a hydrologist, which is to say that I study the movement of water in the world, on the surface and beneath the earth, and I'd been doing research for multinational companies for nearly half a decade by the time I met Yoshi in Jakarta. We'd fallen in love the way it is possible to fall in love overseas, cut off from everything we'd known, so the country we inhabited was of our own making, really, and subject to our own desires. *This is the only continent that matters,* Yoshi used to say, running his hands along my body. *This is the only world that exists.* For a year, then two years, we were very happy. Then our contracts ended. Before I found work, Yoshi was offered what seemed at first like the engineering job of his dreams. That's when we moved to Japan, which had turned out to be another country altogether.

I poured myself a cup of tea and took it to the front room, sliding open the shutters and the windows. Night air flooded in, fresh and cool. It was still dark, but the neighborhood was already stirring; water splashed and plates clattered, near and far. Across the narrow lane the neighbors spoke softly, back and forth.

The house shook lightly with the surf, then settled. I sat at the low table and sipped my tea, letting my thoughts wander to the coming day and our long-planned trip into the mountains. In Indonesia, that other country, Yoshi and I had talked of marriage and even of children, but in those vague fantasies I'd always had satisfying work, or I'd been content to study Japanese and flower arranging and to take long solitary hikes. I hadn't understood how isolating unemployment would be, or how much time Yoshi would end up devoting to his own work. Lately we'd been out of sorts with each other, arguments flaring up over nothing. I hadn't realized how persistent the past would be, either, catching me in its old gravity the minute I slowed down. After three idle months in Japan I started teaching English just to fill my days with voices other than my own. I took my young charges on walks, pausing by the sea to teach concrete nouns: *stone, water, wave,* yearning for the days when I'd used those same words with ease and fluidity in my routine work. Sometimes I found myself saying wilder things, things I was sure they could not understand. *Dinosaurs drank this water, did you know that? Water moves forever in a circle; someday, little ones, your grandchildren may even drink your tears.*

Now, weeks later, I was beginning to wonder if this would be my life, after all, and not simply a brief interlude in the life I had imagined.

Across the room, tiny lights flickered on my laptop. I got up to check e-mail, the glow from the screen casting my hands and arms in pale blue: Sixteen messages, most of them spam, two from friends in Sri Lanka, three others from former colleagues in Jakarta who'd sent photos from their hike in the jungle. I skimmed these messages quickly, remembering a river trip we'd taken with these friends, the lush foliage along the banks and the hats we'd fashioned from water lilies to block the fierce sun, filled with longing for the life Yoshi and I had left.

Three sequential messages were from home. The first, from my mother, surprised me. We were in touch quite often and I tried to visit once a year, even if briefly, but my mother used the Internet like an earlier generation had used the long-distance telephone: seldom, succinctly, and only for matters of certain importance. Mostly, we talked on the phone or sent slim blue air letters, hers posted to wherever my nomadic life had taken me, mine landing in the mailbox outside the rambling house where I'd grown up, in a village called The Lake of Dreams.

> Lucy, I was in an accident, but it was minor and you are absolutely not to worry. Take any news from Blake with a grain of salt, please. He means well, of course, but he is being overprotective and kind of driving me crazy. I'm nearly sure my wrist is sprained, not broken. The doctor said the x-rays will confirm one way or the other. There's no need at all for you to come home.

I read this message twice, imagining my mother at her solitary kitchen table, somehow injured. Though it wasn't fair—nearly ten years had passed and we had all moved on, at least on the surface—I felt myself drawn back to the summer after my father's death. We'd gone through our days doing the usual things, trying to create a fragile order. We made meals we hardly touched, and passed in the halls without speaking; my mother started sleeping in the spare room downstairs, and began to close the second floor down, room by room. Her grief was at the center of the stillness in the house, and we all moved carefully, so quietly, around it; if I allowed myself to weep or rage, everything might shatter, so I held still. Even now, when I went back to visit I always felt myself falling into those old patterns, the world circumscribed by loss.

The next e-mail was indeed from Blake, which alarmed me. Blake spent his summers living on his sailboat and working as a pilot for the cruises that left from The Lake of Dreams pier every two hours; he spent his winters in St. Croix doing much the same. He liked Skype, and twice he'd flown across the world to visit me, but he didn't like e-mail and almost never wrote. He gave more details about the accident—someone had run a stop sign, and he described my mother's car as totaled—but he didn't sound overprotective to me, just concerned. It was my cousin Zoe who sounded a little out of control, but then she always did. She had been born when I was nearly fourteen, and she was so much younger than the rest of us that it sometimes seemed she'd grown up in a completely different family. Her older brother, Joey, was about my age, heir to the family name and the family fortunes, and we'd never gotten along. But Zoe, who was fifteen now and adored the Internet, found my life amazing and exotic, and she wrote frequently to relay dramatic events from high school, even though I seldom wrote back.

It was nearly dawn. I got up and went to the window. Outside, the cobblestones were brightening to gray, wooden houses emerging from the night. Across the street, a subdued rattling of pots jarred me from my thoughts, followed by the sound of water running. Mrs. Fujimoro came out to sweep her walk. I stepped out onto the patio, nodding good morning. Her broom made such firm strokes—swish, swish, swish— that until she paused I didn't realize the earth had begun to rumble again. It was ordinary at first, a large wave hitting the shore, a truck passing down the street—but no. I met Mrs. Fujimoro's gaze. She caught my hand as the shaking extended, began to swell.

Leaves quivered and water trembled in a puddle. A tiny crack appeared below the Fujimoros' kitchen window, zigzagging to the foundation. I held her hand, staying very still, thinking of my mother's accident, of the moment she realized she could no more stop the car from smashing into her than she could alter the progress of the moon.

The tremor stopped. A child's questioning voice floated from the house. Mrs. Fujimoro took a deep breath, stepped away from me, and bowed. She picked up her broom. Her expression, so recently unmasked, was already distant again. I stood alone on the worn cobblestones.

"You turned off your gas?" she asked.

"Oh, yes!" I assured her. "Yes, I turned off the gas!" We had this exchange often; it was one of my few phrases of perfect Japanese.

Yoshi was in the doorway by the time I turned, his hair tousled and an old T-shirt pulled on over his running shorts. He had a kind face, and he gave a slight bow to Mrs. Fujimoro, who bowed in turn and spoke to him in rapid Japanese. Her husband had been a schoolmate of Yoshi's father, and we rented the house from them. On the rare occasions when Yoshi's parents visited from London—his mother is British—they stayed in another flat the Fujimoros owned around the corner.

"What were you talking about?" I asked when Yoshi finally bowed again to Mrs. Fujimoro and stepped back inside. He'd grown up bilingual and moved with fluid ease between languages, something I both admired and envied.

"Oh, she was telling me about the Great Kanto Earthquake in the twenties. Some of her family died in it, and she thinks that's why she gets so afraid, even in the little tremors. She's terrified of fires. And she's sorry if she startled you by taking your hand."

"It's all right," I said, following Yoshi to the kitchen, picking up my empty cup on the way. "The earthquakes scare me, too. I don't know how you can be so calm."

"Well, they either stop or they don't. There's not much you can do, is there? Besides, look," he added, gesturing to the paper, which of course I couldn't read. "Front page. It says an island is forming underwater, and then everything will improve. This is just a release of pressure."

"Great. Very reassuring." I watched him add water to the tea, his movements easy, practiced. "Yoshi, my mother was in an accident," I said.

He looked up.

"What happened? Is she okay?"

"A car accident. Not serious, I don't think. Or serious, but she's fine anyway. It depends on whose story you read."

"Ah. That's really too bad. You'll go see her?"

I didn't answer immediately. Did he want me to go? Would that be a relief? "I don't think so," I said, finally. "She says she's okay. Besides, I need to find a job."

Yoshi fixed me with the kind expression that had once drawn me to him and now often made me feel so claustrophobic: as if he understood me, inside out.

"Next week, next month, you can still look for jobs."

I glanced out the kitchen window at the wall of the house next door.

"No, Yoshi. I really don't want to put it off. All this free time is making me a little crazy, I think."

"Well," Yoshi said cheerfully, sitting at the table. "I can't argue with that."

"I've looked hard," I told him tersely. "You have no idea."

Yoshi was peeling a mandarin orange in a skillful way that left the skin almost intact, like an empty lantern, and he didn't look up.

"Well, what about that consultancy—the one on the Chinese dam project on the Mekong? Did you follow through on that?"

"Not yet. It's on my list."

"Your list—Lucy, how long can it be?"

Now I took a deep breath before I answered. We'd been looking forward to this hike in the mountains for weeks, and I didn't want to argue. "I've been researching that firm," I said, finally, trying to remember that just hours ago we'd been dancing in this same room, the air around us dark and fragrant.

Yoshi offered me a segment of his orange. These little oranges, *mikan*s, grew on the trees in the nearby hills and looked like bright ornaments when they ripened. We'd seen them when we visited last fall, back when Yoshi had just been offered this job and everything still seemed full of possibilities.

"Lucy, why not take a break and go see your mother? I could meet you there, too, after this business trip to Jakarta. I'd like to do that. I'd like to meet her."

"But it's such a long way."

"Not unless you're planning to walk."

I laughed, but Yoshi was serious. His eyes, the color of onyx, as dark as the bottom of a lake, were fixed on me. I caught my breath, remembering the night before, how he'd held my gaze without blinking while his fingers moved so lightly across my skin. Yoshi traveled often for his job—an engineer, he designed bridges for a company that had branches in several countries—and this trip had seemed like just one more absence to add to all the others. How ironic if now his job became a way for us to reconnect.

"Don't you ever want me to meet her?" he pressed.

"It's not that," I said, and it really wasn't. I picked up the empty orange skin, light in my palm. "It's just the timing. Besides, my mother's condition isn't serious. It's not exactly an emergency situation."

Yoshi shrugged, taking another orange from the cobalt bowl. "Sometimes loneliness is an emergency situation, Lucy."

"What do you mean?"

"I mean that lately you seem like a very sad and lonely person, that's all."

I looked away, blinking in surprise as my eyes, inexplicably, filled with tears.

"Hey." He touched my hand; his fingertips were sticky. "Look, Lucy,

I'm sorry, okay? Let's not worry about this. Let's just go up to the mountains, like we planned."

So we did. It was muggy near the sea but grew into a high, bright, sunny day as the train switchbacked up the mountain. In early spring, plum trees and cherry trees had blossomed against this landscape, blanketing the ground with white petals, and my vocabulary lessons then had been like poems: *tree, flowers, falling, petals, snow*. Now it was late enough in the season that rice had risen from the watery land near the sea, but in the mountains, spring lingered. The hydrangeas were just beginning to bloom, their clusters of petals faintly green, bleeding into lavender and blue, pressing densely against the windows of the train.

We hiked to an open-air museum beneath a canopy of cedar trees and ate in a mountain village built on the rim of a dormant volcano, and our talk was easy, relaxed, and happy, like our best times together. It was nearly dusk by the time we reached the *rotemboro,* an outdoor hot springs, and parted at the door. The changing room was all clear pine and running water, tranquil, soothing, and almost empty. I scrubbed carefully from head to toe, sluicing warm water to rinse, walking naked to the rock-lined pool. The air was cool, and the moon was rising in the indigo sky. Two other women were lounging against the smooth stones, chatting, their skin white against the wet gray rocks, their pale bodies disappearing into the water at the waist. Their voices were one soft sound; the trickle of water from the spring, another. Farther away, from beyond the wall, came the splashing and the voices of the men.

I slipped into the steaming water, imagining the patterns of underground rivers that fed these springs, thinking how everything was connected, and how our lives here had grown from such a casual decision made during my first weeks in Jakarta well over two years ago. I'd come back tired from a week in the field inspecting a canal system, and I dropped my suitcase on the cool marble floor, imagining nothing beyond a shower, a plate of *nasi goreng,* and a drink. My housemate, who worked at the Irish embassy, was leaving for a party and invited me to go, promising good food and better music. I said no at first, but at the last minute I changed my mind. If I hadn't gone, Yoshi and I would never have met.

The party was in a large house that buzzed with music and laughter. I wore a dark blue silk sheath I'd had made, a perfect fit and a good color for my eyes, and for a while I moved through the rooms, laughing, talking. Then I passed a quiet balcony and, on an impulse, slipped out for some air. Yoshi was leaning against the railing, gazing at the river below. I hesitated, because there was something about his stance that made me wish not to disturb him. But he turned, smiling in that way he has where his whole face is illuminated, warm and welcoming. He asked if I wanted to come and watch the water.

I did. I crossed the tiled floor and stood beside him at the railing. We didn't speak much at first, mesmerized by the swift, muddy currents. When we did start talking, we found we had a lot in common. In addition to our work and love of travel, we were the same age, and we were both allergic to beer. Our conversation flowed so swiftly that we didn't notice the people who came and went, or our empty glasses, or the changing sky, not until the monsoon rain began to pour down with tropical suddenness and intensity. We looked at each other then and started laughing, and Yoshi lifted his hands to the outpouring of the skies. Since we were already drenched, there seemed no point in going inside. We talked on the balcony until the rain ceased as suddenly as it had begun. Yoshi walked me home through the dark and steamy streets. When we reached my house he ran the palms of his hands across my cheeks to smooth away the water, and kissed me.

At first it was easy enough to keep the relationship from gaining traction. I'd had enough of the transitory, long-distance love affairs that happen inevitably for people who travel so much. Then the rains began again. They came early that year, and with an unusual ferocity, overwhelming the city's open canal systems and flooding the streets. Much of Jakarta was low-lying and susceptible to water, and the sprawling development around the city—a loss of trees and green spaces—had left few places to absorb the rain. The water rose, and rose. One morning fish were swimming in the flooded lawn, and by noon water was five inches deep in the living room. My roommate and I watched on the news as the flood washed away cars, the fronts of buildings, and an entire village of 143 people.

As the water began to recede, Yoshi and two coworkers organized a cleanup at an orphanage. He picked me up in an old Nissan truck he'd borrowed and we drove through the drenched and devastated city. The orphanage grounds were awash in mud and filled with debris. It stank. We worked all that day and all the next, and Yoshi was everywhere, shoveling mud and orchestrating volunteers. Once, he paused beside a boy in a worn red shirt who stood crying in the mud, then picked him up and carried him inside.

When he brought me home at the end of that second day, the skies opened again. Running from the car, reaching for my house keys, I slipped and grabbed a mango tree to keep from falling. A cascade of leaves and twigs showered down, scattering seeds and pollen, desiccated stems. I was already a mess from cleaning. Yoshi took my arm and we fumbled our way inside. *You're shivering,* he said, *come here.* We let our wet clothes fall by the steaming shower. *Close your eyes,* he said, stepping behind me, the warm water pouring over us, and then his hands were moving in my hair, working the shampoo through every strand, caressing my scalp, massaging my shoulders, the cold and grime draining away, my tension and uncertainties draining away. My arms eased under his touch, he held my breasts like flowers, and I turned.

And now we were here, all these days and miles away, Yoshi's voice, his laughter, drifting over the wall that divided the hot springs pool. I slid deeper into the water, resting my head on the damp rocks. My limbs floated, faintly luminous, and steam rose; the women across from me chatted softly. They were mother and daughter, I thought, or sisters born years apart, for their bodies were similar in shape, and their gestures mirrored each other's. I thought again of my own mother, sitting alone in her house.

Lately you seem like a very sad and lonely person. The comment still smarted, but I had to wonder if it was true. I'd left for college just weeks after my father died, numb but determined to escape the silence that had descended on the house like a dark enchantment. Keegan Fall had tried again and again to break it, but I'd sent him away harshly, two times, three times, until he stopped calling. In the years since, I'd moved—from college to grad school, from good jobs to better ones and through a whole series of romances, leaving all that grief behind, never letting myself slow down. Until now, unemployed in Japan, I had paused.

One by one, the women stepped out of the pool, water dripping onto the stones, causing little waves. I remembered my dream, the faces just beneath the surface of the ice. My father used to tell me stories where I was always the heroine and the ending was always happy. Nothing had prepared me for the shock of his death. He had fallen, it was determined in the autopsy, and hit his head on the boat and slipped beneath the water, a freak accident that could not fully be explained, or ever undone. His fishing pole had been recovered days later, tangled in the reeds at the edge of the marsh.

I left the pool and dressed, but Yoshi wasn't outside yet, so I started walking idly down a path of stones alone. It followed a narrow stream and opened into a pond, as round as a bowl and silvery with moonlight. I paused at the edge. In the darkness on the other side, something stirred.

Not for the first time that quake-riddled day, I held my breath. A great blue heron stood in the shadows, its long legs disappearing into the dark water, its wings folded closely against its body. Then the pond was still, gleaming like mica. Another, smaller heron stirred beside the first. I thought of the two women in the spring, as if they had stepped outside to the pond and been transformed into these silent, beautiful birds. Then Yoshi called my name, and both herons unfolded their wide wings and lifted off, slowly, gracefully, casting shadows on the water before they disappeared into the trees.

"Lucy," Yoshi called again. "If we hurry, we can catch the next train."

The heat closed in as we lost altitude, and the hydrangea blossoms against the windows grew older and more ragged, as if the slow, incremental season had been compressed into a single hour. By the time we reached our stop by the sea, the blossoms had disappeared completely, leaving only glossy foliage. We walked home along the narrow cobblestone lanes. Crickets hummed and the ground shook slightly with the surf. Twice, I paused.

"Is that the sea?" I asked.

"Maybe."

"Not an earthquake?"

Yoshi sighed, a little wearily, I thought. "I don't know. Maybe a very little one."

A vase of flowers had tipped over on the table. Several books were scattered on the floor. I wiped up the water and gathered the petals. As I stood, there was a single quick, sharp jolt, so strong that even Yoshi reacted, pulling me into the doorway, where we stood for several minutes, alert again to the earth, its shifting, trembling life. I was so tired; I dreaded the night ahead, with its earthquakes and its dreams. I dreaded the next day, too, all the little disagreements flaring out of nothing, and the silence that would press around me once Yoshi left for work. I thought of the herons at the edge of the pond, spreading their dark wings.

"Yoshi," I said. "I think I will go see my family, after all."

Chapter 2

TWO DAYS LATER, WE LEFT FOR THE STATION BEFORE DAWN, the wheels of my carry-on bumping along the cobblestones in the early morning mist. We walked along the curving lane, past the fruit seller and the vending machine that sold sake and beer, past the temple with its garden of little statues and the shop where they made tofu by hand. Yoshi was dressed in his salaryman attire, white shirt, black suit, which I'd once found amusing, but which had begun to seem like a true part of his identity over these past months. Was it just my imagination that with every day we stayed in this place Yoshi was pulled a little further from the person I'd known? Or was he simply becoming more himself, a self I hadn't seen when we lived in that country of our own?

The trip into Tokyo took about an hour, and we were pressed closer and closer together as the train filled. Yoshi slipped his arm through mine so we wouldn't be separated when the doors opened and we poured out with the crowd. We'd been very kind to each other, very formal and polite, but on the platform, in the flow of impatient people, the unending river of mostly men in dark suits, Yoshi stopped and turned to face me, slipping a little package into my purse.

"A Webcam," he explained. "So we can talk while we're traveling.

I'll see you there in two weeks." He took my shoulders in his two hands and kissed me, right there, amid the streaming people. "Travel safe," he said. "Call soon." Then he entered the river of commuters and was gone.

I found a seat on the airport shuttle. Though I tried to hold on to the memory of Yoshi's touch, it faded gradually as the rainy landscape flashed by the windows. I settled into the seat and turned my thoughts to the trip ahead, my family. I tried to visit every year, but the move to Japan had interrupted things, and I hadn't been back in almost two years. Wanderlust was in my blood, I suppose, at least according to the stories I'd heard all my life. My great-grandfather, Joseph Arthur Jarrett, was sixteen years old when Halley's Comet returned in 1910. Despite the worldwide panic around the comet's return, he had a clear head and an adventurous spirit; that night he snuck out of the house and walked to the church on the hill, determined to witness history. He was young, a dreamer, and he had a gift that, like his unusual eyes, he would pass down through generations: he could listen to a lock and understand its secrets. The cylinders in the bell tower door turned and clicked in response to his seeking wire. They fell into place, the door swung open, and he climbed the worn limestone steps to the roof. Above, amid the familiar stars, the comet arced across the sky. He lifted his face to it. *Like a blessing,* is what he thought. *Like a gift.* The word *orbit* came from Latin—from *orbis,* meaning wheel. To my great-grandfather, destined to be a wheelwright like his father and grandfather before him, this strange light seemed to him a sign.

The days that followed turned in familiar cycles of work and meals and sleeping, yet the memory of the comet remained, hidden but present, like a star at noon, like a bright coin in a pocket. When a huge elm was felled by lightning later that summer, my great-grandfather touched its trunk and a dream bloomed, bright and urgent, spreading its leafy arms around him, its thick blossoms luminous, incandescent, soft against his skin. *Build a trunk,* he seemed to hear, and so he took a section of the tree and hid it in his neighbor's barn. For a year he measured and cut and planed, in secret. He bound the new boards with strips of hot iron and fashioned thick straps from leather. His heart sang and trembled on the night he finally left, traveling by ship and then by train to The Lake of Dreams, where a distant cousin, Jesse Evanston, no more than a name on a slip of paper, was standing on the platform in the watery air to meet him.

That was the story, anyway. As I checked in for my flight, I wondered how he'd felt, pinning his dreams on such a faraway unknown—no telephones back then, no e-mails, and no going back. For me, nearly a century later, there was such a careless ease about distance. At almost the same time as our takeoff from Tokyo the day before, we landed at JFK, its corridors bustling with amazing human diversity. After another hour in the air, the lakes came into view, long, narrow, and deep, deep blue—pressed into the low green hills like the slender fingers of a hand. North-flowing rivers once, they had been deepened and widened by the slow work of glaciers. I studied them until they disappeared beneath the silver wing of the plane, remembering the cold, clear shock of the water, the layers of deepening cold and deepening color, the shallows of the shores giving way to the blueness of the depths, turquoise and indigo and finally midnight blue.

I'd e-mailed my brother that I was coming, and as I rode down the escalator to baggage claim I saw Blake waiting, studying the descending people, his hands shoved into the pockets of his jeans. His face opened in a smile when he saw me, and he waved. In some ways Blake had been hit hardest by our father's sudden death. He'd done well at the Maritime College, and he'd taken some good jobs on big boats in the Great Lakes, but he kept circling back to The Lake of Dreams for summers, a kind of holding pattern he couldn't seem to break.

"Hey, Sis," he said, wrapping one arm around me in a hug. He's six foot four, and even as tall as I am, I had to stand on my toes to hug him back. "Mom's at the doctor, or she'd be here, too."

"She's doing okay?"

"She's doing fine. It turned out to be a sprain, after all. She'll have to wear an Aircast for a couple of weeks."

My bag circled by on the belt and I pulled it off, remembering the moment, just a day before, when the luggage service had picked it up from my tiny patio in Japan. A world away, it seemed already. I started toward the car rental area, but Blake caught my arm.

"You can use Dad's old car while you're here," he said. "No need to bother with a rental."

"Really? The Impala?" I asked, as we made our way out the automatic doors to the parking lot. "Has Mom actually started that thing up? It's been sitting in the barn for years."

"I know, but it still runs. Mom had it checked out a couple of months ago, thinking she might sell it, I guess. It's all tuned up and in good shape."

"I'm surprised she'd think of selling it."

Blake glanced at me, his eyes—the family eyes, a changeable blue flecked with green, with long dark lashes—both serious and amused. "Things move on, Luce. You'll see. Lots of changes this time." He tossed my bag into the back of his truck. "How about you? How's your life these days? Do you miss Indonesia at all? I think about my trip there all the time. Especially that park we went to—the one with wild-looking trees, and the volcanoes."

Blake had come to visit me just after I'd met Yoshi, and we'd gone snorkeling on the coral reefs, hiked through the lowland rain forests. It had been Yoshi's idea, actually. He'd gone with some friends a few weeks earlier and thought Blake and I would enjoy it.

"We had a good time, didn't we?"

"We sure did. It was steamy hot, though. What's Japan like? And how's my good friend Yoshi these days? Things okay? I like him, you know."

"I know." They'd hit it off, Yoshi and Blake, drawn together by a love of sailing and all things nautical, as well as by a kind of carefree approach to life that sometimes drove me crazy. They'd both been enamored of rambutans, the hairy red fruits piled high on roadside stands like shaggy Ping-Pong balls, and had pulled over five or six times to buy baskets full, peeling them to reveal the sweet, translucent fruit within. "He's planning to come, you know. In a couple of weeks."

"No joke? That's great, Lucy. I'll be glad to see him again."

"Me, too." I told Blake about my life then, about Yoshi and the geothermal springs, the incessant trembling of the earth, talking in a stream because I was so tired and so happy to see him and so disconcerted, as I always was, to be back in this place I'd known so well, where life had gone on quite steadily without me. Blake filled me in on the businesses that had opened or closed, the classmates who'd had babies or gotten married or divorced, all sorts of local gossip.

We'd left the main roads to climb the low rise between the lakes. The landscape was deeply and comfortingly familiar, the country roads following ancient trails through the lush green hills and fields, broken by white farmhouses, red barns, silos. The Iroquois had lived on this land once, and they had named the lakes: Long Lake, Beautiful Lake, Place of Blessing, Stony Place, Canoe-Landing Place, The Lake of Dreams. After the revolution, their villages were razed and burned to the ground—blue and gold historic signs marking General Sullivan's brutal campaign were scattered every dozen miles or so. The land had then been allotted to the vanquishing soldiers, who carved farms from the forests, braving the long winters for the brief, exquisite months of summer. Along the shores, summer cottages and rough fishing camps had sprouted, and over the years these had been replaced by ever larger and more ostentatious commuter homes. Still, we drove primarily through farms; from the county line at the top of the rise, we followed the road down a long hill, through green fields that ended at the silvery blue edges of the lake.

"Your old friend Keegan is back, by the way."

A pulse then, the familiar quickening I always used to feel.

"Is he? I haven't seen him in years." This was true, though it didn't feel true.

"He is. He opened up a studio in the old Johnson glass insulator factory by the outlet. That whole building's been renovated. Restaurants, galleries. Very trendy." Blake glanced across the cab at me. "You remember Avery, right?"

"*Your* old friend."

Blake smiled, nodded. "Right. We're back together, you know. She's a chef in a new vegetarian place in the Johnson building, too. Did I ever tell you that when we broke up the second time she went to culinary school? She's really good."

By then we had reached the intersection with the lake road, near the entrance to the depot. The lake was deep enough for battleship training, and during World War II hundreds of families had been relocated under eminent domain, their houses and barns razed like the Iroquois villages before them, airstrips and Quonset huts and weapons bunkers rising almost overnight out of the land amid the corn. Usually this stretch was deserted except for the dull green military vehicles that came and went on their mysterious errands, but now dozens of cars were parked on the grassy shoulders, and a small crowd had gathered at the open gates.

"What's going on?"

"That's the other big news," Blake said. "See what happens when you stay away so long? The depot closed, just last week. It was announced three, four months ago."

I was still thinking of Keegan, the way he used to speed his motorcycle flat out on this stretch, the wind tearing at our sleeves, so it took me a minute to process this news.

"Is that possible? I thought the depot was a fact of life."

"Yeah, weird, isn't it? The economy is lousy here anyway, and now it'll only get worse. This place employed a lot of people."

I looked south along the shore at the miles of undeveloped land behind the formidable fences. Our mother's grandparents had been among those evicted when the land was taken and we'd heard stories of that loss all our lives. We'd grown up traveling along the depot's miles-long fence with its barbed-wire summit, the world within a secret place we could never enter. Blake slowed to maneuver through the unexpected traffic, then stopped, waving over a guy wearing jeans and a jacket with the logo of the local television station.

"Hey, Pete. What's happening?"

"Hey there, Blake." Pete was short, with wiry dark hair, and he sprinted across the road, ducking to look in the truck window. "It's a rally—save the black terns, or something." He gestured to the south, toward our land, toward the marshes. "One group is trying to get all of this designated as a protected wetlands area. I don't know what the rest want yet—about six other groups have showed up. You here to watch the fireworks?"

Blake laughed. "Not me. I'm on my way back from the airport. My sister just got in—this is Lucy. Lucy, Pete."

I nodded hello.

"Developers here, too?" Blake asked.

Pete nodded. "Oh, yeah. All kinds. Plus, the Iroquois want it back, and there's a coalition to protect a herd of rare white deer that's living on the land. Some of the descendants of families who got evicted during the war have filed claims, too. You sure you don't have a dog in this fight, Blake? Everyone else seems to."

Blake grinned. "Nah. Haven't even figured out who the dogs are yet."

Pete laughed. "Plenty to choose from, that's for sure. Well, good seeing you. Good to meet you, Lucy."

He slapped the side of the truck as he stepped back. Blake drove slowly through the crowd, picking up speed as the road cleared. Glimpsing the shallow reeds where my father always loved to fish, where herons hid in the rustling grasses, I was pierced suddenly with grief, remembering the long, thin sound of the line flying through mist.

"I used to love it when Dad took us fishing."

Blake took his right hand from the wheel and gripped mine for a second.

"I know," he said. "I did, too."

It was a deep and yet comforting silence that rose between us, one I could have shared with no one else. When we reached the driveway, low-hanging branches of the apple tree scraped the truck roof. The grand house, Italianate, with two wide porches and a cupola, sagged a little, as if it had exhaled a deep breath. Paint was peeling on the trim and the porch. My mother's moon garden had run completely wild. It had once been a magical place, white crocuses, daffodils, and freesia poking from the mulch, the angel trumpets and night-blooming water lilies carried outside once the air had grown as warm as skin, everything fragrant and luminous, the blossoms floating in the dusk. Now, the trellises were broken and leaning at crazy angles; the moonflower vines cascaded over the fence and tangled in the overgrown roses. The peonies were in full bloom, extravagant and beautiful, and the lavender and lamb's ears had spread everywhere, straggly in the center, ragged at the edges.

Our mother was sitting on the side steps in the sun, her legs extended and crossed at the ankles, her right arm in a bright green cast cradled across her ribs. I'd come back to visit many times in the decade since I'd left for college, and she'd been to see me in Seattle and Florida. Each time I was struck by how familiar she looked, and how young. Her face was almost unlined, but her hair had turned a silvery gray when she was still in her twenties. She wore it pulled back, silver at her temples and running in a thick rope down her spine. She stood up when we pulled in and came right over to meet the truck.

"Lucy!" She hugged me with her good arm as I got out, her cheek soft against mine, smelling faintly of oregano and mint. I hugged her lightly in return, remembering her broken ribs. She kept her good hand on my arm as we walked. "I'm so glad to see you, honey. Oh, you look so good, so beautiful. Did you get taller? That's not possible, is it, but you *seem* taller. Come in—are you starving? Thirsty? You must be just exhausted."

We went through the screened-in porch to the kitchen; I dropped my bag near the door. Everything seemed just the same, the wide windows overlooking the garden, the table pressed against the wall, the turquoise-

and-white-checked curtains I'd made in middle school still hanging in the window of the door. My mother filled tall glasses with ice while Blake cut wedges of lemon and poured sun tea from the big glass jar she always kept on the sunny counter in the summer.

"To Lucy," she said, lifting a glass with her good hand. "Welcome home."

"Is that Lucy already?" a voice from the dining room called.

Art, my father's brother, older by a less than a year, came to stand in the doorway. Even as I realized who it was, I was shocked. He had aged, his broad face slackening, and his hair, gone gray at the temples, cut short and bristling. Somehow in this aging he had come to resemble my father so closely it might have been his ghost standing in the doorway. I couldn't speak. Art didn't seem to notice, though. "Here's the wanderer," he said, stepping into the kitchen to give me a quick, tense hug. "Home at last. How long are you staying?"

"A couple of weeks," I said.

"Good. You'll have to come see us—lots of changes afoot."

"I was telling her." Blake was leaning against the counter. "There's a big brouhaha over at the depot today, did you see it?"

Art nodded. "I did. They wanted me to sign a petition. Wetlands—well, damn. I told them that's prime real estate, a once-in-a-lifetime chance to build."

Blake laughed and agreed, and I glanced at my mother, who was standing with her injured arm across her waist. She caught my eye.

"Art was kind enough to replace the bathroom faucet today," she said.

This meant: *Don't make a scene, Lucy, please.*

Undeterred, I was about to tell Art exactly what I thought about losing the wetlands, but then the ancient freezer on the porch shuddered on, forcing me to consider the muttering old house, its demands and complaints, and the kitchen renovation, which had been less than half-finished when my father died, walls torn out, appliances in boxes, dust from the Sheetrock gathered in the corners. Art and my father had never gotten along, but Art had come to finish the kitchen job. Twice in those numb weeks after the funeral I'd walked in and seen my uncle's legs sprawled out from beneath the sink, tools spread out around him as he struggled with the couplings, and thought it was my father.

"Dad loved those marshes," was what I finally said.

Art was a big man, with long arms and hands thickened from years of work. He drummed his fingers on the counter, looking in my direction but not quite at me; his gaze traveled past me, to the scene outside the window, to the lake.

"He did. Your father did love that place, I know, Lucy." He drummed his fingers a little harder, and then slapped his hand flat on the counter. "We used to go there when we were boys. It was our go-to place, I guess you could say, whenever we needed to think something through, or just to get away. Fishing wasn't bad, either," he said, lost in thought for a moment before he shook his head and rejoined the conversation. "Now, Blake," he went on, changing the subject. "I'll see you later today, right?"

"Not today. I can come tomorrow."

"Be early, then. There's plenty of work." Art turned to my mother. "Evie, I fixed the window sash in the bathroom, too. I'll stop back next week to put on a coat of paint. But it should be okay in the meantime. Come and take a look."

"I appreciate it, Art," my mother said, following him into the other room.

"What was that about?" I asked Blake once they'd gone. "Are you working at Dream Master now?"

Dream Master Hardware and Locks was the business our great-grandfather had founded in 1919, turning his intuitions about the internal mechanics of locks into a thriving enterprise. In its heyday the Dream Master factory shipped locks all across the country. Like most of the other industries in the area, it was gone now, but the hardware store remained, and Art owned it. My father had once owned it, too, but in 1986, the year the comet came, when I was almost ten, he had come home one morning with a box full of things from his office, and he'd never gone back, or said a word to me about why he left.

Blake ran one hand through his wild curls and glanced after Art. "Walk me outside," he said.

We went through the porch and down the steps, and then Blake kept right on going across the lawn to the shore. The day was clear but windy, the water punctuated with whitecaps like commas, the buoys singing their hollow metal songs. I caught up with him at the end of the dock.

"What's going on? Did you quit your job on the boat?" I asked.

Blake kept his gaze on the water, watching the rippling patterns change, a distant flock of ducks floating light on the surface.

"Not yet. I've agreed to pilot through the summer, but just the evening cruise. I might quit after that, though. I'm thinking about it. Art offered me a job. A good job. He stopped in a couple of weeks ago to ask me in person. Took me by surprise, I can tell you."

I didn't say anything, trying to sort out why this news felt so upsetting.

"Art's helped Mom out a lot," Blake went on quietly. "I know they always argued, he and Dad, and we were never close to Art growing up. But lately I've been thinking I haven't been quite fair to him. Maybe none of us have."

"Well, so what? When did anything between Dad and Art ever end up fair?"

Blake shrugged. "We were kids, Lucy. We don't really know. Art probably feels bad about the way things turned out. It's got to haunt him, being on such uneasy terms with Dad before he died. Suppose he's just trying to make things right?"

I felt it then, the pull of the family history, an invisible gravity, almost irresistible.

"But what about sailing, Blake? You love to travel. What about winters on St. Croix? You're just giving all that up?"

"Like I said, things change." Blake glanced at me, embarrassed, assessing. "Long story short, Avery is pregnant. The baby's due in October. So, I have to think differently now."

I was too surprised to say anything at all.

"That's right," Blake said. "We're having a baby. Good wishes appreciated."

"Sorry. I'm sorry, Blake. Of course I'm happy for you. It's just a lot to take in."

He gave a small smile, nodded. "That's okay. I had the exact same reaction, actually—stunned silence." We stood in the wind off the lake.

"Are you happy about it?" I asked.

"Sometimes. It's exciting, sure, but a surprise. The timing is bad for us both."

Wind rattled the ropes on the dock, and I tried hard to remember Avery, a slight, energetic girl with dark brown eyes and hair.

"Look," Blake said. "This thing at Dream Master, the way I see it— it's just a job. Not a forever job, just a good-for-right-now kind of job."

"Right, I get it. It makes sense."

He smiled then, his charming old smile, and gave my shoulder a playful push.

"Water looks nice," he said.

"Oh, you wouldn't!"

"Wouldn't I?"

He pushed me harder then, and though I could have kept my balance I grabbed his arm and let myself fall, dragging him in after me. We hit the clear, cold water and came up laughing, shaking bright droplets from our hair.

"Oh! It's freezing!"

"It's June—what did you expect?"

"Not to be swimming." I skimmed my hand across the surface, sending a glittering arc of spray. Blake ducked, then sprayed me back.

"Truce!" I finally called, staggering out of the water onto the gray shale beach. Blake followed me up the lawn, catching my arm before we reached the driveway.

"Mom doesn't know," he said, looking at me seriously with the beautiful dark-lashed family eyes, blue irises mottled with green. "No one else knows. I promised Avery I wouldn't say anything until she's ready, so keep it quiet, okay?"

I nodded slowly. "Okay. I won't say anything."

"Thanks. Hey—it's good to have you home, Luce." He gave me a hug as we reached the driveway, and then headed toward his truck.

"Aren't you even going to dry off?"

"I'll drip dry," he called back. "And I'll see you later, okay? Welcome back."

I waved, watching him pull away and disappear.

Art had gone, too. I found my mother in the kitchen making up plates with chicken salad, lettuce, and grapes, working slowly because she could use only one hand.

"Just a light supper," she said, and then she looked up and saw my wet clothes, my hair. "Oh, the two of you," she said, laughing, biting her lips because it hurt her ribs to laugh. I could tell she was happy, though. "There are towels on the sun porch. And could you pour us some wine? You must be tired, Lucy, but it's so good to see you that I'm not going to let you sleep, not yet."

After I changed we ate on the patio, weighing the napkins down with forks because the breeze was still brisk, cold in my wet hair. The setting sun had emerged below the clouds and the lake had turned from gunmetal gray to the color of sapphires, waves lapping gently at the shore. My mother's face softened in the golden light, her silver hair glinting amber.

"So," she said. "Here you are. And this Yoshi of yours is coming, too, I hear. That would be a first, Lucy, meeting one of your parade of boyfriends. Sounds like it might be serious?"

"Oh, I don't know. I mean, yes, I suppose. We're at kind of a crossroads, I guess." I paused there, surprised at my own words. Was it true?

"Well, you don't want to wait too long," my mother said.

"Too long for what?" I regretted the words the minute I spoke them, because my tone was sharp. My mother averted her gaze, ran her finger around the rim of her glass.

"I'm sorry, honey," she said, her voice mild. She looked up and smiled at me. "I don't mean to pry. And I don't mean that you have to find happiness in a relationship. Not at all. But I do want you to be happy. Wherever you find that happiness, I want it for you. That's all."

Now I had to look away, out to the tranquil waters.

"I think you'll like Yoshi," I said, finally. "He and Blake really hit it off. His job has been really consuming, so that's been kind of hard, especially since I don't have any job at all just now. It seemed like a good time for him to come, that's all."

"I can't wait to meet him."

We talked a little more about work, and then I asked about the car wreck.

"Not serious," she said, waving her good hand. "It could have been, but I was lucky. The ribs are the worst, it hurts to laugh or take a deep breath, and there's nothing I can do but let them heal. Still, I don't know why everyone got quite so upset. Except maybe it reminded us," she added. "About how quickly things can happen."

Again, silence fell between us. I was the first to break it. "I still miss Dad," I said.

"I know."

"What do you think of Blake?" I asked after a moment. "Working for Art, I mean?"

She was looking out at the water with its dancing nets of light, and shook her head slightly. "I try not to get too involved, now that you two are adults. Art has been a terrific help to me, Lucy. You haven't been here to see it, but it's true. I guess your father's death made a powerful impression on him. I think maybe they always imagined they'd have time to patch things up, time to find a way to get along, but then, just like that, it was too late."

"Whatever happened between them, anyway?"

"Oh, honestly, honey, it's hard to pinpoint. There was always tension. I remember when your father brought me here for dinner and announced that we were getting married, Art made a point of taking me aside to tell me all your father's faults. It was strange, almost like he was jealous and wanted to keep things from working out. That didn't really make sense, because he was already dating Austen. But anyway, I didn't think much of Art for doing that, I can tell you. As an only child myself, I always wanted to have siblings, so I've never understood why they couldn't get along. But that's just the way it was for them, growing up, maybe because they were born so close together."

"And Dream Master?" I asked. "That happened later?"

My mother glanced at me, her expression somewhat guarded. "It did."

"Well?"

"You were always such a persistent child," she observed. "No wonder you're such a success around the world."

Long stems of white gladioli stood in a vase on the table. I touched a petal, feeling hurt rather than complimented; my mother had argued against my living overseas, especially after 9/11 happened while I was in Sri Lanka, and it was still a sore point between us. Golden pollen coated my finger.

"These are pretty. Secret admirer?"

To my surprise my mother laughed, color rising briefly in her cheeks. "Not so secret. Someone I met in the emergency room. His name is Andrew. Andrew something or other. I was pretty spacey from the pain pills. We had a lovely conversation, of which I remember almost nothing."

I opened the florist's envelope and pulled out the little card.

"Yes, go ahead," she said. "Feel free."

Dear Evie, thank you for the good conversation on a very bad day. As discussed, these are Apollo gladioli. Hope you like them. Yours, Andrew Stewart.

"Why Apollo gladioli?" I asked, catching the envelope as it skidded across the table in a gust of wind that rattled the wind chimes and slammed waves against the shore.

"Well, we talked about the moon landing, that I do remember. Where we were in 1969, that sort of thing. I suppose I must have mentioned my old moon garden, though it all went to seed years ago. But maybe that's why he sent these."

"Looks like you made a big impression." I put the card back in its envelope, suddenly very sad. My parents had met as volunteers in a community garden just as my father was about to leave for Vietnam. Over the next year, they wrote. My mother savored his letters, the onion-skin pages in their thin envelopes filled with his slanted script. She had known my father so briefly that it was as if she had made him up to suit herself, and when she wrote back it was with a reckless freedom, telling him things she'd never shared before—her secrets, fears, and dreams.

Then one day she had looked up to see my father silhouetted against the door of the greenhouse where she worked. He was so much taller than she remembered, disconcertingly familiar and strange all at once. He crossed the room and stopped in front of her, but didn't speak. The scent of earth gathered in her throat. Water dripped in the sink.

"I'm transplanting zinnias," she'd finally said. As proof she held up her hands, dirt beneath her nails, her fingertips stained brown.

My father had smiled. Then he leaned down and kissed her. She kissed him back, pressing her wrists against his shoulders, her earth-stained hands lifted like wings.

I'd heard this story over and over, growing up, so I didn't really like it, not one bit, that some man I'd never met was sending my mother flowers. Jet lag traveled through me like a wave and the world suddenly seemed vibrant and strange, as if all the colors might burst from their shapes. I put my hand on the table to steady myself.

"You okay?" my mother asked.

"Just a little tired, that's all."

"Of course you are, honey. I'm surprised you lasted this long. I made up the couch on the screened porch for you."

"What about my old room, can't I use that?"

"Do you really want to?"

She sounded reluctant, and I remembered she'd told me once that in the silence of my father's sudden absence, the voices of the house had begun to whisper to her constantly, the trim crying out to be painted, the driveway sputtering about cracks and pits, the faucets leaking a persistent dissatisfaction. *Love,* said the kitchen cabinets my father had built from quarter-sawn oak. The lights in her sewing room, the slate tiles of the patio, the newly sanded floors, all of these persisted, saying *love, love, love,* and when the gutters clogged, when the shutters broke loose, when a windowpane cracked, she could not bear to alter the things he had last tended; nor could she stand to listen to the clamoring of the house. That was why she'd closed off the second floor, turning the glass doorknobs, clicking the metal bolts shut.

"Would you mind? I'll make the bed and everything."

"Of course I don't mind," she said, though I sensed that she did.

I found the key ring hanging inside the kitchen cupboard. The keys made soft metal sounds as I carried them to the second floor, which was warm and stuffy, the doors all closed. When I entered my old room I went from window to window, pushing up the sashes, struggling with the combination storms, letting fresh air pour in. I put a fitted sheet on the narrow bed, unfolded the flat sheet, and tucked it in, fatigue throbbing through me like a pulse.

It was faintly light still, not quite nine o'clock. I lay down without undressing, punched speed dial, and closed my eyes. Yoshi picked up on the second ring, his voice low and smooth, like river stones.

"Moshi Moshi."

"It's me. I got here just fine."

"Good. I miss you, Lucy."

"Me, too. What are you doing?"

"Walking to catch the train. It's raining a little."

I imagined the lane, the river he'd cross before the station. If I were there I'd be lying in bed watching rain drip from the copper eaves, planning my vocabulary lesson for the day.

"I haven't set up the Webcam. Maybe tomorrow. My mother isn't very high-tech."

"How is she?"

"Okay. Fine, really. But the house is very quiet."

"You see. I was right."

"I do see. She's glad you're coming. She wants to meet you."

"Just a few days. I want to meet her, too. How's your brother?"

"He's good. He says hello. He's having a baby."

"What?"

"It's true. Top secret, though. I'll be an aunt in October."

"Congratulations. I didn't know he'd gotten married."

"He didn't. Not yet. I mean, I don't know if he will. It's all a surprise."

"Well, tell him hello."

"I will. Have there been more earthquakes?"

"A few, not so bad."

"Hey. Did you turn off the gas?"

He laughed. "Yes," he said. "Yes. I turned off the gas. Look, I'm almost at the station now, I have to go."

"Okay. Call me tonight?"

"I will. Send me an e-mail if you can, okay?"

"I will."

"Love you."

He really must miss me, I thought, startled—Yoshi wasn't much for endearments, especially on the phone. "Love you, too," I said.

I pressed the button and there was only space, all the miles between us filling up with darkness. I put the phone on the bedside table without opening my eyes, remembering the little concrete house we'd shared in Indonesia, its garden filled with mango trees and lush, swiftly growing plants I couldn't name. We always met there when we got home from work, and shared a drink as the moon rose, listening to the rustling sounds of lizards in the tall grass. I wanted to reach out now and catch Yoshi's hand in mine, to walk with him back into that tranquil life. But he was in the middle of a day and ten thousand miles away. I pulled the blankets up and fell asleep to the sounds and scent of water.

The dream began as a long and wearying journey in the rain, full of airports and frustrations, missed connections and clocks ticking, perilous deadlines. I was being followed, through corridors, first, and then through a forest. My suitcase, old-fashioned and made of leather, hit a tree and broke open, spilling everything. In panic, I started crawling through the foliage, the earth damp and loamy. I searched wildly through the velvet leaves of cyclamen, blossoms flaring around me like birds in startled flight. What I'd lost was important, somehow vital to me, life or death, and even though footsteps and voices were approaching, growing louder and more menacing, I couldn't stop, pushing leaves away and digging in the earth with my hands, until the voices were upon me.

I woke, so frightened and disoriented I could not move.

Gradually, slowly, I remembered where I was. Still, I had to take several deep breaths before I could swing my legs over the edge of the bed and stand up. In the glaring light of the bathroom I splashed water on my face, studying my pale reflection in the mirror. My eyes, like Blake's, were large and blue, but shadowed with fatigue.

The house was still, the closed doors in the hallway like blank faces. I unlocked them all. Everything was caught in time, as if the world had stopped the summer after my father died. In my parents' room, the bed was neatly made. Blake's room still had its posters of the moon and the earth, our luminous blue-green planet floating in the interstellar space of his walls. In the guest room, packed boxes were stacked high against one wall, so perhaps my mother had been up here after all, starting to go through the old things. When I opened the door to the cupola, stale, hot air spilled down the narrow steps, as if nothing had stirred in it for decades. It was like a tower in a fairy tale, where the princess pricked her finger, or spun straw into gold, or lowered her thick hair to her lover below.

No breath in that tiny rooftop room. Here, too, I opened all the windows, sweeping away the dead flies that had collected in the sills. When the room was full of the lapping sounds of the lake, full of wind, I sat on one of the window seats, breathing in the fresh air. The lake was calm and smooth, almost opalescent. I watched dawn come, the sun catching on the ring of keys I'd left splayed out against the painted seat: new keys and ancient keys, formed for locks that no longer existed, kept because they were beautifully fashioned, or because no one could remember what they opened and thought they might be needed someday.

My father's lock-picking tools hung from the ring, too, folded like a Swiss Army knife into a compact metal case. They were a kind of inheritance, passed down from my great-grandfather, Joseph Arthur Jarrett. I opened them, wondering when my father had used them last. As a girl I would sometimes go to his office at Dream Master after school and do my homework in the corner, happy to be near the swirl of conversation and the scents of metal and sawdust, customers coming in for nails or tools or chicken wire or a special order of tile. Sometimes they came with their secrets, too, stored in metal boxes from which the keys had been lost. My father's expression was always intent and focused as he worked, his scalp visible beneath his cropped hair in the harsh light, his face breaking open in satisfaction, finally, as the tumblers clicked and fell into place. He charged five dollars for this service, ten dollars for house calls, and people paid happily, so eager that they almost never waited to open their boxes in private: Bonds or jewelry or wills; a few times, nothing at all.

My father had taught me what he knew, letting me sit in his chair and press my ear against the smooth wood or metal of a shuttered box on his desk, instructing me how to listen to the whisper of metal shifting, something like a wave, smooth and uninterrupted, until suddenly the frequency changed slightly, became weighted, suspenseful. What was or wasn't inside never really mattered; it was the whisper of metal on metal that he wanted me to hear. The first time I succeeded, the box springing open beneath my touch, he'd let out a cheer of delight and lifted me up in a hug.

Beneath the lip of the window seat, almost hidden beneath layers of paint, but visible now that the cushions had been stripped away, was a little keyhole. I slid down and squatted on the floor amid the dust motes and the carcasses of flies, slipping a thin metal tool into the keyhole and pressing my ear against the wood. I closed my eyes, imagining my father on those long ago days, making the same motions I was making now, listening in this same intent way. When the last tumbler clicked into place I exhaled a breath I didn't realize I'd been holding, feeling a relief so intense it was almost like joy, and pulled open the cupboard door.

The space seemed empty. In the soft glow of sunrise, I reached inside and felt along the floor, worrying about dead mice or, worse, finding nothing but grit. Then my wrist grazed a stack of papers and I pulled it out. Dust streaked my hands and permeated the papers. At first I felt a rush of excitement; surely, if someone had taken such pains to hide these, they must be important. Yet aside from the mild scholarly interest they immediately evoked—they were mostly flyers and little magazines that seemed to have been written by or for suffragettes—the pamphlets were disappointing, more like insulation than a true find. I closed the cupboard, the lock clicking back into place, and carried the keys and dusty papers back to my room. I lay down on the bed, meaning to read through them, but I got caught in the mysterious tides of jet lag, and fell asleep instead.

Chapter 3

MY MOTHER WAS ON THE PATIO WHEN I GOT UP, WEARING A dark purple jogging suit and drinking coffee; her silver hair was pulled back in a purple scrunchie. She had moved the vase of glads with their supple pink throats to a shady spot beside a low stone wall. The lake was as smooth as glass, silvery blue. It felt good to be outside, in so much space and fresh air after the density and bustle of Tokyo.

She pushed the list she was making out of the way and poured me some coffee from the thermal pot, the rich scent drifting over the table.

"Did you sleep okay?"

"Thanks." I took the cup, sipped—it was strong, very hot. "That's good. Thanks. I slept okay, I guess. I was up a lot—jet lag."

"No wonder. Such a long trip."

"Not so long. At least I didn't have to walk." She laughed, and I missed Yoshi. "What's that—a grocery list?"

"It is indeed. You're just in time for the solstice. It's the day after tomorrow—everyone will want to see you."

"Oh, the solstice party—that's right." All the years I was growing up, my parents had star parties whenever there was a minor celestial event—an eclipse of the moon, an alignment of planets, Venus drawing close. The adults brought telescopes and had bonfires on the shore and we children ran until we were so tired we fell asleep on blankets on the grass or curled up in the hammock. I remember being carried inside from those parties, my father's arms so strong around me, falling into the softness of the bed, sleepy and safe, into clean sheets that smelled like wind. "I forgot about the solstice."

"Then you've been away too much," she said.

"So you say," I replied. "Every time I come to visit."

"Oh, don't be so sensitive," she said, and finished her coffee. "Sweetie, I need to go to work today. I wish I didn't, but I've missed so much time with the accident. So here—take these." She slid a set of keys across the glass-topped table, the bones of her hand moving visibly beneath her skin. "The Impala," she explained, though I knew. "It's all tuned up, ready to go. There's an extra house key, too."

"Thanks." I remembered my father taking us for drives on Sunday afternoons, hours when we'd meander with no particular destination, taking in the bursting forth of spring or the trees with their autumn leaves, golden or orange or fiery red against the deep blue sky. "Blake says you might sell it?"

She nodded. "Probably. It's hard to let it go, but it's time. No one in the family wants it, and it's silly to have it just sitting out in the barn." She paused before she spoke again. "I'm thinking of selling the house, too."

I didn't answer right away. "Seriously?"

"I know—it must be shocking. For a long time I couldn't think about it. Your dad is so much a part of this place. And what you said yesterday is true, he loved the lake, and the marsh, especially. So it's hard. But look at this place, honey. I've become pretty handy over the years, believe it or not, but I still can't keep up with it all. I've been thinking about it for quite a while, but it was talking about the gardens in the ER—how beautiful they'd once been—that finally made me realize how far gone things really are. You see something every day, and you don't notice. But when you really look"—she gestured to the tangled jungle of vines and weeds and flowers, the peeling paint on the porch—"I have to admit that it's beyond what I can handle."

"But wouldn't you miss living here?"

"Of course I will. But I won't miss the responsibility. Or the taxes! Anyway, I'm just starting to think about it, honey. No need to panic." She smiled. "It would probably take a couple of years just to clear the place out."

"It might take a couple of decades, actually," I said, trying to keep my tone light. "There's so much stuff everywhere."

"Well, you don't want it," she said thoughtfully, and I realized she really was quite serious about selling. "You're off gallivanting around the world, and Blake can hardly leave his boat for dry land, much less take on the upkeep of this place. Still, it'll be the end of an era."

I didn't say anything for a few seconds, trying to sort out how I felt. Everything my mother said made sense, and yet I hated the thought of someone else living in these rooms, even though it was true that I didn't want to live in them myself.

"The end of several eras," I mused, thinking of Blake and Avery with a baby on the way, which I could not mention. "Oh, speaking of old stuff, I found something last night that I want to show you."

Upstairs, I collected the pile of dusty pamphlets I'd left on the table by the bed. When I came back my mother had been deadheading the flowers, and spent blossoms were piled on the stone wall; she was talking on her cell phone, laughing.

"They're beautiful. They're right here in front of me. Thanks so much—so thoughtful. And your stitches? Oh, good. Tonight? I'm sorry, I can't. My daughter just got in and I don't know our plans."

I splayed the papers and pamphlets out against the glass table, trying to pretend I wasn't listening in on my mother's conversation. In full daylight they looked older and more worn, the paper brittle, the edges stained, the dust of decades woven into the fibers.

"Your secret admirer?" I asked when my mother finished.

"Andrew," she said, flipping the phone closed. "He's very jovial this morning." My mother put the phone down so she could pick up a leaflet.

"It's okay if you want to have dinner with him tonight."

She looked up and smiled, amused. "I know."

"Okay with me, I mean. You don't have to entertain me twenty-four–seven, that's all."

"I know, sweetie. Thank you." She went back to the pamphlet. "My goodness—this was published in 1913."

"Interesting, isn't it? I found these in the cupola this morning. Stuffed away in a window seat."

She met my gaze, her eyes pale gray and curious. "I didn't realize any of those seats opened."

"There's a little keyhole below the lip of the seat facing the lake. With the cushions gone, you can see it. Dad's tools are still on the ring."

"Ah—you picked the lock?"

"I did. First try."

She smiled, her expression suddenly wistful. "Your father would have been very proud."

I looked out at the lake until I could speak again. "Mostly, that's why I tried to open it—just because he'd taught me how. Nothing inside but dust, though—and these."

We sat at the table and leafed through the papers, drinking our coffee. It was an eclectic collection. There was an obituary for the last passenger pigeon in Cincinnati, Ohio, in 1914, and beneath a drawing of her was the word *extinct*. There was a page listing all the births in the county in March and April 1911—I scanned it, but none of the names seemed familiar. I found the wedding announcement of my great-grandfather to Cora Evanston, who was noted in the article to have shaken hands with Teddy Roosevelt when she was five years old. She was the widow of my great-grandfather's cousin, Jesse Evanston. The rest were pamphlets, most published in New York City between 1911 and 1914, though there were a couple of flyers from much earlier, and some from other cities. Two little magazines were devoted to the work of women artists. One flyer, more intense in tone, advertised a rally in support of the right to vote for women, to be held in Canton, New York, in May 1914, with Carrie Chapman Catt as the featured speaker. "Just think," I said, handing that one to my mother. "Maybe a suffragette lived right here in this house."

"Maybe so," my mother said, pulling a pair of reading glasses from her pocket. "Well, this was certainly the area for that sort of thing. I'm trying to remember—I think the house was built in the 1880s, and then fell into disrepair for a while." She waved her hand at the verdant chaos in every direction. "Not unlike now, perhaps. That's how your great-grandfather got it for a song, or so the story goes. I think he bought it around 1925 and set about restoring it."

At the bottom of the stack, several more newsprint articles were held together with a rusty paper clip, the paper so brittle it crumbled at the edges, the type blurry.

"Listen to this," I said, touching my mother's hand. "From 1913. It's hilarious.

"'Fortunately, we have come to realize that healthy outdoor play is as good for the little girl as it is for the little boy, and the ideas of our grandmothers' day—that boys were to play ball, ride horseback, swim, shoot, etc., while the girl's play was restricted to sedentary pursuits, such as sewing, doll-playing, etc.—have been placed on the relic heap, and the girl today keeps pace with her brother in physical freedom and activity.'"

My mother laughed. "Well, I'm glad I was born when I was," she said. "No way could I have made you play with dolls all day, Lucy."

"Imagine living in this house and not being able to swim in the lake."

"I bet they snuck out and swam anyway."

"I hope so."

Between the last two articles I found a small envelope, square, made of heavy paper, the size of an invitation. The flap was tucked, not glued, and inside was a single sheet of paper, folded once. A dried flower, mostly brown but faintly purple in the center, slipped out and crumbled into fragments as it touched the glass-topped table.

The handwriting was faded, pale brown, the letters slanted, sharp, and certain.

21 September 1925

If Iris is to leave your household, Joseph, then I beg you, do not have her go to strangers, but have her come to me, or if she will not, send her instead to the address I enclose, to Mrs. Alice Stokley, a friend of my friends here, who will provide her with schooling and employment suitable to her age—she is only 14.

My heart aches to write this. I understand the expenses you list of clothes, books, and housing, but I cannot see how the money has not been enough. I have sent all I have. If you say it is so, then it must be, though today I cannot sign this note with love, R.

I read the words over and over, trying to puzzle out a meaning, my image of a well-dressed suffragette quickly fading. Joseph must certainly be my great-grandfather, the dreamer, who had climbed the church tower to view the comet. But who was R, the writer of this note? And who was Iris? The letter was forceful, intimate; this was no passing acquaintance.

"Do you know who these people are?" I asked, handing my mother the paper.

She read the note, shaking her head, while I wondered about the author of this note, and who had saved it. Was it perhaps Cora, my great-grandmother, who had hidden these papers? Maybe she had even attended this speech by Carrie Chapman Catt. We knew very little about Cora—only that she had married my great-grandfather Joseph Jarrett after her first husband died in a fall. Like so much of the rest of the family, she existed largely in the shadows cast by my great-grandfather's unremitting light, so it was exciting to consider her inner life, to imagine her sitting in the cupola, reading avidly, sliding her pamphlets into the window seat if footsteps started up the stairs. "No. I've never heard them mentioned. There are so many Jarretts here and there and everywhere, maybe I've forgotten—but no, I don't think so. I've never heard those names."

"Poor Iris," I said. "Whoever she was. Being sent off to work at fourteen."

"That's what happened in those days, though. It happened to my grandmother, too. Relatives took her in when she was orphaned, but not out of kindness. They needed an extra pair of hands. I don't think she was treated very well."

"I wonder if Iris was orphaned, too?" I said softly.

"I wonder." My mother was thoughtful. "You know what? There's a note I found, years ago, that might be connected to these papers. Let me get the key, and I'll see if I can find it. It's packed away upstairs in the trunk."

"Everything's open," I said. "I unlocked all the rooms."

"Did you?" She considered this, an expression of sadness and then annoyance passing swiftly over her face. I knew I'd crossed a line. "Well. I suppose I'll have to look at that stuff sometime, won't I? Anyway, hang on a second. I'll be right back."

Her footsteps sounded lightly on the steps. I wondered how many years had passed since she'd been up there, what she'd feel to find the rooms all open again. I went through the articles, reading more carefully. A slip of paper, inscribed with the same sharp, slanted handwriting of the previous note, fell out from between the pages.

I have read these pages so many times. I have to write it down, how I feel. No one has ever spoken about these things, not in my whole life. We had no mirrors in my parents' house—my own body, and I had never seen it. So I locked the door. There is a mirror on its back. I took off my jacket and my skirt, and folded them on the bed. And then my shift, my drawers, my stockings.

I think I am thin, my skin is so white. Am I beautiful? I cannot say. The room is very dim. I seem to collect all the light.

My cheeks, my collarbones, like wings. Those drawings show wings inside the body, too, a mystery. My body has a pattern. I did not know. Oh, I knew so little, I knew nothing at all! The air was so still and hot, and the door was so far away. I wanted to leave but I did not want him to hate me, and I was afraid. In that strange light he walked around me, his eyes never left me, saying beauty my beauty, I'll marry you, I will. And I believed him.

I read the brief note twice, caught up in its anger and loss and passion, which stood in such contrast to the factual articles in which it had been hidden.

My mother came back out, the screen door slapping shut behind her, holding in her good hand a small package wrapped in dark blue paper and tied with light blue grosgrain ribbon. She put this on the glass-topped table and took her seat again.

"Here's the card that was with it," she said, handing it to me. "Years ago, when I redid that old trunk, I found the package behind the lining. I think the handwriting is the same." The faint scents of cedar and lavender and must floated up when I opened the envelope and took out the single piece of cardstock.

Dearest, this was fashioned for you with love.

I studied the sharp slant of the letters, the loops of the *l* and the *e* almost collapsing on themselves. "Yes, I think it's definitely the same writing. That's really interesting, because while you were gone, I found this," I added, showing her the scribbled note. "It's the same handwriting, I think, though the tone is really different."

My mother read. When she finished, she put the paper gently down on the table.

"This poor woman," she said. "Imagine never having seen your own body in a mirror. I suppose even reading these articles about physiology would have been scandalous at the time. I think it may have been illegal to publish them. No wonder someone stuffed all this in a window seat."

I nodded. "So, what's in the package?" I asked.

"It's beautiful. Wait until you see." My mother untied the ribbon and the papers rustled like leaves as she opened them, layer by layer. "I found the famous trunk your great-grandfather made hidden away back when I was first married. It was in the loft of the barn, pretty beaten up, the bands all rusty, everything coated in dust. I had this crazy idea I could fix it up and earn my way into the family's good will—what a disaster! The trunk was out there in the first place because no one could agree who it belonged to. Your grandfather thought it should go to Art, but your father wanted it, too, and your grandmother took his side for once. After the argument had gotten pretty heated and gone on for several weeks, your grandfather hauled the trunk up to the loft and left it there. He was none too pleased to see it again, let me tell you. But at least the experience wasn't a total loss. By then I'd found this, tucked behind the tattered lining. Here."

She caught the edges of a cloth and stood, letting it unfurl, silvery white and delicate—not sheer, but finely woven. A row of circles in a slightly thicker texture floated like overlapping moons along the border, caught in tendrils of woven flowers and vines.

"It *is* beautiful," I said, reaching to catch its edge, as soft as silk.

"Isn't it? The minute I found this it felt like mine. I never told anyone about it, except for your father, of course." She ran her fingers along the edge. "All these moons, these nests of flowers. This was the inspiration for my moon garden, actually. That, and Virginia Woolf." She smiled and recited, "Every flower seems to burn by itself, softly, purely in the misty beds; and how she loved the grey-white moths spinning in and out, over the cherry pie, over the evening primroses."

I just nodded. I didn't want to think too much about my mother's moon garden, run ragged with neglect. "I wonder who made this. Because it's hand-woven, I think. A very fine flax, maybe."

The cloth lifted on the breeze for a second.

"I don't know. I think of her sometimes, though, all the care she took."

"Maybe she lived here; maybe she's the one who collected all these pamphlets."

"Maybe. Funny that you found these other papers, hidden away all this time."

"See? You can't possibly sell the house—not until we know who wrote these."

My mother didn't answer, but smiled a faraway smile.

"It was a joke," I said.

"I know." She glanced at her watch and sighed. "I really have to get ready for work, much as I don't want to."

"What time do you have to be there?"

"In about an hour. Can you take me into town? Would you mind? I'm not supposed to drive with this cast, and I forgot to ask Blake to pick me up."

"Sure. I'll take a quick swim first, while you get ready."

"But it's so cold, Lucy. June cold, melted-ice cold."

"Right, I know. I was already in, remember? It'll wake me up."

She shook her head, smiling, and carried the coffee pot inside.

I hadn't thought to bring a bathing suit, but I found an old one of my mother's in the summer porch where we always used to hang them to dry. I walked across the lawn and out to the end of the dock and dived straight into the water without missing a beat, so the cold shock happened all at once. This was the best way; by the time I surfaced, the water felt warmer than the air. I dived deep one more time, through the layers of water, cold and growing colder, until my foot touched a moss-covered rock on the bottom, and I came back up, shedding memory and desire, seeking nothing but air.

I dressed quickly, collecting the papers in an old file folder and carrying everything upstairs. The cloth was as light as a fragment of mist, as the remnant of a dream. Then I went out to the barn to start the car. The Impala was canary yellow with a white top and chrome trim like arrows along the sides. It had been polished to a gleam and smelled like stale air freshener. I had to pause, getting in, because the front seat was still set for my father's legs, longer than mine, and I remembered how he'd slide in and turn the ignition with a flourish, and what a treat it had been those rare times I got to ride with him in the front seat, listening to him talk about this or that while we drove into town, meandering, as if we had all the time in the world.

When I finally pulled myself together and adjusted the seat, the Impala started right away, hardly making a sound as I backed out of the barn. My mother came out onto the porch steps, pausing to lock the door behind her. She was dressed in a straight dark blue skirt and a blouse printed with tiny gold flowers, a briefcase in her good hand, her bright green cast in striking contrast to her serious outfit. She was the chief loan officer at the bank, a position she'd worked up to from her initial job as teller.

"This feels strange, doesn't it," she said, sliding across the white leather seat.

"It's like a cruise ship," I said. "It must get about five miles to the gallon."

"Probably. No seat belts, either. He just loved tinkering with it, though. It wasn't ever really about getting from one place to another."

I drove toward town, passing the miles of depot land, the rolling fields verdant beyond the silver chain-link fence, butterflies and goldfinches darting through the tall grasses. At the curve before the entrance I slowed, half-expecting more protestors, but it was quiet, the gates closed, no one in sight.

"I see you brought those papers," my mother said, opening the folder on the seat between us. "I was wondering if the historical society could shed some light on them. You could ask Art if he knows anything, too."

"Art doesn't exactly seem like the family history type." We were traveling through the outskirts of the village by then, the houses closer together, the road hugging the lake. "So—what happened? Between Dad and Art, I mean."

"Oh, why does it matter, Lucy?" she asked. "I don't really like thinking about that time, honey. It can't be changed, right? Life goes on."

"Well, of course." Though I could feel her reluctance, I couldn't back away. "But don't you think it matters to remember?"

"I don't know, Lucy. Maybe. Probably. But it doesn't help me, not anymore."

I pushed again; I couldn't leave it.

"I just don't get it. I guess I'm thinking about Blake, Mom. Working for Art at Dream Master—it can't possibly end well with so much history."

"Suddenly the past is so important," my mother observed drily, and I knew she was thinking again of all the years I'd been gone.

"Ah. Why not just tell me? I'm afraid for Blake. I mean, Art's never going to make a real place for him at Dream Master. He'd never displace Joey, not even a little, to do that."

There was a brief silence. I turned onto the main street into town.

"All I really know is that Art didn't go to Vietnam," my mother said, finally. "That's the main thing. There was the draft, and your father's number came up, and Art's didn't. It was a terrible time, when I think back, waiting to hear if you'd been born on a good day or a bad day, all those young men all over the country, connected by a random date. A terrible time, and terrible luck, too. Your father was supposed to have an equal share at Dream Master, that was always the plan, but while he was in Vietnam your grandfather had a stroke, and your grandmother gave power of attorney to Art."

"Why would she do that?"

My mother shrugged. "Maybe she just got nervous. Your father was fighting a war, after all, half a world away. In any case, by the time your father came back, Art owned the controlling share of Dream Master. He'd already started having conversations, quietly, about selling the lock factory and all the patents to a rival company. He never said a word to us, and your father didn't realize what was going on, not for years. He came back and we got married and he went straight to work, just glad to be home. Glad to be alive. When he finally found out what had happened, he was so mad. He thought about selling out and leaving, but then your grandfather died and your grandmother moved into town and gave us the lake house and the acreage. It felt like a consolation prize, but she was shrewd; it was just enough to keep us here."

"That's when everyone stopped speaking to each other?"

"More or less. The beginning of the end, you could say. Your father stayed on at Dream Master for a few years even after the lock business was gone, thinking maybe he and Art could build something new. They hardly spoke, though. The final straw came in 1986. You know, when the comet came back? The local paper ran a big story about your great-grandfather and how he'd come to this country and started Dream Master after the comet of 1910. Art was featured quite prominently in the article. Your father wasn't even mentioned. I remember he threw the paper on the counter, went to work, and came back two hours later with his things in a box. He never went back."

"I remember that."

"Really? You were so young."

"I remember lying in my room and hearing people arguing downstairs. I remember how weird it was when Dad didn't go to work for a long time."

She was quiet for a moment. "We always talked about moving away. Maybe we should have. Instead, we stayed and tried to work it out. That's when I painted the house. Do you remember that? I started with the cupola and never stopped. If we were going to live in that house, I was damned sure going to make it ours."

"You planted gardens," I said softly, feeling terrible.

"Yes, I did, didn't I? Lots of gardens. Beautiful gardens, weren't they? And your father sold his share of Dream Master and bought the marina. We made a good life from a very unfair situation, we really did."

We were entering the village now, driving past the Victorian houses with their expansive lawns, past the lakeside park, through the center of town with its brick-faced buildings, which had once housed the feed store, the grocery, the five-and-dime, and which were now filled with gift shops, florists, and restaurants. The old movie theater had been turned into condos. I parked behind the bank, maneuvering the Impala into the last spot at the very end of the lot, far away from everyone. My mother got out, smoothing her skirt with her good hand and then picking up her briefcase, already shifting into a professional persona I hardly recognized. I got out, too.

"Aren't you going back to the house?" she asked.

"Not yet. I thought I'd get some coffee. Should I pick you up this afternoon?"

She hesitated, smiling a private smile that somehow excluded me from her day. "Sweetheart, thanks, but I've got a ride. Andy's picking me up."

It took me a minute. "The secret admirer?"

She laughed. "Yes, but for heaven's sake, Lucy, he's just giving me a lift."

My mother kissed my cheek good-bye and crossed the parking lot. I watched her climb the steps and disappear into the bank, trying to sort out my feelings. She was only in her early fifties, attractive, vibrant; there was no reason she shouldn't move on with her life. Maybe, while I was gone, she already had. This was a good thing, at least in theory. So why did it leave me feeling so unsettled? First Blake with a baby on the way, then my mother with a budding romance—it made me feel left behind, as if, despite my constant travels, I'd really been standing in place.

I locked the Impala and walked through town, looking for a coffee shop. Blake was right, there were changes everywhere. The sandwich shop where I'd worked in high school had been replaced by a sushi bar. I paused and looked through the windows, as if I might catch a glimpse of my former self behind the counter, fixing sandwiches and wrapping them in squares of white paper, dreaming of college and freedom. Any minor humiliations, any desire to rage at the general injustice of life— my cousin Joey was among those who regularly came in on the way to a carefree day of swimming or sailing—I'd stored away until Keegan Fall stopped by with his motorbike to pick me up each night at closing time. We flew down the narrow roads around the lake to whatever empty barn or waterfall or field party we could find, the wind rushing over us, cold and thrilling.

A waitress tapped on the glass, startling me from my thoughts. I walked on. Some of the empty storefronts had new businesses—a travel agent, a jewelry store with handcrafted items, a real estate agent with a window full of lake properties. Gone were the little cottages that used to dot the shore; instead there was one minor mansion after another. I could hardly stand the thought of selling the family house, and found myself calculating how my savings—half in yen and half in euros—might translate into dollars. Even if I could afford it, though, I'd be so far away most of the time. And the tax rates was sobering, too. My mother never discussed finances, but for the first time I wondered how much of her salary went into the house and the land, and how much more independence she would have if she sold.

The lake breeze was stiff. At the park, several people were sitting on benches, holding their newspapers tightly against the wind. Sailboats already dotted the water, distant and colorful, like butterflies against the whitecapped blue. Blake's boat, the *Fearful Symmetry,* was moored in the slip he rented at the marina, but when I went on deck and called his name there was no answer, so I walked on.

Dream Master Hardware and Locks was the first building on Canal Street. Dark brick, it rose two stories above the high paned windows of its storefront. Its original name, DREAM MASTER LOCKS 1919, was etched in the broad stone lintel above the door. Blake was probably inside, but I couldn't bring myself to go in; if the family history had a shape, it would be this building.

Instead, I followed a group of tourists past a green space with benches to the renovated glass insulator factory, which took up much of the block. Abandoned and falling into decay for years, the building had been beautifully restored. The brick had been cleaned and tuck-pointed, the windows replaced, porches and balconies added. Colorful signs listed the businesses that had opened there. I found Avery's right away:

The Green Bean
Eclectic Vegetarian Cuisine

It was bright and open, the high rafters exposed and ceiling fans moving gently. The walls were brick and the windows and doors were trimmed out in pale oak. The last time I'd been here the building was condemned, full of broken windows and abandoned machines. Now a line of people waited on the chic scarred wooden floors, and the display cases held scones and muffins and biscotti, all bathed in a soft gold light. The air was full of rich scents, coffee and eggs, balsamic vinegar and sweet brown rice. Avery was busy behind the counter, slight and deft, moving with swift purpose from one task to another. I went out onto the deck and got a table overlooking the water. A waitress with a bright green cap and apron took my order: a roasted artichoke, green bean, and egg-white omelet. She brought hot coffee in a bright green mug. I sipped this, leafing again through the yellowed papers I'd found, wondering who Iris was and what had ever become of her, while water from the lake flowed by steadily.

My laptop was in my bag; other people were working at their tables, so I took it out and found an Internet connection right away. There were twenty-seven e-mail messages, three from Yoshi. He'd sent one from his phone the night before—*having a drink, wish you were here*—and I imagined him at one of the noisy after-work places he liked to go for yakitori or noodles and drinks—really, an extension of the corporate day. The other two were brief and businesslike, forwarding queries from potential students. To the last one he'd attached a photo taken from the balcony outside our bedroom, catching the copper roof of the Fujimoro house and the glint of the distant sea. *At night I wake to the sound of trains passing. I miss you.* I saved that message; I missed him, too.

The waitress brought my order, with a cinnamon roll on the side. "Compliments of the chef. Avery's busy, but she says hello."

"Tell her hello back. Hello and congratulations. This place is terrific."

And it was, the omelet tender, the roll so rich and buttery it melted in my mouth. I ate slowly, savoring the food and the fresh air and the patterns of the water. I was nearly finished before Art came in with my cousin Joey and took a table across the deck. If Art had come to resemble my father, it was equally true that Joey and Blake could have been brothers; Joey had the same curly hair, though his was darker, and the same striking, long-lashed blue-green eyes.

I didn't want to see Joey. I didn't even want to think about him. Though of course I'd seen him at the funeral and the wake and then in passing over the years since, I'd hardly spoken to him since we'd run into each other at the gorge on the night my father died. That night Keegan and I were standing in the curve by the falls, water roaring around us, so we didn't hear the car doors slamming, or the voices coming closer. It wasn't until they started gathering on the shore that we saw them, milling on the broken shale, their faces briefly visible in the flare of lighters as they pulled out cigarettes and joints, their laughter cutting through the night air, through the rush of water. There were a dozen or so people from the in crowd that hung together at lunch and downtown after school. They were mostly wealthy, dressed in boat shoes and designer jeans and polo shirts, driving brand-new cars. Keegan and I stood, as quiet as deer, until the beam from a flashlight caught me in the face.

"Oh, it's just Lucy. Lucy Jarrett and Keegan Fall."

We had no choice then but to make our way to them.

"Hey, cousin," Joey said, emerging from the group as he cracked open a beer. Someone had lit a flare and his face was strangely shadowed in its flickering light. Since the rift between our fathers we'd passed each other in the school halls as if we didn't even know each other, and I didn't trust his sudden friendliness. "How about that? Why'd you cut your hair so short, cuz?"

"Because I wanted to," I said.

He laughed; it wasn't his first beer. "I hear you're heading west."

"That's right."

"I hear you got a big scholarship, too."

"I did," I said; the letter had come just the day before, and the thought of it still made me flush with pleasure.

"That's good. Glad it worked out." And then, before I could say thanks—I was actually about to thank him—he added, "I mean, since you needed it so bad."

"Come on, Lucy," Keegan said softly. His strategy for dealing with fights—his mother was a very vocal member of the Seneca Nation, so he'd had his share of taunts over the years—was always to slip away and disappear, but I stayed where I was, the stream breaking around my ankles.

"What do you mean, Joey? I earned this scholarship."

"Sure," Joey said. He was a shadow on the moonlit shore. "You do what you have to do in life, right? If you have to work, you do." He shrugged and lifted his beer. "I'm glad you'll get to go to college after all, Lucy. Cheers to you." And he drank.

Keegan caught my arm. "Let's go," he whispered. I let him pull me away, but we didn't leave the gorge. I couldn't let it go. I knew even then that I was caught up in something beyond this moment of foolish insult, some dark dynamic I'd inherited as surely as I'd gotten the Jarrett eyes, the gift of listening to locks. Keegan and I crouched a few feet away in the dense green summer foliage; I waited until Joey and his friends shed their clothes and waded out to the falls so they could dart beneath the pounding water or linger in the pools it had formed in the rock over time. When I was sure they wouldn't see us, I scrambled to the shore, grabbed Joey's clothes and keys, and ran. "Is this a good idea?" Keegan asked, but I didn't hesitate. I flung his clothes to the highest branches. His red shirt was a distant flag, his trendy jeans flopped over an unreachable branch, his keys sailed far into the darkness, rustling dense brush as they landed. At that moment I didn't care if Joey walked home naked. He could search for his clothes all night; he could climb to the top of the falls and crash to the bottom for all I cared.

My cousin still dressed well, in parachute-cloth pants and a dark blue cotton shirt. When he smiled up at the waitress, his eyes crinkled at the corners, charming and flirtatious. Her answering laughter floated over the deck. Some things didn't change, after all. I closed my folder with its dusty discoveries from the past, packed up my computer, and paid my bill, trying to slip out amid the crowded tables before they realized I was there. It was too late, though. Art saw me, called my name, and waved me over. To my surprise, Joey stood up when I reached the table and swung one arm around my shoulders. I wondered if he even remembered what had happened at the falls.

"Home for a while?" he asked.

"Couple of weeks. How about you?" The last I'd heard, Joey had been unemployed, bumming around L.A. studying filmmaking, which had made me feel quite satisfied, sitting in my sleek Jakarta office as I read the family news in my mother's letter.

"I've roped him into working here for the summer," Art interjected. "I'm trying to start a dynasty. Why not? Between Joey and your brother, the business could have a pretty bright future. You're not interested, are you, Lucy? Because there's always a place for you, if you ever want."

I smiled politely, wondering what Joey thought of Art's sudden magnanimity, deciding not to point out how he'd been quite happy to slam the door on the idea of a dynasty when my father was alive. "Thanks. I'll keep it in mind. Big project?" I asked, nodding at the rolls of drafting paper on the table.

"Oh, that." Art waved his hand. "Just some ideas we're working out. Always dreaming something up, you know. Staying on the cutting edge."

Joey had been scanning the deck, which was full now, and he didn't look at us as he spoke, taking in the crowded tables. "That's right. Trying to stay one step ahead of the curve. Speaking of which, Avery's sure got a gold mine here," he added. Then he looked up and winked at me. "I may just have to give Blake a run for his money with her, what do you think?"

A joke, I told myself, just a joke. But I remembered in that moment why I'd been so happy to steal Joey's clothes and hide his keys. I remembered my distaste and anger.

"I think you two look busy," I said, forcing a smile, moving away. "Guess I'll see you around."

Chapter 4

"I HEAR HE'S FABULOUS," THE WOMAN SAID, SO ENGROSSED IN her conversation that she nearly ran into me as I left the restaurant. She was carrying an outsized patchwork bag over her shoulder and I stepped back into the doorway to let her pass.

"Oh, he's very good," another woman said. "I was here last spring, when he first opened. They'll let you try it, you know. It's really an experience. They walk you right through it. You hardly have to use any air at all. It's not like blowing up a balloon or anything. I made a glass egg."

"Did you? I want to do that."

"I'm sure you can."

"He really must be good."

"Oh, he is, he's won awards."

They were past me then, walking through the midmorning sunlight to the other end of the renovated factory. I knew they were talking about Keegan, and I followed them as they sang his praises.

It wasn't hard to find the entrance to Keegan's studio; a group had collected five deep outside the tall glass windows at the corner of the building, waiting for the next tour to begin. A sign hung from the doorway with a single word engraved in colorful script: *GLASSWORKS*.

When I looked more closely I saw it was a mosaic made of tiny glass chips fused together. I couldn't see much over the gathered heads, just trees and water reflected in the window, the distant glow of fire beyond. Those in the front rows appeared spellbound, emitting sighs of appreciation. There were many well-heeled women like the two who had passed me, but there were also several young people dressed in plenty of black, and two groups of teens that looked like they'd come on a field trip.

It was frustrating not to be able to see, and I was just about to leave when a tour leader finally pushed open the double glass doors, inviting us to enter. The group shifted and began to flow inside; I went with the current. A rush of heat poured over us as we filed into the vast room and took our places behind the observation railing. In the open space, several figures moved in a slow dance with fire. The guide raised her voice, but I could hardly make out what she was saying over the roar of the venting hood, the flames.

Against the far wall, three ovens glowed with a deep red-orange fire. A man wearing goggles, his dark hair pulled back in a ponytail, crossed the room and eased open a door on the glass furnace, revealing an interior of deep golden orange. Heat shimmered in a veil between his figure and the fire. He selected a pipe from a nearby vat of water and plunged it into the furnace, turning it slowly several times before he pulled it out, the glass on the end molten, glowing.

Subtly, as thick as caramel, the glass shifted shape as he carried it to a long metal table and began to roll it, smoothing and elongating the soft glass against the steel. The color slowly faded, the glass growing clearer with every movement, until it was completely transparent. He sat, still turning the pipe very slowly, then lifted it, pressed the tip to his lips, and began to blow.

It happened very gradually, almost imperceptibly, that the molten glass began to swell, growing round like a soap bubble, the surface thinning and becoming faintly iridescent, as large as a kumquat, then as large as an apple. Twice the glassblower checked his progress and went back to plunge the growing shape into the furnace, softening the glass, our guide explained, before returning to the table to shape it further with his breath. The assistant came up with a wooden paddle dripping wet and pressed it to the base, steam rising in a cloud as the wood began to smolder. She pulled the paddle away, leaving the glass flattened slightly at the base. This process was repeated several times, and slowly the rough shape of a vase evolved. The glassblower transferred the glass to another pipe, using metal tools to widen the opening, while the assistant turned. The vase was released with one swift tap, and the assistant, ready with gloves, whisked it into the annealer to cool.

This process was mesmerizing to watch, and was going on in various stages all through the room. The tour guide announced that there would be time for questions in a few minutes, and that afterward we'd be given a chance to blow glass, if we wished.

It was only then, when he plunged the blowpipe back into a vat of water, his motions fluid and precise amid the sudden burst of steam, that I realized the person breathing shape into the glass was Keegan. Yes, there was the triangular scar above his elbow, and those were his hands, emerging now from the heat-resistant gloves, steady and strong; hands that had curved around the handles of the motorcycle, hands that had slipped beneath my jacket on cold spring nights and traveled across my skin.

Keegan had been a tense and disaffected teenager, attractive in a brooding way, but now he moved with an easy sureness, comfortable with the ongoing dance of the workers and raging fires, calling out directions to the apprentices. The rebel with his leather jacket and his silence and his sweet, crooked smile was gone, it seemed, but the feelings I'd had for him all those years ago surged up as if I'd never left, never gone to college and graduate school and traveled the world.

Keegan took off his goggles and approached our group. His arms were muscled from all the work with glass. He was leaner than I remembered, and he seemed taller, too. I watched, fascinated, as he gestured to the furnaces and equipment, answering questions, but I wasn't really paying attention to anything he said. Instead, I was remembering how it always was with us, Keegan waiting in the shadows of the parking lot while I locked the sandwich shop and stripped off the plastic gloves, the orange and brown polyester uniform. While I scrubbed away the smell of ham, the grease and salt of chips, while I shook my hair free from the hairnet and slipped into my jeans, a tank top, my black leather jacket. I crossed the parking lot and straddled the motorcycle, pressing the length of me against the length of him as we took off into the night.

People started lining up to take their turn at glassblowing, but I held back, watching. One by one, Keegan helped them each create an iridescent sphere. These were set aside to cool, and then the tourists were guided out through the gift shop. Finally, I was sitting alone. The assistant, a young woman dressed in a rust-colored coverall, her dark red hair cut short and her cheeks flushed from the heat, came over.

"Sorry, but we're about to take a lunch break," she said. "The gift shop stays open, though. You might want to check it out. There's some great stuff."

"Actually, I was hoping to say hello to Keegan. He's an old friend. I haven't seen him in years. If he has a minute?"

She studied me for a second before she nodded and turned, her gestures nimble and precise, stepping between the equipment to where Keegan stood by the furnace. When she pointed in my direction he looked up, nodded, wiped his hands on a cloth he'd pulled from his back pocket. I could tell he hadn't recognized me, and I wondered if I'd changed that much. A few feet from the railing he paused and really took me in, his brown eyes crinkling at the corners.

"Lucy?" he said, his smile deepening. "Lucy Jarrett. Wow. What a surprise. What's it been—a million years?"

"Hey there," I said. So much time had passed that it was a shock as well as a pleasure to hear his voice. I felt it straight through my body, head to toe. "How are you, Keegan? How have you been?"

He stepped over the railing and sat down next to me, smelling faintly of heat and sweat, and looked at me intently, pleased and amused.

"I'm good, doing well. I've got this new place."

"So I see. Not bad. People are standing five deep outside."

He nodded. "Yeah, so far so good, anyway. I've been here about six months. I'm giving myself three years, but they say the first one is the real make-or-break time. But you never know—a cold summer and all the tourists will stay home; there's a lot I can't control." He grinned. "But then again, I've never been terribly afraid of risk."

"Yes, I seem to remember that about you."

"And you? I hear you're a world traveler."

I told him a little about the places I'd lived and studied, the jobs I'd taken, about my life with Yoshi, in Jakarta and Japan, which suddenly seemed very far away.

"You know," I said, interrupting myself, overcome with regret suddenly for the way I'd ended things between us. "I'd like to tell you more, and I'd like to hear how you came full circle to end up back here—I know you were traveling, too—but before I say another word I want to apologize."

"For what?"

"For being such a jerk to you after my father died."

"Oh, Lucy." Keegan shook his head, studying his hands, lean and calloused, which were clasped between his knees. "Look, it's understandable—even if I didn't understand it at the time. And it's true, I didn't. But you were in shock. I know. It's major, losing a parent, and I shouldn't have pressed you."

"No, really, I was awful to shut things down like that. I've thought about it off and on for years. I'm sorry."

He nodded but didn't speak. I put my hand on his arm and he looked over at me, a question in his smile, and I remembered how we'd pull over in some deserted place, still trembling from the wind and the ride, and pulled my hand away.

"You were leaving at the end of the summer anyway," Keegan said. "We didn't ever talk about it, but I knew. So. What do you say we just let the past be the past?"

Could it? I wondered. Could the past ever be just the past? Still, I felt relieved of a burden I hadn't realized I'd been carrying.

Keegan's attention had been drawn elsewhere. *Back to the furnaces,* I thought at first. Or maybe his assistant, her short red hair swinging as she worked, was more to him than an employee. But then I saw that his gaze had gone even beyond the furnaces to the far wall, where a door had opened in the brick. A small boy with curly dark hair stood in the doorway, dressed in jeans and a T-shirt, barefoot. A young woman waited behind him, her hands on his shoulders. She pointed in our direction and the boy waved, and Keegan waved back, standing up.

"Damn. I asked Tina not to bring him down here. It's too dangerous." Keegan was already swinging one leg over the rail. He called back over his shoulder, "Lucy, if you've got another minute, come on and meet Max. Meet my son."

Most people had gone by then, but a couple had stayed to tend the furnaces, keeping them stoked until the next round of tours. They kept an eye on me as I navigated the edges of the room, careful to stay far from anything that glowed, still trying to get over the shock of hearing Keegan say "my son."

I caught up with him at the doorway. He was squatting, talking to Max, who looked to be about six or seven years old. He had eyes as dark as Keegan's and he was holding something in his fist. Slowly, Max opened his fingers and Keegan picked a beetle up from his small palm.

"Very nice," he said. "Did you bring it for lunch?"

Max laughed, clearly delighted. "That's silly, Dad."

"Silly? Why so? Lots of protein in bugs."

Max dissolved into giggles. "Dad."

"I told him it was gross," Tina said, "but he wanted to keep it."

"This is my old friend Lucy," Keegan said, handing me the beetle with its shiny brown sides. "Maybe she'll stay for lunch. Should we invite her? She might like bugs."

"You know what?" I said. "One time I did eat bugs for lunch. Deep-fried crickets, to be exact."

Max was wide-eyed. "Did you like them?"

"They were crunchy," I said, putting the beetle back in Max's small, damp palm.

Keegan chuckled. "Seriously, come on up, Lucy, if you have time." He stepped aside so Tina could leave. She was slender, waiflike, and very quiet, her hands plunged into the pocket of her hoodie as Keegan pulled bills from his wallet and thanked her for coming on such short notice. He pointed Max back toward the stairs. "Bugs or not, I need to get you some lunch. The next babysitter's supposed to be here at one o'clock. Mom's sick, isn't she, buddy?" Keegan said, ruffling Max's hair.

"I shouldn't come up, then," I said. "I don't want to disturb her."

"Oh, she's not here," Keegan said.

"Mom lives in Auburn," Max confirmed.

"We're separated," Keegan explained. "We have been for about the last year. The regular babysitter couldn't make it on such short notice, so we had Tina, and this afternoon we'll have Tracy. Max and I also worked out a deal, didn't we? A little bit of coloring, a little bit of Play-Doh, a visit from Dad every hour, and a video."

"Plus the cell phone."

"There you go," Keegan said, tapping his pocket. "It's right here."

We entered a loft space with soaring ceilings and beautiful golden pine floors, sanded and polished, scars and all. The vast paned windows I remembered from the factory were still in place across one wall, and Keegan had set up little living areas, using furniture to mark off spaces. A couch faced the windows overlooking the canal, flanked by a coffee table and two chairs. Adjacent to this was an area dedicated to television and games, with beanbag chairs and low tables all around. This was clearly the space Max had been frequenting, for there were crayons everywhere, stuffed animals and plastic blocks, an open box of animal crackers, and a wealth of crumbs on the rug.

On the opposite side of the loft, the windows were much higher, light drifting down from another story. Here, Keegan had installed a kitchen with a counter that opened onto a dining area. His furniture was garage-sale eclectic, the cabinets stainless steel, the dining room Danish modern from the 1950s. Against a white wall there were shelves displaying rows of molded blue glass insulators, all lined up like little glass hats; these had been made in this factory in the town's glory days, Keegan explained, before oil prices went sky-high and fiber optics were invented and businesses fled south. He made a habit of collecting them. I touched the sea-blue glass, clear and full of air bubbles, trying to imagine myself back in a time when these rooms had been filled with the roar of machines, the heat of glass, the voices of the workers calling. Silence now; the waters of the canal flowed below.

Keegan had gone right to work, placing slices of wheat bread on the counter, slathering on peanut butter and jelly.

"Want a sandwich, Lucy?"

"No, thanks." I slid onto a stool, watching Keegan slap the sandwiches together, feeling right at home. I thought that it must be good to be Max, to have a father as silly and interesting and attentive as Keegan was. "I just ate."

"Apple? Glass of milk?"

"I'm fine."

I wanted to ask Keegan whom he'd married, but not with Max in the room.

"This will sound crazy," I said instead, "but this feels like exactly the same space where you used to hang out. The same view from the windows anyway."

Keegan cut Max's sandwich into quarters and looked up.

"You have a good eye. This *is* just the same space."

"Really? Your old crash pad?"

"My home away from home," he agreed, opening the refrigerator for some milk.

Max asked for apples, and I wandered back to the space with the overstuffed furniture, gazing out at the canal with its steady waters. In high school Keegan had discovered this place and carved out a spare retreat, furnished with a battered leather sofa and an orange crate table, amid the abandoned machinery and debris. He came here to clear his head, he said, but the one time I'd come here with him I'd felt claustrophobic, the heat of the day trapped in the motionless rooms and the water, unconcerned with anything, drifting by outside. I preferred the thrill of the motorcycle rides, or the nights when we took the canoe out onto the dark lake, paddling deep and then letting the boat drift, trying not to capsize when we kissed.

"Lucy?" Keegan had crossed the room and stood beside me. "You okay?"

"Memory lane, that's all," I said. "It's all so different than it was."

"Isn't it? It was a shock to me, too. But the way it happened was very serendipitous. I went to art school, you know. In Chicago. I never got to tell you. I was wait-listed all that spring, but I kept quiet about it, because in those days I didn't really believe that the things I wanted for my life would happen. But I got in, and scraped together enough money and scholarships to go. The first couple of summers, I took a job on freighters, mostly traveling to Mexico and South America. I lived in Mexico for a while, too."

"Sounds exciting—why did you come back?"

"My mom got sick. Cancer. She was so young, too. She died four years ago, and she was sick for a few years before that. I used to take the bus back to see her every couple of months. One of her nurses was Beth Rowland. Do you remember her?"

"Didn't she have a brother? Dave?"

"That's right, Dave. Well, one thing led to another. I transferred back here, to Alfred University, and Beth and I got married. Too fast, and we were too young. Way, way too young." He folded his arms, and gazed out the window at the water. "By the time Max was born our marriage was on the rocks, pretty much. It was a bleak time for me. One day I was out walking along the canal and I saw FOR RENT signs on this building. The units weren't finished yet, and no one else had bought one, so I had free choice; they wanted an anchor tenant, so the price was right. A place to live, and studio space—it was like a gift. So here I am."

"I'm sorry about your mother," I said. "I didn't know."

"She always liked you, you know."

I smiled, thinking about Beth Rowland, whom I remembered only vaguely—a graceful athletic girl with wavy brown hair. Max resembled her, it was clear, and for some reason that made me feel suddenly bereft. I'd never let myself think about what might have happened if I hadn't cut Keegan off so abruptly. I'd needed to leave and I had, and yet our lives had been so deeply woven that last spring before my father died. It could have been me marrying Keegan, sharing this steady and interesting life he had made.

"Can I have some animal cookies?" Max called.

"Depends on how many giraffes you already ate," Keegan called back. "More than eleventy zillion and you have to quit." Max laughed. "I drive his mother crazy," Keegan added to me in a softer voice. "But when he's here, I want him to be happy."

I asked where the bathroom was and Keegan gestured beyond the kitchen to another open space where beds were set up, a large one and a trundle bed, for Max. The bathroom was beyond, partition walls hardly taller than I was, and all rough plumbing. I dried my hands on a stiff white towel and came out, glancing around for a mirror.

That's when I saw the windows, beautiful stained-glass windows propped against the larger windows of the loft. Two were contemporary, with bright colors and geometric shapes. I guessed that these were Keegan's work. The third was very different, a lush, brilliantly toned scene in the Art Nouveau style. It depicted a story that seemed vaguely familiar, two men ripping open a sack of grain to reveal a silver chalice hidden in the center. A crowd was gathered, including several women, one, in a green gown, standing apart from the others. The artistry of the window was evident even to my untrained eye. Though it was very dirty—a corner had been cleaned, but that was all—the colors were rich and strong. However, that was all secondary, as far as I was concerned. What stopped me was the border, intricate, a pattern I'd seen for the first time just that morning: a row of overlapping spheres in white, interlocking moons nestled amid lacy vines, bright flowers.

"Keegan," I called without moving. "Where did you get this window?"

"Which one?"

"The window with the grain and the chalice. The window with the border."

"The Joseph window?" Keegan came into the bedroom. Max followed, climbed up on the trundle bed, and lay down on his stomach, watching us with his head resting on his folded arms.

"Tired, buddy?" Keegan asked. He pulled a blanket up over Max's shoulders. "How about a rest? I'll put your tape on."

"I don't want to," Max said, but he didn't move.

"I know. Just for a minute, close your eyes."

Keegan pressed a tape into an old machine and a cheery song about an animal parade came on. With a nod to me, he picked up the window with the border and carried it to the living area, where he leaned it up against the wall of windows. The colors were even stronger here.

"It really needs a cleaning, as you can see. They took it from the chapel on the depot land. For some reason it wasn't ever installed—they found it in a closet in the back. You know the depot is closed, right?"

"I saw a protest there the day I flew in."

He nodded. "Yeah, there'll be a fight over that land, I'm sure. But when the base was built—when that land was originally taken—there was a thriving village there, and a small mission chapel that had been built by the church in town. After Pearl Harbor, the land was cleared fast to create the base. It was a war effort, and though it's kind of hard to believe it these days, people simply packed their personal things and left, and everything—houses, barns, shops—was razed. But the church officials protested, arguing that the building and the land were a sacred trust. Plus, there was a small cemetery, as well as an Iroquois burial ground right next to it. So when the village was razed, the church was simply boarded up and left standing, and the cemeteries, too; that was the compromise. A few months ago someone went inside, for the first time in decades, I suppose. They found this window leaning against the wall behind the altar and started to take the protective boards off the others. They've been pretty much forgotten all these decades. Everyone has been amazed by the quality of the glass art. There are nine other windows in addition to this one. Those I've seen so far are quite exceptional. Stunning, really. I was hired to do an early assessment of their quality and to recommend a studio for restoration, which they desperately need. Since this one wasn't in the wall, I brought it here to have a closer look."

"Do you know who made it?"

"A few ideas, but nothing solid. Why?"

I sat down on the floor in front of the window, studying the colorful scene dimmed with grime.

"It's this border," I said, tracing a section with my finger, the pale, interlocking spheres of glass, thickened in places, the vines and flowers made of leading. "There was a piece of cloth in a trunk in our house. My mother found it, years ago. It's got this same pattern woven into the fabric. I've never seen anything like it, have you?"

"No, I haven't. Not in glass, anyway."

"I suppose it could be a common pattern for the era. I'd have to do some research. But the coincidence is so striking. It seems there must be a connection."

Keegan squatted down beside me, so close I could feel the heat of his arm.

"The church might know something about the donor. There's at least one other window with this border motif. Much larger and grander, actually; it also came from the chapel, and they've already had that one restored. It's on display in the church downtown for the time being, so people can see it while the other windows are assessed and cleaned. I think they're hoping to raise some more money. The restoration is pretty expensive. You really should see it, just because it's so beautiful. I'm working there tomorrow, if you want to stop in."

"Thanks. I'd like to. Keegan, why did you call this the Joseph window?"

He laughed. "That's what the rector calls it. Otherwise, I have no idea. I think it's the story about the coat of colors, when Joseph gets tossed into the well and taken off to Egypt. As I understand it, this particular scene comes at the end, when his brothers finally find him during the famine."

"Really? I don't remember a chalice in that story." The glass near the base of the window was thick and slightly buckled, as if it had begun to slip and pool. "It looks as if it's melting," I added.

"It is, kind of. Glass isn't really a solid. It always longs to return to its fluid state. Over time the lead weakens and gravity pulls at it—that's why restoration is so necessary. Otherwise the glass will eventually flow out of its shape and the window will be lost."

A buzzer sounded. Keegan stood up and opened the door to the studio. He had a quiet but hurried conversation with the new babysitter, during which I gathered my purse and the papers I'd been carrying around all day, feeling the tempo change, feeling both excited about the window and suddenly in the way.

"I'll see you tomorrow, then?" I asked, starting down the stairs, and Keegan paused to smile and wave and tell me to meet him at St. Luke's at ten.

The next tour had already started, the furnaces roaring, the guide explaining the process to a new group of mesmerized tourists. The only exit was through the gift shop, and I stopped to look at some of the work—vases and plates, stained-glass sun catchers and delicately blown spheres. As I turned, my purse caught the edge of a display, and when I reached to catch the perfect glass egg I'd jolted loose, I hit another display and started a cascade of plates tipping over one by one until the last one fell against a dark red bowl and sent it crashing to the floor.

"Hold still," the sales clerk said, raising her hands, palms open as if to push back a wave. "Just stand still, and take a deep breath."

I did, watching while she gathered up the pieces.

"Just one bowl," she said, finally, and refused to let me pay. "It happens."

I was very careful as I left, chagrined, suddenly exhausted, too. It was still a beautiful day, windy and changeable. The clouds that had threatened to gather were more scattered now, and the early afternoon was sunny. The Impala floated over the low hills, the lake flashing through the trees. I hadn't expected to be so moved by seeing Keegan again. Maybe it was simply that things had ended so abruptly between us, with no sense of closure or any kindness on my part, but all the old stirrings from those last wild days of spring were present again, forceful and unsettling.

When I got home, the house was empty. My footsteps echoed, fading in the layers of space, above and below, and I had a moment of understanding why my mother had locked up so many rooms. I went upstairs and slept a deep, post-jet-lag kind of healing sleep, no dreams.

By the time I woke up it was late afternoon. My mother still wasn't home. The windows were open in her narrow downstairs bedroom, fresh air flowing in through the pines. A yellow dress was tossed on the bed, half-slipping off the corner. Her closet door was open and clothes were askew on the hangers, hanging off the doorknobs, a kind of exuberant chaos that seemed completely out of character. Restless, I changed into the same bathing suit I'd used the day before, cobalt blue and still faintly damp from my last swim, then went down to the lake.

The boathouse doors swung back with a great groan, and I stepped into the cool darkness, water lapping just below the motorboat, which was in its hoist. I lifted my dark green kayak from its hooks and hauled it through the wide doors to the beach. Half in the water and half on the stony shore, it moved lightly with the waves. I waded into the lake and climbed into the boat, pushing my paddle against the rocky bottom until the water grew deep enough to stroke. There was a small breeze, and my muscles moved in a rhythm as familiar as breathing. Leaves fluttered against the vivid sky.

I skimmed across the dark blue water, traveling along the shore as it curved outward into the lake, to the place where sediment from a stream left a trail of silt and the marshes began—a stand of cattails, broken by purple flowers, songbirds flitting in and out, sharp reds and yellows and blues against the muted reeds. This was where we'd always stopped before, the invisible boundary between our land and the forbidden depot. My arms ached. I rested the paddle and let myself drift. The shadows of fish flashed below. Bass, maybe perch; my father would have smiled to see them. Wind rustled the reeds and waves lapped at the boat. On the shore trees had grown up, ending abruptly in fields that were themselves overgrown and rippling.

It happened unexpectedly, as moments of beauty so often do. As I sat quietly, adrift, piecing together the stirring discoveries of this strange day, the deer began to emerge from the trees. The legendary white deer, wild and elusive; I'd never seen them before, and I held very still. One by one, until there were five of them, quivering for a moment at the edge of the trees before something startled them and they leaped high, running like swift clouds through the fields.

Chapter 5

THAT EVENING MY MOTHER CAME HOME IN A PALE GREEN
Prius, laughing as she slipped her good hand through the flimsy plastic
handles of the bags, standing and smiling at the car as it backed out,
because one arm was in a sling and the other was full, and she couldn't
wave. The driver did, however, and stuck his head out the window
to call good-bye. His face was angular and kind and he had salt-and-
pepper hair, and my mother stood in the driveway until his car
disappeared out of sight.

We ate our simple dinner—French bread, pitted kalamata olives,
smoked Brie, and a green salad—at the counter, exchanging stories of
our day. Hers were about people who'd been in and out of the bank,
people I might remember; mine were about the changes all over town.
She'd taken a tour of Keegan's Glassworks last spring and showed me
a plate she'd bought—bright yellow glass with a scalloped edge. Afterward, we cleaned up our few dishes, then poured some more wine and
went out to the patio, where my mother supervised while I hung deco-
rations for her solstice party: tiny lights nestled amid the bushes and the
plants, even cascading from the overgrown peonies in her old night
garden. I thought about my father as I worked. The last time I'd been
here for this party, the summer before he died, he'd hung lanterns all

along the shore and built a bonfire that lasted all night. I placed a few flowering plants in white baskets from the branches of the trees. I tied ribbons on the branches, too, and rearranged the furniture.

In the morning we got up early and I filled balloons from the party-sized helium tank my mother had bought, tethering them to the lawn and porch railings and the branches of trees, where they floated like small planets gone adrift. We drove into town a little early so I could meet Keegan at the church by ten. After I dropped my mother off, I parked and sat for a few minutes in the Impala, checking messages on my phone. Yoshi had e-mailed the dates for his Indonesian trip and a couple of suggestions about when to fly here. I started to text back, but suddenly I wanted to hear his voice, maybe to anchor me in the midst of all these unexpected dynamics from my past, so I called him instead. He picked up on the second ring, his voice so steady and familiar that I felt a rush of comfort, a surprising longing to see him.

"Hey, where are you?" I asked.

"In the kitchen. Having a drink. Going over some paperwork."

"In the kitchen," I repeated. "I wish we were dancing."

"Ah. Me, too."

"Yes—I'd like to be dancing in the darkness with you."

Yoshi laughed, pleased, I could tell.

We talked for a moment about his travel plans, and when I hung up the air all around seemed clear and empty, somehow new.

Tourists had begun to stream into town for an art fair in the park, and I walked against the current to the church. Its doors were shaped like an arch, rounding upward, tapering to a point, painted dark red. They had old-fashioned hinges and hardware, with ornate patterns and deep keyholes, made to resemble workmanship from much longer ago. The intricate iron stood out sharply against the deep red color of the door. Inside, a rush of silence, a deep stillness that made me want to listen, and the scent of wood and wax. I paused at the threshold, adjusting to the quiet, the muted light. The floor was made of rust-colored ceramic tiles, the pews of dark polished oak, and the stained-glass windows were luminous, alive in the dimness of the church.

I closed my eyes for an instant, remembering. As a child, I had come here twice a week, for choir practice and for the slow Sunday service. Blake and I sat fidgeting in the pews, passing notes and drawings on the backs of the offering envelopes, our parents casting disapproving glances. I remembered the standing and the rising and the kneeling, the prayers spoken in unison, the same each week, and then the silent prayers, more mysterious, when I knelt self-consciously, aware of the breathing all around. In those days God seemed as silent as my father, as disapproving as my uncle, as distant as the portrait of my great-grandfather in the hall; when I closed my eyes, those were the gazes I felt, and I was always nervous. Still, at eight, ten, twelve, I did my best, praying for the usual things: grades, crushes, the baby chickadee fallen from its nest, its tiny life trembling in my palm. In seventh grade, alarmed about pollution, I prayed hard for the rivers and the lakes.

Yet even though the stories all seemed to exclude me—in my childhood, the only formal place for a woman in this church was helping with the altar cloths or singing in the choir—I was still drawn to something here I couldn't name, the deep silence, perhaps, or the sense of mystery the silence evoked. Even as a teenager, riding wild with Keegan Fall, I still went to church. When the church rules finally changed—it had been a controversy, a bitter decades-long fight—I was among the first girls to become an acolyte. I remembered slipping into the white cotton robe falling in smooth folds to my ankles, tying the rope belt around my waist, lifting the heavy brass cross and leading the choir slowly down the central aisle. I felt both happy and defiant, my hair cut short that last spring I was home, wearing cutoff jeans beneath the flowing robes.

Then my father drowned. I sat in the usual pew during his funeral, his casket in front, piled with flowers.

Grant us grace to entrust thy servant, Martin. . . . We filed up for communion, one by one, the church echoing with the sound of our shuffling steps, the muffled coughs and cleared throats. We knelt together at the railing, my mother on one side and Blake on the other, and in the pause between the wafer and the wine I listened to their soft breathing, my sadness and longing so great I imagined it would split me open. The priest moved behind the wooden railing, offering the wafers and then the chalice, lip to lip. *The Body of Christ, the Cup of Salvation.* I didn't believe that literally, it made no logical sense, and yet nonetheless I had often felt a sense of mystery, of longing and longing answered, in this ritual, this place.

So I waited, kneeling between my mother with her red-rimmed eyes, her silver hair pulled severely back, and Blake in his suit grown a few millimeters too short on the sleeves. I waited, but when I stood up, the wine both sweet and bitter in my mouth, and walked through the narrow corridor around the organ and back to the sanctuary, I did not feel healed of my grief. Nor did the world appear transformed. I paused at the front of the church and looked at the rows of pews, full of familiar faces, among them my cousin Joey and Uncle Art, his wife Austen holding Zoe on her lap, everyone dressed in black, some weeping or wiping their eyes. The same people were wealthy, the boat owners and the business owners who had depended on my father to open their locks, to reveal their secrets and their treasures. And the same people were poor. They had the same dreams and secrets and losses and frustrations. My father was gone, forever gone, but in a few minutes we would all step back into our lives, and the day-to-day would close over his absence as seamlessly as water over a rock.

Lucy, my mother whispered, slipping her arm through mine. *Lucy, honey.* She took a step down the aisle, and I did, too.

That was the last time I had been inside this church.

The air was still and hushed. In India and Japan I'd visited temples that held this same expanding silence, a quiet that invited stillness and careful listening; in Indonesia the call to prayer had wavered through the shimmering air five times a day. Yet it had been years since I'd encountered my own traditions, and the church felt familiar and new all at once—the sanctuary lighter, the windows more vibrant. I started down the center aisle. There was scaffolding in the front, by the window nearest the baptismal font, and the floor beneath this window was strewn with tools on a piece of canvas. The window itself was filled with plain glass. A moment later, Keegan walked through the narrow doorway that led behind the organ, whistling lightly.

"Hey," he said, breaking into a smile when he saw me, his voice echoing.

"Hey."

"How did you get in?"

"The door—it's not locked."

"Really? It should be. Just one second."

He half-ran down the aisle. When he came back, he gestured to the blank window. "This one was taken out for repairs; it's coming back this afternoon. I'm just getting rid of some of the old caulking to make the process go faster."

"Is this one of the windows with the border?"

"No, those are all still at the chapel on the depot land. All but the largest one, which was sent out to be cleaned and is on display here for a little while. Want to see it?"

"I do, but I'm afraid I'm interrupting you."

"That's okay. I like showing off the window. It's just in the other room, back where they keep the vestments and the wafers and the wine. Follow me."

I did. Everything about Keegan was so familiar, the shape of his ears, the swing of his arms, the hair slipping out of the dark blue rubber band he'd used to pull it back. *Do you remember?* I wanted to ask as I followed him through the narrow passage, up three steps into the room. *Those nights when we went out on the lake to watch the moon rise, letting the waves and currents push us where they would?*

Keegan unlocked the door and waited for me to step through into the little room, which was oddly shaped, with cupboards and shelves filling all the walls.

"I used to put my robes on in this room. By the way, don't use that sink."

Keegan smiled. "Yes. They warned me. A pipe straight to the earth. Communion wine only. No cleaning of brushes."

"It's interesting—as if the earth is sacred, like the wine."

"It is."

"Interesting, or sacred?"

Keegan considered this. "I meant interesting. But both, I'd say. Come, check out the window—it's hanging just around the corner, in the alcove."

I passed the cupboards full of vestments and stopped as I turned the corner, taken aback by the size and beauty of the stained-glass window. It was hanging against a large clear window overlooking the lake, so the mosaic of leaded glass was flooded with light, and colors slanted down from it, falling on my arms and all across my body to the floor. Birds flew through a deep blue sky, and below, multicolored fish swam in a darker sea; vines climbed the edges and flowers bloomed in brilliant hues, and amid the flora there were animals of all kinds, zebras and lizards, rabbits and elephants, surrounded by lush trees whose variegated leaves seemed to flutter. Human figures, too, growing like the trees and flowers from the dark red earth, visibly human but not visibly male or female, standing with lifted arms, their hands transforming into leaves, the leaves in turn forming letters I did not understand. Bordering the lower edge was the familiar row of vine-laced moons. Above these interlocking moons was a single sentence in letters of light-filled gold.

"For she is a breath of the power of God . . . she renews all things."

"I had no idea it would be so stunning," I whispered.

"Isn't it something? The other window—the Joseph window—will be spectacular when it's finished, too. I can't wait to see the others in the chapel. This one is the creation story. It hadn't been completely covered, and when I first saw it, the glass was so filthy I couldn't even make out the images. Do you see these patterns?" he asked, gesturing to swirls of clear light woven through and around the images. "That's wind, I finally realized. At first, when the glass was still so dirty, I thought maybe pieces had been broken and replaced, but this glass is original, organic to the design."

I reached through bands of color-filled air to touch the border of overlapping moons, the intricate vines and flowers of lead. "Here it is again, that pattern."

"Yes. It must have been a commissioned work. It's nice stained glass," he added. "Not Tiffany or La Farge, though there are traces of those influences, but still—very, very good. Whoever made this window was an excellent craftsman, a fine artist. And whoever ordered it had a lot of money."

I stepped back as far as I could and took some photos with my cell phone. They'd be grainy, and I wished I'd thought to bring my camera.

"Is it very old? It looks old."

"Well, it's an Art Nouveau design, but because of the glass I'd place it later than that, maybe 1930 or 1940. The techniques used to make stained glass are ancient, but in the nineteenth century people started simply painting the glass, dropping the leading entirely for a few decades. Then, around the turn of the century, there was a revival of the old ways, which still continues."

"And the one in your studio? The Joseph window?"

"That's the same period. The same artist, too, I can almost guarantee. It was probably part of the same commission, along with the windows that are still in the chapel. I don't know why it wasn't installed."

Light fell across me in vibrant patches of blue and green and yellow, and I thought of the fabric with its matching border. The writer of the notes may have woven that cloth, and perhaps she had made these windows, too, or at least been involved in their design. But who was she, the elusive R? Who was she?

"The pattern is so distinctive," I said. "I'm sure there's a connection."

"You know, Lucy, donors used to have artists put figures of loved ones—or even of themselves—into biblical scenes. I'm wondering about the women in the other window. Were they at all familiar?"

"I don't know. That's an interesting thought, but I wasn't really paying attention to the faces. I'd have to look again. But it would take more than a face, anyway. I need a name, a story. I wonder—Keegan, can I go to the chapel to see the other windows?"

"That, I don't know. It's still pretty restricted. But I'll find out."

Footsteps had been echoing distantly in the sanctuary, then in the hallway; now they drew close and we turned as a woman entered the room. She was tall, though not quite as tall as me, wearing a clerical collar, and maybe a decade older than me. Her blond hair swung near her shoulders.

"Oh," she said. "Keegan. I didn't realize anyone was here."

"Hey, Rev," he said, smiling. I could tell he liked her. "This is my old friend Lucy Jarrett. We were wild and crazy about each other, once upon a time."

She smiled and shook my hand. "Suzi Wells."

"That would be the Reverend Dr. Suzi," Keegan said.

"Suzi will do," she said.

"We were just looking at the window," I explained.

"Ah—I've been away all week. I haven't seen it yet. May I?"

I stepped back as she entered the alcove and paused, stunned, just as I had been, by the breathtaking beauty of the patterns in glass and light.

"Oh, my. It *is* beautiful. Gorgeous. Keegan, is this really the same window?"

"Cleaned up nicely, didn't it?"

"I can't believe it. It was so dark before."

She stepped closer and touched the human figures, their upraised fingers turning into leaves, into language.

"What does it say?"

"It's Hebrew. *Tehillah,* or praise. *Adamah.*"

"As in Adam and Eve," Keegan suggested.

Suzi nodded. "Yes, though, actually, *adamah* simply means arable land. In English it translates roughly as *hummus, human*. I think that must be why these figures are growing right out of the earth." Suzi leaned closer. "So it means something like 'The People Praise God.' When did you say this was made?"

"In the 1930s or '40s, maybe."

She straightened, thoughtful. "Really? Yet the imagery seems very contemporary. The imagery and the use of that quote."

"I wondered about the quote," I said.

She nodded without taking her gaze from the window. "I'd have to look it up to give you the exact chapter and verse, but it's from the book of Wisdom, praising Wisdom's many virtues. Some traditions call her Sophia, which of course is the Greek word for *Wisdom*. According to the Scriptures, Wisdom was present at creation. No, I'll amend that— she was not just present, Wisdom was actively involved in creation. Delighting in it. She's described as an all-powerful, all-seeing, vivifying force. I imagine that's what this wind weaving through the scene is all about. Wisdom is associated with the Holy Spirit, too; and *spirit* is a word that also has feminine roots—*ruah* in Hebrew, meaning breath. Present in all things, renewing all things." She turned to Keegan. "This was made in the 1930s—are you sure?"

"I'm almost certain."

"Well, that's remarkable. In recent years there's been so much interest in recognizing the female imagery and metaphors woven all through Scripture, which have been largely ignored. It wasn't so common in the 1930s or '40s, though. I wouldn't have expected to see it in the artwork of that time. So I'm very curious about this window. It's just so fascinating."

She laughed at herself then and stepped back from the window. "Okay—fascinating to me, as a priest and a scholar. Maybe not so fascinating to either of you."

"Well, it is," I said. "Though to be honest, for different reasons." I pointed out the border motif, and told her about the fabric and the papers I'd found stuffed away in the cupola. "I'm startled to find this pattern here, and I'm walking blind, really. I don't know anything about this person, except that whoever she was, she must have been connected to the family."

"And to the church as well, I would guess."

"Right, that's exactly right. So I was wondering if the church has any records of these windows? Any documents about the original gift?"

Suzi held up her hands. "I really don't know. That's a good question. All I know for certain is that the chapel on the land that eventually became the depot was established as an extension of this church sometime in the 1930s. So the dates fit, don't they? Still, that's all I can offer. I'm relatively new here. But why not ask Joanna—she's the church secretary." Suzi slipped a cell phone from her pocket and checked the time. "She won't have left for lunch yet. Joanna is very good, and she's been here several years—if there's something to be found, she'll find it."

We stepped into the hall, which was lined with windows on one side and the framed black-and-white photos of the rectors, going back to 1835, on the other.

"I'll see you next week, Rev, when the window is ready," Keegan said. "Tuesday sound right?"

"It does." She smiled then, standing in the doorway. "You know, Keegan—you're welcome on Sunday. You, too, Lucy."

I didn't answer—the long line of rectors gazing down from the wall made me nervous—but Keegan laughed, as if this were a familiar and comfortable exchange between them. "Thanks, but I don't like organized religion. No offense. I prefer to pray my own way."

She smiled. "Let me ask—how is that?"

He grinned. "Well, I take my boat out. I sit on the water and think about the things in my life that haven't gone so well, and how I could have done some of them differently. And then I think about good things in my life, one by one. I feel thankful."

The Reverend Dr. Suzi Wells laughed. "Well, I'm not going to argue with that," she said. "Still, come sometime. I think you'd be surprised."

Still smiling, she stepped back into the vestment room. Keegan offered to show me the office, but I told him I knew where it was.

"Thanks, though—and for bringing me here."

He smiled, and held me in his gaze for a moment, and I had the strange sense that time was falling away, that this moment was connected quite directly to the days when we'd been so free and easy with each other. It was all I could do to keep from taking his hand, as I would have done so easily when I was seventeen.

"It's good to see you, Lucy. Really good. Let me know what you dig up, okay? And I'll find out about access to the windows in the chapel. Good luck on the treasure hunt, meanwhile."

The hallways were byzantine, one addition connected to another, but I made my way to the office without getting lost. Joanna, the secretary, was a short, stocky woman with shoulder-length hair full of streaky blond highlights. We'd been talking for several minutes before I realized she'd been a year ahead of me in school, a girl who sat next to me in Spanish class. Now she was married, with two children; her husband worked for the town. I told her the same story I'd told Suzi, about the border in the cloth and the windows, about the notes I'd found. She rummaged through a file cabinet for a few minutes but came up with nothing. "Let me check the archives," she said, standing up and smoothing down her skirt. "That's a fancy way of saying I need to go poke around the basement. It shouldn't take too long."

I waited in the office, gazing out the arched window where the branches of a gingko tree were swaying, their fan-shaped leaves rippling in the breeze, feeling restless and excited, stirred up in a way that made me think of my early days with Yoshi in Indonesia, when it was becoming clear that life was shifting, changing in some vital way. One discovery by itself—the cloth, the letters, the windows—would have been something to note and then forget, but together they raised questions about my past, which I'd always imagined to be written in stone. It was seismic, in its way, as jolting and unexpected as the trembling of the earth.

Footsteps sounded on the stairs, and then Joanna appeared, a little breathless.

"Well, there wasn't much of a record," she said. "At least, not that I could find right away, though I'll try to look again if I have time. The chapel was built in the late 1930s as an extension of this church. It's in the church history; ground was broken in April 1938. I have an idea, too, that it was funded by an anonymous donor, though I couldn't find anything down there about that. All I found was this one receipt with the name of the artist who made the windows."

She handed me a piece of paper with a formal heading and pale blue lines. The script was neat and careful, the prices logged in columns on the side. It made me think of bills of sale from my childhood at Dream Master, the gray steel case that held the invoice forms, the listing of purchases, all written carefully by hand, whisper-thin sheets of carbon paper layered between the invoice pages.

This invoice was dated October 6, 1938, and listed three items.

8 Stained Glass Windows @	*$250.00*
1 Stained Glass Window @	*$650.00*
Total purchased	*$2,650.00*

Across the bottom was written *Gift, Anonymous Donor,* and below that was a stamped notation of the artist:

FRANK WESTRUM, GLASS ARTISAN
ROCHESTER, NEW YORK

"Thanks," I said. "This is really very helpful."

"Good. I thought it might be. I'll make you a copy. Also, I had a kind of brainstorm after you told me your story, so I figured while I was down there with the mice I'd pull the baptismal records from 1910 to 1920. Just to see, you know. We had a flood a few years ago, so there are some gaps in the records, but I thought you might want to take a look. Here."

I thanked her and sat down on the overstuffed couch and opened the folder, inhaling its scents of dust and mildew, leafing through the ornately printed certificates, each one decorated with the delicately outlined image of a winged dove, haloed, descending toward what looked like a shell. Some certificates were water-stained, some yellowed. The old-fashioned names flashed by: Gloria, Herbert, Evan, Lloyd, Stuart, Susanna, Norman, Earl, Ivy, Bertha, Homer, Gladys, Oscar, Grace. There were no Jarretts, though I saw plenty of last names or middle names that I recognized from families who still lived in the town, or had when I was growing up—the ancestors of my classmates. I tried to imagine what it would have been like to live here in 1910, before the great wars and before the depot was built, when the lake shores were undeveloped, wild land flowing straight down to the water's edge. There would have been no paved roads. The children whose names were flashing by would have attended one-room schoolhouses and pumped their water out of wells and used lanterns at night.

While flipping through May 1911, I glimpsed a familiar name and went back to check, a pulse of excitement rising as I read. The baptismal certificate was on thick paper, stained at the upper right corner but otherwise intact:

We Do Certify

That According to the Ordinance of
Our Lord Jesus Christ, We Did Administer to

IRIS JARRETT WYNDHAM

On   *31st day of March A.D. 1911*

The Sacrament of

HOLY BAPTISM

With Water
In the Name of the Father, and of the Son,
and of the Holy Spirit

In	*St. Luke's Episcopal Church*
On	*11 May 1911*
Signed	*Reverend David Prescott* †
Parents	*George Isaac Wyndham (deceased)*
	Rose Jarrett Wyndham
Sponsors	*Cora Stuart Evanston*
	Walter Jesse Evanston

"Find something juicy?" Joanna asked, pausing to look over my shoulder on her way to the copy machine.

"Yes, actually—I think I did. I found her name. Rose Jarrett." I thought of the papers from the cupola, the letter about Iris going away, signed with the single letter *R*. This must be her—Rose. I felt such a sense of frisson then, as if this woman who had lived and dreamed and suffered a hundred years ago had just stepped into the office. "She must have been my great-grandfather's sister. We never heard a thing about her, yet here she is in 1911, a widow with a daughter."

Joanna sighed. "It gives you chills, doesn't it, really? When you see these forms, black and white and just filed away in boxes, and then you think how all these people were here once, maybe standing right where we are now, having conversations, living out their lives."

I nodded, thinking of the cloth, wrapped in layers of paper, hidden behind the lining of my great-grandfather's trunk. Maybe it had been for Iris. A baby blanket, perhaps—that made sense, given its size, its delicacy, and the care put into its weaving. But why had it been hidden away? "I wonder what happened to her—to them both?"

"I hate to say it," Joanna said, handing me the copy of the receipt, "but I can check the burial records if you want. Lots of children didn't make it in those days. She'd have just been little when the flu epidemic hit."

"That could be," I said, feeling oddly relieved; as sad as that story would be, at least I'd have an answer. "That would explain why no one in the family ever talked about them." Then I remembered the other note, the one about sending Iris away, but I asked Joanna to check the records anyway.

"Could I have a copy of this birth certificate, too?"

"No problem." She slid it onto the glass and closed the lid. "I won't get back to the archives today. Maybe not tomorrow, either. But if you leave me your number, I'll call when I can and let you know. You could check the cemetery records, too. Marriage records, that sort of thing. Newspaper archives."

"Thanks very much."

"Glad to help. It's kind of a fascinating mystery, isn't it?"

It was, I thought, but it was more than that, too. I felt such a quickening to think there was a family story I hadn't yet heard, a way of thinking about the past that might break open everything I'd understood. It was exhilarating and a little frightening, too; alluring.

"Yes," I said, taking the papers. "Yes, indeed, it is."

Chapter 6

IN A LABYRINTH, WALKING THE SINUOUS PATH THAT LEADS finally to the center, people once carried clews, round balls made of twine, to help them find their way back out. As I left the church, I felt I'd just discovered such a clue, tangible and full in my hands, unraveling slowly to mark my way through this unexpected landscape of the past. I threaded my way back through the byzantine corridors, questions about Rose Jarrett and the artist Frank Westrum rising one after another. She must have known him, somehow; she must have been responsible for the border in the windows, a kind of signature. She might even have commissioned the windows, or been involved in their design somehow. If the papers from the cupola were any indication, she'd been an adventurous person, passionate and thoughtful, interested in women's suffrage. It was as if a window had appeared where I'd imagined only a wall, so now I could look through it to discover another way to see the story. Whatever had happened to Rose had happened long ago, was ancient history, really, yet I felt instinctively that there was a connection to my own life, and this was both thrilling and a little frightening, too—because what if in the end I discovered something I didn't want to know?

I wanted to see the window again, to see if there was anything I'd missed. Keegan had already gone, however; the door to the vestment room was locked. I probably could have eased it open if I'd tried, but the eyes of all those rectors lined up along the wall made me too uncomfortable. I had a sense, also, that I should not trespass, which echoed the feeling I'd always had growing up that the mystery of this place was ultimately sealed against me, no matter how much I might long to enter. I was a girl, and so my picture would never look like the long line of men whose faces lined the wall and whose domain this seemed. Though in the Episcopal Church women were regularly ordained starting in 1976, Suzi was the first female priest I had ever met. Likewise, in my family, the stories never had women at the center, which was one reason why the discovery of Rose—an ancestor I'd never heard of before—felt so astonishing and intriguing.

I walked on. The sanctuary was very still, my footsteps echoing on the tiles. Near the front doors, at the end of the aisle, I paused and turned. Light filtered through the stained-glass windows, muted and serene. Each one told a story, invisible in darkness, taking life only when the sun rose and filled the colors, and each was the story also of the people who had given it, long dead now, whose names ran along the bottom in gold letters. *In honor of James, Hannah, Our Beloved Mother, The Evans Family, Sarah, Virginia, child of Susan and Samuel.* What had Joanna said in the office as she handed me these papers? *It gives you chills . . . all these people . . . standing right where we are now . . . living out their lives.* My father had grown up in this church, and his father. My great-grandfather Joseph had walked these aisles before anyone alive today was born.

And Rose. She had stood here, too, decades before the chapel on the depot land was built yet somehow connected to it, holding her infant daughter, trying to soothe her perhaps, tucking the edge of blanket closer against the coolness radiating from the stone walls, even in May. Then she had walked out into the world and disappeared.

A door fell shut; footsteps sounded on the choir stairs, and then the Reverend Suzi emerged into the sanctuary.

"Ah, Lucy," she said, looking momentarily startled. "Still here? Can I help you with something?"

"I'm just leaving. I just wanted to stand in the church for a minute, I guess. I hope that's okay. I was thinking about all the people who've stood here before me. I haven't been here since my father died," I added.

"Of course it's okay. I heard about his accident," she said. "I'm sorry. It must have been very hard."

I nodded. "It was. But it was a long time ago."

"Some moments resonate in powerful ways," she said.

Our voices were soft amid the stone walls, the wood. I didn't know what else to say, and anyway my throat had thickened with the memory. Suzi let the silence gather for a moment.

"You're Evie Jarrett's daughter, aren't you?" she asked, finally. "How's your mother doing? How's her arm?"

"She's fine," I said. "Better than I could have imagined, actually; she's even got a date this afternoon."

Again, Suzi didn't respond right away, which made me really have to think about the words I'd spoken, to hear the sharp edge my tone had carried.

"You know, your mother's very glad you're here," she said. "I went to see her after the accident and she was so excited that you might come. It must be a little strange for you, though. Are things very different?"

"Oh, very! Everything has changed so much. Even here. Maybe especially here. It wasn't that long ago, but I was the first girl allowed to be an acolyte in this church."

"Really? So you were breaking new ground." Suzi spoke rather pensively, which made me wonder about the path she'd taken.

"I suppose I was. I didn't think about it that way, though. I just wanted to be an acolyte. I hate to say it, looking back, but it didn't cross my mind even then that women could be priests."

"Some changes take a very long time. Like water on stone. That's why I'm so especially interested in these windows." She nodded at the manila folder Joanna had given me. "Did you find anything?"

"Yes, actually. I did." The photocopies of the baptismal certificate and the window receipt were still faintly warm from the machine when I handed them to her. "Rose. Her name was Rose Jarrett. She would have been my great-great-aunt, though I've never heard of her before. She had a daughter, Iris."

"Reverend David Prescott—he's in one of the photos on the wall," she noted, pointing out the signature. "Such a long time ago. No one would remember her, which is too bad. Whoever she was, she seems to have found a way to see herself—and women in general—in the sacred texts. To imagine herself into the story, so to speak. I think that must have been exceptionally difficult at the time."

"I know. I wonder what happened to her. And to Iris, too. Plus there's the border pattern, which is so fascinating. Keegan said the windows dated to the 1930s, but the papers I have are much earlier."

"Keegan, yes." She nodded, smiling, as she gave me back the photocopies. "Well, he would know, wouldn't he? I've become very fond of Keegan, working with him on these windows. He has enormous expertise, and he's been good enough to donate his time, which is a real blessing. The windows are a treasure, but they turn out to be so incredibly expensive to maintain."

"It's been good to see him again," I said, remembering Keegan lifting Max into the air, their jokes back and forth, their laughter. I thought about Blake and Avery with a baby on the way, the elegant vase of gladioli sent to my mother by a stranger, the mysterious old papers, fragile and gritty to the touch.

Her cell phone rang, shattering the quiet, and the Reverend Suzi slipped it from her pocket, glancing at the number.

"Sorry—I have to take this," she said, gesturing toward the door. "It's good to meet you, Lucy. Come by anytime. And keep me posted on whatever you find, okay?"

Outside the muted sanctuary, the world seemed bright, newly washed and vibrant. Summer traffic was already backing up the hill and the sidewalks were crowded with tourists in their loose bright cotton clothes. I walked without intention for a while, absorbed by my discoveries, wandering through shops without really seeing what I was looking at.

In the park I wove my way through the art fair to the seawall and tried to call Keegan; he didn't pick up, so I left a message about the baptismal certificate as I wandered on through the village. At last I found myself at the pier where Blake moored his boat. The *Fearful Symmetry* was graceful, thirty feet long with a tall white mast, bobbing gently on the water. I stepped down onto the deck and called his name, but the voice that floated up from the cabin was Avery's, light and questioning. She appeared at the bottom of the stairs wearing jeans and a gauzy yellow blouse, her dark hair pulled back in a ponytail.

"Oh, Lucy," she said. "Hi there. Blake's at work. I was just going over some papers. Come on down, if you want."

The stairs were narrow, opening into a paneled room as compact and complete as a studio apartment, with a v-berth in the bow, a galley kitchen, a tiny bathroom, and a sitting area. I'd always marveled at how sparely furnished Blake's life was. He didn't care much for things; he liked the uncluttered feeling that came from owning very little. Avery moved some pillows to make room on the built-in sofa. The table was covered with drawings, and I recognized my mother's drafting paper, her neat lines and handwriting.

"Want some iced tea?"

"I'd love some, thanks," I said.

Avery moved as deftly in the narrow galley as she did in her restaurant. She piled up all the papers on the table and placed tall glasses of tea, with sprigs of fresh mint, on two bright yellow coasters she pulled from a drawer. I had to smile: never in a million years would it have crossed Blake's mind to buy coasters. "Those are some sketches your mom did," she said as she sat down. "They're plans for organic vegetable gardens, actually. That's my dream someday—to have organic gardens to supply the restaurant. I hate paying to ship all that stuff, using all that energy just to move produce around. She drew these up for me for my birthday last month. It was really nice of her."

I sipped my tea: cold, faintly raspberry. I remembered Avery from high school as quiet, so shy she'd hardly spoken the few times we'd met before. But that was years ago, before she'd gone away to school, before she and Blake had ended their romance and started it again several times. She seemed so different now, confident and sure of what she wanted. She was at least two years younger than I, and yet she already had her own business and a baby on the way. I felt a pang of unexpected envy. Envy, and the feeling I'd had so often in Japan that despite my wild adventures, I'd really been circling around the same still point for years.

"I think you're brave," I said.

"What? Dating Blake?"

"Well, that, of course." I laughed. "No—taking all this on, I mean."

"I'm nuts, actually." She laughed, too, relaxing back on the cushions. "Really nuts, I sometimes think. It's exciting, sure, but there's so much pressure. And it never ends. Still, I love working with food. I love it when the place is full and I look out and see everyone happy, eating healthy things."

"My meal was so good."

She grew serious. "Thanks, but it could have been better. If I had everything fresh, it would have been *tons* better. Your artichokes were canned, I don't like that. We were hoping—Blake and I were hoping— that maybe we could get some acreage when the depot land is sold. Or else down the road, when your mother sells her place."

I caught my breath a little to hear how far my mother's plans had traveled, trying to sort out my complex feelings before I spoke. Loss, of course, and anger that I hadn't known, and the feeling that I'd been left out, which wasn't fair; I'd been gone for years, after all. Avery didn't notice and went on speaking.

"Not the lake lots, of course. Too pricey. But that land is black earth, as rich as Iowa soil, and it used to all be farms, before all the bunkers and airstrips. There's a black walnut tree just inside the depot gates—my great-grandfather planted that tree decades ago when that part of the land belonged to him. I'd like to get it back."

There was wistfulness in her voice, and hard determination, too, and

I thought about the day I'd arrived—was it only two days ago?—Pete leaning into the truck and saying, *You sure you don't have a dog in this fight, Blake?*

"Were you at the rally?" I asked.

She shook her head and gave a short laugh. "It seems I'm only ever at the restaurant anymore. But I heard about it—people came in for lunch after it was over. Were you?"

"I saw it, that's all. Driving by with Blake the day I arrived." The boat swayed gently with a wave; one of my mother's drawings slipped from the table and I leaned over to pick it up. "So many people were there."

"*So* many—it's true. It's a huge controversy. The wetlands people may be getting together with the white deer people, though. They had lunch together, anyway—eggplant soufflés and white wine."

I thought of the deer emerging from the trees and moving like clouds against the sea of tall grass. My father used to tell us stories about them, growing up, and sometimes we'd go out in the evenings to search for them, driving slowly on the gravel roads around the depot. People came to school with stories of having glimpsed one standing in the road or disappearing into the trees, but that was rare, and in all our searching, we'd never seen one. I asked Avery if she had.

"Just once. A long time ago. We were on our way home early one morning when one leaped in front of our car. My father slammed on the brakes, barely missed it. We watched it disappear into the trees, and then five or six others followed, pure white. I was little, so they seemed magical, like unicorns or something. I remember we all just sat there, not speaking, for a long time. Even my dad."

I sipped my tea and studied the three framed photos on the wall behind Avery. The first had been taken on the deck, Blake standing behind Avery with his arms around her waist. Her head was tipped back against his shoulder, she was laughing, and he was smiling down at her, the wind sweeping a piece of her hair across his cheek. The other two were more formal, the two of them standing side by side, smiling at the camera in front of a lighthouse, an anchor.

"Do you like those?" Avery asked, turning to look. "I just had them framed last week. Those two on the left are from the trip we took to Nova Scotia last spring."

"You look so happy, both of you." I was hoping she would tell me about the baby, so I could stop pretending that I didn't know.

"We were. It was a good trip, mostly." She paused, as if choosing her words. "Lucy, is Blake very much like your dad was?"

I thought about this. I never would have said so before, but knowing that Blake was working at Dream Master made me reconsider. He'd given me his reasons, and they made sense, but all the same I wondered if the lure of the past had something to do with it; he could have worked anywhere else in town. "I don't know. In little ways, maybe. The same laugh, the same eyes, that sort of thing. But I can't really say. Why?"

Avery sighed. "I guess I'm just trying to figure him out. Sometimes he just seems so far away. So lonely, somehow."

I didn't answer right away. *A very sad and lonely person*—those were Yoshi's words to me. I liked to think that the past had no power over me, but maybe I was caught in it, too. Avery half-stood and reached to the counter for a bag of pistachios, and I glimpsed the faint swell of her stomach beneath the gauzy blouse, so slight I might not have noted it unless I already knew. When Blake had visited me in Indonesia, he and Avery had broken up, and one evening he'd struck up a deep flirtation with a woman at the next table. I wouldn't have guessed then that he'd be here now, back with Avery, about to have a baby. The boat swayed gently, making little ripples in the iced tea, and I thought of the waves that had run through the earth, and of Yoshi's hand running the length of my thigh as I woke amid the earthquakes. I thought of his kindness, and his kiss on the train platform, which seemed a very long time ago.

"Lucy?" Avery said, offering me the pistachios. "Earth to Lucy? Did you want some of these? Some more tea?"

"No, thanks." I smiled. "Sorry to be so spacey. I guess I'm still a little jet-lagged. I should probably get going, actually."

"Well, it's good to see you. Can I give Blake a message?"

I shook my head, imagining the sort of message I could leave: *Discovered lost ancestor, please call ASAP.* "That's okay. I'll track him down eventually."

Upstairs, I lingered on the deck, thinking about Yoshi, about loneliness, mine and Blake's and maybe everyone's. It was still a clear day, but low clouds were scattered on the horizon and the wind had come up; the lake was decorated now with whitecapped waves. The fire siren sounded; it was noon. Even though I didn't want to go to Dream Master, I did want to tell Blake what I'd discovered, and so I left the pier and crossed the main road, following the outlet away from the center of town.

For all his talk of progress, Art had let Dream Master go quite a bit. The plate-glass windows were filmy, and one of the gutters on the third floor was hanging askew. The brick needed tuckpointing, too, and the grass in front was long. It struck me that maybe Art's hiring of Blake was less an act of generosity than it was of desperation. There was something weirdly comforting about that thought—there seemed to be some sort of balance in the universe as long as Art was doing poorly—except that now Blake was involved. I took a deep breath, cut across the gravel parking lot, and climbed the concrete steps. A little bell rang when I opened the door, just as it had in my childhood. I paused on the threshold, taking in the scents of metal and paint and sawdust, the underlying odor of dust.

Aisles of locks and hardware and tools—hammers and saws, planes and screwdrivers—ran the length of the store. There were bins of nails in addition to the prepackaged kinds. Wooden rulers and yardsticks sat beside tape measures in their flashy yellow cases. Dozens of different light fixtures hung from the ceiling.

I took a step and called out, "Hello." Nothing. "Hello?" I called again, louder, but no one came.

I walked up and down the aisles, noting the little changes. Art had put gray speckled linoleum down over the planked floor I remembered; he'd taken down the old flypaper strips, probably long ago. The offices were still there, though, off a corridor that ran behind the storefront, still paneled in dark wood. My father's, at the end of the hall, was completely changed—the rolltop desk gone, the windows shaded with plastic blinds, and a new conference table set up in the middle of the room, shiny black laminate, with sleek black chairs around it. A nondescript gray carpet covered the floor. I looked hard for the room where I'd played with Blake and Joey, the room where my father had unlocked so many secrets, but I found no trace.

"Lucy?"

I hadn't heard Art coming, and I started. Tall and broad-shouldered, he blocked much of the hall. Again, he looked so much like my father that I found it difficult to speak.

"I was looking for Blake," I said.

"I sent him to take an order in Union Springs. He should be back pretty soon."

"Oh. I see." There was an awkward silence. "Do you have a minute, then?" I asked. I realized I hadn't really spoken to Art in years—even at my father's funeral we'd exchanged only the most formal of condolences—but maybe my mother was right and he'd be able to shed some light on the discoveries I'd made.

He glanced at his watch. "A few minutes," he said. "I've got to meet with the zoning office. But come on in, why don't you, and sit down."

I sat in a leather chair with wooden arms. It would spin, I remembered; we used to play on it when we were kids.

"So, Lucy," Art said. "It's been a while. What's on your mind?"

"It has been a long time, hasn't it? Well, I guess I just had some questions."

He put his elbows on the desk, made a tent with his fingers, and nodded.

"Happy to help if I can," he said.

I was still carrying the papers from the church. Rose Jarrett would have been Art's great-aunt; Iris would have been some kind of cousin. Yet I found myself reluctant to mention Rose, the discovery of her existence still too new for me to want to share it. Instead, I explained about the papers and pamphlets I'd found in the cupola and asked if he knew anything about them.

Art listened closely. "In the cupola, you say? What sort of papers?"

"Oh, a hodgepodge, really. Old newspaper articles, some magazines. I was interested in them because they looked like they had to do with the women's suffrage movement. I thought they might be historical. I thought you might know."

His lower lip jutted out slightly as he thought, and he shook his head. "Doesn't sound at all familiar. Before my time, of course."

"Right. I thought they might have belonged to my great-grandmother—your grandmother. Cora, wasn't that her name? The dates seem about right for that. I never knew her, of course. I don't even remember hearing stories about her."

I'd found the key; he relaxed back into his chair.

"My grandmother was a lovely person. At least as much as I remember her. I was only about ten when she died. She loved children, doted on us. She made beautiful pies, too; it seemed there was always a fresh one on her kitchen counter. That was in the house you lived in, which was where I grew up, too. We moved in after our grandfather died; Grandma Cora was a widow by then and not in good health. She slept in the big room at the front of the house—I think you've got the piano where her bed used to be—and my mother took care of her until she died. Now, my mother—your grandmother—she was a wonderful woman, too."

I nodded, remembering the story my mother had told me about what had happened while my father was in Vietnam. My grandmother had died when I was seven, and all I could conjure of her was a fluttering sleeve of a polyester print dress, her eyebrows arching as she laughed, and the fleeting dark red color of her fingernails.

"She didn't like to swim," I remembered, suddenly.

"No, she did not. She made sure we learned, though, me and Marty."

"You know, the strange thing is, there was a note with these articles. It seemed like it had been written by a member of the family—it was written to your grandfather, in fact—but it wasn't signed. It was passionate, though. A note about a girl named Iris, being sent away."

He didn't answer for a moment, and when he spoke, it was slowly.

"Well, I suppose it's no secret that every family has its skeletons; you know that by now. There was some sort of scandal, way back when. My grandmother's sister, maybe? I'm just talking from what I've gleaned, growing up, overhearing a bit of this or that. It's probably as much conjecture as truth. But something did happen that got hushed up. Had to be hushed up, that's how I understood it, for the sake of the family. It never interested me much, to be honest. I'm much more concerned with the here and now, with what's right in front of my face."

I thought about what was right in front of us, this building with its layers of the past, and all the things that had gone unspoken for so many years.

"What happened?" I asked, the words slipping out despite my best intentions. "What happened between you and my father?"

When Art finally met my eyes his face was anguished, grief welling up, the creases on the side of his mouth deepened, his eyes darkened with pain.

"I will not speak ill of the dead," he said. "That is one thing I will not do. But I'm sure you've heard only one side of the story. Your father was a good man, but he wasn't easy. He especially wasn't easy for me. Maybe I wasn't easy for him, either. I don't think we'd have gone into business together if it hadn't been expected of us from the time we were born. Still. What I did back then, while he was off fighting the war—it was wrong. I can't undo it. But I can make a place here for you and for Blake. I was—I am—absolutely serious about that."

I didn't know what to say; his impassioned remorse caught me off guard. I wanted both to defend my father—against what, I didn't quite know—and to comfort my uncle, who seemed consumed by the past in ways I hadn't ever considered. My emotions were so intense and so conflicting I didn't realize right away that he hadn't really answered my question, not at all.

"I can't work here," is what I finally said. "If that's what you mean. I appreciate the offer, I suppose."

He nodded once, ran his hand through his bristly gray hair.

"Just think about it, Lucy. There's always a place for you here. Remember that."

I told him I would and then I stood up, saying good-bye, touching the papers I'd found, just to be sure they were still in my bag.

"Don't be a stranger, Lucy," Art called as I left, and I waved.

A few customers had entered the store and were browsing in the aisles. To my surprise, Blake was behind the counter, listening intently to a woman describing the kind of plumbing supplies she needed. When he finished filling her order he came over, smiling, rolling his eyes a little at the situation. I thought of Yoshi, who had been so pleased when I told him about Blake's impending parenthood. When we'd talked of children it had always been in an abstract sort of way, and now I found myself wondering what Yoshi would be like as a father.

"What's up?" Blake asked.

"Yoshi says hello," I said. "He's going to try to smuggle in some rambutans."

Blake laughed, and I told him briefly about the letters in the cupola and the windows in Keegan's studio and the church. Again, I didn't mention Rose. Blake was interested but distracted, too; he kept glancing around the store to see if there were any customers in need of help. Then Zoe came in, ringing the little bells on the door, and when she saw me she ran over and hugged me with the exuberance of early adolescence, then started talking a mile a minute about a play she was in. She'd grown so tall since I'd last seen her, and wore dangling earrings, and once in a while she spoke of herself in the third person—"Zoe is so excited!"— as if she were posting on Facebook and not talking to me in person. She looked a lot like Joey, with the same intense Jarrett eyes, her dark hair. Blake smiled, raised his eyebrows slightly, and drifted off.

I promised Zoe I would see her again before I left and she said she was coming to the solstice party with her parents. Then I left Dream Master and walked back into town, got a sandwich and drink from the grocery store, and sat on a bench by the outlet while I ate. Light made dancing patterns on the water and a few seagulls hovered on the concrete seawall, waiting for crumbs. I tossed them little pieces of bread, thinking about my discoveries at the church and my conversation with Art.

When I finished eating, I wadded up my lunch papers and tossed them out, pausing in the shade of an oak tree to look at the pictures I'd taken of the Wisdom window on my phone. The resolution wasn't very good, but still the imagery was vibrant, striking. Had Rose designed them? And who had she been?

Yoshi had sent several messages regarding his flights. I didn't call because it would be after midnight there by now, but I went to my saved messages and played the two he had left, telling me about a job he'd heard about, one I might like, and that my students missed me and he did, too. I closed my eyes and played them again, listening to the cadence of his voice.

Keegan had left a voice message, too, about the windows in the chapel. I tried to call him back, but he didn't pick up.

When a break came in the traffic, I darted across the street and slipped into the library, which had once been a private home. Built of gray stone, it had a deep front porch facing the lake and a wooden screen door that creaked and slammed shut behind me, causing the librarian, a young man with short hair, to glance up. I passed the bulletin board thick with flyers: lost cats, town meetings, a poster from the white deer consortium, an open meeting of the Iroquois coalition. I sat at one of the long cherry tables where I used to do homework. Now there were computers at every seat. I typed in "Frank Westrum." To my surprise, several articles appeared. Though I couldn't trust them all, I read the first entry with some excitement anyway. Westrum had existed, clearly, and as more than a local artist who'd faded obscurely away.

Frank George Westrum, 1868–1942. Glass artisan. Associated with the studios of La Farge, where he apprenticed 1894–1901. Married Beatrice Mansfield in 1896, and in 1919 moved from New York City to Rochester, New York, to open an independent glass studio. Consultant to Corning Glass. Two children, Marcus Westrum b. 1896 and Annabeth Westrum b. 1897.

At the end of the article there was a link to the Frank Westrum House in Rochester. A photo came up of a stained-glass window, a simple sphere in shades of ivory against a dark square background. A long-stemmed tulip followed the inner curve of the sphere, the leaves fluid, as if floating, the single red flower blooming. The patterns did not match the border pattern on the windows in Keegan's studio or the church, but stylistically the resemblance was clear. Below was a single paragraph.

Home and studio of glass artist Frank Westrum from 1920 until his death in 1942, this house contains 27 striking examples of his stained-glass work in wide variety, from the grand windows in the stairwell to modest transoms. Sold to private owners in 1945, this dwelling was purchased by the Frank Westrum Preservation Society in 1968, on the 100th anniversary of his birth. The Society is dedicated to the collection and preservation of his body of work, which exemplifies the resurgence of the art of stained glass and the influences of William Morris, Charles Rennie Mackintosh, and the Art Nouveau movement. Open May through September, Tuesday and Thursday, 2–5.

I read this over twice, thinking of the window with its cascades of vines, its animals and swimming fish, its brilliant colors, and its row of familiar lacy moons along the bottom. Rochester was about an hour away; I'd have time to get there. Sunlight filtered through the leaves, making an ever-changing pattern on the glossy table. The librarian gave me an amused, perplexed smile when I asked him what day it was, just to be sure.

"Wednesday, last time I checked."

So much for making it that afternoon. And anyway, there was my mother's party.

On an impulse, I went back and typed in "Beatrice Mansfield." Sometimes I hated the Internet, which made it possible to give in to every momentary distraction or flight of mind. But to my surprise she, too, was listed with a brief entry.

Beatrice Mansfield, b. April 23, 1873, Seneca Falls, NY. Design school in New York City. Married glass artist Frank Westrum in New York City in 1896. Active in the fight for women's suffrage, corresponded with Elizabeth Cady Stanton, Amelia Bloomer, Margaret Sanger, early mentor to Vivian Branch. Two children, Marcus and Annabeth. Died April 10th, 1919, of influenza.

Nothing came up when I typed "Rose Jarrett," however; not a single thing. When I checked the library's online catalog—the card catalog of my childhood, with its oak cabinet and thick rectangular cards in neat rows, was long gone—there was nothing there about her, either.

I sat back in the chair for a few minutes. The ceiling fan clicked softly above me, stirring the warm air. An older couple, probably retired, sat in stuffed armchairs by the bay window, reading magazines and looking up to chat with each other now and then. A group of teenage girls drifted in, moving together like a flock of beautiful birds. It was so calm and tranquil here, and I considered just staying for the afternoon, finding a good book and a comfortable chair. Those were some of the simple pleasures I'd imagined when I decided to make this visit. Yet the past kept welling up, as persistent as a spring, and my curiosity to know what had become of Rose and her daughter, and how their lives might have helped to shape my own, now became as insistent as hunger. It was partly the pure mystery of it, a desire to put all the pieces into place and solve the puzzle. Yet it had to do with my own life, too, all the scattered fragments that might come into focus if I had a clearer lens. All these years I'd taken such comfort in my wandering life, but really I'd been as anchored to the night my father died as Blake had been, circling it from afar, still caught within its gravity. Now Blake was moving on, and my mother was, too; the feeling I'd been fighting all day, this feeling of being adrift by myself in a vast dark space, engulfed me for a moment.

I closed my eyes, listening to the fan and the squeak of the screen door as it opened and fell shut with a sharp slam, the soft, excited voices of the girls, the rustling pages of the paper. The air smelled of new leaves, leather, and wood and bloomed with quiet. I stayed, finally. I stood up and crossed the room to the librarian, who looked up, smiling, as I started to talk, telling him the story.

Chapter 7

WHEN I GOT BACK TO THE HOUSE, AFTERNOON LIGHT WAS already pouring into the west windows, polishing the lake with a golden sheen. The solstice party would start at seven o'clock and last until the sky faded into blue dusk and then deepened into twilight, revealing its stars one by one. Avery was bringing the salads and dessert and I'd stopped to pick up some groceries, mostly drinks and chicken to grill. I parked near the side porch, hauling the bags up the wide, weather-beaten steps. The grocery store, expanded twice while I'd been gone, had been disorienting, full of artisan breads and cheeses and high-end deli items, with a tank of lobsters, a salad bar, a sushi bar, and a hot-foods bar. Tourists sat at little tables with cups of coffee as I wandered, disconcerted, amid the unfamiliar aisles.

The screen porch door was unlocked. I pulled it open with my foot and dropped the bags on the wicker sofa, searching in my purse for the key. A package wrapped in dark red paper was propped against the main door to the house, and a note was taped to one of the windowpanes.

Here's the recipe for my grandmother's rhubarb pie, and a little something I thought you might like. My regrets about this evening, I'm sorry I can't come. Will call, my fond regards, Andy

I shifted the groceries inside and put them in the refrigerator—the plump chicken breasts, so unnaturally huge, as large as whole chickens would be in other parts of the world, the numerous bottles of wine and sparkling water. I left Andy's note and the red package—it was light and soft—on the counter where my mother would see them right away. Then I went back outside to get the books I'd checked out from the library and the photocopies I'd made from their microfilm collection, souvenirs of my afternoon journey to the past.

The librarian had been very helpful, directing me to some histories of the feminist movement in the general collection, as well as to a local history of the village, all of which I'd checked out. He'd also showed me how to pull up periodicals on their rather ancient microfilm machine, and I'd spent a couple of hours scanning old editions of *The Lake of Dreams Gazette*. Finally, in the reel marked 1938 to 1940, tucked between articles about the threat of war in Europe and reports of local crop yields, I found a brief article about the dedication of the chapel in Appleton, the small village that had later been razed to build the depot. There was even a photograph of Frank Westrum standing outside the arched doors, bearded and thin and dressed in a suit, looking seriously into the camera. The rector, Rev. Timothy Benton, stood with his wife, and an unidentified woman was by his side. Though the donation of the funds for the windows had been made anonymously, in a later article the *Gazette* reporter had discovered that the patron was local, one Cornelia Elliot of The Lake of Dreams, widow of a prominent doctor and a veteran of the fight for women's suffrage. "A sensibility which will perhaps explain," the article, written in 1938, stated archly, "the very unusual— indeed, the quite droll and eccentric—nature of her gift."

I thought of the Wisdom window, with its rich colors and harmonious design, its human figures reaching upward, hands turning into leaves, into language. *Extraordinary* was one word that came immediately to mind. *Vivid, lush,* and *gorgeous* followed, but not *droll* or *eccentric.* I wondered what the rest of the windows looked like—a chapel full of such art would have been stunning, I imagined. I'd gleaned from the librarian and a few more references he'd found that Frank Westrum had been hugely out of favor in those years, his work finding its way into thrift shops and jumble sales, so maybe that explained the comment, and also why the church had left the windows when the chapel was closed. I looked closely over the next months and years, hoping for something to elucidate the article, but found nothing.

After a couple of hours my eyes ached from scanning the tiny type, so I took a break and went back to the desk to ask the librarian about Cornelia Elliot. He started nodding in recognition before I'd even finished, asked me to wait a minute, then unlocked the special collections room, which was no more than a closet behind the stairs. He came back with a brown booklet, the paper cover brittle and stained, the title in sharp black: *Recollections of a Dangerous Woman,* by Cornelia Whitney Elliot. Cornelia—who went by Nelia, he explained—had been a well-known and controversial figure locally at the time. She had self-published only fifty copies of this memoir, so they were rare. I couldn't check it out, but he could photocopy it for me for fifteen cents a page, if I wanted.

I did.

So I had this to read, along with some records I'd photocopied from the town clerk's office: the certificate of marriage of my great-grandfather Joseph to Cora Evanston, in December 1915, and records also of Cora's birth and death, as well as of the death of her first husband, Jesse, who had fallen from the roof of a barn, suffered for weeks, and died in late May 1915. A brief, yellowed obituary had been clipped to this death certificate. That meant Cora had married my great-grandfather only seven months after her husband died, which was startling. She was seven years older than he, which was surprising, too. Everyone, including Rose and Iris, was listed in the local census taken that year, but in the following census, taken in 1925, Rose was gone, and Iris's last name was Jarrett, not Wyndham. I'd made photocopies of all these documents, too.

I carried all these papers in from the Impala—they were hot from sitting in the backseat in the sun for so long—and spread them out on the dining room table. I opened wide the French doors to the patio, let-ting in fresh, damp air from the lake, then went upstairs to collect the papers I'd found in the cupola. When I came back down, I noticed that the answering machine was blinking with three messages, and I paused to press the PLAY button. There was a message from the orthopedist regarding my mother's next appointment, a call from a contractor regarding an appraisal for a new roof, and then a man's voice floated into the room.

"Andy here. Guess I'm missing you again. Ha—that sounded a little weird, didn't it, kind of too much like a country music song. I meant we weren't crossing paths yet, but maybe I meant it the other way, too. Anyway, I wanted to make sure you got my note. Happy solstice, Evie—a very happy solstice to you."

He cleared his throat then and hung up without saying anything more. I played the messages again, listening to the timber of his voice, his choice of words, trying to picture his face. Gravelly and low, his words were careful and a little formal; he sounded ill at ease, maybe even ner-vous, at leaving a message for my mother, and that was endearing. I imagined him as a large man, someone comfortable in jeans, comfort-able in his own skin. I listened to the messages again so I could consider his voice once more, thinking how strange it was to find myself examin-ing my mother's suitor, wondering about his character, even his intentions. When his voice ended the second time I pressed SAVE, then poured myself a glass of wine and sat down with my treasure trove of papers. It was the photocopy of Cornelia Elliot's little book I reached for first, published in 1927 and dedicated to her older sister, Vivian Whitney Branch.

Vivian Branch. I closed my eyes, seeking the connection, then remem-bered the Internet biography I'd found, and searched through the papers to find it. There it was, in the brief note about Beatrice Mansfield—she'd known Vivian Branch. Here was a connection, and an exciting one, too, for Vivian Branch was a name I vaguely recognized; someone in my high school history class had done a presentation about her. She'd been a nurse as a young woman, and had become very active in feminist circles in New York City at the turn of the last century and beyond; she had known a number of first-wave feminists, as I recalled, but I hadn't realized how deeply she'd been involved in the suffrage movement, or that her sister had lived in The Lake of Dreams. Was it possible that Rose had known her? I turned the dedication page over and began to read:

Readers of this little book will no doubt wonder as to the history and perspective of its author, Cornelia Whitney Elliot. Let me say that I write this as a woman 57 years wise, who has witnessed much in this new century of ours. I write to leave a legacy to generations which will follow me, a first-hand account of the struggles I and my sisters in suffrage faced in obtaining for all women the right to vote. Already a new generation is rising for which this right is never questioned, but is, instead, a fact of life. They can hardly imagine the time, so recently past, when their voices would have gone unheard. While they cannot be truly grateful, having never been deprived, nonetheless they can learn—they must learn—to appreciate the history of their good fortune through the experiences of those who not only witnessed history, but made it. It is for that purpose that this little book is written.

Wow. I put the pages down on the table as if they were flaming. Well, the librarian had warned me about the tone. Just before she wrote this book, Cornelia Elliot had been voted out of the leadership of the group she'd helped to form; younger women had bristled at her old-fashioned and sometimes autocratic ways. She'd been swept aside by a wave of history, and she was understandably angry. I scanned through the rest of the pages, looking for dates or events that were relevant to Rose.

I didn't find any. Nor did I find any references to Frank Westrum.

Instead, most of the text focused, as she had stated in her introduction, on her involvement with the suffrage movement, particularly the events she had orchestrated after she moved to The Lake of Dreams from New York City. Her husband, a physician, loved the natural beauty of the area, but for Cornelia, who loved the amenities of the city, the experience had been a trial. She had compensated by becoming deeply immersed in her social justice work, and it seemed, in the subtext, that the more her activities had irritated her husband, the better she had liked them.

The suffrage march she had organized in October 1914, inspired by the march in Washington the previous year, took up a full chapter and was written about with great vigor and delight. Cornelia Elliot described the marchers, spirited and determined despite the unpredictable and sometimes hostile crowds. She seemed thrilled to have been arrested and thrown in jail, not only for marching but also for distributing information about human physiology and family planning, which was illegal under the Comstock laws at the time.

Distributing information about family planning. I found the note Rose had written when she'd read that simple pamphlet and locked her door to look at herself in a mirror for the first time ever. How shocked she had been by facts that seemed so ubiquitous to me, so basic! Had Rose known Cornelia Elliot then? Had she gotten the pamphlet from her? Had they ever talked about these matters? The note seemed private to me, something Rose had written but never meant to send.

I paused and did an Internet search for Cornelia Elliot, but turned up nothing more than I already knew. Then I tried Vivian Branch, her older sister. This time I found several entries, including one that noted the gift of her collection of papers to Serling College. I wrote a quick e-mail to Special Collections at Serling College, asking if there was any correspondence that might illuminate Cornelia Elliot's life as well as her sister's. Then, because I was starting to feel overwhelmed by all the swirling dates, I took a fresh sheet of paper and wrote down all the names and facts I knew:

Westrum, Frank, 1868–1942

Westrum, Beatrice Mansfield, 1873–1919

Jarrett, Cora, 1887–1958

Jarrett, Joseph, 1894–1972

Jarrett, Rose, 1895–????

Jarrett, Iris, born 1911

Suffrage March in Washington, 1913

Suffrage March, The Lake of Dreams, 1914

Dream Master founded, 1919

Womens suffrage granted, 1920

Iris leaving, 1925

My grandfather born, 1925

Windows finished, 1938

Depot built, chapel closed, 1940

Arthur born, 1952

My father born, 1953

I sipped my wine, considering. The air smelled so clean; buoys clanked faintly. Voices floated across the lawn and into the room. I gathered up the papers and put the pile on the liquor cabinet by the stairs, next to my stack of books. Outside, Blake was helping my mother from his boat onto the dock, holding her good hand while she gained her balance. Then he reached to help Avery, who was carrying two canvas bags over her shoulder; she staggered when the boat shifted and caught Blake's arm in both of hers. Light flashed off the smooth surface of the lake, casting them all in silhouette as they crossed the lawn, making it hard to see them in any detail. Still, as they reached the patio I sensed that something was different about my mother. She was wearing a white linen skirt and a light blue knit tunic shot with silver threads, along with silver sandals and silver earrings. At first I thought she was wearing her hair up again. Then I realized she'd cut it short, very short, so it feathered across her scalp, full and lovely.

"Your hair!" I said.

"Like it?" She tilted her head a bit self-consciously. "I had this moment of inspiration, I guess. Inspiration or pure craziness. I went in just to have it trimmed, but then I found myself telling Josh to take it all off. I love it, I have to say. It's so light. I feel like my head could simply float away."

"It looks good," I said as we walked inside, and it did. "It's just so different."

"Twelve inches came off. I gave it to Locks of Love. What's all this?" she asked, nodding toward the books and papers stacked on the cabinet. She and Avery were already at the counter, unloading the canvas sacks: containers of tabbouleh and hummus, a roasted pepper salad, a pasta salad, loaves of fresh bread.

"Research, that's all. Is it in the way?"

"No, you're fine. Leave it," she said, turning to take a plate of sliced watermelon out of the fridge, the line of her neck long and elegant. How strange that something as simple as a haircut could make her look so different. I found myself wondering how Andy saw her, remembering his voice, low and warm, on the answering machine. "I'm free," she said, smiling and touching the nape of her neck. "I feel absolutely free."

By the time I changed into my only dress and came back downstairs, Blake had fired up the grill and Avery was carrying bowls of food out to the patio. My mother had invited friends from work as well as family and neighbors. People began to arrive, parking on the grass near the road and carrying bottles of wine or plates of food across the lawn to the house. The balloons we'd inflated that morning floated like small suns and moons in the trees, and the tiny lights sparkled like emerging stars.

It was a lovely party, the sort of pleasant evening where the conversation drifted from one topic to another, settling lightly here, then there, laughter floating out over the water. I moved between groups, hugging people who remembered me. Mr. Hardesty from next door patted my back, and I was struck by how thin he'd gotten in the years since my father died, since I'd seen him last, holding on to my mother and Blake that terrible morning as if they might fly away if he let go. He had retired from being a weatherman, he informed me, and no longer looked at weather reports at all, preferring to carry umbrellas and boots in his car and let each day surprise him however it would. Georgia from across the street, however, had hardly aged. She was still making pottery—the wind chimes on her porch and the porches of the neighbors all sounded faintly, even at this distance—and she was excited about Keegan's Glassworks, but she told me she'd started teaching art at the community college, too, for the steady income and the health insurance, now that their son was in college. At this she scanned the party and called out to Jack, whom I remembered as a wiry boy, full of energy, darting across the fields with his friends in games of hide-and-seek, and who was now a junior at NYU, studying acting, his hair pulled back in a ponytail: young, and supremely confident, in a way I never remembered being.

"You know, I invited Keegan," my mother said, pausing on her way to the patio, a glass of wine in her good hand. "He was at the bank today and I thought, why not?"

She smiled, and I thought of the place where Keegan's hair tapered to his neck beneath the ponytail, the heat of his arm against mine as we'd studied the windows.

"Is he coming?"

"He said he'd try to make it. He asked if you'd be here," she added. "I think he was really glad to see you."

I nodded, trying not to reveal the charge I'd felt, knowing he might stop by. Not on his motorcycle, I reminded myself, and maybe with Max, but that only made the idea more attractive. "Keegan's changed a lot," I said. "He's so calm, and so accomplished."

"He probably says the same about you."

Someone I didn't know touched my mother's arm before I could reply and she turned to her guests. Talk and laughter floated. I poured drinks and offered Avery's delicate spinach and goat cheese appetizers. Art arrived with Joey, his voice a notch deeper and louder than the other voices, so I always seemed to know where he was—in the kitchen, greeting my mother on the patio, putting an arm around Lawson, Georgia's husband, who'd come here straight from work, his shiny shoes looking odd against the grass. Joey got a beer and stood by the shore with Blake, talking quietly, while Zoe, with the mercurial moodiness of teenagers, planted herself in the hammock with a book, looking up now and then to gaze at the water. I couldn't tell if she wanted to be left alone or simply to look like a tragic nineteenth-century heroine to the audience of assembled guests.

"Oh, don't give her the satisfaction," her mother said when I asked if she thought Zoe might like some company. Auburn-haired and very thin, Austen had started selling real estate in recent years, and looked glossy to me, burnished. She waved her drink in exasperation at Zoe's moody presence. "She's driving me absolutely crazy these days. I suppose that's her job, right, at this age? But everything's such high drama. From the way she storms around the house you'd think we locked her in a cupboard every night. We *ruin* her life. She has *nothing* that her friends have. Et cetera. Lucy, if you ever want a visitor over there in Japan, I'd be happy to send her to you for a few weeks. Oh, well," she added when I didn't respond, taking a long swallow of wine. "I lived through Joey, who was no saint, so I suppose I'll live through this, too."

I glanced at Joey, remembering our high school days, his careless disregard, his clothes hanging from the branches where I'd thrown them.

We ate, and opened more wine, and the evening deepened into twilight, stars emerging. As darkness fell, the moon, nearly full, rose over the horizon. I thought of Rose, the beautiful border of pale interwoven spheres in the blanket and the windows. Avery started bringing out slices of cake, and my mother put bowls of whipped cream and strawberries on the glass-topped table. I stepped into the shadows, watching the party as if it were taking place on a stage, feeling a strange sense of distance, knowing that this sort of gathering happened all the time and would carry on once I was gone again, as well. I slipped my phone from my pocket to check the time. Almost ten already. If Keegan hadn't come by now, he probably wouldn't; he, too, was in the midst of a life that had gone on quite well without me. I walked down to the dock and kicked off my shoes, sitting on the end with my feet dangling in the water, and dialed Yoshi. He picked up on the second ring, the pulse and murmur of his office in the background.

"Hey there," I said.

"Ah, Lucy."

"I'm at a party," I told him, lying back on the dock. "I'm looking at a sky full of stars. It's the shortest night of the year, you know."

"Not here, unfortunately." His voice was soft. "Look, I can't talk right now. Can you Skype this evening? That would be what—tomorrow morning your time?"

"Sure. Is everything okay?"

He sighed. "Yes. Yes and no. The trip to Indonesia is getting complicated, that's all. I can't really talk about it now. You okay?"

"It's a beautiful night," I told him, searching for the Big Dipper. In Indonesia we'd had a screened balcony off our bedroom where we used to sleep on the hottest nights, under these same stars. "I miss you."

"Believe me, I wish I was there."

"Soon."

"Yes, soon."

He was gone then. I closed the phone but didn't stand up right away, gazing at the night sky, wondering what office politics had distressed Yoshi; he was usually so calm.

By the time I started back to the patio, people had begun to drift away. From a distance it was such a happy scene: candles glowed, and the tables were strewn with paper plates and crumpled napkins. Georgia bustled around picking up before she left, too; Austen took Zoe home to study for a final exam. I lingered in the wild remains of my mother's moon garden, where a few roses straggled out of the greenery, fragrant and pale. A few moonflowers, too; the sprawling lavender released its piney scent when I passed it. I was thinking of my father and our last conversation here, when the garden was still orderly in its wildness, wondering what he would have made of this party, this night, the direction my life had taken. Stilled by sadness, I paused amid the fragrant ruins. The group dwindled until it was only Art and Joey, along with my mother, Blake, and Avery, gathered on the patio around the fire pit, where the embers still glowed. The conversation meandered. Blake had discovered a photo of the founding of Dream Master in an old filing cabinet at the store, our great-grandfather digging a shovel into the earth by the outlet in a groundbreaking ceremony, and they talked about that for a while, passing the photo around. My mother excused herself and went inside, the screen door slapping shut behind her. The answering machine beeped and voices murmured faintly as she paused in the dark house to listen to her messages. I thought of Andy's voice, and imagined her smiling to hear it. On the patio, the conversation stalled. Then Art raised his glass and made a toast.

"To the new venture," he said. "To The Landing."

I'd been about to join them, now that I'd composed myself, but I paused at his words, watching as Joey and Blake and Avery raised their glasses and clinked them together. I thought of the rolled papers between Art and Joey on the table at The Green Bean, and the easel full of drawings for their development in the corner of Art's office. Plans, I'd imagined, plans in their early stages, but this sounded like more, and I waited.

"Isn't it too early to celebrate?" Blake asked, sounding a little self-conscious and ingratiating; I felt a surge of anger that he was trying so hard to be a part of this. "Plenty of things could still fall through."

"No, now that we've got the initial land and the financing is set up, it's just a matter of time," Art said. "Of course, we'll have to navigate the obstacle course of those injunctions, but they'll never hold. As for stage two, I feel quite sure your mother will want to sell eventually, Blake. We've had several conversations."

"Really? I'm not so sure," Avery said. "Not about Blake's mom, but the rest." She repeated the story she'd told me on the boat about the various conservation groups meeting over lunch. "There's that meeting tomorrow. And Keegan Fall has been really active doing grassroots work."

Blake made a dismissive sound. "No one wants the land to go back to the Iroquois," he said. "That's a political dead end. His business may be thriving, but he doesn't have a lot of clout."

"New businesses come and go in this town," Joey noted from his place deep in the low chair. "We'll see if Keegan Fall has what it takes."

"He's doing himself no favors," Art noted. "Lining up with the tree huggers and the land grab. He's going to end up on the wrong side of history if he doesn't watch out. People here have long memories."

"He's already on the wrong side of history," Joey observed, taking a long drink from his beer. "He's just choosing to stay there."

Stung, I touched the lavender again, its fresh scent rising. Keegan was a year older than I was but ended up in my grade because his mother took him away and traveled for a year. When Keegan came back to fifth grade the next fall, thinner, his jeans a bit too short, he sat by himself near the window. He got teased on the playground, mostly by my cousin Joey, who was tall and strong but lacked kindness. He taunted Keegan every day, calling him a dirty Indian and asking him why he had only two shirts to wear. Keegan didn't respond, just kept his distance, his face like a mask, even his dark eyes veiled and far away.

One day I sat on the swing next to his, digging my toes into the scuffed-hard dirt. We'd been to a museum in Syracuse where we'd seen the wide round stones the Iroquois had once used for crushing corn. I told Keegan I thought this was interesting and asked him if he really was an Iroquois.

He glanced at me to see if I was planning to make fun of him, but this happened after the split in my family, so I think he knew I wasn't on Joey's side in this or any other matter. We watched boys in the near distance kicking a soccer ball along the edge of the field. The school was at the top of a hill, and though we couldn't see the lake for all the houses and trees in the way, we knew it was there.

"My mother's grandmother grew up in the Seneca Nation," Keegan said, finally. "You know all that land where the depot is now? That used to be their land."

"Maybe one of your ancestors was a chief," I ventured, thinking of the beads we'd also seen, round and smooth and colorful, which I'd longed to touch.

"Maybe," Keegan said.

We'd been too absorbed to watch our backs, and Joey had crept up behind us. He heard me say this and shouted, "Me Big Chief!" pounding on his chest. The boys behind him hooted with laughter and the mask fell across Keegan's face once more.

"Why don't you hit him?" I asked, softly. "You ought to hit him in the face."

Keegan didn't say anything, didn't even look my way as the bell rang and we filed in from recess. Nothing happened that afternoon, but the next day when Joey started riffing about smoke signals, Keegan turned around, swift as the wind, and punched him in the face.

Both Keegan and Joey got pulled out of school, and when Keegan came back the next day, he sat in his usual place by the window, though a couple of boys were talking to him, asking about the fight and what the principal had said. When they left I went over quietly and sat next to Keegan and slipped him a piece of gum. He took it and looked up, studying me with the same intent expression he'd had the day before, just before he punched Joey, and then a smile lit up his face, though it was so swiftly gone that I was hardly sure I'd seen it.

After that, we were friends. We never talked much and we didn't hang out at lunch, but we sat next to each other in class and took to giving each other things—a pencil, the prize from a box of Cracker Jack, a funny picture. A secret friendship, so we wouldn't get teased.

So there was that history between us, that connection. We talked about it when we met up again years later, sitting next to each other at a basketball game. Keegan was with his friends and I was with mine, and halfway through the game he looked down the row with that funny half-smile he had and passed a note down, hand to hand, until it reached me.

Hey there, Lucy Jarrett. How have you been all these years?

"Damned right on that," Art said, his face shadowed by the faint light from the dying fire. "He's had good luck, but he counts on the summer to get him through, just like the rest of us. Steve Peterson called today, by the way. He's interested in signing on for the first stage, too."

"First stage of what?" I asked, stepping out of the shadows.

There was a silence.

"She might as well know," Art said, finally. "I don't suppose it makes any difference at this point."

"We made a bid on the depot land," Joey said. "On two parcels of land. The first is toward the village, and that's the one we've pretty much got nailed down. The other is adjacent to your mother's property, just over the tree line."

"We've got plans for it," Blake put in, and the muted excitement in his voice made me worry for him. No matter what Art said, I didn't trust him to treat Blake with any fairness. "A housing development called The Landing. This area used to be a stopping point for steamboats. It's historical. Maybe you saw the designs down at Dream Master."

"I saw them. But half of that is marshland," I said, thinking of the beds of reeds and cattails, the swift, graceful shadows of the fish beneath the water.

"So, we drain it." Art's voice was terse, wary. "That's what's got the environmentalists all in a tizzy. But they'll come round eventually."

"It's really about jobs, Lucy," Avery said. She'd been so quiet I'd nearly forgotten she was there. "I'm sure it feels really altruistic and noble to worry about the environment, but we've been hard hit with the depot closing, and things weren't great before that. Maybe it doesn't seem different to you because of all the money on the lakes, but we all know there are two economies here, and one of them is hurting."

"You can join us anytime," Art said. "If that's what's really on your mind. I'm serious, Lucy. That's what I meant when we were talking the other day. No one's keeping you out if you want in."

I didn't say anything. The door creaked open and my mother came back outside, carrying a stack of plastic glasses and another bottle of wine.

"What?" she asked, stepping into the uneasy silence, pausing as she sensed the tension. "What's going on?" Her voice was light, conversational, but because I knew her so well I could hear the wariness in it, too. Or maybe I was the one who was wary, cautious suddenly in the wake of this new information. Did Andy know, I wondered? And how far had these discussions gone?

"Just filling Lucy in," Art said. "Telling her about our ongoing discussion."

"Were you?" My mother's tone hardened a little, and I could tell from her voice that Art had crossed a line. "I hope you told her also that I'm far from making up my mind." She turned to me. "Lucy? Did he tell you that?"

"Not exactly."

"Ah. I was getting to it," Art said. "No pressure, then, Evie. Guess I was just hoping you'd decided," Art said. "Blake and I were both hoping, I should say."

"Well. I haven't. One way or the other. The land is still mine."

In the quiet that followed she went around distributing plastic cups. I was unnerved, and yet it struck me that she was enjoying herself. As long as she didn't make a decision, she had a certain power over Art and everyone else who wanted this land so badly. It was a new side to my mother, and one I wouldn't have imagined, one I wasn't sure I liked. I wondered what she really wanted—what, in the end, she'd decide to do.

"I'm going to pass this wine around," she said, holding up a bottle. "So you can all have a look before we open it. If I'd known this was going to be such an uneasy moment, I might have waited. But here we are, so I guess we'll go on. I found this in the basement when I finally started tackling that maze in the back room. It was stuffed away in a box, wrapped up in a quilt that fell to pieces when I pulled it out. Take a look. And then, I suggest we have a toast."

The bottle passed from hand to hand. When it reached me I held it so it caught a wedge of light. The label was written in dark ink, a slanted handwriting that didn't belong to Rose.

COMET WINE
Langport, England
1910

Art cleared his throat, getting serious, the way people in the family always did when they talked about Joseph Arthur Jarrett and his comet dreams. "My grandfather used to talk about this wine," he said. "I was just a boy, but I remember him telling the story. They went out that fall and picked the grapes that had grown beneath that comet sky. They made the wine themselves, and when he emigrated he brought three or four bottles with him. It's supposed to be special, wine from grapes grown under a comet sky. My, my. I thought it was all long gone."

I imagined my great-grandfather lifting his face, the light from the comet falling all around him as he dreamed of a new life. Like everyone else, I'd always found this story, passed down through the generations, very moving and important. But now I wondered: where was Rose?

"This bottle must have been forgotten, then," my mother said. "Packed away for safekeeping, maybe, and then forgotten. Let's see if they were right about the vintage."

"Evie. I say we save it."

My mother looked steadily across the fire pit at Art.

"It's my wine," she said lightly, though the hardness in her voice was audible now. "I found it in my house, after all. And I want to know how it tastes." She took a corkscrew from her skirt pocket and asked Blake to open it. After a second's hesitation, he did. The cork, nearly a hundred years old, squeaked as it turned against the glass.

My mother took the bottle from him and poured us each an inch of the wine, such a dark red it looked like a piece of the night. I had a childhood memory of when the comet had returned in 1986, of staying up late in the cupola to search the dark sky, our disappointment when we finally located the comet, so faint and far away. That's what I remembered, but maybe the disappointment came from other events at that time; it had been the turning point, the comet and the celebration, the day my father packed his things up at Dream Master and left for good.

"To the solstice," my mother declared. We lifted our glasses, and drank.

The wine tasted dark and sweet. It was okay, rather sharp, edging toward vinegar, not magical. Once we finished people sat talking until Art stood up to leave.

"Evie," he said, and paused. He seemed about to say something more, but then he waved his hand with a laugh. "You sure throw a good solstice party," he said. "Come on, Joey. Let's get going."

Blake and Avery stayed a few minutes longer to help clean up. Then they walked across the lawn, hand in hand, and climbed back into the boat. The sail caught the moonlight like a wing.

"Great party, Mom," I told her as we stacked the leftover trays of hummus and vegetables and dip in the refrigerator. "It was good to see everyone."

"It was nice," she agreed. She met my gaze as the door fell shut. "Lucy, I meant what I said out there. I haven't made up my mind to sell this place, and even if I do, I haven't decided to sell to Art, not by a long shot."

"But you're thinking about it," I said, leaning against the counter. "I suppose that's all right. It's not like it's got anything to do with me anymore."

"Well, that's been your choice, hasn't it?"

"It's been the way things have worked out, that's all."

"You didn't have to go to school on the opposite coast, Lucy. You didn't have to take jobs on the other side of the world. You *made* those choices."

I stared at her in disbelief. "I went to the best programs," I said, finally. "I took the best, most exciting jobs. You told me to go. That summer after Dad died. You gave me your blessing."

My mother ran her hands over her face, down her neck, and sighed. "Yes. Yes, I did. You're right. I wanted you to live your life. I still want that. I worry about you, so far away, it's true. It's hard. You don't realize it, Lucy, but after that tsunami, for instance, when I couldn't reach you, it was terrible."

"I wasn't even in Indonesia then."

"But you see, I didn't know that. I didn't know where you were. For all I knew, you were on one of those devastated beaches."

I'd been in New Zealand when it happened, hiking with Yoshi and some friends, and we hadn't heard about the tsunami for several days. When we got back to Jakarta, Yoshi and I volunteered at the orphanage where we'd worked the year before, where children who had lost their families were being sent. We did what we could, whatever they needed, though we still felt helpless in the face of all that loss.

"Okay," I said. "I'm sorry. I'll try to do a better job being in touch."

My mother shook her head. "You're a grown-up, Lucy. I trust you to know what you want. But it goes both ways, don't you see? I have a life, too. Maybe you'd feel happier if I rattled around in this old house forever, and spent every waking hour trying to keep it up, but I will not do that. I'm telling you. Will I sell this place to Art? I don't know. I might. I might sell to someone else. Or I might wait another year, or two, before I do anything at all. I won't be pressured, that is one thing I do know. Not by you, or Art, or anyone."

The air was so charged. "All right, then. But what about Andy?" I asked, surprising even myself.

She held up her hands. "What about him?"

"Does he know about all this?"

"No. Not that it's any of your business, either, Lucy. But the fact is, I just met Andy. It's fun, going out, that's all. I'm having fun. Why is that a problem?"

"It's not. I didn't mean that."

"Then, what did you mean?"

I took a deep breath, listening to the hum of the refrigerator, the distant lapping of waves against the shore. I'd spoken without thinking, and I didn't really know why I was so upset. It had to do with the land, yes, and all the intricate and difficult family history. It had to do with Blake so willing to go along with Art, and even with Avery being pregnant. The dark taste of the comet wine was still in my mouth. I'd never told my mother about meeting my father on the night he died. I'd never told her that he'd asked me to go fishing. In some alternate universe there was the day we might have had if I'd said yes, a day when we came back at dawn with a line full of fish, an easy day of sunshine and grilling trout and dinner on the patio—a day that would have led us somewhere else, not here.

"I don't know," I said, finally. All the energy seemed to have drained from the room now, but maybe it was just jet lag. "I don't know what I meant. It's just—you know, a lot of changes, very, very fast."

She nodded, but didn't speak right away. "Not so fast," she said, finally. "Not really, Lucy. But it must seem fast to you. I get that."

I almost told her then how it might have changed everything if I'd gone fishing that night, how we'd be in a completely different place if I had. But she was happy now, that was the thing, maybe as happy as I'd ever seen her. In this moment, at this time, she was happy.

"All right. Who knows—maybe selling the land, even to Art, would be okay. I mean, Blake and Avery can't raise a baby on a boat."

She turned and looked at me hard. "What did you say?"

I closed my eyes for a second and swore silently to myself.

"Look, I wasn't supposed to say anything. But that's why Blake took the job. And that's why Avery didn't even sip the comet wine."

"Oh, you're right. Oh, my! It makes sense. But I didn't realize—"

"Don't tell him you know, okay? He'll be upset. I promised him. And he promised Avery. She's looking forward to making some sort of formal announcement."

"I'm the grandmother-to-be. They won't care that I know. I'm sure they won't."

She paused and pressed her hands against her face, her silver rings flashing. She shook her head once, let her hands fall.

"Oh, it's very exciting, isn't it? What a shock. Though now that I know, I guess it makes perfect sense. You're right," she added. "They absolutely cannot raise a baby on a boat. Where's my phone?"

"Oh, please. Don't tell him I told you."

"I won't. I'll say I guessed. You're right, she didn't drink. When's she due?"

"October, I think."

My mother was already punching numbers into her cell, and didn't seem to notice when I left the room and climbed the stairs.

I lay awake for a long time, the events of the evening running through my mind, before I finally fell asleep. Later that night a thunderstorm came in, and in my restless sleep I dreamed another dream like the one on my first night here, the urgent seeking of round things hidden beneath the leaves in the forest. But this time I found them, beautiful spherelike shapes tucked beneath leaves, as delicate as rain but made from glass, so beautiful it was painful to look at them, filled as I was with yearning. When I picked them up they turned liquid in my hands and fell to the earth, and rolled away in tiny beads, and I crawled after them, my heart breaking to think of all that beauty lost. I gathered all the fragments together and sat on the forest floor, trying to put them back together, to mend them with glue, to fasten them with metal rods, but time and again they melted at my touch, and disappeared.

Chapter 8

I WOKE UP EARLY, TO A GRAY DAWN, RAIN COMING DOWN SO hard and the clouds so low that it was hard to tell where the sky ended and the lake began. The rain had knocked the balloons from the trees, and the paper lanterns we'd strung by the patio sagged, heavy with water. I went downstairs, the residue of my dream lingering, all beauty and loss, and made a cup of tea, moving as quietly as I could. My mother was sleeping in; she didn't have to be at work until ten, and it was something of a relief not to see her after our argument the night before. Some of the food from the party was still out on the counter, so I snacked on Brie and crackers and took a cluster of grapes when I went upstairs. I closed the door to my room and sat cross-legged at the head of the bed, sipping at the orange pekoe while I gazed out the window, the rainy lake mist-covered, the grass dark green, drenched, and flattened. Yoshi had promised to be home by seven, and it was five minutes before that. I dialed into Skype and he answered right away, his face filling up the screen.

"I brought home some noodles," he said. "I'm here in the kitchen. Do you mind if I eat while we talk? I'm starved."

"From that place down the street?" I asked. It was a small shop, paneled in light wood, with stools pulled up to the counter where they served big bowls brimming with noodles and broth. Yoshi and I liked to go there on weekends.

"Yes. I got your favorite, curried noodles," he said, lifting the spoon to show me before he ate a mouthful. "Too bad for you that you're so far away."

"I have my own pleasures," I said, holding up the grapes. "You forget it's early in the morning here. It's not at all a curry time of day. So, how are you?"

"Not so great, in fact," he said. "Sorry I couldn't talk earlier, but the office was a little tense when you called."

"What happened?"

"It's the Indonesia project. There were those objections from the people in the village, you remember that? They don't want the site destroyed, because they think it's sacred. So, we spent the last week drawing up a set of alternate plans that would let the bridge go around the site. Win-win, right?"

"Sounds that way to me," I said.

"Hang on just a second," he said, and disappeared. I thought of all the times I'd been warned not to go out at dusk in Indonesia—a transition time, when it was easy to lose your spirit or suffer some sort of danger. It had always made sense to me, illogical though it was, and it made more sense now that I was in this other kind of transition, drifting between the past and the present, between the life I'd been living and whatever sort of life was to come, a time when I sometimes felt I might lose myself entirely.

Yoshi was on the screen again; he'd gotten a bottle of sake. "Right, exactly: win-win. That's what the engineers all thought. Completely good solution. But the manager disagreed. It would add too dramatically to the cost; and they already own the rights to the land in question anyway, so they don't have to compromise."

"You were vetoed."

"Yes. And worse—I argued."

"Ah. I see." There were any number of expats in Yoshi's company, so it was more flexible than many, but with his looks and heritage and fluent Japanese, Yoshi was expected to walk a different walk. It seemed to me that he overcompensated, staying longer at the office and going out drinking with his business clients more often than anyone else, trying to offset moments like this, when the differences in his training and philosophy broke through. "It's not a big deal, though, is it? I mean, they're not going to fire you."

I was half joking, but Yoshi didn't smile.

"No. At least, I hope not. It's just very quiet around me right now. The fact is, when they hired me they expected my experience in Indonesia to be helpful to them, but they didn't expect me to advocate for the Indonesians. So now I've been assigned a partner when we go to Jakarta next week."

"Really? A chaperone?"

"Something like that. I'm not too happy. So, no, it's not a big deal in some ways. But to be honest, I've been giving some thought to quitting."

"Quitting? Really?" I laughed, but in fact it filled me with a rush of panic to imagine us both adrift in the world.

"Some thought, yes. Not real serious thought, mind you. Just the late-night thinking after a bad day."

"If you quit, we'd both be unemployed," I observed.

Yoshi must have heard the flare of panic in my voice, because he smiled into the computer, across ten thousand miles. "I'm just frustrated, that's all. Let's change the subject. What's been happening with you? Is it pouring? I've been checking your weather."

"It is." I glanced out the window. The sky was beginning to lighten at the horizon, a pearly gray-white line above the green, and I hoped it would clear. "I've been making fascinating discoveries about my ancestors," I said, and told him about the windows I'd discovered and the trip I planned to Rochester to visit the Westrum House. Yoshi was interested, though he was having a hard time following all the various relationships.

"She's your great-grandmother, this Rose?"

"No. My great-grandfather's sister. I guess that would make her my great-great-aunt? We never heard about her. I think there was a scandal."

"Sure you want to know?"

I considered this because it echoed so clearly my own apprehension, my initial sense that the past might have been covered up for very good reasons. "You know, I really do. I'm not sure I can explain exactly why. Just that it feels like an important piece is missing from my family. I mean, if the scandal had to do with Rose being a suffrage leader, then that's remarkable. We could use some more heroic women in the family." As I said this I thought of my own struggles all these decades later, pale in comparison and yet real enough, especially for a woman in science. Times when I'd been interrupted in the middle of a presentation, or given all the paperwork to finish, a kind of corporate housekeeping, or had been excluded in a routine way from important conversations outside of work.

We talked for a little longer about his travel plans, and then Yoshi said he had to go. There were reports he had to look over before he could relax. He took a long drink, looking tired, I thought, sapped.

"You should get some sleep."

"I will. Once these reports are done, I'm going to crash in front of the TV. Mrs. Fujimoro asked after you, by the way. She noticed you were gone."

I remembered the press of her hand, the earth trembling beneath our feet.

"How is she? How are the earthquakes?"

"There was a biggish one yesterday. When I came home the bookcase had fallen over, and the rest of the plants in the kitchen."

"I can't say I miss the earthquakes," I said. "I miss you, though." And I did, thinking of the long June dusks there, the walks we'd take sometimes in the evening, by the sea.

"I wish you were here," Yoshi said, his voice wistful.

"Soon," I said. "Love you."

"Likewise," he said, and before I could give him a hard time about his lack of romantic impulses, he'd switched off Skype, and the screen went dark.

Downstairs, I had a quick breakfast with my mother, then drove her into town. We were a little formal with each other, guarded. She said Blake had seemed glad to talk about the baby, though he'd asked her to keep it quiet because Avery had been planning to announce it more formally.

"Does he know I told you?" I asked as I dropped her off at the bank.

She winced a little. "Well, maybe. I didn't say so, but maybe he guessed. He seemed a little taken aback at first that I already knew. But Lucy, I really don't think it will be a problem."

I watched her hurry up the steps in the rain, clenching a plastic coat around her to protect her cast.

From there I drove to Rochester, first on local roads, winding through the countryside, cows grazing in the fields like black-and-white clouds, the new corn trembling in the steady rain. Route 20 connects the northern tips of all the lakes, roughly following the route of the old Erie Canal. It travels through the nineteenth-century towns strung like beads along the tips of the lakes, so beautiful and faded, having grown and prospered a hundred years ago when the streets were unpaved and full of horses, barges floating down the canal and stopping at these ports to load crates of glass or garments, pumps or rope, fresh from the assembly lines. Now, with so many factories closed and so many businesses having left, the towns were stately but worn, some thriving with tourists, some with their windows empty or boarded up or given over to transitory businesses that offered fast cash advances against payday. Their outskirts trailed on for miles, full of strip malls and fast-food chains.

The Westrum House didn't open until two o'clock, so I stopped to visit the Sonnenberg Gardens in Canandaigua, and I had lunch there, too. Then I got on the highway into Rochester and found my way downtown. The Frank Westrum House was tucked away on a street full of tall brick homes, hidden by a row of overgrown forsythia bushes. The path was made of flagstones leading past the bushes and through a garden full of nooks and alcoves, hidden benches, and wisteria trailing from trellises. The house was immediately distinct, two stories, built in a style reminiscent of Frank Lloyd Wright, with lots of horizontal lines and windows everywhere. It was so quiet that I worried that despite the hours posted on the Web site the house wouldn't actually be open. Yet when I finally walked up to the entrance—a portico, really, with several long beams extending over the stoop—a little sign with red cursive letters said *OPEN*. I stepped into the hall, called out, "Hello." My voice echoed.

Newspaper articles, framed and hung along the wall, documented the history of the house, and I studied these as I waited. The neighborhood had been built in 1873, and the brick houses along the street dated from that time. However, there had been a fire on this site in 1910, one house kindling another and both fires raging most of a night, burning the houses to their shells. No one died in these fires, but the families lost everything. The lots sat empty until Frank Westrum bought them in 1920 and began building this house, which had taken him the better part of a decade to complete due to scarce funds. The final framed article talked about the restoration of the house in the 1960s, when it was purchased from private owners and the search for the glass art of Frank Westrum to fill it had begun.

There were distant footsteps, hurrying, and then a tall man clad in khakis and a white shirt stepped into the hallway. He had short, wavy flaming-red hair that made me think of the fires that had burned here, and his skin was pale, freckled. His name tag said STUART MINTER in thick block letters. Stuart was about my age, and he gave a nervous smile as he approached, speaking so quickly he was almost hard to follow.

"Hello and welcome, sorry to make you wait. It's usually a pretty quiet time of day, so I wasn't really expecting—well, sorry, as I said. Did you come to take the walking tour?"

"Yes, I would like to do the tour," I said. "But I have some questions for you first." I told him about the windows I'd seen in The Lake of

Dreams, each with their distinctive rows of moons and densely woven vines and flowers along the bottom.

"Here's the motif. Does it look familiar at all?" I asked, bringing the digital image up on my phone. "It's a little hard to see. But the church had documentation—an original receipt—that indicated Frank Westrum made these windows on commission in 1938."

Stuart Minter took the phone and studied the image. "No," he said, finally. "We have nothing like that here, nor have I ever seen that motif in the Westrum archives. I'd remember it, I'm quite sure. It's unusual, isn't it? But even with this image—it's very fuzzy—I can see trademarks of Westrum's work in the window. Look, there's this distinctive pattern of leading. You can just barely make it out, but if you look closely you can see how the pieces of stained glass come together here and there in a kind of flower shape. You'll see this again as you take the tour, as well. That pattern is in every Westrum window, something of a signature, as the audio guide points out."

"That's very interesting," I said, making a mental note to mention this detail to Keegan. "Is there any way to trace how Frank Westrum came to make these particular windows on commission? Do you have those records here?"

He bit his lip lightly, thinking. "I don't know, but the archives are pretty extensive. I'll check while you're looking around, if you want."

"I'd appreciate it."

"Not a problem." He smiled. "It's rather exciting, isn't it? Something unexpected to liven up the day, anyway."

Stuart gave me an iPod with the audio tour, along with a map of the Westrum House and its exhibits, then disappeared back down the same corridor he'd emerged from, marked STAFF ONLY, his footsteps fading. The house was not large, but it was open, empty of furniture and with extensive windows against which the art glass of Frank Westrum hung, casting colorful patterns on the opposing walls, the ceilings, and the floors. I started the audio and walked from piece to piece, through bands of light and color, learning about Westrum's life, his childhood, his brief but significant apprenticeship with John La Farge, his equally significant break with his mentor, his marriage and two children, the death of his wife, and his move upstate. Clearly, from his windows, Frank Westrum had entertained a passion for water; the stained-glass scenes were full of its calm sheen or swirling currents or white-tipped waves. He'd liked vines, too, which tended to climb the long sides of glass panes he'd made to flank doors, and he liked flowers of all kinds. Much of his work was architectural, transoms or narrow panels to be inset above picture windows. In the middle of his career, he had experimented with geometric shapes as well, a counterpoint to the lush and intricately patterned scenes of his early work. In a series of square windows he had worked with green and blue and the white glass shaped into diamonds and triangles, arrowhead points.

There was something very calming about his work. In part it was the effect of the room itself, its white walls and vast windows everywhere. But it was also the glass art, with its radiant colors, its images of earth and leaves and water, the human figures in their flowing clothes, the geometric patterns with their soothing continuity and order.

The audio tour took me through the four downstairs rooms, and then instructed me to return to the foyer and travel down a short hallway. I did this, still glancing at the pamphlet, but I stopped, transfixed, when I reached the base of the stairway. Its open risers backed to a wall of glass; there was light everywhere. An enormous stained-glass window hung in the landing, radiant gold and green, purple and vermilion, pale blue and dark amber. It depicted a woman walking on a path of bluish-gray pebbles in a garden, holding a sheaf of many-colored long-stemmed flowers in her arms. Her hair was loose, falling to her shoulders in a dark cascade. Her simple dress was a golden green, falling to her toes, tightly belted at the waist in a darker green. Her feet were bare, her eyes cast toward the flowers, and her arms, her face, were done in a soft white glass that made her seem to glow, like the flowers in my mother's old moon garden. I noted the flowered leading pattern that Stuart had mentioned in the lower left corner, and again in the edge of her sleeve.

However, what held me still was her stance, the way she stood half-turned, gazing outward as if she recognized someone beyond the frame. Her face was familiar, too, rather long, her downcast eyes large, dark blue. I got my camera out and scrolled quickly through the saved images until I reached the one I'd taken of the Joseph window. Yes, one woman stood out amid the others, turned just this way, her face the same shape, though the image was much smaller, of course. Cupping my hand over the screen to darken it, I glanced from the phone to the stairwell with a growing sureness and excitement. Yes, I felt certain—these two images, in two very different scenes, had used the same woman as a model.

Footsteps sounded in the corridor, and a moment later Stuart appeared with several green file folders in one arm, running a hand through his flash of dark red hair, looking a little worried that he'd left me alone for so long.

"She's exquisite, isn't she?" he said, pausing beside me. "This window came from a private collection in New York City, quite undocumented. We think it's from rather late in the Westrum opus. He must have done it during his retirement; certainly after he moved to Rochester. At least that's the speculation among art historians."

I nodded, slipping my phone back into my purse. I didn't want to tell Stuart, not yet anyway, about my own discovery.

"She's incredibly striking. Not beautiful exactly, but very unusual. You don't know who the model was?"

"Unfortunately, no. We don't know much about that period of Westrum's life. He'd fallen out of favor and retreated here for the last twenty-some years of his life, after his wife died. No one was paying much attention to his work, sadly enough. We assume this woman was someone from the family who commissioned the window, but that's only a guess. It may also have been Westrum's daughter, Annabeth. The colors are particularly powerful in this piece, do you agree?"

"Yes. And I see the pattern in the leading."

"That's right. Here's the other thing I just love in this window—look at the gradations of color in the flowers. It's the spectrum of the rainbow, red to violet. Which is a wonderful visual pun, because the flowers are irises, and of course in Greek mythology Iris was the goddess of the rainbow."

"That is wonderful to know," I said quietly, trying to hide the thrill of excitement, electric and alive, that ran through me as he pointed out the flowers. *If Iris is to leave your household* . . . "Did you find anything interesting in the files?" I asked, nodding at his folders.

"Well, yes and no. Come back to the desk and I'll show you."

I followed him through the narrow hallway to the console, where he opened the folders and spread out the papers. There was a copy of the letter of receipt and thanks from the church for the chapel windows, clipped to a series of other letters.

"These are the commission requests," Stuart said. "I only had a chance to glance at them quickly. You're welcome to look further, of course. But the windows seem to have been ordered by a V. W. Branch in 1936. The address is in New York City, so Westrum probably knew him there. There's not much more information—just a detailing of the dimensions, some sketches of the images requested, that sort of thing."

I looked through the letters, all typed, all signed in black pen by V. W. Branch.

"Not him," I said. "Her. V. W. Branch is probably Vivian Whitney Branch, an early feminist." I was trying to speak very calmly, but I felt the sort of excitement you feel when the pieces of a puzzle are about to come together and make sense. "She had a sister, Nelia Elliot, who lived in The Lake of Dreams. That's probably the connection to the chapel windows. Nelia Elliot was active in the suffrage movement, too."

I went through all the papers carefully, one by one, hoping for a more tangible link to Rose, but I didn't find anything.

"Well, that's disappointing. I'd hoped the person who commissioned these might be an ancestor of mine," I explained, for Stuart was looking very perplexed. "But nothing here has her name, or her handwriting. I found a few letters of hers at my mother's house—I didn't bring them, unfortunately. But I'd recognize the handwriting."

"Well, it's quite unlikely that your ancestor would have known Frank Westrum," Stuart observed, a little affronted, taking a page from me and studying the script. "Not unless she lived in New York City before 1920. Or here thereafter."

"I don't know where she lived," I said. "But I do have a feeling she knew him."

"Ah, feelings," he said indulgently. "Wonderful, ephemeral things, feelings."

Annoyed, I pulled the phone from my purse and scrolled again to the image of the Jacob window. "Look at this—look at the woman behind the sack of grain."

Stuart studied the screen, two spots of color surfacing on his cheeks.

"I see what you mean," he said quietly, at last. "She's very familiar, this woman."

"I know. She almost has to have been the model for both windows."

"And you say she's an ancestor of yours?"

"I think so. Maybe. As I said, I found some letters in the house. She's never mentioned in the family stories, Rose Jarrett. But there's a record of her in the church—a baptismal record. She had a daughter in 1911." I didn't tell him the daughter was named Iris; I felt secretive about that discovery, so private and so exciting. I couldn't imagine sharing it, not yet. "Then she disappeared altogether."

"Where did you say the church is?"

"St. Luke's, right downtown in The Lake of Dreams."

Stuart nodded without commenting. It was always interesting to mention The Lake of Dreams to people from the area because the town had a reputation for being exclusive and rather snooty, for holding itself—the purity of its waters and the beauty of its village—above the other lakes and villages nearby. People either aspired to The Lake of Dreams or resented it. I couldn't really tell what Stuart thought, but I imagined he'd be among the former.

"I see." Then he gave a little laugh and sighed. "Well, actually, I don't see, not at all. I still don't understand why you think there's a connection between your relative and the woman in the window in the church."

"It's the border along the base of the window," I said. "Here, have another look. See—all the moons and vines I mentioned earlier? That same motif recurs in a piece of fabric I found in our house. There's also a note she wrote that was with the fabric."

"Yes, well. That's hardly proof."

I laughed. "I know. This is not proof at all. I'm going on gut instinct, an intuition that says these pieces must fit together. Of course, I could be totally wrong."

"May I?" He took the phone and scrolled to the Wisdom window again. After a moment, he nodded slowly. "You know, I think you're probably right, proof or no."

"I know I'm not supposed to—it says no photos right here—but given the circumstances, I wonder if I could take a picture of the window in the landing?"

Stuart grew clipped again, professional, and handed the phone back to me. "Oh, I'm afraid you can't. The museum directors—"

"Extenuating circumstances, don't you think?"

He hesitated, glanced at his watch. "I'll have to call and ask," he said. "I was thinking I should call them anyway. They'll be interested in your photos, your Rose." He walked around the console and hit a number on the speed dial, keeping his head turned, his voice hushed, as he conferred with whomever answered.

"All right," Stuart said as he hung up. "That was the chair of the board of directors, who also happens to be a Frank Westrum scholar. He agreed you could take one photo, as long as you leave a copy of the church window photo with us here, and some contact information, too. He's quite interested, you see. I thought he would be."

"I'll e-mail it right now." I took a business card from its little holder on the granite counter and punched the e-mail address into my phone. "By the way, what's in those other folders?" I asked.

"Ah, right—not so much, really. Orders for glass in various colors."

I looked, but Stuart was right. Not much to go on. I copied down the address in New York City so I could check it against Vivian's other letters once the archivist at Serling College got back to me. I took my single photo of the window, framing it carefully, and gave Stuart my name and phone number before I left.

It was after five o'clock by the time I stepped outside. Low clouds had gathered, and the wind-stirred leaves seemed lurid against the maroon brick across the street, the darkening sky. I paused beneath a trellis covered with wisteria; a butterfly floated past, then drifted to the ground like a leaf.

As I was puzzling over Frank Westrum and Beatrice Mansfield, and how the equally mysterious Rose Jarrett might be connected to them, a shiny black car drove up and parked on the street beyond the gates. A tall man, rather plump and beginning to bald, got out and hurried into the house, glancing at me with an assessing interest as he passed. He disappeared into the building, but a moment later he was on the steps again, hurrying along the flagstones, the wind catching at his tie.

"Pardon me, are you Lucy Jarrett?"

"Yes, I am."

"Pleasure," he said, extending his hand. "I'm Oliver. Oliver Westrum Parrott." He grimaced slightly when I smiled and said, "I know it's a ridiculous surname, but what can you do? I'm chief of the board of directors. I am also Frank Westrum's great-grandson. Stuart called me just now, and I was able to dash over straightaway. I wonder, could I see the photo of the window you've found? If it's truly a Westrum window, there will be great interest, you see."

"I sent an e-mail copy," I said. "But yes, here, it's on my phone. Have a look." I pulled up the image, surprised at how possessive I felt about this information suddenly, about Rose. "The quality isn't great, I'm afraid." I handed him the phone; he stepped back beneath the shadows of the wisteria to see more clearly. For a moment he didn't speak, but a muscle started twitching in his cheek.

"I see," he breathed, finally. "Yes, this is very exciting, I'd say." He looked up then, his eyes dark brown and avid. "Lucy. Pardon me, Ms. Jarrett, could I call you Lucy? Could I buy you a drink? I think perhaps it would help us both if we were to exchange stories."

I glanced at my watch. "I don't know—I have an hour's drive."

"I won't keep you long, I promise. Plus, I know more about Frank Westrum than anyone else in the world."

I nodded, intrigued. "All right."

I followed Oliver Parrott and his black car for several blocks to an old section of the city that had been revitalized, the brick storefronts full of restaurants and shops. He parked, and so did I; we met outside a little café with big plate-glass windows. Oliver held the door open for me, then threaded his way through the after-work drinkers to the back, which opened onto a little patio overlooking the water. Due to the breezy weather, several tables were free. We took one with an umbrella and ordered—gin and tonic for Oliver, sparkling water for me.

"So, please—tell me about Frank Westrum," I said as the waitress left. "I have to confess I've never heard of him until a few days ago."

Oliver nodded, settling back in his chair. "He was a fascinating character. I'm biased, of course; it's fair to say his legacy shaped my life, something my wife and children will attest to, with some frustration, I'm afraid. Not that I'm an artist," he added, waving one hand as if to dismiss any aspirations he might once have had. "I've dabbled, but it became quickly apparent to me that I didn't have the talent. Or the interest, really—it's not an easy life. I went to law school, thinking I would work for arts organizations, and that's what I've done. When there was an opening on the Westrum House board, I took the post gladly. My great-grandfather has been an avocation, really.

"He was an immigrant to this country from Germany, one of a great wave of artisans. He arrived in 1885 when he was seventeen, and started working in a glass factory outside of New York City, where several master glassworkers were reviving the art of stained glass, which had been virtually forgotten. They set about trying to re-create formulas for glass as it had been made in medieval times. Frank Westrum worked for one of these men, and in that way he started to come into contact with Art Nouveau. The style suited my great-grandfather, who loved the fluid, sensuous lines of the natural world, and who was a romantic at heart."

"I have a friend who makes glass from old formulas—Keegan Fall."

Oliver's face brightened. "Yes, of course—I know Keegan Fall. He does wonderful work. He's doing well? I certainly hope he makes a go of that studio. I suppose if you can make that sort of thing work anywhere, it would be in The Lake of Dreams, with all its charm and tourists."

"So far, he seems to be doing okay."

"Delighted to hear it. I've used his glass now and again for restoration work." He took a long swallow of his gin and tonic before he went on. "Anyway, my great-grandfather did very well for about a decade and a half, creating commissioned windows for the wealthy, but he didn't change with the times. Art Nouveau flashed hot for a while, but after the war, it definitely went out of favor. Plus, Frank Westrum was irascible, fierce about his own vision, and stubborn in his convictions. He felt opalescent glass defeated the central beauty of stained glass, which gets its power from its translucence, and he held fast to his aesthetics even when history seemed to be passing him by. One has to admire him for that. Nonetheless, he did maintain a small but loyal following, enough to let him earn a living, but he wasn't well known in his lifetime. This," he added, leaning forward, "is what makes your find in the church so utterly fascinating. Now tell me about this ancestor of yours."

"Rose Jarrett. She had a daughter, born in 1911. That's all I know."

"Now, don't be coy," Oliver said.

I laughed in surprise, glad I hadn't given Iris's name. "I'm not sure I know how to be coy. It was my search for information about Rose that brought me here, to the Westrum House. He used a motif that was important to her. A motif she may have designed. I'll show you." I found the image on my phone again and pointed it out to Oliver. "I'd love to know more about her, but I don't have much to go on, just a note she wrote in 1925."

Studying the motif, Oliver grew thoughtful. "Frank was in Rochester by then," he said. "He moved here because it was cheaper, you see, after his wife died. Also, maybe, for a fresh start. She had relatives in the area, so he knew about it. And as you may have surmised from his work, he loved the landscape here, and all the water."

"Beatrice Mansfield."

"Yes, you know of her? Beatrice. My great-grandmother. My mother was named for her. We—the family, that is—have always speculated that she was the model for the window, actually. It's possible she was the model for your window, too. It's even very likely, given how closely they resemble each other. Don't you agree?"

"I suppose," I said, reluctant to let go of my image of Rose Jarrett. But I didn't persist, because I realized what it might mean if Rose had modeled so extensively for Frank Westrum, what sort of intimacy it might imply—an intimacy Oliver Parrott might not wish to entertain. The wind fluttered our napkins, blew one off the table.

"Ah—looks like we're in for some more weather," Oliver said, picking up the check, refusing with a smile and a wave of one hand when I offered to pay.

The windy air tasted of rain; a few scattered drops hit my cheek. We stood up and I shook Oliver Parrott's hand. He gave me a business card and asked me to call him if I found anything else, and mentioned that he planned to visit St. Luke's quite soon. At this I felt a sudden ripple of panic; I'd been so absorbed in my own questions that I hadn't even considered the things I might be accidentally setting in motion. Once Oliver saw the Wisdom window and the Joseph window, he'd want them for the Westrum collection, of course; he'd want the windows from the chapel, too, if he found out about those. And though I didn't know for certain, Oliver Parrott's polish and his ease with money led me to imagine that the Frank Westrum Preservation Society might have enough money to make the church an offer it would have a hard time refusing. I don't know why this felt so wrong to me, or why I felt as if I'd inadvertently betrayed something vital and essential with all my blind searching, but it did, and I worried about it all the way back, along the interstate and then the smaller highways, through all the towns with their beautiful storefronts, their tattoo parlors and dollar stores and fast-food joints, the real estate offices and grocery stores and coffee shops and gift shops and old opera houses.

The storm that had been threatening came through with a sudden intensity as I turned down the lake road, the rain pounding down so fiercely that I could hardly see. I made it to one of the scenic overlooks and pulled off. When the rain eased, I got out of the car and walked to the guardrail to look down the length of the lake, which stretched for miles, slate blue and rough with waves, amid the curve of hills. A partial rainbow had formed in the dazzling, water-struck air, the spectrum of color clear but transparent behind the dark trees. It was breathtaking, a wild beauty emerging out of nothing, and it filled me with a powerful nostalgia for a past I hadn't even known. And why was that, I wondered? There was such force and beauty in the windows, such unsettled sadness in what little I knew of Rose's life, all her longing, her distance from her daughter. Just knowing she had existed opened new and uneasy possibilities within my understanding of the story I'd always thought I'd known by heart. And I felt responsible, too. Whoever Rose had been, she was gone, unable to speak for herself, fading into the past as surely as these rainy colors were diffusing, even now.

It was late evening by the time I got back, the sun half behind the opposite shore, the west side of the house cast in reddish gold. I found my mother sitting on the patio, glass of wine on the table, the bottle in a silver ice bucket on the floor, in easy reach. She had been reading a novel, and when I came in she put the paperback facedown on the arm of her chair; I glimpsed an ethereal baby dress against a background of black and thought of Iris. My mother was wearing a white T-shirt and chunky silver and turquoise jewelry that looked beautiful with her hair.

She leaned down to the bucket where another glass stood on the patio and handed it to me. "Before I forget, Keegan called. Something about the windows, he asked you to call him back. He's doing very well, isn't he?"

"He is. It's great. Do you know his son, Max?"

She smiled. "Sometimes Keegan brings him into the bank. Sweet boy. Lively, like his dad. He's a good father."

"I thought so, too. You sound very fond of Keegan these days."

"I always liked Keegan. I just thought you were too young. You were."

"I was."

"And now?" she asked, giving me an assessing look.

"Now I'm waiting for Yoshi to come," I said, not wanting to go any closer to the complex feelings that seeing Keegan again had evoked.

She handed me the wine and I poured myself a glass—a Chardonnay, from local grapes. It tasted faintly of pear and raspberries.

"Very nice."

"Isn't it? Andy brought it by. He should be back any second—I sent him out to fix the slats in the fence by the shed. He made the mistake of volunteering, poor guy."

"Really? He's here?"

"You sound disappointed. I thought you wanted to meet him?"

"I did. I do. I've had a very exciting day, that's all."

"Rose Jarrett?"

"Yes. Rose, here and there and everywhere." Quickly, I sketched out my day, my trip to the Westrum House in Rochester. I'd just begun to tell her about the woman in the window on the landing and my drink with Oliver Parrott when she smiled past me and waved. I turned to see Andy, a tall man, broad but lean, dressed just as I'd imagined he would be, in jeans and a cotton sweatshirt, coming up the lawn from the lake. His hair was cut short, glinting silver-gray in the late afternoon light. He was carrying a hammer and a sack of nails. I stood as my mother introduced us. He had a firm grip, a quick, engaging smile, and he asked about Japan with genuine interest. I had no reason to dislike him, yet I found myself feeling cautious, wary, reserved.

"Let me get another glass," my mother said.

"I'll get it," I told her, realizing suddenly that I was the intruder in the evening. The glass she'd had waiting by the wine hadn't been for me at all.

I sat with them for half an hour or so. My mother kept telling me and Andy things about each other—my work in hydrology, his pilot's license, my travels, his travels—to keep the conversation going. He'd grown up in the area and had left young, living up and down the East Coast as an air traffic controller. He had three grown children; his wife had died of a heart attack two years before. My mother touched his hand when he said this, and he flashed her a quick smile.

"So where were you?" I asked in the awkward silence that followed, nodding at the vase of glads. "On the night of the moon landing, I mean?"

He looked startled at this, and my mother cast me an irritated glance, but after a moment he cleared his throat and laughed.

"Well, I was right there, actually," he said. "In Cape Canaveral, I mean. I went down for the liftoff with a bunch of college buddies. We were all in our midtwenties. We all had jobs, some of us had families. But it was a great moment in history, so we went. It was astounding, I have to say. We went out on the beach the night after they'd landed, took our telescopes and imagined we could see them there, walking in the Sea of Tranquility. You know, this town was named after a place on the moon, at least in part. The Iroquois called this the place of dreams, and when the settlers came, they altered the name based on the lakes of the moon. I'm sure you know all this," he added. "The Lake of Dreams. Just down the road from The Bay of Rainbows and The Sea of Ingenuity."

I'd studied Blake's posters often enough to know all the names on the moon, fearful as well as beautiful. I thought it would put a damper on the evening to bring this up, but then I did it anyway. "The Ocean of Storms, The Marshes of Decay, The Lake of Death," I said. "Not exactly cheery."

Andy just chuckled. "I guess you know your lunar geography," he said mildly.

"I was fifteen that year," my mother said, ignoring my comment. "We went outside, too, out into the fields. We'd been watching the moon landing all day. We took our blankets out and stayed there all night, drinking diet soda and gazing at the moon. We were low-tech—no telescopes. Nothing seemed changed, yet we knew that it was."

"I wonder where Dad was that night," I mused, because I didn't know and couldn't ask him. It wasn't until the words left my mouth that I realized how they'd sounded, how maybe I'd even meant them, without consciously deciding to do it—as an intrusion, and interruption, a reminder of the life my mother had once led.

"I don't know," she said. "That's one thing we never talked about."

Andy took her hand, and she smiled.

I stayed a few minutes longer. They invited me to dinner, but I declined, saying I was tired, which was true. Andy's Prius hybrid was as different from my father's car as it was possible to be. I waved as they drove away, then went inside and made myself a peanut butter sandwich in the deepening dusk, without turning on any lights. I ate at the counter, drank a glass of milk, washed my few dishes. It was dark by the time I finished, but I went outside anyway, leaving the unlit house, walking barefoot through the wet grass. I wanted to swim, though I didn't have the energy to go back up to the house and change. After wavering for a minute, I shed all my clothes on the dock and dived into the water. The lake was cold and frothy, still stirred up from the storm. I was shivering a little by the time I climbed onto the raft, but I sat there for a long time, glad to be in a place where no one would find me, adrift in the water and adrift in the air, sorting through the unexpected events of my day. To the south were the marshes and the miles of darkened depot land where a village had once been, where the chapel still stood, unused for decades, the windows boarded up. I needed to go there, to understand how Rose was connected to the windows. In all fairness, I felt I needed to warn the Reverend Dr. Suzi about the charming and disarming Oliver Parrott before he showed up with his stories and his checkbook and his persuasive manner.

For the moment, though, my questions were simpler: who was Rose Jarrett exactly, and if she had come to this country with my great-grandfather Joseph, why had I never heard her story? Why had the delicately woven blanket been hidden away? Oliver Parrott could think what he liked, but the woman in the windows was familiar, connected to me like someone I'd known in another life, in a dream, and I wondered if tracing this story to its source might be a way to settle the restlessness that had been with me since the night my father died.

The raft moved gently, soothingly, on the waves. The moon, almost full, cast the sprawling old house in mild light. I was cold, but I didn't want to leave. I lay there for a long time, watching the sky clear and the stars emerge, taking their places in the night.

Chapter 9

MAYBE IT WAS THE NIGHT SWIM OR THE FACT THAT MY JET
lag had finally eased, but I slept very well that night and woke feeling
like myself again. I checked my e-mail before I even got out of bed,
wondering what Yoshi had decided about his travel plans. My mailbox
was almost full, because he had forwarded me photos from our friends
Neil and Julie, sitting on a white sand beach, the azure ocean stretching
to the horizon. There were underwater photos, too, of fish in neon
colors—yellow and bright blue—swimming amid the swaying coral.
They'd gone snorkeling near an island about three miles from the Indonesian coast, and they had liked it so much that they'd invited Yoshi to
go with them while he was there. He wanted to know if there was any
reason for him not to do it—he'd arrive two days late if he did.

There wasn't really, and if the situation were reversed I knew I'd
want to see Neil and Julie, to visit that beautiful beach. I wrote back that
it was fine with me, but in truth I felt for the first time how very far
away he was, and I was filled with a desire to be there with him, diving
into water as warm as breath. To try to ease the distance I called him,
and we spoke for a few minutes. He was waiting for a train and it was
noisy, so I didn't tell him much about what I'd discovered in Rochester,
though I did promise to e-mail him the images of Frank Westrum's
windows and said we'd go see them when he was here.

All the time I was talking, my mother had been moving downstairs. I heard the shower go on and then off, the closet doors opening, the tap of her heels. It was chilly, the floor cold against my bare feet, so I poked around in the drawers where some of my old clothes were still stored. I hadn't brought enough sweaters; in Japan the heat was already dense, and I'd forgotten about the chill that lingered in the lake air long into the summer. I found an old sweatshirt, dark blue, with the words *Night Riders* in orange across the front. That was the team name for The Lake of Dreams High School. Dreamers didn't have much punch, and Nightmares had been decreed too negative, so we were the Night Riders, a name Keegan and I had taken literally often enough in that final year, traveling out on his motorcycle, or slipping the canoe into the midnight lake and climbing in, riding the slow waves, the pulse of the night, out into the water.

My mother was already dressed when I came downstairs, standing at the counter eating leftover bean dip on wheat crackers, drinking a glass of milk. The recipe card Andrew had left was on the counter, too, and a silk scarf, in a beautiful rhubarb shade, was pooled beside it. She was lost in her own thoughts, though after an instant she looked up and smiled.

"Morning," she said, wiping off her fingertips and reaching for the glass.

"How was dinner?"

"Very nice. We didn't go far, just downtown. We ate at that new place, the one that juts over the water? It was good. I wish you'd come with us."

"It just didn't feel right," I said. "So much romantic tension in the air." I was trying to joke, but the words sounded flat and wrong even as I said them.

She looked at me for a long moment, maybe remembering our argument. "Oh, nonsense," she said finally, lightly. "Really. I hardly know him."

"You seem to like him."

"Yes, I do."

"So. Well. That's good. Anyway, I was tired last night, and I had a lot to think about. The windows are so stunning, Mom. You'll have to see them." I poured myself some coffee. "It's chilly this morning, isn't it? I had to dig this old sweatshirt out of the bottom drawer."

"Are your drawers still full? How ridiculous is that, after all these years? You know, I was just thinking we could start going through some of this stuff while you're here. There are decades of clothes and bric-a-brac and old papers, generations of it. I haven't had the heart or energy to tackle that project, but it really needs to get done."

So she could sell the house and the land, I thought, but didn't say.

"I guess we could do that. This weekend, maybe? Before Yoshi gets here. He's been delayed a couple of days, so once he gets here I won't want to spend time organizing."

"That's too bad he's delayed. Everything okay?"

"Everything's fine."

"Okay. I don't mean to pry. Just thinking that we could clean out a room for him, too, while we're at it."

I looked at her.

"What?"

"Mom, we've been living together for two years."

"I know. And you can arrange things however you want. But it's still my house, and I'm setting up a room for him."

I laughed, and then she did. "Oh, Mom. Whatever."

It was misty as we drove into town, the fog collecting in the dips of the road so that we drove through clouds, the hood of the Impala the color of egg yolks amid the viscous white until we emerged on the tops of the hills and it took its place with all the other colors—the deep green of the corn, the flashing red of barns, the blue patches of sky that were trying to break through. My mother and I didn't speak much, though she reached over and squeezed my hand when I dropped her off. I parked in the same place in the lot, far away from everything, and then walked down the street to Avery's for a cup of coffee. She wasn't there, so I couldn't apologize for having slipped up and told my mother about the baby. As always, the air in the restaurant was fragrant with butter and honey, yeast and coffee, and this morning the inside tables were full of people talking quietly over the food, wet umbrellas folded at their feet. When I stepped outside, Dream Master rose stark against the gray sky, the brick darkened with rain.

The glassworks was closed to tours on Friday mornings in order to catch up on special orders and give everyone a chance to get ready for the waves of weekend tourists. The gift shop was open, though, the door ajar and a display of new bowls in the window—bright ruby, sapphire, and amethyst—but I didn't want to go in. Instead, I walked a few feet to stand outside the plate-glass windows, where I could watch the artisans plunging their pipes into the furnace and pulling out the molten glass, forming it with their breath, the vessels taking slow shape, one by one: a vase, a wine goblet, a clear glass bowl. I rang the bell twice, but if they heard it they ignored me; they didn't even glance up. Keegan wasn't working—at least I couldn't see him—but I wanted to tell him about my trip to Rochester and meeting Oliver Parrott. I wanted to tell him about Rose. After a minute of standing in the drizzle, I remembered that he'd had given me his cell number when we were at the church. I fished around in my purse until I found it, punched the numbers in. He answered on the fourth ring, and when I told him I was downstairs, he buzzed me in.

The glassblowing room was hot, despite the high windows open all along the canal and the huge fans moving constantly. Courtney, the assistant, glanced up and nodded, turning her attention almost immediately back to the shape emerging from her blowpipe, the swelling glass a deep iridescent green, like a mallard's neck. I paused for a moment, watching her fluid, expert motions, the glass that shifted and grew as if alive, before I crossed the room and went upstairs.

Keegan was sitting on a beanbag chair, his long legs extended and crossed at the ankles. Max was sitting next to him, caught in the curve of his father's arm, while Keegan read out loud. It wasn't a board book, or even an early reader, but rather a collection of Greek myths. They were reading the story of Demeter and Persephone, the girl's sudden vanishing and the mother's desperate search, the way she'd stopped the world from growing until someone told her what had happened to her daughter. When Persephone returned, the pomegranate seed was already on her tongue; the moment she bit it she was destined to spend half the year in darkness. It seemed a little complex for a boy as young as Max, but he was riveted. Keegan glanced up and smiled as I came in, without interrupting the story. I leaned against one of the steel supporting beams and listened to his voice, so animated and soothing. Max listened, too, avidly attentive, and now and then he glanced up at Keegan with a satisfied and adoring expression.

When the story was done, Keegan closed the book and stood up, stretching.

"Read another one, Dad," Max said. "I didn't get enough stories."

Keegan laughed. "Not enough stories? You *never* have enough stories, Max. I could read to you all day and all night and you'd still want more."

Max laughed and shouted, "More!"

"How about you watch cartoons for fifteen minutes while I talk to Lucy?"

Max cast a level and assessing gaze at me before he reached for the remote. Keegan came over and kissed me on the cheek, a friendly kiss, nothing more, but one that took me back in time anyway. I felt the warm press of his lips, smelled his familiar scents of soap and sweat and now of fire.

"Nice sweatshirt," he said.

"Thanks. I found it at the bottom of a drawer. We missed you at the solstice party," I added, remembering how the night had been woven with the glittering possibility that he might come. Did I sound too disappointed? I touched my cheek where he had kissed me.

"Your mother was just being nice," he said. "Besides, it got busy here at the end of the day. A special order, place settings for a bridal shower."

"She likes you," I said. "She wasn't just being nice. It was a good party."

"I'm sure it was. Well, maybe next year. Need some more coffee?" he asked, nodding at my cup as he walked toward the kitchen.

"Love some." I followed him to the counter—he moved so fluidly, with the same athletic grace he had while working the glass—and sat down, pulled the plastic lid off the cup so he could fill it. "My mother said you left a message?"

"I did, actually. Good news. I got permission to take you to the chapel. Not until Wednesday, unfortunately, but they'll have the boards off the rest of the windows by then. I'm eager to see what they've got there, and I thought you would be, too."

"That's fantastic. I didn't get to tell you the details, but I found out who made the windows, and I think I found the connection with my family, too. I have this ancestor I've never heard of before. Her name is Rose. She had a daughter, too, born in 1911. And then she seems to have disappeared. They both did. Though I think I found some clues," I added, remembering the woman with her arms full of irises.

Keegan looked surprised. "That's really amazing, isn't it? I mean, the way your family is, all interwoven and clannish, it's hard to imagine there's a forgotten ancestor."

"Really? Are we like that?"

"Kind of, yeah. No offense or anything."

"It's okay. But am I like that?"

Keegan shrugged, amused and perplexed. "I don't know, Lucy. It's been a long time. But sure, you used to be pretty focused on all those complicated Jarrett dynamics."

I nodded. It was probably true. When I came back I always felt as if I were standing on the edge of a river, watching the swirling currents of the family interactions from a safe distance. Now I wondered if I'd slipped into the midst of them again.

"The thing is, Keegan, I don't think Rose was forgotten. I think she was covered up. Obscured. I think she was an early feminist—interesting and maybe scandalous. By the way, have you ever heard of Frank Westrum?"

"Westrum? Sure. Are they Westrum windows, then?" Keegan put down his coffee, his voice threaded with excitement. "They are, aren't they? It crossed my mind, actually—it would make perfect sense—the style and the era are right. The church had records?"

"They did. The original receipt. I drove to Rochester yesterday, to the Westrum House. I met Oliver Parrott, by the way. He sends his regards."

"Oliver Parrott, what do you know." Keegan, smiling, shook his head. "Isn't he something? Was he wearing a bow tie?"

"He was."

"What a character. I like working with Oliver because he really cares about the quality of the glass, about making the repairs authentic. But he's, shall we say, quite persnickety. He'll make you do a thing over and over and over again until he feels you've got it right."

"He's really excited about the windows," I said. "I maybe said too much, though. It didn't cross my mind until I'd left that he'd want them for the Westrum House, but of course he will. I'm thinking I should call the church, let them know he might show up."

"I wouldn't worry about it too much. The Reverend Suzi is pretty savvy. Oliver was bound to find out sometime anyway."

I picked up my cup, which Keegan had filled to the brim, and coffee sloshed onto the counter, onto a stack of papers. I grabbed a dish towel and sopped up the spill, drying off the top few papers, though a faint brown stain radiated across the center of a flyer. It was a copy of the one I'd seen hanging in the library, advertising the town meeting and setting out the Iroquois position on the land. At first I thought Keegan had just picked one up, but then I realized the whole stack was made up of these flyers.

"Yours?" I asked.

"Yep. Don't worry about the spill. I've got plenty more."

"I didn't know you were involved in the land issues," I said, remembering the solstice party, how Art and Joey—and yes, even Blake—had dismissed Keegan as being on the wrong side of history.

"I'm moderately involved. They asked me to help post these, and I said sure. Since Max was born it's seemed more important to me, to have that heritage. To pass it along. And I happen to believe in this particular cause."

"I guess the land is pretty valuable," I said. "I think most of my relatives are angling to get it."

"Thick as thieves," Keegan said, cheerfully. "I was surprised at Blake, but there he is, right in the middle of it. The Landing," he added, somewhat derisively. "Even the name is stuck in the past."

"Well, what do you think the land should be used for?"

"That's just it. That's the point exactly. It shouldn't have to be used for anything, not farms, not weapons bunkers, not high-end homes. It should just be."

"Not casinos."

"No, I agree with you. We'd like to keep it in some kind of preserve, if we got it. The thing is, Lucy, we see that land as a sacred trust. We want to protect it. And this is a rare opportunity. Even though they've had weapons and bombs and who knows what buried there all these decades, a lot of the land has been left alone. There's a herd of white deer that's evolved over the decades within those fences, and there's a nesting place for black terns, which are endangered. We've been working with the conservation groups, and that's been good. But the developers are hungry. Famished. To be fair, a lot of people have been hurting for a long time, and it got worse when the base closed. You don't see it so much in town, because of all the tourists and the money on the lake. But drive out into the countryside, and it will hit you."

"I kayaked a little way into the lake by the depot, but I was afraid to go too far. I saw the white deer, though. Five of them, disappearing into the trees. Beautiful. I noticed several streams; I hadn't realized they were there. I wonder—has anyone done a hydrology study of that land? There's been so much development on the lake in the last couple of decades. At some point, all the demands—the septic tanks, the piping of water—starts to be too much for the ecological system to handle. Plus there's the issue of runoff." I thought of Indonesia, the rising waters. "Build too much and there's no place for water to go, and you get floods."

"Well, that's interesting. There's been some flooding toward the south end of the lake, but I don't think anyone has connected the dots to all the new houses. And I'm not sure about the runoff issues." He smiled. "Maybe you should come on board as a consultant."

I smiled, pleased at the compliment. "I'm sure there are local hydrologists who know the land better."

"Well, maybe. I think you'd have a lot to offer, though. Want to see the whole thing, see what you think?" Keegan asked. "I was planning to take Max for a boat ride; his mother's still sick and his babysitter can't get here until noon."

He smiled then, invitingly, his eyes crinkling at the corners, and I was taken back to that long ago spring when we'd spent so many nights on his motorcycle, in a boat, the wind in our faces. Except it didn't feel so long ago now that I was back in town, finding reasons to drop by and say hello. *Stop,* I cautioned myself. Because I had this other life in another country, and where could anything with Keegan ever lead but heartache? *Just stop.*

"Sure," I said.

"Great," he said. "Let me get my keys."

Downstairs, Courtney, the assistant, was carrying the green glass vase to the annealer. She lifted her protective glasses and called out to Keegan as we passed. Her eyes were pretty, dark and large, and her features were prominent, widely spaced; she was sturdy and strong, as well as striking. Keegan paused, talking with her for a minute, while Max and I lingered at the edge of the conversation. Then Courtney came over to stand with Max, and Keegan took my hand. "Want to try?" he shouted over the roar of the fire, and I nodded.

Keegan went through all the motions of the dance, gathering the molten glass, turning it against the metal table to start its shape. He placed his lips against the pipe, and the glass began to swell. "Your turn," he shouted, then handed me the pipe. I put my lips where his had been, the metal warm against them. Keegan leaned close to help me turn the pipe, and I blew lightly, the glass growing larger. Back and forth we went, his lips on the metal, mine, our breath mingling, swelling the glass. Finally he tapped off the beautiful piece we'd created, the shape of a raindrop, and carried it to the annealer in heat-resistant gloves. I was trembling—from the weight of the pipe, from the heat, from the press of Keegan's arms against mine. I thought of my dream, the spheres that had turned liquid in my hands. Keegan's sure and steady touch with something so fragile was breathtaking. He came back with Max, and we stepped outside into the fresh, rainy air.

"That was just amazing."

He smiled. "You did a great job. No two pieces are ever exactly alike—that's the part that really appeals to me. It's a pretty nice way to make a living."

"When will it be done?"

"A couple of days. How about I come up and drop it off?"

"Good," I said. "That would be good."

Max was running on the grass, making wide circles.

"So," Keegan said. "I have this supplier coming. Courtney reminded me. He just called from downtown, and he'll be here any minute. It shouldn't take long, but I have to see him. Would you mind taking Max for a walk, say, just down along the outlet? I'll catch up in a minute, and then we can take a ride."

"No problem," I said. Though I'd spent very little time with small children, Keegan was a good father so effortlessly that I figured it would be a piece of cake. "I love that walk and I haven't done it in years."

"Great." He turned back, disappearing into the glassworks, and I went down the sidewalk to catch up with Max, the warm pressure of the pipe still tingling on my lips.

"Where's my dad?" Max asked.

"He's got to do some work. He said we should take a walk and he'll catch up."

"I want to wait for my dad."

"I was a friend of your dad's, you know. A long time ago."

"My dad knows everyone in town."

"I'm not surprised. Shall we go?"

"No."

We stood there for a moment in the misty air. Finally, I said, "You know, Max, your dad tells me you're very smart. He said you know where the trail is. But I didn't believe him."

It was too easy, so easy I almost felt bad for having done it. Max stamped one foot on the sidewalk and said, "It is *so* true," and then he took off.

The trail was narrow, gravel-covered, winding its way through the trees, which were still dripping a little from the morning rain. We followed the outlet, veering away from it and then drawing closer again. Max refused to hold my hand. He said he wanted to walk a few steps ahead because I didn't know where I was going.

So I let him, watching him half-run, half-skip over the gravel. He was wearing jeans and a puffy red jacket and his shoes had little lights in the heels that flashed with every step. Max moved with the same lithe agility as his father.

"Maybe we should wait here for your dad," I suggested as we made a slow curve that took us out of sight of the old factory buildings. There was a historical marker noting that this was the site of worker dormitories and later individual houses back at the turn of the century, when factories were thriving in The Lake of Dreams. The ruins of one such house had been left. Another structure, just the framing, a ghost of a building, stood beside it. "Hey, Max!" I called as the distance between us grew; he had gotten quite far ahead. "Come look at this!" He didn't even turn around. "Hey!" I called again. "Wait up. You can't go by yourself."

"My dad lets me," he said, his small voice drifting back to me. "My dad does, all the time. Besides, I'm the leader."

"Right. Okay. You're the leader. Wait up anyway."

I jogged to catch up and we walked awhile longer, Max staying just a few feet ahead, the path drawing near the outlet, which rushed in its banks, the surface as smooth and molten as glass, then moving back into the trees. My thoughts kept circling back to Keegan, to his lips against the metal pipe, to the swelling glass, to the play of fire reflected on his skin. We walked, and then my phone rang and I stopped to rummage in my purse.

"Hey, Max, hang on," I called. He turned as I flipped open the phone and paused beneath the trees to talk. It was Keegan.

"What's up?" I asked.

"Sorry, Lucy, slight change of plans. The supplier just called and he's running late. So, why not just bring Max back here? Whenever you're ready, I mean, there's no rush. Everything going okay?"

"Everything's fine. He's a fun kid. Has a mind of his own."

"Yeah, I know. I like to think he takes after his mother that way."

"I'm sure. He must get the charming part from you, then."

Keegan gave a low, familiar laugh. I closed my eyes for a moment, remembering his breath on my cheek, my lips against the metal.

"Glad you still think so."

"Really, he seems like a sweet boy."

I smiled as I spoke, then looked up, expecting to see Max in his red coat poking his stick impatiently on the ground. But the path was empty. He was nowhere in sight. I took a step, scanning the foliage—surely he was hiding somewhere, or had stepped off the trail to look at another bug. With the phone still against my ear I started hurrying.

"Well, bring him back whenever," Keegan was saying. "I'm sure he'd love to stay out all day, but I know you must have things to do."

"It's okay," I said, though it wasn't—I'd rounded the curve and still didn't see Max, and panic was beating through my blood. It was the panic of my dream. "Hey, do you let him walk ahead? He says you do."

Keegan laughed. "He can tell you're a novice. Don't let him push you around."

"All right. We'll be back soon," I said, already closing the phone, already starting to run, calling out for Max. The wet leaves flashed and slapped my arms, the gravel slipped under my feet. I shouted, but my voice faded in the dense wet air. There was no answer. He had stepped into the trees, perhaps, like a child in a fairy tale, lured by some treasure my grown-up eyes overlooked. I was thinking with terrible panic of stolen children, too—anyone could have been here, could have pulled him into the trees and be holding him there right now, even as I ran past shouting, calling his name.

The path curved again. I glimpsed Max's red coat and felt a rush of relief. I slowed down a little, catching my breath, trying to still my racing heart.

Then I saw where he was.

There had once been a bridge across the outlet, but it had long since fallen down. Now there were only two piers remaining, one on the shore and one set a few feet into the river, with a little platform connecting them. Max was standing on this platform, right at its very edge, his hands clasped behind his back as if he were an old man, peering calmly down at the churning water below.

I kept walking, taking a deep breath to calm myself, because it mattered to be calm, I knew.

"Hey, Max," I said, as evenly as I could, when I got close enough. "Hey there, fearless leader. What're you doing?"

He turned and looked over his shoulder, smiling with excitement.

"I'm watching the water. It's neat. I can see shapes in it, can you?"

"That really is neat," I said, climbing up on the nearest pier, slowly, so I wouldn't startle him. I didn't step onto the concrete platform because I couldn't tell how strong it was. Max was looking down again, studying the water, swirling and brown. I could see why he was so fascinated; at this point the outlet narrowed, and the water was forced through the banks with a wild rushing force, shape-shifting and mesmerizing. The tips of his flashy sneakers extended an inch into thin air. *Please,* I thought, *let me say the right thing.* "Hey, could you step back a little, Max? 'Cause your dad just called, and I have something to tell you."

He didn't. For a long moment we both just stood where we were, Max staring at the mesmerizing water, all its froth and force, tree branches and litter traveling on its surface, pulled abruptly under.

"Max?"

He turned around. He took one step, then another. I took his hand, and wouldn't let him pull away when he tried to.

"Let's jump," I said, and we did, landing on the muddy earth.

"Ouch," he said. "That was too far."

"Hold my hand again," I said, in a firm but friendly way. This time he did.

"What did my dad say?"

"Oh, he said it's time to come home."

"He did?"

"He did."

"Okay."

Max pulled away from me again on the way back, but not until I'd made him promise to stay close, and this time I kept up with him, I didn't let him get out of reach. I was exhausted by the time we reached the glassworks. Keegan was standing at the edge of the road, talking with a man who had brought a load of sand. I was still shaking from what had almost happened. Max ran up and flung his arms around Keegan as if nothing had happened, and Keegan reached down absently, tousling Max's dark curls while he kept talking. Finally, Keegan shook the supplier's hand and took a step back, turning his full attention to Max.

"Hey, Max. How was the walk?"

"I showed her the trail," he said. "I told her I knew the way, and I did."

"He did," I agreed, and then I told Keegan briefly what had happened, how Max had run ahead and found a lookout place right above the swirling waters. Keegan listened, his face growing as masked as it once had when we were children bearing schoolyard taunts, and when I finished he squatted down and took Max by the shoulders.

"Max. What do you think would happen if you fell in the river?"

"I didn't fall."

"I know. And I'm glad. But what if?"

"It would take me away like the branch," Max said.

"It would take you away," Keegan agreed, very serious. "And you wouldn't be able to get back. And I would be so sad. My whole heart would break. Don't do that again, Max. You understand? You don't go near the water. You know that."

"I'm so sorry," I said. "I nearly stopped breathing when I saw where he was. I just keep thinking how horrible it would be if—"

"Lucy. Stop." Keegan's voice was calm, but firm. He stood up and sent Max to sit on a nearby bench for a minute, then caught my hand, his palms calloused from his work with fire. "Look, nothing happened, right? Trust me, if I spent every moment of parenthood doing the what-ifs, I'd drive myself absolutely crazy. Max is a handful. I should have gone with you. But everyone is just fine. So that's a moment where we don't have to linger."

"All right," I said, though I knew I'd carry that image of Max standing so calmly at the edge of the roiling water with me for the rest of my life. "You're pretty good at this, you know," I added. "This fatherhood stuff. You make it look easy."

He laughed. "I'm totally winging it," he said. "Everyone is. What do you think? Do you still have time? Want to take that boat ride?"

Keegan took one of Max's hands and after a minute I took the other, and we climbed into the boat Keegan kept moored by the glassworks, at the docks where barges had once pulled up to load their wares. I sat next to Keegan near the bow, and Max, bundled securely in a bright orange life jacket, sat between us. The day had brightened and there were patches of blue, but it was still mostly overcast. I hugged my arms against the wind, glad to have my ratty old sweatshirt as we traveled out across the water, spray in our faces as we hit the white-crested waves.

We traveled several miles down the lake, and I recognized the point where we crossed the border of the depot land into waters that had once been forbidden.

At first the green hills, forested or covered in swaying grasses, sloped down to the wide shale beach. Soon, however, the landscape began to change, grass-covered concrete bunkers rising out of the land in evenly spaced intervals. Even covered in sod they looked unnatural, rising out of the earth like the steady sound of a machine, like identical notes in the most boring piece of music in the universe. Their hunkering shapes and monotonous regularity made them seem ominous, too. Weapons bunkers, they must be; I'd seen an editorial from 1940 describing the soil as having been "seeded with bombs instead of wheat." They were empty now, the weapons transferred, but even so I felt uneasy looking at them, the wild, organic beauty of the landscape lost to this precise and repetitious order.

Just past the last of the bunkers Keegan cut the motor, letting us drift with the waves. A cluster of machines, the yellow and orange and vivid green of crayons, stood on the shore. They had torn grass from the earth like a scalp, discarding it on one of the artificial hills, exposing the dark, rich soil. The area they had uncovered was large, and puddles had formed across it in the recent rains, so that in the overcast light it looked barren and uninhabitable; bleak, a quagmire.

"They sure don't love the land, do they?" Keegan asked. "That's the first stage of the first development. Not the one your uncle and Joey and Blake want to build, but a different company. We got a court order to have construction stopped temporarily. We're trying to prove that the sale of those parcels was invalid."

"I hope you can. You really should look into the groundwater. Because there's a layer of shale beneath the soil that drains this whole area, and it looks like they're damaging that here. Plus, the kind of development you're talking about will strain the whole fragile ecosystem of the lake, which is already under stress. And this whole watershed drains into

Lake Ontario, eventually. That's the thing with water systems. Everything's interconnected. Everything affects everything else."

"Really, we'll have to put you on the committee. I mean it—I called some friends while you were with Max, and it turns out the conservation groups have filed papers about the water table. That, along with the wildlife protection, is their main issue."

"That's good. What do you think? Will you win?"

"I don't know. But here's hoping."

He turned the motor on again and took us past the lurid machines, past a forested section of land and a cluster of buildings, to a clearing. Here, the chapel stood by itself on a hill. It was built of red stone; the paint had peeled away from the doors, leaving them a weathered gray. A small graveyard, enclosed inside an ornate iron fence, stood beside it.

"There it is," Keegan said. "I can't wait to see the windows all uncovered. It's a good thing they were boarded up, or we'd have lost them. I'm glad it's far from the airstrip, too—less chance of damage from vibrations."

"It looks so strange, here all by itself."

Keegan nodded. "Believe it or not, the chapel was in the center of town. There was a blacksmith, a grocer, a seamstress. More than five hundred people lived there, and they were all scattered to the winds overnight. And before they came, the Cayuga and Seneca lived here, fished and hunted here."

"I'm hungry," Max announced.

"Granola bars and juice in the backpack," Keegan said. "It's up there, under the bow." Max lifted a curtain and scooted into the cavelike space.

"He likes it in there," Keegan said. "He'll stay there the rest of the ride, I bet."

We passed more forested land, more fields, and came to the shoreline my mother owned: the boathouse and my kayak on the shale beach, the wide lawn up to the house with its porches and French doors, its cupola.

"Remember that night you snuck out?" Keegan asked. "I was waiting right here in the canoe, trying to stay in the shadows. You were wearing a white dress."

"I nearly tipped the canoe trying to get in," I said. "I got soaked."

"It was a warm night, as I remember."

"It was," I said, remembering how we'd sat spooned close together, me leaning back and Keegan's arms around my waist, and the moon floating above us.

"We were so young, weren't we?"

"Yes, we were. We were indeed." Keegan lingered for a moment longer before he turned the boat in a wide curve and headed back, the damp wind rushing over our faces.

We docked, and Keegan lifted Max from the boat as we talked, making tentative plans to meet at the chapel on Wednesday. We parted at the sidewalk, but I stood watching them walk, Max skipping again, his shoes flashing, as they went hand in hand back to the glassworks, back to the fire and motion.

The Impala was stifling. I opened all the windows and doors to let it cool while I took out my phone to check my e-mail. Nothing more from Yoshi, which made me a little uneasy. Maybe he was just busy. I pulled up an earlier message and then a photo of the two of us, taken by a stranger outside the hot springs. Yoshi had his arm around my shoulders, and we were both smiling, and there was nothing in the picture to reveal our languorous dance in the dark kitchen, or the little flares of anger, or the trembling earth.

There was a message from the Serling College Special Collections office confirming that they had possession of the collected papers of Vivian Branch, and saying also that they were in the process of researching my request. Last was a message I didn't expect, from Oliver Parrott. It was very formal, inviting me to visit the museum again to go through some of the images from his archives. Stuart would be there, he assured me, though the house wasn't officially open on Saturdays, and I was welcome to bring someone, too. He had spoken to the church, he said, and felt quite passionately about the connections that were emerging.

He could not wait to see the other windows, and he had stood for a long time this morning before the window on the landing of the woman with her arms full of flowers.

Full of irises, I thought.

Yes, I wrote back. *I will come.*

Chapter 10

SOME DREAMS MATTER, ILLUMINATE A CRUCIAL CHOICE, OR reveal some intuition that's trying to push its way to the surface. Others, though, are detritus, the residue of the day reassembling itself in some disjointed and chaotic way, and those were the sorts of dreams I had the night before I drove back to see Oliver Parrott—dreams of chasing after Max, whose laughter I kept hearing in the trees, floating over water; dreams of running across the depot land, trying to climb out over the fences, which kept growing higher. Yoshi was in the dreams, too, trying to help, unable to find me. Frantic dreams, they left me tired, and I woke grouchy to another rainy day, the sky so densely gray and the rain so thick that I couldn't see the opposite shore.

I pulled on the only pair of jeans I'd brought, my last clean T-shirt, and the same dark blue Night Riders sweatshirt. In the gray light, the color made me look bleached-out and tired. I brushed my hair and teeth, collected a basket of dirty laundry, and made my way downstairs.

Though it was Saturday and she had the day off, my mother was already up and dressed, her short hair moussed into spikes. She was sitting on the floor of the living room, near the door to the sleeping porch, a cup of coffee steaming by her side and several big boxes lined up at the edge of the rug.

"I'm taking it on," she said. "I don't have to work today, and so I thought I'd start digging into this mess. Want to help?"

"Oh, not really. It's such a funky, rainy day. It's put me in a bad mood."

"Well, have a quick look anyway. Blake's coming by in a few minutes to take a few things."

I got a cup of coffee and sat down beside her on the floor, pulling open the flaps of the box closest to me. It was full of books, children's books. I pulled out *The Little Engine that Could, The Very Hungry Caterpillar,* and *The Cat in the Hat.* They were worn from many readings, the cardboard corners dented in places, the pages soft.

"Oh, that's a good one," my mother said, reaching for *Goodnight Moon.* "I loved this one. So did you. I must have read it out loud three hundred zillion times. Anyway, I promised Blake this box of books, now that he'll have a use for them. I'm glad you told me, Lucy, even though it was awkward at first. I mean, yes, Blake was a little upset, but I think he really wanted to talk about it, too, and when he realized I was happy about the whole thing, he relaxed. Really, I can't wait," she went on. "People always say how thrilling it is to know you're going to be a grandparent, but I didn't imagine it really would be. I've set another box aside for them already, filled up with old toys."

"What about me?" I meant to say it in a kidding way, but even to my own ears I sounded a little shrill. Seeing my mother so excited made Blake and Avery's baby seem very real, and although it was ridiculous, I felt left out, or left behind, the sweep of life moving on while I kept doing the same things over again in different places. "Sorry," I said. "I'm in a lousy mood—I didn't sleep well. I guess I just mean that if I ever have a baby, everything will be long gone."

"Trust me—people will pass things on." She looked at me then, and added softly, "But if there's anything special you want to hold aside—you know, for some day—go ahead. Blake and Avery won't even notice."

"It's okay. Maybe that mobile Dad made when I was born. I'd like to keep that."

My mother nodded. "It's already in a box in your closet. I put it away—oh, a couple of years ago. And the trains he made for Blake. I put those away, too."

She reached into the box in front of her, pulling out a handful of folders.

"So—you and Yoshi have any plans?" she asked, trying to sound offhand and failing so miserably that I laughed.

"New plans every day, it seems. But no. If you're talking about settling down and having children, no."

She nodded and rested her hand briefly on my arm, which irritated me because I was afraid she felt sorry for me. "Just curious," she said, pulling away.

"Need help with any of that?" I asked, glad to change the subject, as she caught a slipping folder. "How's your arm feeling, by the way?"

"I'm fine. I saw the doctor yesterday. I'm healing nicely, he says. If all goes well, I can get rid of this Aircast next Wednesday, hooray. Oh, look at this, Lucy."

She handed me a poem written carefully on wide blue-lined paper, back when kids still practiced cursive writing. I'd decorated the edges with dolphins and fish, waves and seashells, even though I'd never been to the ocean.

"Guess my inclinations were clear even then."

"Guess so." She glanced at several files full of business papers left from my father's time at Dream Master and chucked them into the recycle bin.

"Ah, report cards." I gave her a stack of Blake's, and pulled one of mine out, from fourth grade. "'Has strong writing skills and loves science. Needs to work on sitting still.' That was Mrs. Blankenthorpe," I said. "I remember her. We used to call her Mrs. Battleship."

"That's terrible," my mother said, though we were both laughing.

We kept going, refilling our coffee cups one time, then again. The porch roof was leaking, and every now and then my mother went to check the bucket she'd put out to catch the drips. I suggested that she could install rain barrels, and she sighed.

"It must be hard to keep up with this place," I said when she came back from having dumped the half-full bucket onto the lawn.

"It is." She sat down again. "But I truly haven't decided what to do, Lucy. Art has his ideas, but they aren't necessarily my ideas."

I didn't answer; I didn't want to argue again. Despite what she said, it felt like an understanding had already been reached, even if my mother hadn't quite come to terms with it yet.

By the time Blake stopped by the rain had eased, but he was soaked from doing some caulking on the boat. We took a break and ate some scrambled eggs along with more leftovers from the party: tabbouleh and French bread, now a little stale, spinach hummus on crackers. Then we went back to sorting out the boxes. The phone rang; my mother reached into her pocket and smiled when she saw the caller ID.

"Back in just a second," she said, then went into her room and closed the door.

Blake and I didn't speak for a while, listening to our mother's murmuring voice. Tension, either from the party or from my mistake in telling the news about the baby, was in the room, invisible but real, limning everything.

Finally, Blake asked what I was doing with my day. I told him I was going to visit Oliver Parrott and invited him to come.

"Today?" He waved his hand, dismissive. "This may surprise you, Sis, but some of us actually have to work."

I decided to let it pass, not to mention the work he seemed to be doing with Art and the developers. Because Blake was doing his best, probably, doing what he thought would make a good life for himself and for Avery and the baby in the midst of a rotten economy.

"Well, sometime, then—you should go see this place. Take Avery; it would be a nice drive. The stained glass is really striking, even if there turns out to be no connection to Rose. And I'm totally curious to know what Oliver Parrott thinks he's discovered."

"He seems a little off to me, this guy—dedicating his whole life to the study of another person, some dead ancestor."

"Well—it's not the person he's dedicated to. It's his legacy."

"Same thing. It's weird."

"Well, it's really no different than you and Art, is it?" I asked, keeping my voice pleasant even as I lashed back. "Doing everything you can to keep Dream Master alive."

Blake didn't answer. His jaw was set and he was staring out the window at the lake. It took a few minutes for him to speak.

"I'm just trying to make my way, Lucy—got a problem with that?"

I let the silence gather, too, trying to figure out why Blake was so upset, and why Oliver's choices were explicable to me while Blake's were not.

"No," I said, finally. "I don't have a problem with that. But it was strange—really disconcerting—to find out what kinds of deals were being cooked up with this house and all the land, all these plans you and Art and Joey are making, all those conversations happening, and I had no idea. Not that it's any of my business."

He gave a short, angry laugh. "It's not. That's the thing, Lucy, it's not your business, at all. You seem to think we're trying to pull a fast one, but we're not. The deal would be good for Mom, if she decides to take it. You haven't exactly been around to help, you know, these last years when she's been rattling around in this old house, trying to hold it together."

"True." I bit my tongue then. I didn't say what I so deeply wanted to say: *I haven't been going around in circles, either, tethered to the past.* But then Blake, encouraged perhaps by my agreement, stepped things up.

"You know, Lucy, you'd do yourself a real favor if you were more willing to embrace change, not resist it."

"Are you talking to *me* about change?" I asked. I put down the papers I was holding and stood up, barely able to contain myself. "Do you have any idea how many places I've lived in these past years, Blake? Two states, four countries, seven different jobs. New cultures, new communities, new people, every time. You think *I* can't handle change?"

"Oh, I know all that. But this is different. This is a different kind of change. A letting-go kind of change. Not a running-around kind of change."

Was it? Yes and no. I loved my life, but I also thought about how I'd felt earlier, talking to my mother about our old books and toys.

I was still standing face-to-face with Blake, so angry I couldn't speak immediately; I imagined taking the old swim trophy from the table and hurling it across the room to smash against the wall, I was that furious.

"That's enough."

We both turned, startled. My mother was standing in the doorway, her cast held close to her chest, the phone in her good hand.

"I'm just expressing some concerns," I said.

"Right. So altruistic. Like I'm not," Blake countered.

"Stop it! You seem to forget, the two of you, that you're fighting over something you don't control. I'm not an imbecile, and I'm not behaving like a teenager, either, unlike the two of you. I'll keep my own counsel, thank you. And I will not listen to this senseless bickering in my house. *My* house, you understand?"

She stepped out of the doorway, strode across the room, and sat down in the overstuffed chair where she used to read to us as children.

"Now," she said. "I'm going to continue sorting these things. Blake, I'm sure Lucy would help you carry those boxes out."

Blake refused my help, but I walked out with him anyway. I stood there in the mist, hands in the pockets of my jeans, as he put the boxes of toys and books in the passenger side of his truck and slammed the door. Blake didn't get angry easily, but when he did, it was hard for him to let it go. Maybe he would have said the same about me. The times we'd seen each other over these years, either here or meeting up in exotic places, we'd been on our best behavior, not admitting any tension. Now we were being our teenage selves.

"I don't want to fight," I said.

"Then maybe you shouldn't have mentioned the baby to Mom. I asked you not to do that. Avery answered the phone and you can imagine how she felt."

"I'm sorry. It was after the solstice party and I'd had a couple of glasses of wine, and it just slipped out." All this was true, but it was also true that I'd been angry in that moment, as I was in this one, about Blake's collusion with Art about the land.

"Okay, then," he said, finally. "All right. Truce, okay? That stuff I said about change? I didn't mean it."

"I figured," I said, stepping back to let him climb into the cab.

"We're good, then?"

"We're okay."

"Okay. Good."

He waved as he backed out, and I waved back, watching him drive away, his red truck disappearing into the mist.

When I went back inside my mother stood up from where she was sitting on the floor amid piles of paper. She stretched and said she was tired of the dusty past. When I told her what I was doing and asked if she'd like to come along, she surprised me by agreeing. I went upstairs for my purse and my papers, and by the time I came back down she had changed into dark jeans and a crisp white blouse, the rhubarb scarf flowing around her neck, silver earrings dangling. We popped open our umbrellas and ran to the barn for the car. The rain made the Impala feel cozy, heat pouring out of its vents.

"Did you and Blake patch things up?" she asked in the middle of our conversation, halfway to Rochester.

"More or less. I still think it's a mistake, the way he's attaching himself to Art, to Dream Master. It didn't end well the first time, and Blake can't fix it now. Plus, I don't care what Art says, I can't imagine that he'd share things he could give to his children equally with anyone else."

My mother sighed, looking out the window at the rainy landscape. "I don't know. There are forks in the road that I've second-guessed for years. But I can't do any of it over. We made the best decision we could at the time. And even if you're right, Lucy, even if Blake is making a mistake, it's his mistake to make. I have to stay out of it. And honey, so do you."

I didn't answer, and we drove the rest of the way in silence. It was still raining when we arrived at the Westrum House. We huddled beneath our umbrellas under the dripping portico as the bell sounded deep in the empty rooms. It was several minutes before we heard footsteps; then Oliver fumbled with the keys for a little while longer before the door finally swung open. If he was surprised to find I wasn't alone, he didn't show it, but graciously shook hands with us both. He stepped back, pulling the door wide open, and ushered us inside.

The house was utterly still, even more silent than it had been on my last visit, and our quiet footsteps—my mother's flats, my sandals—echoed. Stuart gave us a brief tour of the main rooms and served us tea. Then we climbed the open stairs with Oliver, lingering on the landing to take in the window of the woman with her arms full of flowers.

"She looks like you, Lucy," my mother said softly. "Don't you think? If your hair was different, pulled up like this, she would look a great deal like you."

"I suppose," Oliver said, a bit reluctantly. "I guess I can see the resemblance. But then, she might look a great deal like a great many women, if they had their hair pulled back. I'll show you a picture of Beatrice when we come back down. He loved her very dearly, and he used her image a few times after she passed away, working from photographs. I have several photos of his daughter, Annabeth, as well. She modeled for him frequently, and we always imagined he'd used one of them for this window. I think you'll see the resemblance."

Oliver turned then, and took us down a narrow hallway to an interior room, windowless, with a projector set up in the back. He explained that he'd been through the slide archives of windows that were either owned by the Westrum Foundation and currently in storage, or still privately owned but whose Westrum provenance was sure and whose owners had agreed to have the windows documented. We took our seats in the middle of the room like students in a class, my mother folding her hands in her lap and me jutting my feet out, crossed at the ankles. "Sit up," my mother admonished in a whisper, but I paid no attention.

The first image that came up on the screen was of two very large doves with gray bodies and reddish-orange heads and chests. They were facing each other; between them was a bush with dark orange berries. The window in which they appeared was square; a pattern of blocks in alternating colors ran around the edge.

"This window is still in a house in Mount Vernon, New York," Oliver explained, his voice soft, the cone of light illuminating the dust in the air. "It was custom-made for the house in 1919, to commemorate the passenger pigeon, which had become extinct. The owner of the house was a naturalist—indeed, he had been a founding member of the Sierra Club before he moved east from California—as well as a patron of the arts. In the 1800s passenger pigeons were so profuse a flock would darken the sky like a storm, but they were zealously overhunted and their habitats were destroyed, and finally, in September 1914, the last one died in a zoo in Cincinnati. This is quite a good replica, and the colors of the glass are especially worth noting here. We hope to purchase this someday—I would like to have it in the entrance—but the current owners don't want to part with it. Never mind—we will persist."

He clicked through several more pictures, pausing to comment on a design feature or a point of history of each. His knowledge of his great-grandfather and everything concerning him seemed utterly inexhaustible. The room was warm, and the projector made a quiet hum. My mother pressed back a yawn, and even though I was fascinated and curious, I did, too.

"Let me hurry us along here," Oliver said, as if he sensed the way sleep was settling on the room. "What we want is slide number eighty-nine. Numbers eighty-nine and ninety-seven, actually. Those are the operative images, the reason I contacted you, Lucy. I went through everything again after we last spoke, because it was nagging at me so, once I saw the woman in the photo you'd taken of the window Keegan Fall had found. Here we are." He stopped clicking through the images, which had rushed by in a blur of shape and color, settling on a long, rectangular window.

The image of this woman was stylized. She was tall and thin, and she gazed down at her cupped hands. Her auburn hair, piled on top of her head, escaped in tendrils; her dress was deep blue, falling to her ankles, with an empire waist. Her toes were straight, and her hands and face, her arms and feet, were a pearly opalescent white. She was looking down at three pale blue eggs in her palms and her eyes seemed almost closed.

"I don't know," I said. "The angle is so different, it's hard to say if she's the same woman or not."

"I have to agree," my mother said. "She seems a little bit generic. Maybe the similarities are in the artist's style?"

"Yes, yes, I know," Oliver said, both excited and a bit impatient. "In this one, I'm not looking so much at the face. You're right, it's ambiguous, maybe yes, she's the same one, maybe no. But I think she is the same woman, and this is why: look at the pendant she is wearing. Look at the bracelet on her left wrist. They are the same."

He was right. The pendant was oval, like the eggs, a nugget of dark blue lapis lazuli resting against her pale chest. The bracelet, too, was a deep vibrant blue, made of oval-shaped beads strung together. I'd been concentrating so much on the face and the flowers in the other windows that I hadn't really paid attention to the jewelry and couldn't remember if it had appeared in those or not. But Oliver knew. He clicked to the next slide, which was of the woman in the stairwell. The bracelet was not visible beneath the flowers in her arms, but the lapis lazuli pendant clearly was.

"You see," he said, and then clicked again to an image of the Joseph window, which Keegan had sent at Oliver's request. Here, the woman was much smaller, but the resemblance of her stance and facial shape and features to the women in the other two windows was very strong, and Oliver was right—she wore the lapis lazuli pendant, too.

"Now, one more," Oliver went on, after giving us a minute to absorb the image. "This last one is a very recent acquisition, a couple of months ago. I found it at an auction, actually, an estate sale right here in

Rochester, just a few miles away. The proximity of course makes me think that the owners must have known Frank Westrum, at least professionally, but the executrix of the estate didn't seem to have any information. She's the niece or grandniece of the owner of the house, quite elderly herself. I asked her to check, but she phoned a few days later to say she had nothing that connected the window to Westrum— or to anyone, for that matter. So, we are going on style."

He clicked to the final image.

This window was large and, like the window in the stairwell, featured the now familiar image of the woman. Here, she stood on steps, one sandaled foot pointing down to the next stair. She wore a tunic, caught tightly at the waist, fastened at one shoulder and leaving the other one bare. She was looking at something out of the frame, smiling, her hands lifted as if to catch something falling from the sky—raindrops, or snow, or the rays of the sun. She wore no pendant, but the dark blue bracelet hung from her wrist. A tangle of vines and flowers climbed the side of the window, scattering dark red petals and blossoms on the stairs around her feet.

"Roses," I said. "She's walking on roses."

"I suppose it could be," Oliver said. "They might be climbing roses, or maybe they're clematis. Still, I concede roses as a possibility. The trouble, though, is that there's no concrete evidence that Frank Westrum knew Rose Jarrett personally. None whatsoever."

"Maybe he didn't," my mother suggested. "Maybe she just modeled for him."

"Unlikely. He didn't typically work with hired models. He liked to work with people he already knew."

I looked back at Oliver, who was studying the image on the screen.

"You said you talked to the executrix of the estate?"

"I did," he said, shifting his gaze to me. "As I said, I was quite specific about connections to Frank Westrum. I took photos of his other windows to show her, but she had nothing to share."

"But I wonder if you asked her about Rose."

Oliver ran one hand through his hair and shook his head. "No, of course not. This was weeks ago. I didn't even know about Rose. But I really don't think it would have mattered."

"Well, I think it could. It's a stone unturned."

"Well, by all means look into it, then," he said curtly, and moved on through the slides. He didn't believe in Rose, I could tell. That she'd existed, yes, but not that she'd mattered at all to Frank Westrum or these windows.

I watched Oliver, whose hair was thinning, and who, despite his careful and elegant attire, looked tired in the light from the projector. Blake's dismissal of his passionate interest in the past did make me wonder, for the first time, why Oliver had invested his whole life in preserving the reputation of his famous ancestor. He was so deeply invested in the family history he'd pieced together that he wouldn't welcome any disruptions to his vision of the world. He'd asked me here to learn something, I felt sure of that, but I wasn't sure what he wanted to know. Clearly, it didn't really have to do with Rose.

Oliver turned off the slide machine.

"There's one more place I want to show you," he said. "If you have enough time?" When I nodded he said, "Good, I'm glad. This is off the tour, of course. I seldom take anyone to Frank's studio, but I'd like you two to see it."

Oliver led us down the stairs and through a narrow hallway that opened onto the back porch, where he handed each of us a compact umbrella. The path to the carriage house was made of pebbles that shifted under our feet as we hurried through the spitting rain. Oliver held his bright blue umbrella high, and the wings of his bow tie, a dark gold, fluttered as he ran. We followed him through wide doors, pausing in the empty open space that smelled of dust and old leaves, the concrete floor cold beneath our soles.

"It's upstairs," Oliver said, shaking the rain off his umbrella and waiting for us to do the same. Then we climbed a narrow flight of stairs to the studio. The space was wide open, one large room without walls, flooded with light from the windows and a central cupola. Even on this rainy day it was bright. Several easels stood at one end of the space, and at the other was a kind of sitting area with a cluster of winged chairs around a low table. The center of the room was taken up by a grand workbench with multitudinous narrow drawers. Oliver beckoned us over, and slid some of the drawers open to reveal fragments and panes of brightly colored glass and layers of translucent drafting paper.

"This is where he worked," Oliver said. "He designed this studio himself, renovating this old carriage house, which didn't burn in the fire, while the main house was being built. This was in 1920. He was grief-stricken at the loss of Beatrice, and I think he simply couldn't stand to stay in New York City once she was gone. You can see how organized he was, everything arranged by year. It's been an invaluable resource as we've worked to reconstruct his creative process. Now, here's what I wanted especially to show you." Oliver pulled open another of the long, narrow drawers and took out a framed photograph of a woman. She was tall, her hair hidden by a cloche hat with a flower over the left ear. She was standing outside, turning to look back over her shoulder, laughing, carefree and appealing.

"This is Annabeth Westrum, my grandmother," Oliver said. "It was taken in 1923, in the garden out front, beneath the wisteria trellis, which had just been installed. Here's another one, a frontal view, taken on the same day. It was her wedding day. She was twenty-six. You see the resemblance, I'm sure, to the women in the windows. I have always felt quite certain that she was the muse, as it were. The model."

I studied the photos, Annabeth's long face, her laughing eyes gazing across the decades. I could see what Oliver meant. In a very general way, she did resemble the figure in the window; it was a natural conclusion to draw. Yet I wasn't quite convinced, nor did I really want to be. After a polite moment, I handed the photos to my mother and wandered the perimeter of the studio, pausing by the easels. Had Rose ever been here, standing in the clear light while Frank Westrum sketched her? My mother and Oliver were talking, their voices low and steady, first about the photos, and then about the contents of the drawers. Oliver had gone through those marked 1936 to 1938, the years when Frank would have been working on the chapel windows, but he'd found no sketches, no prototypes. Odd, Oliver said, it was very odd; all the other commissions had a clear paper trail. Beautiful, my mother murmured more than once, the papers rustling as she sifted through them. I ran my hand along the frame of an easel, imagining Frank Westrum, precise, contained, meticulous, standing here, his pencil flying over the paper as he drew her.

"Lucy," my mother called. "Look at these!"

She was standing over a pencil drawing of wild irises with their narrow, swordlike leaves, their pendulant, opulent blossoms. "Look, there's a whole sheaf of them," my mother said. "Irises mostly, but also a couple of sketches of roses." Before I could speak, she turned to Oliver and added, "Rose had a daughter, you know. A daughter named Iris. I think Frank Westrum must have known her, don't you?"

Oliver's expression closed up a little bit, growing inward, and thoughtful. I had the same plummeting feeling I'd had after telling him about the windows in the first place. I'd hardly had a chance to look at the sketches—fields of irises, banks of them, a single iris in a vase—before he gathered them up again and slid them back into the drawer labeled 1938. "Well, that's very interesting, I have to say. You hadn't told me. Even when you saw the window in the landing, you didn't mention it."

"Does it really matter?" I asked, because I could see that it did, that the mention of Iris had triggered some memory or piece of knowledge he didn't want to share.

"Oh, probably not."

He glanced at his watch and suggested that we spend a few more minutes with the windows themselves before we had to leave. I didn't object, turning this new piece of the mosaic over in my mind as Oliver hurried us down the stairs. It was clear to me that Frank Westrum and Rose had been close, though the evidence was only anecdotal, only a few sketches and a sheaf of irises in a window.

At the open doors of the carriage house we paused. The rain was pounding down outside, splashing in the puddles that had begun to collect in the gravel.

"My umbrella," I said. "I left it upstairs. I'll catch up in a second."

I ran back upstairs—my umbrella was by the easel where I'd left it when my mother called me over to see the sketches. And though I hadn't done this by design, I couldn't help myself—I went back to the work-table and pulled out the drawer labeled 1938. There were nearly a dozen sketches, the penciled lines smeared in places. He'd been playing with the contrast between the sharp leaves and the lush flowers in drawing after drawing. I didn't dare to take them, and when I heard Oliver coming up the stairs I slid the drawer shut again in a rush of panic and left.

Back in the museum, Oliver was very attentive to my mother, witty and charming, telling stories about the place the Westrums had liked to vacation in the Thousand Islands. I walked from window to window as they talked, half listening, looking for any further evidence of Rose, wondering what Oliver was holding back from us. It was physical, almost, my desire to know who she was and how she had lived, what had ever happened to her and to her daughter. From this point in time, almost a hundred years later, the events of her life looked fixed, determined. And yet, in her brief notes I had recognized a restless passion that seemed familiar, mirroring my own seeking, my own questions. My great-grandfather's story had been long established by the time I was born, and I'd never had the sense that he'd questioned his choices or made a single mistake. Yet here was this ancestor, hidden from view all these years, who seemed more like me. I was more determined than ever to track down Rose—to know her story, to understand how her story had helped to shape my own.

Before we left, Oliver gave me the contact information for the executrix of the estate—her name, Joan Lowry, as well as her address; he even gave me directions to the house nearby where the estate auction had been—probably because he was so sure I'd turn up nothing more than he had. He wrote the information on an index card, holding the pen oddly with the tips of his fingers, copying the address carefully from a Rolodex on the credenza—no BlackBerry for Oliver—and handed it to me, asking in an offhand way what day we planned to view the chapel.

"Wednesday at nine o'clock," I replied, regretting the words even as I spoke them, feeling I'd somehow walked into a trap. Maybe this was why I'd been invited.

"Oh, good," he said. "Keegan mentioned it would be happening soon, but your Reverend Suzi hasn't let me know when. Maybe she didn't get my messages. That's fine, though, that date. I'll put it in the calendar right now. And I suppose I'll see you then."

He held out his hand and I shook it.

My mother's hand he kissed, saying that he'd been enchanted, which made her laugh in a flustered way.

"He's slippery," I said as we opened our umbrellas—it was raining hard again—and made our way down the wide stone steps. "He probably arranged this whole meeting just to get that information about the viewing."

My mother slipped into the passenger seat. "Sweetheart," she said. "I don't think so. You're starting to sound a little paranoid. I thought he was charming."

She shut the door and I started the car, letting it warm up for a moment, wiping away the condensation that had begun to gather on the windshield.

"He was certainly charming to you. He likes you, I think."

My mother smiled, but didn't reply.

"Anyway, I'm not paranoid. I'm suspicious. Wary. There's a difference."

"Suspicious of what, though?" My mother looked up from the damp pamphlet in her hands. "I mean, really, Lucy, what difference does it make if Oliver Parrott ends up with these windows? Maybe they belong here. After all, it is a museum. It's not like he's selling them on the black market or grinding them up."

"I don't know," I said slowly. I opened the map and searched for the address Oliver had given us. "I feel possessive about Rose, I guess. It's personal for me, probably in the same way Frank Westrum is personal for Oliver. To find this woman, Rose, who was part of the family story, but never included—well, it matters to me, that's all. *She* matters to me. Plus, I think Oliver knows more than he's revealing. Did you notice how he reacted when you told him about Iris? I wish you hadn't done that."

"Why in the world not? I didn't notice anything strange at all. It was fine."

"I don't want him to know everything we know," I said. "I just don't trust him, that's all."

"Oh, Lucy. That's ridiculous. Well, I hope you can find out what happened," my mother said. "And I hope you aren't disappointed if you do."

I gave her the map and the directions and she navigated us through the city. We drove by a tall brick town house just a few blocks away, where Oliver had found the windows. Then we headed out of town. Joan Lowry's retirement community was just off the highway, in a modern three-story building with porches made of dense plastic formed to resemble wood and windows with plastic strips made to resemble panes. It was an assisted living unit, where you lived in your own apartment as long as your health was good, though the nursing home was right there, in another building, should the need arise. It made logical sense, but I didn't like to think about it.

We found Joan in good spirits. She was in her own apartment, and when the desk clerk called upstairs and explained who we were, she said she'd be glad to see us right away. My mother and I took the elevator up to the third floor and walked down a hallway with wide wooden railings along each wall until we reached number 354. Joan opened it almost before we'd finished knocking, a slight woman with thick gray hair and stylish glasses. She was dressed in blue polyester pants and a dark blue sweater, sturdy shoes. Her apartment was small, painted a neutral beige, filled with furniture she must have taken from her old house, a velvet couch and a massive entertainment center across from it, a heavy round table with carved legs, set for one. She made a pot of tea and insisted that we sit on the sofa while she carried the pot and cups to the coffee table on a wooden tray. I glanced around as she poured, her hands shaking slightly. There were Scottish terriers with red bows everywhere—in framed prints, stenciled onto the wall in a border, in the fabric of the curtains, statues perched along the windowsills.

"Aren't they cute?" she asked wistfully when I remarked on them. "I used to have a little Scottie. I always had one, actually, but when the last one died I didn't get another. No pets in this place," she explained, sitting across from us in a wingback chair. "Though I do think Mr. Kitteredge down the hall is hiding a cat."

My mother and I sipped at our tea while she talked, filling us in on the residential gossip. I was grateful to my mother, who managed to keep the conversation focused. I saw why Oliver had felt frustrated, and kept trying to steer her into conversation about her aunt. Her great-aunt, it turned out.

"It must have been quite a task to settle the estate," I said. "We've been going through a few boxes at our own house this morning, and I'm already exhausted."

"Oh," she said. "It nearly did me in, I can tell you. There were boxes and boxes and more boxes of things—in the attic, in the basement, in the extra rooms. She was a pack rat. All sorts of memorabilia, everywhere. She never married, so there was no one else to see to it all. And she had been so active, in so many different things. Plaques from this and certificates from that. Plus, I had all the stuff from her former housemate; all of her boxes were in the attic, too."

I put my cup down carefully on its saucer. "Did you say she had a housemate?"

"Yes, from ages ago. She died a long time back. In the 1940s, I think. But all her things were still there."

"Do you remember her name?"

"Oh, yes, her name was Rose. They were great friends, apparently. Even at the end of her life, my aunt used to speak of her. They were radicals together, you see. Free spirits, thumbing their noses at convention, that sort of thing. My aunt was something of a black sheep in the family," she confided. "You know, never marrying, having a career. In those days, it wasn't the done thing. She was making a statement, at least that's how other people felt. Really, though, she was just living her own life. She said she liked me because I showed some spirit, and when I went to college she sent me money for books every semester. We kept up a correspondence."

"She sounds remarkable."

"Indeed, she was. She was a suffragette, you know, and the first woman in this county to cast her vote in 1920. There was an article about her in the newspaper." She gave a wave of her hand. "I saved it here somewhere."

"I wonder," I said, trying to sound more casual than I felt, "what happened to all those things that belonged to Rose?"

Joan pressed her hands together for a second. "Well, let me see. I had the auction people come—they took the stained-glass windows, for instance, that your Mr. Parrott was so keenly interested in having. They took all the biggest furniture, too. Then I had a great big garage sale. You know, pots and pans, glassware. My neighbor Bobbie Jean helped me get it organized. She's good at that sort of thing, a little bossy, but she means well. And after everything was gone, there were still boxes and boxes of papers. Bobbie Jean took them all. She said she was dropping them off at the Women's Rights National Park in Seneca Falls. Because you realize my aunt, Lydia Langhammer, was arrested once and thrown in jail overnight. I remember how she used to like to tell that story. It was something she and Rose had in common, too. One of the reasons they were such good friends."

I'd been letting the commentary wash over me, listening for key words, and at this I interrupted.

"You mean Rose was arrested, too?"

"Well, yes. I think that's what Aunt Lydia said. More than once, as I recall. Aunt Lydia used to call Rose the fire to her oil. Or maybe it was the oil to her fire. It's terrible, you never think to write these things down and then later they're just gone. Poof!"

I let my breathing slow, forced myself to be calm as I asked the next question.

"I wonder—did they take those boxes full of papers? The Women's Rights National Park?"

"As far as I know, they did. Bobbie Jean didn't say otherwise. More tea?" she asked, as she saw me glance at my mother.

"No, thanks so much."

"I'm afraid we have to get going," my mother added.

"I wish you'd have more tea. I wish you'd stay a little longer."

"We're already late. It was so nice of you to see us, though."

She walked us to the door, talking all the while, and didn't stop even when we'd stepped out into the hall. Finally, I put my hand on her arm. She glanced down and paused in the stream of words.

"Thank you," I said. "I'll let you know if we find out anything."

And before she could start talking again we were striding down the hall. I took the steps two at a time, and burst out into the cool, damp air. The rain had stopped and the sky, though overcast, was lighter.

"She seems very lonely," my mother said.

"I know," I said, glad for my skin, my clear eyes, but aware of how fleeting youth is. There had been a photo of Joan as a young woman on the wall above the table; she'd once been just as strong and agile as I was now.

We took the highway back, passing the signs for Geneva, Seneca Falls, Waterloo, winding through the countryside on local roads for the last few miles. There were deep puddles in the gravel driveway, and rain dripped from the foliage, so dense around the fence. The bucket on the porch was overflowing; inside, the boxes waited, their contents strewn across the living room floor.

"It's this hour I don't like," my mother said. "This, and when the wind is up, that's the other time this house seems like a hostile place."

"You'd be happier somewhere smaller?"

"Absolutely," she said, turning on the lights. "A maintenance-free condo, that's what I have in mind. It's beautiful here, but sometimes this house feels like my enemy."

That night I lay awake for a long time, listening to the steady rain on the roof, thinking over the events of the day, so excited about the boxes at the Women's Rights National Historic Park that I couldn't sleep, worried because I hadn't heard from Yoshi in two days, except for his brief e-mail. When I called him, he was packing, heading for his flight, so we didn't talk long; he'd be in Jakarta by evening. I closed the phone and lay awake in the darkness, remembering my argument with Blake, what he'd said about change, wondering what it was I'd set in motion, and whether I'd be glad, at the end, that I had.

Chapter 11

I WOKE UP THE NEXT MORNING TO A SUNNY DAY, THE AIR
washed clear by the rain, the prisms I'd hung in the window years ago
casting dozens of little rainbows on the ceiling and the walls. It was still
early, just chilly enough for a blanket. I stretched, then relaxed back into
the narrow bed. Outside, Andy arrived to pick my mother up for brunch,
gravel crunching under his tires, the car door slamming shut, his steps
on the stairs. The screen door slammed shut, too, and my mother's
laughter floated out, hers and then Andy's, followed by a silence when
I imagined that they kissed, standing in the sunny kitchen. More doors,
floating voices, their footsteps on the stairs. I sat up to watch them depart,
Andy walking around the car to open the passenger door, my mother
smiling up at him as she slid into the seat.

I sat crossed-legged on the bed and pulled the laptop from the table,
glancing up at the lake while I waited for the slow Internet connection,
whitecaps scattered here and there against the sapphire blue. Wind
chimes sounded distantly. Rainbows danced along my arms, the sheets.
Yoshi had e-mailed from Jakarta that his trip had been uneventful. It
was evening there. I imagined him having dinner on a terrace full of
potted ferns and rattan furniture, the tropical dusk settling fast around
him. We used to like to wander the outdoor night markets, picking out

sticks of satay or plates of grilled fish or steaming bowls of noodles, but Yoshi's company preferred the ubiquitous international hotels; he'd be lucky if he got out even once for a shaved ice covered with syrup and corn, his favorite. That life we'd shared, those slow and careless days, seemed so far away. I tried calling him on Skype, but he didn't pick up.

Downstairs, my mother had left the coffee warming, a bowl of fresh blueberries in the fridge, and a note saying where she'd gone. I ate at the counter, the blueberries firm and sweet, leafing through the latest *Lake of Dreams Gazette,* which featured articles on Keegan's Glassworks—he was standing by the furnace, the glory hole he called it, with his arm tight around Max—as well as a four-page insert on the history and evolving controversy around the depot land.

The Women's Rights National Historic Park is in Seneca Falls, just over an hour's drive away. It's open on Sundays, and after I washed my few dishes, I gathered up all my notes and photocopies, along with the original documents I'd found in the cupola, and set off. It seemed unlikely that they'd still have the boxes Joan Lowry had given them, or that those boxes would shed any light on Rose and her life, but I still felt optimistic as I drove through the rolling landscape and the canal towns that had prospered a hundred years ago, when Rose was young. She had perhaps been here, too, which filled me with deep excitement. Whoever she had been, whatever she had done, her story was part of the whole, and might illuminate my own.

In Seneca Falls I stopped first at the Elizabeth Cady Stanton home, where she'd lived from 1847 until 1862. A tour was just starting. The ranger took us through the simple rooms with their wide-planked floors and deep windows, which had overlooked the flats, a booming industrial area, as well as the two acres of orchards and gardens Elizabeth Cady Stanton had overseen while raising seven children. Her husband traveled with the circuit court and was often gone; she had written of how she suffered from an intellectual hunger that the busyness of her days did nothing to alleviate.

I lingered on the lawn after the tour, imagining the Stanton children scattered in play and Elizabeth striding about in her trousers and knee-length skirts. I imagined her sitting in the parlor after her guests had departed, after her children had gone to bed, writing out the Declaration of Sentiments in the long twilight evenings of early July, and then standing up to proclaim this declaration to an audience of hundreds. It must have felt exhilarating; she must have left the Wesleyan Chapel on a wave of excitement, filled with a sense of achievement and purpose. Her beliefs and her actions had opened the way for Rose two generations later, and had made my life of study and travel possible, too. But I wondered if she'd known this. It had taken seventy-two years longer for women to earn the right to vote, and not one of the speakers at the first Women's Rights convention in 1848 had lived to see it.

In the main park building life-sized statues—of Elizabeth Cady Stanton herself, Lucretia Mott and her sister Martha Coffin Wright, the McClintocks and the Hunts and Frederick Douglass—gathered in the lobby as if arriving for the convention 158 years ago. The ranger at the front desk escorted me upstairs to meet the archivist. Her name was Gail and she was tall, with a low voice and dark, intelligent eyes. She listened with a thoughtful expression as I explained my story and asked about the boxes.

"Well, let me check," she said. "We deal mostly with events and artifacts connected to the 1848 convention, so if the boxes didn't contain anything like that we probably didn't keep them." She pulled a ledger from a low shelf and opened it, tracing down the lines with her index finger. "Yes, okay, here it is—Joan Lowry, did you say? I have a record of three boxes donated."

"Really? Are they still here?"

"No, I'm afraid not. We went through those boxes four months ago. We did find three items relevant to the convention, apparently, but those are being processed. The rest—let's see. Yes, here it is. The rest we sent to the Lafayette Historical Society. We often pass things on to them. Sometimes they find illuminating items that are of no use to us. You might try there."

"You can't tell me what the relevant items were?"

"Not at this moment. I'm sorry. I can check for you, if you like."

"That would be really helpful, thanks. What about these?" I asked, opening the folder and showing her the pamphlets and flyers. "Are these of any interest?"

She looked through them slowly, giving careful attention to each document.

"To me they are," she said. "We wouldn't keep them here—they're from the wrong era—but you should hold on to them. Maybe check with the people who have Margaret Sanger's papers—these articles about family planning were written by her, probably around 1912 or 1913. This is an early copy, and they're relatively hard to find. Later they were censored by the post office. They violated the Comstock obscenity laws, which made it illegal, even for physicians, to explain the basic facts of reproductive health. Sanger went to jail. Her sister, Ethyl Byrne, did, too, and almost died from the hunger strike she undertook in protest of those laws."

I thanked her and gave her my address and phone number in case anything turned up. Then I drove through the expansive streets with their grand houses and wide lawns to the Lafayette Historical Society. It was located in an ornate Queen Anne house with intricate trim along the roofline, well kept but in need of paint; the second step sagged as I walked to the door. I was lucky, as it turned out. Though the building was usually closed on Sundays, it was open for a genealogy class. I stepped into a foyer that had been perfectly restored, with deep mahogany wainscoting and wallpaper with a tiny green floral print on cream. A young woman with a pierced nose and lip sat behind a vast desk, reading, and she finished her paragraph before she finally put her bookmark in the page and looked up, the little diamond below her lip catching the light.

"I think I know those boxes," she said once I'd explained what I wanted. "I was here when they dropped them off. I don't think anyone's gotten around to looking at them yet. Come on upstairs to the reading room, and I'll check."

I followed her up the staircase, wide and curved, to the second-floor reading room, which was lined with bookcases. A grandfather clock stood against one wall, ticking softly, and a wide cherry table with heavy matching chairs took up the center of the room. The windows were bare, the glass mildly warped. She disappeared up another set of stairs and came back a few minutes later with a large box. There were two more, she said. I couldn't wait, and started going through the first one while she went up to get the others. A jumble of papers, file folders, articles: I took them out one by one.

"There you go," she said, heaving the last box onto the end of the table and brushing off her hands. She gestured to the papers I'd placed on the table. "Nothing's been sorted, like I said. It's probably a lot of receipts and ledgers and cryptic notes to self. But you're welcome to look. We close at four o'clock."

I glanced at the clock; it was already past two o'clock. "I'll have a quick look," I said, and so I began.

Lydia Langhammer had been a hoarder: everything from receipts for purchases to recipes and loose clips resided in the box. I went through it all carefully without finding anything of interest.

The second box was similar, as if someone had dumped the contents of a desk and several filing drawers. Here I did find references to Rose, however, who began appearing in the ledgers as having paid for certain expenses, and to whom some of the receipts were made. These accumulated in a low pile, though after the initial excitement of seeing her name, my eagerness slowly faded. What did these bits of paper tell me, after all, that I hadn't known before? I kept digging and sorting, mindful of the changing light in the room and the ticking of the clock. Near the bottom of the box I came upon a leather binder, tied shut with a ribbon. Another ledger, I thought, or a collection of bills, but when I opened it letters fell out, several of them, all in different sorts of envelopes but written in the same hand, a script I recognized at once from the cupola notes, sharp and slanted: Rose. With trembling hands, I opened the one on top. The paper was coarse, yellowed, the pages filled with her handwriting, the black ink faded to the color of bark. It was dated September 21, 1914.

Dear Iris,

Beautiful girl. I left you this morning. You were in the garden, making a pile from the gravel by the fish pond, wearing the dark yellow dress I made for you. You are only three years old and you are so smart. You pulled the petals from an orange marigold and scattered them on the water. Feeding the fish, you said. I held you very close. Your hair, like dandelion fluff when you were small, lies flat now, so smooth and shiny. You smelled like soap and sunshine. Then Mrs. Elliot arrived and Cora called you inside for lunch. You climbed the steps one by one—they are too tall for your little legs. You turned, laughing, to wave to me. Then you disappeared beyond the door.

Mrs. Elliot called to me to hurry but I could not. I kept looking at the porch, willing you there, but you did not come.

I used yellow ribbons on your dress. I have one tied around my wrist. It flashes beneath my cuff as I write. The other passengers don't notice, they go on with their business. They seem very ordinary and I wonder if I seem that way myself. It makes me wonder what secrets they carry in their hearts. The old woman across from me, who gazes out the window—what is she remembering? Or the gentleman beside me, adding numbers in his ledger, or the young farmer and his wife exclaiming at the sights—what are their secrets, their dreams?

I am dressed plainly—my one suit, brown, a blouse the color of goldenrod. I sit quietly with my satchel at my feet. What do they see, looking at me? They could never imagine you, turning, laughing, to wave one last time from the stairs.

You did not know I was leaving.

It is better that way. I tell myself again and again.

I promise—I promise—I will come back for you soon.

Meanwhile, I will write every day. Maybe you will never read these letters. Maybe I will be back so quickly that you will not remember I was ever gone. Still, I will write. Someday when you are older you will have these to keep and see how much I loved you, even though today you woke up from your nap, stretching in that patch of sunlight that falls across the bed in the midafternoon, to find me gone.

They will take good care of you, I pray.

Despite the scandal, Joseph loves you, because he loved your father. And Cora, though she does not like me, dotes on children since she has none of her own.

There was a page break, and I paused. Muted voices and laughter floated up from the genealogy class. My hands were shaking a little. The story I'd imagined hadn't included Rose leaving Iris. The note I'd found in the cupola had been dated 1925, eleven years later, when Iris would have been fourteen. It seemed Rose had never come back. I thought of my mother's warning, *I hope you aren't disappointed,* and realized that I might be, that Rose could turn out to be less heroic and interesting than I'd imagined. The letters fanned out against the polished cherry table. I took a deep breath, turned the page, and read on.

At the station, Mrs. Elliot gave me a poem. She copied it from a magazine. A poem for travelers, she said. The poet is a woman but she is called only HD. Mrs. Elliot always says I am thirsty for words and she gave me books. I read this poem again and again. "Wind rushes over the dunes, and the coarse salt-crusted grass answers." I do not understand it really, yet the words say the sadness I feel.

Iris. Where are you at this moment? I named you for the flowers. They are the color of your father's eyes. This is the story I want you to know. Your uncle cannot tell you, he doesn't understand.

Also, he would begin with the comet, which is the wrong place to start.

The story begins earlier. An ordinary summer day. I was weeding in the vineyard. I paused to drink from the bucket. That's when I saw the line of rising dust, the bright flashes of silver through the trees.

"What's that?" I asked. My friend Ellen stood, too.

"I don't know."

"I think it's an auto-mobile!" I was excited, I had never seen one before.

"It must belong to the Wyndhams."

"It must."

"Let's go and see."

So we left our work and ran to the village.

By the time we reached the commons people were coming from their shops and homes, shading their eyes to look. Mr. Marcus, the grocer, said it was a Rolls Royce—a Silver Ghost, he called it.

The vehicle drew closer. It made no sound at all, not even when it stopped at the village green, bright as a mirror. Everyone who looked at it saw something different reflected back—a dream of speed, of a factory job, the promise of change. Your uncle leaned over the engine. I stared at its silver hood where a small silver woman with silver wings stood about to leap, to soar.

"Do you like her?" Geoffrey Wyndham was next to me. I nodded, too shy to speak. His family owns most of the village. In the church graveyard you can see tombstones with their name all the way back to 1134. One winter we skated on the pond and Geoffrey chased me until the color of the ice changed suddenly, from opaque to clear, the darkness of the water visible. He shouted and grabbed my arm, pulled me away from that dangerous edge. Now he was tall. My chin only reached his shoulder.

"Go ahead," he urged. "Touch her."

So I ran my hand over her silver form.

At supper that night all we talked of was the auto-mobile. Our father sat in the middle of the conversation like a boulder in a current. Finally he dropped his fork and stood.

"There's still work here to do, and plenty of it," he said to Joseph. "Let's go."

"Ah—for what?" Joseph's voice was rough. "Who will need wooden wheels for wagons when auto-mobiles travel twice the speed on rubber tires?"

It was as if the air left the room. Father turned without speaking and went into the shop. Joseph rose and followed him. A few minutes later the argument began. We cleared the table, not speaking, as the words rose and ebbed and rose again.

It is night now, I can hardly see to write. The young couple has gone to the dining car. The old woman took off her hat and ate a beef sandwich spread carefully on a cloth napkin she unfolded from her bag. The accountant next to me has begun to doze. For a time we passed endless rows of houses and flats, moving so slowly that I caught glimpses of people eating dinner at their kitchen tables, or reading in a chair, or reaching to close their curtains. Then we picked up speed as the flats ended and factories began. Then it was dark again. I ate a roll, trying not to notice the scent of roast meat.

Time is different when you travel. This night is less like last night, when I lay awake in our little room, listening to your soft breathing, than it is like the night years ago when Joseph and I were traveling to this new land. On that trip I woke each time we stopped, lights and voices from the stations drifting down the darkened aisles.

Joseph was sleeping, his eyelashes dark against his cheeks, his coat folded carefully beneath his head. He looked like the carefree brother I knew before our troubles, before he changed, and I changed, and everything we knew was lost. The train moved on then, into the night, taking us closer to our new lives. I closed my eyes, matching my breathing to my brother's. When I woke the sun was golden on the new wheat, on the dark blue lakes.

You are there still, in that place. My hand aches from this writing, my heart from the steady turn of the wheels.

> Love from your mother, Rose

I sat back in the chair, still holding the fragile paper with its careful, slanted handwriting. Toward the end of the page the letters became wider and more wobbly, and twice the words ran off the page entirely. The pages trembled in my hand and I put them down, pressing my palms to my face and running my fingertips along the arch of my eyebrows, down my cheeks and the curve of my neck.

Everything changed with this letter. The story that had shaped my entire life and the lives of everyone I knew had changed. *He would begin with the comet, which is the wrong place to start.*

Then what had happened, I wondered, to make them flee everything they had known? What were the troubles that put them on that train, Rose with my great-grandfather, dreamy and carefree in his sleep? I flipped through the remaining envelopes in the binder. I imagined Rose bent over these pages, writing in the dimming light, her heart tightened with loss.

The little clock on the mantel struck four, delicate tones falling through the air, muffled in the carpet. A moment later the light footsteps of the curator sounded on the stairs. Without letting myself think what I was doing, I slipped the remaining letters back into the leather binder and shoved this into my bag. Blocks away, the town clock started ringing the hour, and then she was in the doorway, the low afternoon light catching on the silver hoops that climbed her ears.

"Wow, how many earrings do you have?" I blurted out, nervous; the letters were visible inside my bag, if she thought to look.

Startled, she touched her pierced lobes, then smiled.

"Eight in the left ear, nine in the right. Last week I pierced my navel, too. I haven't quite gotten up the nerve to do my tongue."

"Doesn't it hurt?"

She smiled a little wearily, as if she heard the question often. "Not so much. The very tops of my ears, a little. How did the research go? Did you find anything?"

"A letter," I said, tapping the unfolded pages on the table. "Amid lots of other papers. It has some references that are useful. I wonder—could I take it for a few days?"

"I'm sorry." She shrugged, then crossed the room and picked the letter up. I didn't want her to touch it, and kept my hands clasped in my lap with great effort as she scanned the lines. "It hasn't been cataloged, you see. Probably I shouldn't have let you see it at all. Is it important?"

"To me it is. To my family. Probably not to history—you know, with a capital *H*. It's personal, that's all. That's why I'd like to borrow it."

"Sorry. Really—I would if I could."

"Okay. I'll come again tomorrow."

"Sorry, we're not open tomorrow. Usually we are, but because of this class, we're not. It's kind of an experiment, to see which days get the most traffic. We'll be open Wednesday and Friday, though, nine to one."

Slender filaments of panic fanned out around my heart; there was one more box I hadn't seen at all, but Wednesday was the day Keegan had arranged to see the chapel on the depot land. Friday was the soonest I could come back. But I smiled and shrugged, sensing that it would be better not to make too big a deal of this.

"Ah—that's too bad. No exceptions?"

She hesitated, glancing from the boxes and back. "I would, you know, but I'm leaving town. I'm going camping with my boyfriend." She roused a little, curious now, and read the last part of the final page out loud. " 'You are there now, in that place. My hand aches from this writing, my heart from the steady turn of the wheels.' Sounds like a love letter."

"It is, kind of. A mother to her daughter, actually."

"Are you sure it's not important? Maybe I should call the director."

"Oh, no, don't bother. Really." I stood up, making myself step away from the boxes with their tantalizing contents. "Like I said, it's nothing earth-shaking. Not important to anyone but me. I can wait, though I can't come until Friday. What time did you say?"

"Nine o'clock."

"I'll be here."

I crossed the room and started down the stairs before her, holding my bag close to me, my left hand running down the carved and polished railing. She followed me to the door with its panes of etched glass; the lock, I noticed, was electronic, well beyond my expertise. I really would have to wait.

The car was stifling hot and smelled of dust, having been sitting in the sun all afternoon; I opened the window to the lake breeze. My stomach growled—I hadn't stopped to eat all day, I realized. Still, I slipped the second letter from its envelope.

Across the street, the door of the museum opened. The curator came out, slipping on sunglasses. She paused to make sure the door was locked behind her and hurried down the steps toward her adventure, car keys dangling from her left hand. She walked swiftly, passing one Victorian home after another, slipped into a lemon-colored VW convertible, and drove away.

I imagined Elizabeth Cady Stanton walking these very same streets with her children in tow, words like an undercurrent in her mind, rising up, pressing, as she bought flowers or stopped for sugar and eggs, hurrying home and leaving her packages scattered on a table as she made some swift notes, catching the idea that was pressing itself, necessary, essential, jotting down the words I'd read earlier that day: "We come into the world alone, unlike all who have gone before us. . . . Nature never repeats herself, and the possibilities of one human soul will never be found in another." Children, calling in the background until she sighed, put her pen down, and went to them. I imagined her standing on the street corner with Susan Anthony and the scandalous Amelia Bloomer in the daring split skirt that allowed her the ability to move unconstricted—scandalous, all of them, Elizabeth, Susan, and Amelia, three young women with their fierce intelligence and their dreams, talking together on an ordinary summer day.

I turned the letter over in my hands. Rose Jarrett stood behind that veil of time as well, traveling in her brown suit and yellow blouse—where, exactly? Why had she left her brother and gone off without her child? In the midst of what scandal had she fled? It worried me, not knowing what had happened to them both. And I wondered, also, with a growing sense of anger, why I'd spent my life not knowing Rose Jarrett had existed, when I might have learned from her life something about how to live my own, something beyond the bright fleeting streak of a comet and the parameters of life fixed in place. I had so many questions. How had she come to influence Frank Westrum's beautiful windows, those mosaics of glass filled with light, and to write these passionate letters? The historical society was quiet behind its wrought-iron fence, holding its secrets fast.

A breeze flowed into the car, smelling of water. I thought of my little charges in Japan, our walks beside the sea, the words I had taught them—*wave, water, stone*—and the words they had not understood: *someday, little ones, your grandchildren may even drink your tears.* I unfolded the second letter, written on a ledger page with faint blue stripes and columns, and began to read.

22 September 1914

Dearest Iris,

What a gloomy letter I wrote last night. But I woke feeling better.

My accountant's head drifted to my shoulder as he slept. He was so embarrassed. He has given me a blank page torn from his book of numbers to apologize. He lives in Poughkeepsie and he does accounts for a paper company. That sounds like a dull life, but he seems happy. He told me all about the city. He has a house there and has never married. He looked at my hand and saw no ring and began to ask more questions. Briefly, I imagined setting up housekeeping in his tidy house. Then I told him about your father, fighting in France. Missing there.

He nodded, as if I'd moved a set of numbers from one column to another. He went back to work. I ate two apples from my bag.

Mrs. Elliot can see the window of your room from her house. She promised to watch over you. She promised to give you the blanket. I wove it at night when I knew I must leave. Joseph was gruff and did not say good-bye, but he left a note in my pocket with five dollars. I could buy an egg for breakfast, but I will save it instead. Each penny brings me closer back to you. I am not to worry, Mrs. Elliot said. Her friends are kind and will meet me at the station. I am not to worry, but I do.

The tracks are close to the river, a muddy silver blue. There was a river near our village, too, it flooded almost every spring. For a few strange days and miraculous days we could catch fish in the streets and set the withy baskets in the fields for eels.

I must finish my story. I was walking along this river with a basket of eggs when Geoffrey Wyndham drove over the rise. Joseph was beside him.

"Rose Jarrett!" Geoffrey called, stopping the vehicle beside me. He laughed, sunlight falling through his straw hat and making patterns on his face. He invited me to have a ride. I nodded yes and climbed into the back of the silver machine.

"Hold on to your hats," Geoffrey said, though Joseph and I weren't wearing any hats. Then we drove.

The speed! We flew, the landscape blurring into long smears of gold and green and blue. I gripped the seat, black leather, wind pulling my hair loose, making my eyes water. I had never gone so fast, or imagined it possible.

At last Geoffrey stopped next to a broken stone fence, woven with weeds and tumbling out of its shape. He turned around, one arm on the back of the seat, smiling.

"Scared?"

I nodded, I still couldn't speak. Geoffrey laughed and got out of the car, reaching to give me his hand. I took it and stepped down out of the silver car like a girl in a story.

"I wasn't scared," Joseph said. "It was like flying."

"Flying—yes. Just so. Do you see that?" Geoffrey asked, pointing to ruins in the midst of the shimmering green fields. "It used to be a monastery, long ago. Henry VIII had it sacked. They built it here because when the floods come during the summer sea the place becomes an island, sometimes for weeks. I wanted to see it."

He started off. Joseph went with him and I followed. The sun was hot.

Twice, we disturbed dragonflies in the tall grass, they rose up in great clouds and drifted away.

The abbey made us quiet. The roof was gone, but some walls were still standing. Geoffrey slipped between the wire fences and disappeared into a corridor. Joseph hurried after him. I followed more slowly. The stones beneath my feet were dusty and smooth. Rain had streaked the stone walls. Old leaves littered the floor.

The page ended, and there wasn't another one in the envelope. I pulled the other letters from my purse, worried that the second page might still be in the box, or lost altogether. I was avaricious for the story by now, half here in the hot Impala, half in the Silver Ghost of a hundred years ago, bumping over dirt roads to the ruins of the abbey. It must have felt so astonishing to ride in a car for the very first time, though they were probably going only ten or fifteen miles an hour. Whatever sadness was to come, Rose wouldn't have known it in this moment of exhilaration, this sunny day filling up with an adventure. I sorted through the letters as if they were playing cards. Toward the middle of the stack a page matching the page in my lap jutted out of another envelope. I pulled it out and opened it, sighing with relief to find it continued the story.

We turned a corner. Stairs rose, ending in the blue sky. Through gaps in the wall we glimpsed the grassy fields, moving in the wind. We reached a large room with a vast fireplace. Geoffrey stood in the middle, looking around. His cheeks had reddened in the sun. "I can almost imagine the monks," he said. "Can't you?"

"This place is too quiet," Joseph said.

"That's because it has a secret. My uncle told me. He says everyone who comes here has to tell their secrets, too."

"What's your secret, then?" I asked. Though I could hardly speak before, in this place I was free, as if all the invisible lines between us had fallen away. I could say anything.

Geoffrey spoke up slowly, a faraway look in his eyes. "I want to go to India," he said. "I'm to go to Cambridge next year, then work here with my father, but I don't want that life. I want to see the world. I'm joining the Royal Navy as an officer instead. That's my secret."

Joseph began to speak almost before Geoffrey finished. "I'm going to America. I have a cousin there, and when I raise ten pounds, he'll sponsor me."

I was startled. I knew who he meant. Once a year our mother's cousin sent us a bundle of knickknacks and candy, sometimes coins. She kept his brief letters in the kitchen drawer.

"Is it true?" I asked.

Joseph looked at me. "If you tell, Rose, I'll make you sorry."

"Rose won't tell," Geoffrey said. He tossed a pebble into a corner. "She won't, because she'll share a secret, too. What is it that you dream of, Rose? Tell us. Do you want to be a princess?"

I don't know what made me answer as I did. Perhaps it was the silence, the layers of the past that seemed to well up from the stones, the years of prayers that had been spoken here.

"A priest," I said, without even thinking, but as I said the words I knew they were true. "I would like to stand up in the church and say the words, and be a priest."

A long silence followed, wind moving in the sunny air.

Then they laughed.

"A priest!" Joseph repeated, scornful. "Don't be daft."

"Girls can't be priests," Geoffrey agreed, though more kindly.

My cheeks flamed and I didn't speak. I hadn't known how deep this longing was until I spoke it. Though I had always understood that it was beyond rules or even words, how I felt when I walked into the silent church to mend the robes or repair the altar cloths—more alive, more listening, than I ever felt in other places.

I paused in the reading and looked out the window, watching two young men on bicycles travel down the quiet street and disappear around the corner. What Rose had put into words was something I'd felt, too, something I'd been thinking about since I'd seen the Wisdom window with its beautiful rendition of creation. Now I was more convinced than ever that Rose was connected to those windows, remembering their vivid colors, the swirl of wind, the sense of divine life and motion in the world: *ruah,* breath, spirit.

"All right," Geoffrey said. He leaned against the stone wall. "I'll tell you another story. Once there was a beautiful woman from a noble family. She fell in love with a man who had no prospects and was sent away. A few years later she visited this very monastery and was shocked to find her beloved had become a monk. They started to meet in secret." He paused here, lowered his voice. "When they were discovered, she was sealed up in a wall right here, alive."

Now Joseph was as quiet as me. He was staring at Geoffrey Wyndham's soft leather boots. I knew just what he was thinking—not about the horror of the story, which I didn't believe, but about the noble girl, the man who had no prospects, the ruin of it all. My shame deepened, for our boots, Joseph's and my own, were old work boots, cracked and muddy. We had no prospects either.

We listened to the wind move in the grass.

"I'm leaving," Joseph said. He walked past the broken stairs and disappeared into the corridor. When I went to follow him, Geoffrey caught my arm. There were dry leaves under my feet and the sky opening above.

"Don't be angry," he said. "I think you're too pretty to be a priest, that's all." Then he leaned down swiftly and kissed me. I was startled by the feeling, like flowers opening to the sun, and I did not pull away.

"That's my real secret," he whispered, his breath in my ear, his cheek against mine. "A secret only for you, Rose Jarrett."

This is how it began, then, a year before the comet.

It is nearly noon. My accountant has gone. He gathered up his things and bowed slightly in my direction before he disappeared into the crowd. He slept so soundly, his head resting on my shoulder. I feel a little sad to

think that I will never see him again, or know what happens to him or
probably, once I leave this train, ever think of him again.

There is more, but it must wait.

This letter was not signed, but ended with a penciled drawing of a
rose.

I ran my fingertips along its upper edge. *This is how it began, then, a*
year before the comet. So much for my great-grandfather's luminous dream,
which we believed had started everything. So much for the family history,
drawn in a straight line from one generation to the next—history that did
not even mention Rose. I felt as I'd so often felt in Japan, waking to earthquakes in the middle of a summer night, as if the world were an unsteady
place, about to split wide open. I thought of the beautiful cloth with its
row of vine-encrusted moons trembling with the breeze from the lake.

My mother had found that cloth wrapped in plain paper, hidden in
the lining of my great-grandfather's trunk, with the handwritten note
inside. Whatever answers these letters provided, the questions they raised
were even greater. For now I could imagine Rose sitting in a cold parlor
in the middle of the night, weaving, her breath visible, her fingers growing numb. I could imagine all this, but not why she had left, or how the
blanket had passed through the years, unopened, ignored. As much as I
wondered what had happened to Rose, I wondered also what had
happened to her child.

I glanced at my watch. It was already after five. I'd been sitting in the
car reading these letters for almost an hour. There were more, but I felt
I'd taken in as much as I could for the moment. I slipped the pages back
into their plain envelopes and the envelopes back into the binder, which
I left on the seat beside me. Then I turned the key in the ignition and
drove out of town, traveling on the local roads again, my windows open
to the breeze, trying to sort through everything I'd learned, to refocus
my lens on the world.

When I reached The Lake of Dreams there was a regatta and the
streets were crowded with cars and tourists. There was a detour away

from the lake, and on an impulse I turned down the outlet street. The Green Bean was full, people standing on the sidewalk with buzzers in their hands, waiting for a table; clouds of laughter and voices poured from the patio by the water and drifted across the road to me. The glassworks was busy, too.

I parked in the gravel lot behind Dream Master, ignoring all the NO TRESPASSING signs. It was closed for the day, and a kind of stillness had settled around it. I slid the binder beneath the seat and locked the car, pushing down the chrome buttons and checking twice to make sure I still had the keys. The gravel was rough under my feet, and heat rose from all the tiny stones. I thought of going to see Keegan, but I'd see him Wednesday, after all, when we went to view the windows in the chapel. He'd be busy now, either with work or with Max, and if he wasn't he'd be stretched out on the sofa or his open bed, a fan clicking in the high ceiling. As I imagined that, I imagined myself there with him, how he might turn to me in that space, as he had so long ago, learning about each other amid the ruined machines as the light faded from the windows. It shocked me, the strength of the image, the desire I had to see if it might happen this way—though I couldn't tell if it was really desire in the present or left over from the unfinished past. Not just the past with Keegan, and a desire to know what might have happened between us if I'd stayed, but the more uncomfortable past where I kept on leaving—countries, jobs, people I loved. I kicked at the gravel and walked to the back of Dream Master instead.

There was a loading dock there. It used to seem so high, we used to jump from it on a dare. There was the old Coke machine, too, empty now, its long vertical door ajar. I climbed up the steps to the back door. The locks here hadn't been changed since Art had sold the lock-making business decades ago. The wire I always carried was in the bottom of my bag and it took me only a minute or two to work the mechanism inside. There was nothing fancy here, nothing tricky. The door swung open into the warehouse room. Boxes were stacked on the shelves and light flowed in through the paned windows and a skylight far above.

I let the door fall shut behind me; the aisles were wide enough for fork-lifts, my footsteps echoing against the walls.

The door to Art's office was open and I walked in, as I had walked in so often as a child, freely, as if the building were our playground. Once I'd hidden in these cupboards, which had been in my father's office, during a game of hide-and-seek. I'd been crouched in the dark, listening to distant voices calling my name, when the office door opened and my father came in with Art. Their voices were sharp; I closed my eyes and imagined the words as knives slashing at the air, and when I opened them again, the darkness was still present. I was afraid, huddled in that small dark space, too scared to move even after the argument ended and Art's footsteps receded. Blake was crying somewhere and my father swore and left to help, the door falling shut behind him. I crawled out then, blinded by the light in the room, my hands tingling, numb.

Now I opened a cupboard door—the shelves were full of papers, files, ledgers—and let it fall shut again. On the easels by the window were the plans for The Landing; on Art's desk was a folder with estimates of costs. I picked this up, let it fall, too. The office was so silent, sun slanting in and making rectangles on the desk, and I wasn't sure if the feelings of apprehension and betrayal, so stirred up within me by the memory of that lost afternoon, had their source in the present or the past—or if it was even possible to draw a line between them.

I left the offices and went to the stairway at the back of the building, climbing up into the factory spaces on the second and third floors, which were empty now, the high paned windows dusty, all the machines long gone. Once, workers had streamed into this place day after day, pressing keys, and more keys, forming the components of the locks, their secret lives going on within them, their actions so familiar that they didn't have to think. In 1919, the year Dream Master was established, my great-grandfather sat below in the same office Art used now, overseeing everything. It was nearly five years after Rose left. Four years before they bought the house on the lake. Six years before my grandfather was born and Iris went away.

I walked over to the window that overlooked the village. The masts of the boats anchored at the pier bobbed in the distance. The air in the old factory was hot and still. I wrote my initials in the dust of a windowpane, then rubbed them out. The Impala sat in the parking lot, a bright bird from another era. I stayed for quite a while, moving from window to window, watching people come and go from the renovated buildings across the street, laughing, careless, as if no other time existed or ever would, oblivious to all the other lives that had been lived over the generations on this very same spot.

The heat gathered; sweat trickled down my neck. I went back downstairs quickly, thinking about Rose and her letters locked in the car, about all the layers of the past. On the landing, I nearly ran into Joey. I gasped in surprise, hands flying to my chest, and he stopped dead, too, looking as shocked as I was. He was dressed in cutoffs and flip-flops, carrying a six-pack of beer, his blond hair already going lighter from the sun. A young woman stood behind him.

"What are you doing here?" he asked.

"Looking for Blake," I said, which was partly true. "The door was unlocked."

Joey touched the handle. "That's weird. It's Sunday, right? We closed at five o'clock."

"Right. Look, I'm sorry. I just thought Blake might still be here. And then, you know, I kept remembering things from when we were kids. When we used to play hide-and-seek here, remember that? I went upstairs to look around. What are you doing here?" I asked, bolder now that I'd recovered a little. "Who is this?"

"Yeah, I remember those days," Joey said, ignoring my questions. "Hide-and-seek. Seems a long time ago."

"It was."

"Well, don't let me keep you, Lucy. I'll check the lock when you go."

And then I was standing on the loading dock in the full glare of the late-afternoon sun, the door clicking shut behind me.

Chapter 12

THE HOUSE WAS EMPTY, HOT FROM THE LATE AFTERNOON sun. I was so hungry I ate out of the refrigerator, tearing off pieces of bagel and dipping them into vanilla yogurt; there was nothing else but wilted-looking carrots and an unopened pound of butter. I ate quickly and without really tasting anything, and drank three glasses of water. Then I gathered all my things, with the rust-colored binder full of letters on top, and made my way upstairs to the cupola. The papers, piled on the window seat facing the lake, fluttered in the light breeze when I pushed open the windows. I'd searched this room carefully for more documents and had found nothing but two stray white buttons and a pair of small metal scissors. Still, I wanted to read these letters in a place where at least some trace of Rose had existed.

There were seven envelopes of different colors and sizes; some had been mailed and others had only Iris's name across the front in Rose Jarrett's now familiar handwriting. The one on top was addressed to Rose in New York City, the postmark too blurry to read. The letter itself was written on thick white paper, one side faintly shiny, the other porous, so that the ink spread out, blurring some of the letters, which had been written in a heavy, rather awkward hand. When I unfolded the single page, a lock of pale brown hair, tied with a piece of string, fell into my lap.

17 October 1914

Dear Rose,

I was on the farm all week. When I came into town your letter was in the silver tray. No one spoke of you, your name is never mentioned. I am happy to know you are safe.

You will be happy to know that Iris is fine. This is a piece of her hair I cut for you. She was playing on the porch, lining up pebbles from the lake from small to large. There were letters made from pebbles, also: R, I, S. I think Cora has been teaching her to spell, she is smart. I hope smart gets her further in life than it has gotten you, that's all.

I am glad you found the money. I will send more if I can. Please send news. Mrs. Elliot goes on here as if nothing ever happened. I do not think she is your friend.

> *Fondly from your brother, Joseph.*

I let the letter fall into my lap and stared out at the lake—smooth this early evening, and deep blue. This brief missive written by my great-grandfather was almost more astonishing to me than Rose's longer letters had been. He had lived here, had worked on the cupola of this house, perhaps pausing to wipe sweat from his face and gaze out at the ever-changing lake, as I was doing now. His portrait hung over Arthur's desk at Dream Master, and though Joseph Arthur Jarrett had died long before I was born, I'd grown up with that image of him as a middle-aged man, successful and certain, the master of all he surveyed, and I'd filled in the rest through imagination and story. The voice in this letter was as different from my image of the man as Rose's story was from the family legends we'd grown up hearing. Kind, he seemed—there was the lock of hair—but also, by turns, terse and judgmental.

I folded the page back up and slipped it into the envelope with the lock of hair, remembering Rose's first letter, where she'd talked about her daughter's dandelion hair. The next letter was to Iris again, and I opened it to find several sheets of plain paper, tissue-thin, the ink once black but now fading to brown, the handwriting slanted, strong, and sure. It had no date, and on the later pages the color of the ink changed and grew lighter, then darkened again, as if the letter had been written over many days.

Dearest Iris,

I am at the station. People come and go. They did not meet me. I waited on the platform, but no one came. After a long time I found a bench and sat. The lobby is vast and grand and there is a clock in the center. I have an address but they are supposed to meet me and I do not know what to do. I must not weep. I must look calm no matter how I feel. So—I will write.

It is late. The station is cold and I keep my coat on.

I think of you warm and safe beneath the blanket. I hope Mrs. Elliot has given it to Cora and that you sleep beneath it, warm and comforted. I wove it all last winter, in the cold attic at night. Across the street, Mrs. Elliot's lights were often on late. They gave me company. Mrs. Elliot is a suffragette and not afraid to say anything. While she is in the room the other ladies are always quiet, but when she is not some of them whisper that she is too extreme. Cora threw away the pamphlets Mrs. Elliot left, but I took them from the trash. I took them up to our room and read them. They made me feel on fire with ideas. After that I tried to stay in the room when Mrs. Elliot was talking, keeping my expression calm even though I wanted to jump up and agree. I think the ladies who came to tea are safe, so they did not understand. They are safe so the world seems safe to them. But to me the world is different and her words were like lamps.

An hour has passed. I am tired, but I must keep writing, that is one way to be safe. When I put my pen down earlier, a man sat beside me and invited me with a wink to share his bed. He shrugged at my outrage.

I am not so desperate.

Not yet, at least.

Oh, I did not set out to be a scandal. To be so alone in a place I do not know.

It is near midnight. I hold myself still. I dozed a little and dreamed of your father disappearing into the bell tower, gone, a silver ghost, and me climbing up and up forever.

He kissed me in the ruins and that moment became like a dream woven into my other dreams, things I yearned for but could never have. I was haunted by his laughter, too. For what he said was true: I could wash and mend the altar cloths or make dinners for the rector or the bishop, but no matter how much I loved the church or God I could not carry the communion wine or bless it or serve it to the people. No woman could. Not even Mrs. Wyndham in her silks. The more I thought about this, the angrier I got. Anger ate a great space in my heart. If the rules of the church made me less—less human—then maybe the rules did not apply to me. I was foolish, I know that now. The rules always belong to those who make them. I was foolish, and so young. I worked, scrubbing or mending, my skin growing brown in the fields. I worked, and in my anger I remembered that kiss. It was like flowers opening and it made me confused. Sometimes I shaded my eyes to watch his automobile flashing through the trees.

On the night of the comet I was fifteen. Our windows were sealed and we were frightened and the air was very still. Everyone was sleeping, but I could not. A sliver of light came in beneath the wool, where I'd left it loose. After a long time I got out of bed and I felt my way in the darkness to the window. When I opened it clean air rushed in, full of the scents of water and the earth.

I crawled out onto the roof to see the comet, soaring like a jewel against the sky, trailing light. Voices rose up and I knew them: Joseph, and another. I hesitated. My hair was loose. I was wearing an old dress I had pulled on, and no shoes. And then I jumped. When he saw me in the garden Joseph's voice turned low with anger.

"You can't come, Rose. Go back to bed."

"I want to see the comet."

"You weren't asked."

"Never mind," Geoffrey said. He was by the hedgerow. I'd heard his voice, but I didn't see him until he spoke. He was carrying a brass telescope.

"Let her come, if she wants. At least there will be three in this village who haven't succumbed to mass hysteria."

Succumbed. I remembered the word. All these years. I looked it up in Mrs. Elliot's dictionary. *To bring down. To bring low.*

Joseph didn't answer. He could not, since Geoffrey was a Wyndham. But he walked ahead of me, by Geoffrey's side. He pretended I wasn't even there.

I think all my life I will remember that night, and the light. It was a new moon, so the sky should have been dark. Instead, the dirt road, the roofs, the trees, all glimmered faintly, as if frosted. From the roof of the church tower we found the comet, its head like the tip of a pencil and pure white, like an eraser in the darkness. The tail spreading out like tresses of hair.

Geoffrey opened his telescope. We took turns looking. The village slept below. An excitement ran through me.

The same sky, I thought when it was my turn and I found the comet in the glass. *Here or India or America, it didn't matter. The same moon and the same stars, and on this night the same wild light on everything.* I felt as if the world were turning and must change. No more sewing, no plucking warm eggs from beneath the chickens, no walls built up against my deepest yearnings. I could study and travel and have adventures and be a priest or anything I wanted, I could give voice to the truest aspects of my nature.

I do not know how long we stood under the spell of the strange light, watching the comet, before birds began to sing in the still-dark trees.

Geoffrey folded up the telescope and looked at Joseph. "You go on," he said. "You go on, Joey. I'll see her home."

"I'll wait," Joseph said.

"No need," Geoffrey replied, his voice reserved, dismissive.

The Wyndhams owned the land. They owned our cottage. Joseph stood for a long moment, his eyes as dark as the sky, before he punched the wall and started down the stairs.

I could not speak. I was as powerless as Joseph. Also, I was full of anger and desire. I was like the bird that senses a cat amid the leaves but can't *resist the brightness of the flowers. We started down the stairs, around and then around again, and at first I thought it would be all right, that we would reach the bottom and he'd see me home beneath this comet sky, as he had promised.*

But at the landing he caught my arm and pulled me into the bell room with its long windows.

That first time he never touched me, only asked me to stand in that faint light, so he could look at me, he said. Step out of that old dress, he said, I only want to look, and after a long time of hesitating, tears in my eyes, I did. That time he kept his promise, walking around me and whispering oh, my beauty, and he never touched me. My fingers were shaking when I dressed.

When I stepped out of the tower, the shapes of things were starting to come out from the darkness. Joseph was waiting. We never spoke, walking home.

I did not seek him out, but he found me that whole summer long. In a clearing, by a stream, in the dusty barn at the end of the lane. Oh, my beauty, I'll marry you one day. He said this each time. I believed him. I understood nothing, I see that now. I told myself I was the princess in a fairy tale, helped from a silver carriage, unfastening my hair in the tower, even though it hurt my heart to do it. Later, when Mrs. Elliot talked about the rights of women, my face would burn at how little I had cared for myself and what might happen to my one and only life. But I was very young, and I had no power, and I believed this was a fate I could not question.

My phone rang, startling me so much that the papers slipped from my fingers to the floor. I had to dig through my bag for it, and by the time I found it the ringing had stopped. Yoshi—it was Monday morning there, early, so he must have arrived, it must be before his first day of meetings. I pulled up the number and pressed REDIAL, standing up to stretch and pace in the little room. The lake was as smooth as glass, a silver gray.

"Hey," I said when Yoshi picked up on the second ring. "Where are you?"

"On my hotel balcony. Overlooking a river of traffic. Where are you?"

"In the cupola at the top of the house, watching boats on the lake. I found her letters, Yoshi. Rose's letters. I'm in the middle of reading them now."

"Are they good?"

"They're amazing. Very moving. I don't know the whole story yet. I wish you were here," I added, though in fact I was riveted by the letters and had hardly been thinking of him at all.

"Why can't I just be there?" he agreed. "Why can't I be there and not here, watching the boats and floating on the water with you?"

"It's just a few more days. How's everything?"

"Not looking forward to the meetings. Otherwise, okay. Look, I have to go, but I've got a break in three hours. Can you give me a call? We can Skype, and I'll fill you in on what's happening."

"Good," I said, "that sounds great. About noon your time, I'll call."

"Are you okay?" he asked. "You sound a little off."

"Just distracted," I said. "It's the letters. That's all."

When I hung up I saw that Zoe had left me three messages, but I was so eager to get back to the letters that I tossed the phone into my bag without calling her and picked up the fallen pages from the dusty floor. I scanned the last paragraphs I'd already read—the comet night, when the whole world changed, the way he'd pursued her all summer long, the way she'd blamed herself although she'd had no real choice—and came to the place where I'd stopped.

It ended when he went on holiday. I stood in the fields as the Silver Ghost passed by. My friends, weeding, said I was pale. They made me sit down to rest, they brought me clusters of red grapes. So sweet, they stained my fingers. The blood of grapes, I kept thinking, those verses from Isaiah, that cry against injustice. The blood of grapes.

It was Joseph I finally told. The Wyndhams had returned by then. Grim, he went up to the manor house.

I waited outside. I waited for Geoffrey. I'd been inside the manor house just once, the ceilings so tall and the furniture all beautiful, and the servants scrubbing floors or making food and serving it on silver trays. Soon I would know how it was to live there, to drink lemonade or chocolate all day long.

I was so young. I see that now. Yet he had promised to marry me. I felt so sure that I could hardly understand what Joseph was saying when he came out alone, an envelope in his hand, talking about the new life we would have, both of us. How we could travel to America and start again. How no one would ever have to know. We would help each other—a whole new life.

He had piles of money. Passage to America. I touched it, then pulled away.

"But he said he'd marry me."

"Don't be daft. Be glad he gave this money to start your life again."

"Start my life again?"

"A new beginning, yes."

I remembered the silver auto flashing in the trees, and the scattered stones of the ruins, and the comet.

"But he said he would marry me. He promised."

"I went to him like a beggar," Joseph said. "You might at least be grateful."

And then I remembered. In the plaster wall behind his bed, Joseph had hidden the few coins he'd gathered, saving for his dream. I'd seen him pull them out, holding them like small silver moons in his palm. I'd seen his longing.

"So. Now you have your dream," I said.

He was silent for a long time.

"You can't go to America alone," he said at last.

"I don't want to go to America at all."

Maybe it was in this moment, as my words drifted off into the dusk, that

*I came to understand how small I was. The manor house across the fields
was like a great ship, and somewhere inside, in a beautiful room full of
light, Geoffrey was laughing, shaking loose his napkin and sitting down to
have his dinner.*

*"I'll go to him myself," I said. "I'll go right now. I'll walk right up the front
steps, and I'll wait until he sees me."*

Joseph's next words were low and hard, like rocks.

"He said he doesn't even know you, Rose. That's what he'll say again."

"He gave you the money, didn't he? That's proof, I'd say."

Joseph caught my arms and made me look straight at him then.

"Who would believe you? Your word against his?"

"It's true!"

"It doesn't matter."

"You'd lose your chance if I spoke out."

"Yes, I would. But Rose, don't you see? So would you."

And so I followed him home.

*I went about my days in a kind of disbelief, watching myself scrub and
sew as if I were outside my own body. I did not see your father again. We
heard he had gone to India. They prayed for him in church.*

*The night before we left I slipped from the house and walked through
the vineyards and then the orchards. The shadows in the moonlight wove
patterns on my skin. It was October, chilly, and leaves crunched beneath
my feet. At the top of the hill I turned to look back. The manor house stood
at the edge of the village, faintly outlined, distant and impassive.*

*I could unlock the oak door to the church just as well as Joseph. The
metal whispers a language of its own. The rows of pews fell away into the
shadows and the high, arched windows caught a faint light. I had polished
every pew and swept every corner, and my stitches were woven into the
white cloths on the altar. I sat down in the velvet-covered bishop's chair.
Always before I had sensed something beyond the familiar in this place,
something silent and just out of sight but present, welling up. But that night
I was so heartsick I could feel nothing else.*

I stayed a long time. Slowly, more light came into the church. The stained-glass windows began to come alive. The silver chalice and plate, set out for communion, were visible, like faraway planets, two silver circles, small and large. I had prepared the altar often enough to know what they said on the bottom: "A Gift from the Wyndham Family." I stood and picked up the chalice. It was heavy in my hands. I ran my fingers lightly across the letters, scratches in the silver. Passage to leave he had given me, yes, but nothing else, and nothing for our child, for you. The silver rim of the chalice caught the faint light. It would be nothing to them, I told myself, to replace one cup. And so I added one more mistake to those I had already made. I slipped the cup beneath my apron, and I walked out the door.

This letter ended abruptly, with no signature, no drawing. I sat back on the window seat. I'd been so engrossed that I hadn't noticed the dwindling light, but the sun had begun to dip behind the opposite shore and there was a faint coolness in the air. I gathered up my papers and carried them down to my room, where I spread them out on the painted floor—Rose's letters in one pile, Joseph's in another, the photocopied documents and the pile of papers from the cupola in the third.

I was so moved by Rose's letter that I read it again rather than starting another, imaging her waiting on the dusk-covered lawn outside the grand house while the negotiations that would determine her life went on without her; imagining her loneliness in the church, and the chalice heavy in her hand. It made me think of the days right after my father died when I'd felt the same lost way. I was remembering the window in Keegan's studio, too, the Joseph window, which had a chalice hidden in the sack of grain, and the crowd full of unnamed women, trying to puzzle out how it connected to the letters Rose had written. I'd looked up the story about Joseph and the coat of colors out of curiosity. He was tossed into a pit because his siblings were jealous of him. He ended up in Egypt, in exile, interpreting dreams. When a famine came, the brothers who had thrown him into the pit came to ask for food, not knowing who he was. He gave them grain, but he also tricked them by having the cup he used for divination hidden in their sacks; when they came back to return the cup, he accused them of theft. Interested, I'd also read Grail stories, and the bones of both narratives seemed very close—disharmony, a land in famine, a quest for healing, and a silver cup or bowl.

Maybe that window was personal, I realized, thinking of Rose sent into an exile of her own, starting a new life in a strange country, exiled again by some sort of scandal, forced to leave her daughter. Maybe that's why it had never been installed. I couldn't know exactly where she saw herself in this story or what, if anything, she had meant to say by choosing it. Maybe it was just the image of the chalice she had liked. I wondered what had happened to the one she'd taken. I wondered what had happened to Rose.

I opened the next letter, dated April 11, 1938. It was from Frank Westrum.

My darling Rose,

The windows progress so beautifully, and my only regret is that you are not here to see them. Dearest, I think they would please you. I have taken all your suggestions about the passages to illuminate, and I have made the border and many of the windows exactly according to your design. Nelia visited yesterday and gave her enthusiastic approval of all we have done. Indeed, she called it a masterpiece. Well, I do not think so. But it has given me great pleasure. First the pleasure of working by your side, all the moments we have shared together all these years somehow woven into this final venture, so close to both our hearts. But there is the pleasure of the glass, too, the days in the glassworks blowing and shaping the sheets, the careful cutting and piecing together. Your templates are quite handsome, Rose, the windows, too. I will come to you on the 30th unless you are well enough to come home. Meanwhile, I send all my love.

Frank

Here it was—proof. She had known him, and she had designed the borders and been integral in the design of the windows. It was such an intimate letter, too, so warm, and it made me feel sure they had been lovers. I wondered how Oliver would react to this news. He'd need to see this letter sometime, though the thought of it made me uneasy. I suspected he wouldn't like this upheaval in all the careful histories he'd written. For myself, I was glad to know that Rose, stranded in the train station, had somehow ended up all right.

The next letter was on the same thick paper as the very first one I'd read of Joseph's, and in his handwriting. It was postmarked March 24, 1915.

Dear Rose,

We were up on the barn roof yesterday. A bright windy day. We were putting on new shingles and almost done. Jesse fell. I heard him shout and then he hit the ground. The barn is high and he landed on his back. We don't know what it will mean but tonight he cannot move.

*   Your brother Joseph*

And then the next, written on the same sort of paper, more than two months later:

25 May 1915

Dear Rose,

I am sorry to tell you that our cousin died yesterday. He has not been right since the fall. The pain is over for him, anyway. Cora does not want people in the house, so hold your visit to a better time. I am sending a picture Iris drew of the flowers in the garden.

*   Joseph*

I checked the envelope again, but there was no drawing inside. Maybe Rose had hung it in whatever place she lived once she finally left the train station.

I heard a car in the driveway and got up to look out the window. It was a slow summer twilight, the shoreline glimmering with tiny lights in the violet dusk. Andy's headlights flashed white against the worn side of the barn, and my mother got out. After a few minutes she came upstairs and stood in the doorway, holding a bag of take-out food in her good hand.

"I can't wait to ditch this cast," she said. "Hungry?"

"Starved."

She sat down on the floor and spread out the containers, handed me a plate.

"We're not allowed to eat in the bedrooms," I reminded her.

She smiled, scooting back so that she could lean against the wall, reaching for the closest box of food. The scent of cashew chicken filled the room.

"I'm mellowing out," she said. "Getting positively decadent. Most nights I don't even bother to cook. I've lost my interest in it, I guess. Andy knew about this place," she added, nodding at the food. "We had lunch there earlier this week. It's good. So we stopped to pick up some takeout."

"He seems nice," I said finally, which sounded lame, and too little too late.

"He is. He's very nice." Her voice was a little reserved. "You know, I don't need you to approve, you or your brother. It's making me a little crazy. You'd both be up in arms if I poked around in your life this much."

I wondered what Blake had said about Andy, but, chastened, decided not to ask. "So, what did you find?" my mother said after a minute. "Looks like treasure."

"It is treasure. These are all letters by or to Rose Jarrett. A couple of them are from her brother, the illustrious Joseph Arthur Jarrett. I found them in the Lafayette Historical Society. The boxes that Joan Lowry donated ended up there. They were closing early, so I slipped this binder into my bag."

"Lucy! You stole them?"

"No, not really. I borrowed them. Though actually, it feels like they belong to us. Or to Iris," I added, thinking of the lock of hair. "They feel like her letters, actually. Could she even still be alive?"

"I suppose it's possible. She'd be quite old. Well into her nineties." My mother put a container down, her chopsticks balanced precisely across the center, and took the letters I handed her, reading through them quickly, shaking her head. "These are amazing to read," she said, letting the pages fall into her lap.

"Aren't they? I've been captivated for hours."

She ran her fingers quickly through her short hair. "Are there more?"

"Just one. At least that I have here. There may be more in the last box I didn't get to see." I pulled the final letter from the binder, a simple square white envelope, addressed to Iris, dated October 12, 1914, written on lined yellow paper. I read it out loud.

Dearest Iris,

I am here now. I am safe. An attic room, pale yellow wallpaper with a pattern in green. The floor is dark gray. I have a white pitcher and basin, and a narrow bed with a plain white cover. I don't need more.

They never came for me. I had the address, I asked directions. It did not sound far but it was. Three miles they said, take a carriage they said, but I walked. The satchel was so heavy. I thought my fingers might fall off. Still, I preferred walking to arriving. I stood a long time on the stoop to gather my courage, checking the address again and again. At last I rang the bell.

Her name is Vivian and she is Mrs. Elliot's sister. She was still talking to someone behind her as she opened the door, laughing, her face turning serious when she saw me. Her skin is pale but not freckled, her hair is the color of oak, creamy brown with a reddish cast and traces of gray, pulled carefully back in a bun. She wore a skirt over softly draping trousers, but otherwise she does not resemble Mrs. Elliot at all.

I handed her the letter.

Her eyes widened. "But you're a day early! And so pale! Come in, come in!"

So I am here. This house is like no other house. It is very simple, almost bare, with little furniture and no rugs. There are paintings on every wall. And books, too, everywhere. She took me into the kitchen. A man and a woman, Hubert and Jane, were sorting papers. She had me sit and bustled around. Hubert offered me a drink and Jane said nonsense, she's just a girl, and Vivian said she's more than a girl, she left her child, give her a drink if she wants it, and put a plate of beef and little egg sandwiches and a glass of warm milk in front of me. I tried to eat it slowly, but could not. They watched me with kind eyes. When I was finished she showed me up to this room. Then I slept all around the clock.

This house has little furniture but it is always full of people. They come and go, there are meetings and suppers and passionate discussions. Some of them do not even knock, they just walk in. And the things they say—Mrs. Elliot is mild in comparison.

The dinners are full of talk and I sit quietly. They are interested in the story of how I came to be here. So I tell them how I used to stand in the hallway when Mrs. Elliot came over and began to talk about the rights of women and the great march she attended in Washington. How I began to slip over to her house when she held her meetings. Cora warned me not to go, but I went anyway. I kept it as quiet as I could. Already my position was in danger; they had not known about you when they agreed I could come. They were sorry for me because they believe I am a widow.

On the day Mrs. Elliot led marchers through The Lake of Dreams, I was working in the garden. The singing came first. Then the women, so many women, maybe three hundred. Their singing voices swelled the air. I put down the garden clippers. I pulled off my gloves, finger by finger. You were upstairs, sleeping. Cora was on the porch and she called a warning, but in that moment I felt such excitement, I did not care. I stepped down the walk and through the gate and I joined them, marching. I sang.

We marched all the way into town, to the park. There was a big table and several women handing out flyers about the right to vote, and other flyers, too, a page I'd seen before and saved. "What Every Girl Should Know." But this time it was blank below the headline, and stamped with black letters at the top saying "NOTHING! Outlawed by the Post Office." I was standing by the table listening to the speeches when an officer came up and took me by the arm and put me into handcuffs. I was very scared. But Mrs. Elliot was arrested, too, and a dozen other women. We spent all night long sitting on the hard benches in the jail, telling stories and singing. They fed us nothing and gave us water in the morning, and by noon the tempers of all of us had begun to fray. That was when we decided we would not be powerless. They brought lunch and we refused to eat it! Dinner, too, we sent away untouched. We declared a hunger strike, and this was reported in the papers.

Joseph came to visit me. He brought food but he was angry. He said I should be reasonable and understand my loyalties. If not to myself, to you. I told him that I was in jail so you might have a better life one day, and then he got a little less gruff, because he loves you, and he said you were safe and well with Cora, even though she was furious with me. So I felt a little better.

Our hunger strike lasted three days. When we were released we hugged one another and spilled out into our separate lives. I walked back to the house, eager to gather you in my arms.

But when I got there, the door was locked. No one answered when I rang the bell and pounded.

I tried the back door, too. I tried the windows and the cellar door, all locked.

They had gone. I did not know where. They had taken you with them.

I did not know what to do. I sat on the porch, too hungry and too hurt to weep.

Mrs. Elliot took me in. Cora and Jesse refused to have me back, they said I was a disgrace and no longer welcome.

So I have come all this way to live with strangers. Mrs. Elliot said I would find work in the city and could save enough money to bring you here, but when I told this to Vivian she shook her head in clear amazement and said her sister was a hopeless romantic and what did she think, there were jobs hanging from the trees?

She asked what I could do and I told her that I sewed. This was the work I did all winter for Cora, her best velvets and silks, while you played at my feet. Some days I staggered out of the room so tired from bending over little stitches that my head felt stuffed with cotton, my eyes burned. But it was better work than scrubbing floors or doing laundry, and you were with me.

"And they paid you how much?"

"They fed us."

She sat back in her chair and swept her hand through the air in disgust.

"I'm very good."

She sighed. "Yes. I'm sure you have the finest stitches."

I flushed, because then I knew she was mocking me, but I did not know why.

"I don't know," I told her, speaking slowly. "I had the finest stitches in my village, yes. But it was a small village."

She glanced at me again, her eyes faintly kinder. "Don't pay attention. It's just—so many arrive, every day. I see them streaming off these ships with their suitcases, and then I see them later, spilling out of the factories that take them in when they can find no other work. Take them in and wear them out. I see them when they are ill. I am a nurse. So I have become cynical, I fear. Trust me—you do not wish to work in a factory."

"Do you like your work?" I asked.

She considered this. "No. I like bringing comfort to people when that's possible, though often it is not. I earn my own money, and that brings me freedom, which I do like." She looked at me then. "Have you any nursing experience?" I said I did not.

"I felt free on the boat," I said, remembering the trip we made across the ocean.

She nodded. "Oh, yes. On a boat you are no place at all." She was quiet for a moment. "But now you are here, and we must decide what to do."

Downstairs, they come and go, talk and argue, voices lapping at my door. Sometimes I join them. Other times I stay alone in my room and sleep, or read, or write. I do not know what will become of me.

"Let me see," my mother said. I handed her the pages and sifted through the papers from the cupola until I found the page Rose had mentioned in her letter, the page that had launched my search, the brittle paper with the dense text discussing basic human physiology, and the scrap of paper that had been folded inside it where Rose had written her startled and impassioned thoughts. Such a simple article, such straightforward facts; I wondered if Cora had ever read these pamphlets, or if she'd been too shocked. Rose had fished some of them from the eggshells and coffee grounds; perhaps they'd been left behind when she went so hastily to New York City, or perhaps Cora had found them only after the move from town to this house on the lake, and had shoved them in the space beneath the window seat—out of sight, out of mind.

We sat up for a few more hours, my mother and I, going through the letters and the papers, trying to sort out the chronology and fill in the gaps. After my mother went to bed, I stayed up even longer, writing down names and dates on index cards and putting them into little piles. I lay down on my stomach on the bed with my chin in my hands, the facts swirling in my mind. I closed my eyes, thinking I would not sleep, just rest.

In my dream that night I took Rose's journey, stepping from a train into an unfamiliar city. I walked, stopping at houses all along the way, but the doors were locked, or the people who lived there did not recognize me and had no idea who I was. Panic was a steady thrum beneath all my actions. I put my suitcase down and it was gone. I walked until I came to a park. It was spring, new leaves on the trees, and a crowd had gathered, held back by waist-high metal barriers. I was trying to see something, we all were, but no matter how I craned my neck or shifted my position, nothing was visible beyond the heads of the crowd. A woman next to me asked my name. I told her, and she expressed surprise. *I have something for you,* she said, reaching into her purse. *Something I've been holding for a long, long time. You must have lost it.* She pulled out a wallet and handed it to me. Inside I found my ID cards, all my identification.

I've been looking for these forever, I said. *Where did you find them? Here,* she said. *Right here, in the museum.* I looked up then and saw that's where we were, that the walls were filled with paintings and the windows with stained glass, and as I watched, the figures in the windows began to emerge, beautiful, luminous men and women stepping into the room. I walked from place to place slowly, because everything, and all the people, were so very fragile. Before I reached the door, I woke up.

I sat up, rubbing my neck, the unease of my dream flowering into the still morning. Letters and papers were scattered all over the floor. The lights were still on. Then I remembered: I'd promised Yoshi that I'd call last night, and I'd forgotten all about it.

It was evening there, and he answered right away when I called him on Skype, his face appearing on the screen with an expression both concerned and annoyed. He was out of sorts to begin with—one of his flights had been canceled, and he'd had to reschedule his whole trip. When he didn't hear from me he'd gotten worried, and his concern came out as anger. We argued, me sitting on my childhood bed, Yoshi in a hotel in Jakarta, ten thousand miles away.

"Maybe I just shouldn't come," he said, finally. "If it's just going to be like this."

"No. No, please come, Yoshi. I want you to come."

"It feels strange, Lucy. Like you've been gone longer than a week."

Had it been only a week? I counted back—yes, but so much had happened that it felt much longer. "When you get here it won't feel that way," I said.

"What's so important that you forgot to call?"

"Nothing," I said, glancing at the cards splayed all over the floor. "Just more news about my family history. I'll tell you all about it when you get here."

"Are you all right?" he asked. "You look terrible."

"Do I?" I looked at all the papers scattered across the floor, covered with dates and facts. I wondered if I'd changed in this short time, if Yoshi would even know me anymore. "I just woke up," I explained. "I fell asleep in the middle of all this research. It was a long day yesterday, I guess."

"Well, it was long for me, too. I was worried when I couldn't reach you. What research are you talking about?"

I explained then about Rose and Iris and the letters, but I was still groggy and the story sounded both confused and boring, too full of detail.

"Anyway," I ended. "How are the meetings going?"

"Okay. We go out to the site tomorrow."

"It will be interesting to see the sacred places," I said, thinking of the chapel and the ancient burial sites on the depot land.

"I don't know if *interesting* is the word I'd use," Yoshi said. "I have a feeling this is going to be confrontational, though probably in a very passive-aggressive way. I have a feeling we won't get much accomplished."

"Maybe that's okay."

"Not if I get fired."

"Are you really worried about that?"

"Not really," he said, but I could tell that he was. "Look, I have to get some dinner, and I need to get some sleep."

"At least you're on your way to a vacation, once it's all done."

"We'll have to see, Lucy." Yoshi sounded tense, but I wasn't sure; it might have been my own scattered feelings I was projecting. "This might turn out to be a bad time for me to leave, job-wise."

"But you already have your tickets."

"I know. Look, let's just wait and see how it goes."

"All right," I said. Everything seemed so fragile now, after the dream, and I didn't want to argue with Yoshi. I couldn't believe I'd forgotten to call him, so lost in the mysteries of the past that I'd neglected what was happening all around me. "Let me know, okay? I'm planning that you'll be here, unless I hear otherwise."

"Okay."

"Okay, then. Hope your meetings go well."

"Thanks," he said. "I'll call you soon." And then he was gone.

Chapter 13

THE REVEREND SUZI WELLS WALKED UP THE GRASSY SLOPE to the chapel, which stood alone in a field, a small red stone building with windows that resembled keyholes, four on each side. She led an odd procession: Keegan followed her, dressed in jeans and work boots and a T-shirt with a small tear at the shoulder. Next came Oliver Parrott in his black bespoke suit and polished leather shoes, stepping gingerly through the long grass as if he might somehow avoid the dew. A bald reporter from *The Lake of Dreams Gazette* walked by Oliver's side, a little recorder clipped to his black leather jacket, asking questions about Frank Westrum, which Oliver answered effusively, in great detail. Suzi had contacted the *Gazette*, maybe hoping for publicity for the church, perhaps as a smart preemptive action to keep Oliver and his acquisitions committee at bay, but Oliver was losing no time in telling the story of his illustrious ancestor and his museum. Behind these two came Zoe, in cutoff shorts and flip-flops and a tank top, a canvas bag over her shoulder, bouncing against her hip. She'd called again, wanting to see if I'd drive her to the mall, and I'd told her about my plans, never imagining she'd want to come. But now here she was, plunging through the tall weeds, pausing to brush away insects or remove grass that had stuck between her toes, tossing back excited comments on the day, the weather, the adventure of entering this church, which had stood empty for so long.

She didn't seem to expect me to answer any of this, which was good, because I was still preoccupied, as I had been for the past two days, caught in the secret history Rose had written, consumed with wondering what had happened to her next. It was frustrating, of course, that the historical society was closed, but it had given me time to read Rose's letters again and again, to think about her life as I kayaked and swam and floated on the raft. Her longing to become a priest, her conflicted feelings when Geoffrey Wyndham's attention—unsought, unwelcome—fell upon her, all the ways she had been powerless to choose her life—her story was poignant, and moving, and unsettling. I wished I could march into the past and set things right. And I wondered, also, what her story had meant to my great-grandfather, how these events had shaped him in ways that were perhaps shaping the family still. I'd kept spreading out the index cards with dates and facts, first in one pattern, then another, as if I might finally reassemble them, like the scattered bones of a skeleton which, if I got the pieces in the right configuration, would suddenly take life and rise up and walk away.

Ahead, Keegan paused, stepping out of the procession to wait for me to catch up. His arms were muscled from his work with glass and fire; he had a long narrow burn just below his elbow.

"Excited?" he asked, falling into step beside me.

"Very. You must be, too."

"Oh, yes." He smiled, nodded ahead. "Not half as excited as Oliver, though."

"No kidding. Have you seen his collections? His archived collections, I mean?"

Keegan glanced at me with interest. "He invited you over?"

"He did. I took my mother."

"You must have impressed him. He doesn't show those images to many people. What did you think?"

I remembered the quietness of the Westrum House, the black

auditorium seats all empty and the doors to the world locked, the images flashing up on the screen. I thought of Oliver's passion and the exquisite beauty of the windows. As uneasy as I was about Oliver's intentions, I'd also left feeling dazzled by the intricate, luminous glass.

"They were exceptional. He needs more display space, though, not more windows. Do you think he'll go after these?"

"Wouldn't you? An interrelated series—that's got to be a very special find. Did he serve you tea?"

"He did. Orange spice. With honey. It was very good."

The tall grass and weeds reached the hem of the only dress I'd brought, short-sleeved and as soft as a T-shirt, the sort of cloth that never wrinkled, good for traveling. It was black, and I wore black sandals, which had gotten soaked within a few steps. Keegan's jeans were wet to his knees, which reminded me of our wilder days, pulling the canoe out of the water, his legs wet and his feet pale against the shale beach. We'd been so carefree. My departure had been fixed even then, but it was still so far on the horizon I felt we'd never get there. That last spring the present had seemed somehow eternal, as if nothing would ever change. I wondered if Keegan ever thought about those days, the innocent world we'd inhabited until my father died.

"How's Max? I keep thinking of him standing above that rushing water."

"He's good. He probably doesn't even remember, so don't be worrying. I thought about bringing him today, so he could see where they were digging." He gestured to the small cemetery adjacent to the church, enclosed within an ornate black iron fence; beyond this fence, unrecognized for decades and now roped off with dark blue tape, was the site where the Iroquois had once lived, before the village of Appleton was built and razed, before the land was taken by the government. Though it was still early, two archaeologists were already standing just outside the taped-off area, drinking coffee from paper cups. They waved. I found myself thinking of the lake, of the earth beneath my feet, which had seen so many people, so many seasons, come and go.

"He didn't want to come?"

"Oh, he'd have come in a heartbeat. Are you kidding? He's totally into digging. But in the end it seemed like a bad idea. He'd just be all over the place." Keegan waved back to the archaeologists, whom he seemed to know. "They found some bowls yesterday, did you hear? Big stone bowls, with granite pestles, probably used for grinding corn."

"That's interesting," I said, imagining the streets and buildings that had once filled this land, and the trails and patterns of the Iroquois who lived here before that.

Suzi had reached the chapel door. She was wearing black jeans and a simple black shirt with a white clerical collar. The ministers of my youth would have been men, dressed like Oliver, and they would have driven cars like the one he had arrived in, too—sleek, quiet, and black. Suzi, however, had a blue compact car and used her bicycle around town.

"Well, that was quite a trek," Oliver said, pulling a handkerchief from his pocket to wipe off his shoes. Keegan caught my eye and we both smiled.

"Totally cool," Zoe said. "How long has this place been locked up?"

"Since 1941," Suzi said, taking a key from her jacket pocket. It was ornate, made of iron, probably fashioned at Dream Master. Our great-grandfather or grandfather might have made this key, but I didn't say so. "No one really expected it to be closed for this long. But as far as I know, no one's been in here since, not until they came to uncover the windows."

The key stuck, and Suzi jiggled it; finally it caught, and the door, stripped of its paint by years of weather, swung open. One by one, we stepped across the threshold into the musty stillness of the chapel. Except for a few pews at the back, the sanctuary was still intact, as it had been when the last services were held so many decades ago. The floor, beneath a layer of softening dust, was tile. The room smelled of cold, damp, and mildew. But I noted these details only later.

What captured me, what captured us all, were the windows.

In the darkness of the chapel—there was no other light—the

windows seemed to float. Like the Wisdom window, the colors were bright and vibrant, the images stylized and elongated in the Art Nouveau style. Each window had the familiar border of vine-encrusted spheres along the bottom, iridescent white against the jewel tones that surrounded them. No matter how much I'd hoped and even expected to see it on these windows, the pattern riveted me even as the others began to disperse through the sanctuary, Suzi to the closest window in the west wall, Zoe trailing behind her, and Keegan and Oliver to the east windows, where the early morning light was strongest.

"Oh, it's certainly Frank's work," Oliver said, his voice both excited and proprietary. "Exquisite work, just breathtaking." He turned in a circle, taking in all the windows. "What a find this is for the Westrum Foundation. What an absolute treasure."

He turned back to the closest window and began to look at the detail. A sense of possessiveness flared through me, too. I didn't think of these as Frank's windows. To me, they belonged to Rose. I couldn't bear the thought that she might be obscured, cast as a footnote to Frank Westrum.

Oliver and Keegan began to speak in low, charged voices, talking about the nature of the glass, the quality of the leading, remarking on how well preserved the windows were, how clean—the wooden panels that had protected them all these decades had only just been removed. The reporter was taking rapid notes. "You see," Oliver said, trying unsuccessfully to mask how thrilled he was. "You see this pattern right here, and here—this is the Westrum trademark, these are his windows, that is certain."

Maybe so, I thought. But they also belonged to Nelia, who had paid for them. And in some way I was only beginning to understand, they belonged to Rose.

The words of her letters were still so present, all the love and loss of her early life. I walked around the chapel once, taking in the images. Suffused with light, the glowing windows cast color across the floor, across our faces and our hands. Luminous colors, the yellow of marigolds, the red of blood, the vibrant dark green of late summer grass. I walked from window to window studying the figures. A woman, pensive, holding an alabaster jar, stood beside Jesus, who was seated at a table, a silvery light around him. In the next window, two women, both visibly pregnant, spoke together in a garden. In the third, a woman turned from a cave, her hands open, her skin pale and radiant, her expression filled with wild amazement. In the last window on this wall, a woman stood in front of a temple holding an unrolled scroll while a group of men gathered around, waiting, listening for her words. I touched the bottom of this window, tracing the row of overlapping vine-encrusted moons.

"They are exquisite," Suzi said softly, coming to stand beside me. Her face was flushed and animated, and it struck me that she was moved by the windows, that for her they were not simply an artifact of the past or a clue to a forgotten life but a connection with the stories themselves, with whatever mystery they attempted to catch. What Suzi seemed to be experiencing in this chapel was something that resonated from my past, the sense that there was something numinous present, real and potent, that I could not understand. Rose, too, must have felt this. She must have felt it strongly to want to be a priest at a time when that was impossible, to have helped create this extraordinary chapel full of windows. I thought she would have liked seeing the Reverend Suzi here. Maybe she would have understood even me, with all my doubts and wrong turns and seeking.

"It's the same glass," Keegan was saying across the chapel. "It has the same tonalities and composition as in the Wisdom window. I'm sure, even without an analysis. Just look at the consistency of the color. These windows were clearly all made at the same time, for the same commission, don't you agree? I wonder—when would you place them, Oliver, in the Westrum work?"

Oliver didn't answer immediately, but stood with his arms folded, considering. Suzi's footsteps echoed softly as she moved from one window to another.

"It's difficult to say. In terms of craft, they're late examples. But in terms of design, he's using this Art Nouveau style that he liked so much as a young artist. They certainly recall his youth. I know you have dates on receipts and so forth, but even so these windows are out of character for the work he did at the end of his life. Actually, they're like nothing else I've seen of his, ever."

I walked across the back of the chapel, past where the Wisdom window would be hanging if it were here, to the east wall. The figures in the four windows on the other wall all featured women, too. The first was familiar, a woman kneeling at the edge of a river, pulling a basket from the water to the shore; that story, the rescue of Moses, I vaguely remembered. The next window depicted a young woman in a sun-struck field, presenting a bushel full of grain to an older woman; the third showed a woman pulling water from a well and offering a cup to the haloed figure of Jesus. Jesus was in the final window, too, sitting across from a woman who listened to him avidly, while behind her another woman stood, holding a basket of fruit.

I studied these images, trying to recollect the stories, taken back to my days in Sunday school, the air full of the scent of paste, the rustle of paper, the teachers' voices as they read out loud. But we hadn't read most of these stories, I didn't think. All I seemed to remember were tales of floods and battles and fleeing through the desert. Aside from Eve, the only woman I remembered was Mary in her pale blue robes; we had all wanted to be her during the Christmas play, even though she didn't have any lines.

I walked slowly from window to stunning window. They depicted such ordinary moments, really—women carrying grain or jars or baskets of fruit; women in a garden, by a river or a well, at a grave—even as they dazzled in their beauty and harmonious design, filling the chapel with shifting shapes of color. There was a cumulative power in the images, too, all these women in pivotal moments of their lives, moments infused with spiritual longing or celebration or fulfillment. In the windows of my childhood church, most of the images had been male; Jesus was male, and the disciples were, too, and the language used in the service had referenced only men. Here, that had been turned upside down. I walked from window to window again, feeling my perspective shift. For the first time ever, I could imagine myself into these stories. At the west wall now, Keegan and Oliver were still talking of glass and the Westrum opus. Zoe, who had been uncharacteristically quiet since we'd entered the chapel, came and stood beside me.

"They're so pretty," she whispered.

I nodded. "They really are stunning. She's related to us, you know," I said, on impulse. "The woman who designed some of these windows. See that pattern along the bottom? That's hers."

Zoe didn't ask me how I knew this, or anything about Rose, not even her name.

"Cool," she said. "You know, I like to draw. I wonder if maybe I inherited it."

"Maybe," I said, feeling possessive about Rose again; I'd already claimed her adventurous spirit for myself.

"What are they all about?"

"I don't know, exactly. We'll have to ask."

As we talked I looked again from window to window, trying to determine if any of the figures resembled the woman in the landing at the Westrum House—that is, if any might be Rose—but none was familiar, nor did they resemble one another.

Keegan turned to me and called softly across the room, "Hey—did you see?"

"You mean the border pattern?"

"Yes, but not just that. Look at their clothes."

I did then, searching. Each figure was dressed in the usual fluid robes, the green of new grass, a deep lake blue. And then I saw what Keegan meant, what I had not seen before: in each window, at the clasp of a gown, at the edge of a belt, or caught in the hair, was the trademark Westrum flower. Roses were in all of these windows, tiny but vivid, and deep, deep red.

"Oh!" I stood up and went over to the closest window, touched the rose floating on the water of the river.

"What?" Oliver asked.

"The signature flowers. They're all roses, in every window."

"Are they?" He stepped back to view them all, thoughtful. A square of purple light fell through the thinning place in his hair.

"All right," he said, finally. "I guess you're right—he must have known her. In fact, he must have known her very well. That's something quite personal, isn't it? All the little roses. He only did that a handful of times, putting a significant emblem in the glass, like a game he was playing with the people who bought his work. Things that no one else would notice, only the person for whom they were intended; sometimes it was even a private joke. For example, one window we have was commissioned by his neighbor. Frank needed money at the time, but he didn't like this man, we know from letters we've retrieved; he found him pompous and self-satisfied and very irritating. The neighbor's name was Baum, which means 'tree' in German. The window is quite striking, and Mr. Baum was delighted with it. He never noticed all the leafless trees scattered throughout the scene; Frank used their bare branches to divide colors."

Keegan, who was standing nearby, laughed.

"Yes, but this is different," I said. "This seems a very beautiful sort of tribute."

"Oh, I agree. He clearly made these windows with great delicacy and intention. Some of his best work, I would have to say. He must have had a great affection for her."

"I think so, too." Remembering Oliver's reticence in the studio, I decided not to tell him about Rose, that I'd found her letters, that I'd learned so much more. I didn't want him to know about Iris, either, how she'd been left behind, how all Rose wanted was to earn enough money to come back and claim her daughter.

Zoe and I sat down. Suzi took a seat ahead of us and turned, sliding her elbow over the smooth wooden edge of the pew.

"This Rose Jarrett, who was she? Do you know anything more? Because if I was curious about her before, I'm just consumed with curiosity now."

"Yeah, me, too," Zoe said. "Lucy says we're related, but I've never heard of her. And these windows are so beautiful, but I don't know what they mean. Can you tell us?"

I was glad she had asked so I wouldn't have to admit my own ignorance. I hadn't gone to church since I was seventeen.

"I can tell you something about the windows," Suzi said. "As beautiful as they are, they're powerful, too. The west wall—it's a wall of prophets, really. All four windows. The first image is Elizabeth talking to Mary. I'm sure you can see that they're both pregnant—Elizabeth, who thought she was past child-bearing age, with John the Baptist, and Mary, a young woman, unmarried, with Jesus. Elizabeth has given a prophecy to Mary about her child, and in this window, Mary's speaking, she's saying the Magnificat, which is prophetic, too, and which talks about justice for the poor. Two women, two prophets, their children about to be born, their lives about to change in ways they can't imagine or control.

"Now, the next window, this woman with the scroll, is Hulda. She's from the Hebrew Scriptures. It's a wonderful story—when the king found ancient documents hidden in the temple walls, he consulted Hulda, who was a prophet, to find out what they meant. There were plenty of male prophets around, but he chose Hulda, for her wisdom and her compassion. See how she's standing on the temple steps, holding the scrolls, the crowd gathering to hear what she says?

"This next one I just love," she went on, nodding to the radiant woman turning from the cave. "That's Mary Magdalene. Look at her expression—the amazement, and the fear. The story is so familiar that I don't know if anyone really hears it anymore. But imagine if a person you loved had died, and you went to the cemetery and saw that person again. That's Mary Magdalene's story—she's the person to whom the Resurrection was first revealed, the one charged with telling others. Very little attention has been paid to the fact that the first person to witness the Resurrection was a woman, but it's so. As I said, your great-great-aunt really intrigues me with her choices."

We were quiet for a minute. I wasn't thinking of the windows, really, but rather of my father on the day they'd carried his body to the shore.

"I thought that was Mary Magdalene in the last window," I said, finally. "I thought she was the woman holding the jar."

"No. It's not entirely clear who the woman with the alabaster jar is. There are different ideas. But it's probably not Mary Magdalene."

I hesitated to ask, but I had to. "You said the women on this wall were prophets, but wasn't Mary Magdalene—you know—a fallen woman?"

"Mary Magdalene was not a prostitute," Suzi said. She spoke calmly but also forcefully. "That's the story you grew up hearing, probably. Around the fourth century one of the early popes conflated all women into one fallen woman, and that image has stuck. But it's not true. It's not anywhere in the Scriptures. This woman, too, with the alabaster jar, has been mislabeled that way for centuries. This story appears in all four Gospels, which underscores its importance, but only in Luke is she described, in a very nonspecific way, as a sinner—a term which, when you think about it, applies to everyone. In John she's identified as Mary of Bethany, sister to Martha and Lazarus. Yet, like Mary Magdalene, she's been labeled as a prostitute for centuries. It's a diversion, I think, a smoke screen. Because if they call her a prostitute, she can be dismissed, and the rest of the story can be dismissed, too. No one has to look any deeper into the narrative. No one seeing this woman standing before Jesus with her jar full of nard, pouring it over his head, has to say, Look, look at this: anointing a king is the action of a prophet. Yet it's true, and that is exactly what she's doing."

We studied the woman, her flowing hair, her robes flowing, too, the alabaster jar cradled in her hands.

"It's such a moment of emotional intimacy," Suzi went on. "Sometimes I try to imagine it: the room fills up with the fragrance of the nard, and she pours it over his head. She anoints him. The disciples protest—she's wasting money—but Jesus defends her. 'This story will be told in remembrance of her'—that's what Jesus says. Yet here we are, millennia later, and we don't tell her story. We don't even have her name."

"A forgotten woman," I said. I thought of Rose, who was no prophet, no saint, just an ordinary young woman walking home in the quiet darkness along the rutted dirt road, the summer air soft on her arms, the strange comet light changing everything. She slipped quietly into the garden, in through the kitchen door and up into the little room where she lay awake all the rest of that night, running the events over in her mind. Everything would be different now, she knew that, but she did not yet know just how. She still believed the story she had entered was her own.

Except for a piece of fabric, she would have disappeared.

"Rose Jarrett wanted to be a priest," I said. "Even though she knew she couldn't, that was her secret dream."

"Really?" Suzi, who had been studying the western wall of windows, turned to look at me again, her expression interested, curious. "Well, that explains some things about the windows. But it must have been frustrating—even heartbreaking—for her. This was in the 1930s?"

"No, when she was younger. It was around 1910, 1914."

"I see. What did she do then?"

"It's a sad story. She got involved with the wrong person. He was older, and he had power over her family, but I think she convinced herself it was love. She was young, fifteen. He was wealthy, and he left her when he learned she was pregnant. A sad story, and an old one, too. She came to this country with almost nothing. I don't know what happened next, or how she came to know Frank Westrum."

"That is sad," Suzi said. "I wonder if she knew women were priests in the early church. There's lots of evidence to support it."

"I don't think so. I think she felt she was trespassing even to suggest it. She stole a chalice," I added. "A silver chalice from the church, because she had no money."

I said this quickly, glancing away as I spoke. I don't know what I expected—shock or anger or dismissal—but Suzi just nodded.

"She must have been very frightened, to have done that."

"I think she was. It haunted her later."

I folded my arms. The air in the chapel was damp and stale and chilly. I wished I'd brought a sweater. Thinking of the images of all these women, all this beautiful art, locked away for decades, I was filled with a sudden sense of emptiness. What, I wondered, had become of all the people who had filled this chapel on that final Sunday morning? What had happened to the whispered prayers and hopes and grief and dreams of this community, now so completely vanished? What had happened to Rose?

"What about the other windows?" Zoe asked. "Are they all prophets, too?"

Keegan and Oliver had drifted to the back of the chapel, where they were talking as intently about glass and dates and Frank Westrum as we were about the lives of these women. The photographer was moving from window to window, taking multiple shots of each.

"Some are. They're all very interesting. I was thinking about it earlier, trying to see the thread connecting them. Here's what I see: they are all strong women who weren't afraid to challenge conventional thinking. For instance, that's the Pharaoh's daughter, pulling Moses from the river in defiance of her father's orders. Next to her is Ruth, presenting the grain she has gleaned in the fields to her mother-in-law, Naomi. When their husbands died they went against expectations for widows and supported each other. There's the Samaritan woman at the well, giving water to Jesus, and crossing all sorts of ethnic, gender, and cultural lines to do so. Again, like Mary Magdalene, she's the one who's given the story to tell. Then, in the final window, there's the story of Mary and Martha, which you may already know—it's the one where Martha complains that Mary isn't helping with the housework, and Jesus stands up for Mary, saying it's all right for her to take off her apron and sit down. To listen. It may not sound like much, but remember that we're talking about a culture that didn't value women as anything more than house-keepers, property. And yet here's Jesus, talking with Mary, taking her seriously. It's so radical. Revolutionary, really—a total inversion of the expectations of the time. Some scholars also think that these two women may not be sisters at all, but rather two women who had important roles in the community that formed around Jesus. It wasn't at all uncommon for women to have leadership roles in the early church, though again, that's been obscured." Suzi turned back to me then, resting her chin on her hand. "So Lucy—do you know anything more about Rose, or how these windows came to be?"

"Not really. I'm trying to find out," I said. I was remembering my dream, the figures stepping out of the windows into the room. I had the sense that it could happen; these women with their bowls of fruit and bushels of grain and alabaster jars were so vividly present. Perhaps this was exactly what Rose and Cornelia and Vivian and Frank had hoped the chapel would do. I was stirred by the windows and I didn't want to leave.

It seemed none of us did. Zoe stood and went to look more closely, but Suzi and I sat for a time in silence. Finally, I leaned forward and said, "It's so beautiful. Compelling, too. But it makes no logical sense, any of it."

Suzi nodded, her gaze still on the windows. "No, it doesn't. But I don't think logic has much to do with it. I love that beautiful line from Ezekiel, about replacing a heart of stone with a heart of flesh. That makes no literal sense either, though we understand it in metaphor. For me, that's the power of the stories—that you can't quantify them. That they keep opening up and revealing something new."

I didn't know what to say to that. I almost told her about what happened the night my father died, how I'd run into him in the garden and he'd asked me to go fishing, how maybe it would have changed everything if I had.

Instead, I talked about Rose. "You know," I said. "She made mistakes, yes, but she was so young. She was just trying to find her way. It seems so unfair that she lost everything she loved."

"Do you know how her life ended?" Suzi asked.

"No, I don't. I'm afraid it might have been tragic."

"I don't know about that. You may be right, but I look around at these windows, and what I see is beauty, and joy, and a kind of deep awareness of these stories. A kind of creative, generative peace, as well. To me it seems she wasn't stuck in loss. She grew. She turned at least some of what she lost, and what she suffered, into beauty."

I didn't say anything, and we sat for a few minutes longer, until Suzi stood, saying she needed to get back for a meeting. We walked from the chapel into the bright clear light of the day. Keegan and Oliver were already outside, and the photographer had gone. A breeze from the lake moved through the tall grass, filling it with waves, like a sea, fluttering the tops of the distant trees. Our little group began to disperse, Suzi and Oliver making their way, deep in conversation, through the grass to where the cars were parked at the entrance. Zoe stood uncertainly at the entrance, then reached into her purse and flipped open her phone. I thought of all the moments in my own life when such a gesture would have been a nice hedge against awkwardness, and I thought of Rose, alone in the train station, trying not to attract attention, pulling out her pen to write a letter. I asked Zoe if she needed a ride, but she shook her head, and when she snapped the phone closed she said that her mother was on her way. Then she started back through the fields, her long legs disappearing in the grass. I lingered for a moment, thinking how young she looked.

Keegan had been talking to the archaeologists; now he came over and touched my arm. "Hey," he said. "Pretty amazing in there."

I nodded, still filled up with the images of all those women in the windows. "It was. It was totally spectacular."

"Suzi's pretty cool, isn't she? She lets me come in and just sit in the sanctuary sometimes, when I'm not working. I like that. I guess I like the silence. It seems real somehow, not like that angry shouting kind of religion you get on the news." He laughed a little, shook his head. "I've got this cousin Becky. I don't think you ever met her. She lives in Orlando and she came to visit once—before my mother died. And my mother made her this beautiful dinner, a dessert with some kind of elegant cake soaked in Grand Marnier. So Becky is eating the cake and really liking it, and she asks for the recipe and my mother is explaining, and the next thing you know Becky is up from the table and in the bathroom spitting out the cake because of the Grand Marnier. Now, see, I just don't get that. I don't see how sucking the joy out of every aspect of life can be pleasing to anybody's god."

"Me, either," I said, thinking of the peace I'd always felt in church as a child, and thinking also of a hike I'd taken with Yoshi to a temple in the mountains that was built of dark wood, with a graceful, swooping roof, the sound of running water in the distance.

"Anyway, this is a real treasure. The windows are totally unique. Did you see Oliver? He was practically swooning."

"I saw him," I said. "He seemed very excited, very—covetous. I bet he's planning an addition to the Westrum House already. Does the glass need much repair?"

"A little. Not much. It's in surprisingly good shape. Here," he added, taking my hand. "This was finished, so I brought it."

He pressed something smooth and rounded into my palm, and in the second before I looked at it I remembered my dream again, and the yearning that had filled it; I flushed, as if Keegan might be able to read my thoughts.

The object in my hand was the shape we'd made together in the studio, fires roaring in their furnaces and the molten glass suspended on the end of the blowpipe. Keegan's lips had been on the rim, his breath forming the glass from within, and then my lips pressed against the metal where his had been, my breath mingling with his in the hot embrace of glass, the sphere blooming, growing. It was curved and heavy, colors sliding over the surface, iridescent, like oil on water.

"I added the curl on top," he said. "So you could hang it."

"Thank you." The curved glass fit perfectly in my palm. "I love holding it. And it's beautiful, too."

"You're welcome." He gazed across the fields at the lake. "I thought I'd take a walk while we're here. Want to come?"

"Can we? Wouldn't it be trespassing?"

He smiled. "When has that ever stopped us in the past, Lucy Jarrett?"

I laughed, and we set off across the field full of wildflowers to the trees.

Once we'd struggled through the underbrush at the transition from field to forest, the space opened up and became gladelike, oaks and maples and chestnuts growing high. The earth was loamy, springy beneath our feet, and carpeted with leaves and pine needles that cushioned our steps, silenced them. We grew quiet, too, walking amid the trees. The wind rustled the leaves high above, but around us the air was still.

"Do you know this place?" I asked Keegan, because he was walking with such an unhurried assurance that I'd simply fallen into step beside him.

"Never been here," he said. "Still, it feels familiar, doesn't it?"

"It's the collective unconscious," I joked.

"Maybe so."

The land sloped gently; the distant sound of running water drew us on. Now and then animals scurried invisibly, rattling the low branches; light filtered in through the leaves and made dancing patterns on the forest floor. One bush was alive with tiny brown birds, which took flight and scattered as we passed. I felt I'd entered an enchanted place, a place out of time. We reached the edge of a shallow ravine, a stream running swiftly over the flat rocks below, and followed it, Keegan slipping down the bank so he could wade. My black sandals were crusted with dirt and debris, and I regretted my black dress, but I kept going. The silence of the forest seemed to extend from the silence of the chapel with its glowing windows, as if the whole world were a sacred place, and I wanted to go on, to see where the stream would end. It grew flatter and wider, the water eddying in shallow pools. I slipped off my sandals and stepped into the water. We walked until the trees began to open, until the stream poured itself into the lake and disappeared.

"Lucy," Keegan said. We were standing up to our calves in the cold water. He turned and pressed one hand against my face and kissed me with the same soft assurance he'd had walking in the forest. His lips on mine, as if no time had passed. I thought of the roar and silence of the glass studio, the dance with fire, and I kissed him back.

"Not a good idea," I said, pulling away. Keegan was hardly taller than me; his eyes, so close to mine, were warm. Kind.

"Why not? I've been wanting to do that since I saw you again."

"For one, I don't live here anymore," I said.

"You're here now," he said, running one hand along my arm.

"Yes." I tried to summon images of Yoshi on our tiny patio or lifting his weights in the living room, a fine sheen of sweat rising on his arms. The cobblestone streets, flowers spilling over fences, the trembling earth, all these flashed through my thoughts and were gone, until all I could remember was the empty static of the last call I'd made.

Keegan's lips were on mine again, and mine on his.

I caught myself, stepped away. Distantly, a boat droned.

"You're stirring everything up," I said.

"I know." He grinned. "I'm all shook up, too." He touched my arm again. "Never mind, Lucy in the sky. We'll head back and pretend it never happened."

Not possible, of course. As we walked back, climbing along the side of the stream and then following our own trail through the trees, I was aware of Keegan with every step, every breath. Once, he stopped in a clearing and pointed out the flattened brush, the faint marks of hooves, and I imagined the white deer gathering here, as dense as snow that covered everything in winter, alive and magical and silent. I wanted to pretend the intervening years had never happened, that Keegan and I were still in that time before loss. We were quieter after that, moving softly through the forest and then across the open field, past the locked and silent chapel, but though I imagined the deer everywhere, as soft as rabbits, as fleeing as gazelle, as white as snowdrifts, we did not even glimpse them.

"Keegan," I said, as he pulled open the door of his van, but then I couldn't think what else to tell him.

He smiled, waved, and drove away.

Chapter 14

ON THE PATIO THAT EVENING, ANDY WAS POURING WINE FOR my mother—it was my mother, though it took me a second to recognize her, her hair so short, silvery gray and feathery, the emerald silk top with a mandarin collar resting so elegantly against her neck. She was wearing white slacks and gold sandals, and though she smiled when she saw me and stood up to hug me, her arm free of its cast and warm against my back, I was disconcerted, as if I'd stumbled into an intimate dinner party between strangers.

"Have a seat, Lucy," Andy said, reaching for the extra glass they'd placed on the table and pouring me some wine. He was dressed up, too, wearing a tie. "We're having a drink to celebrate your mother's losing that cast, and then we're headed off to Skaneateles. Your mother, I discovered, has never had the pleasure of dinner at Doug's, which is without question the best fish fry I've ever had. So we're going to do that, and then I have tickets to a violin concert in a church by the lake. You're welcome to join us." He glanced at my mother, who smiled her agreement. "I'm sure we could pick up another ticket when we get there."

I thanked him and declined, truly regretful, because Skaneateles was always beautiful on a summer evening, the lake a clear turquoise blue, the village carefully preserved in all its charming late-nineteenth-century splendor. "Sounds like a nice evening, though," I added, making a mental note about Doug's Fish Fry, which sounded like a good place to take Yoshi when—or if—he ever got here.

"Are you going out again?" my mother asked.

"Maybe," I said vaguely, though I was. Keegan had called an hour earlier and invited me on a boat ride because it was supposed to be such a nice evening. I said I'd like that, and he said okay, I'll pick you up, and I said no, I'll meet you at the glassworks around eight o'clock. Beneath this conversation, so mundane on the surface, ran the powerful currents of our walk through the forest and our kiss in the stream, and beneath even that were the deeper currents of our history, all the evenings we'd spent as teenagers driving wild through the countryside or drifting on the lake.

I'd spent the day swimming and floating on the raft, filled with the images from the chapel, which lingered so powerfully, and the letters Rose had written. From time to time, I'd come inside, the kitchen dim after the brightness of the sun on the lake, to get a glass of iced tea and check my e-mail. There had been a brief, not very satisfying message from Yoshi, giving me his updated itinerary and not much more; I didn't know how his meetings had gone or exactly when he planned to leave for the island. I was torn between feeling concerned and feeling relieved. That kiss with Keegan in the stream had left me unsettled, unsure of what I was doing or what I wanted, distrustful of even my own motivations. It was better, it seemed, not to talk to Yoshi across all those vast miles until I'd come to terms with whatever was going on in my own heart.

Each time I closed the computer, I noted my feelings of both disappointment and relief. I went back outside and read passages from Rose's letters over again, trying to imagine myself into her story, into her dreams and struggles. She must have felt so angry and abandoned, standing alone in the church, the chalice heavy in her hands, so alone and frightened that she betrayed the one part of her life she'd held most dear, slipping the silver cup between the folds of her skirt, slipping away.

They had given up so much to make this journey—friends and family, everything they'd known. They'd come seeking prosperity, a chance to remake their lives, but as logical as that vision sounded from my place in history, it seemed that, for those early years at least, she and Joseph had been little more than servants. It was easy to imagine Rose sitting on the periphery of a meeting or a tea, the talk of equal rights stirring her heart even as she kept her head bent over the mending and the hemming. Perhaps she'd stayed awake late into the night to read, the pamphlets and magazines she'd collected both shocking and alluring, drawing her back again and again, until it all welled up within her that morning of the march, when she left her gloves on the bushes and joined that crowd of women without measuring the cost, knowing only that this was a chance for her voice to matter in the world.

"Here's to your mother," Andy said, putting the bottle down and raising his glass. "To being cast-free!" My mother laughed and shook her head, raising her glass with the arm that had healed, and we drank.

"Well, I'm glad to have it off," she said, her fingers lingering on the delicate stem of the glass. Nets of light reflected from the water made patterns on the table. "But you know, Andy, if it weren't for the accident, we wouldn't have met, would we? So I can't regret it completely."

They shared a private smile. I took a long swallow of wine.

"Sweetheart," my mother went on, turning to me. "Are you sure you don't want to join us? It'll be fun. Plus, I feel like I've hardly seen you, even though you've been here over a week. Before you know it, Yoshi will be here. I can't wait to meet him, but then you'll be gone again. When does he get in?"

"He's supposed to come Saturday," I said, deciding not to mention that Yoshi had been vacillating about this the last time we spoke. I'd been avoiding thinking about our last conversation, which had all the early marks of so many of my breakups, the way I allowed distance to bloom up until I could justify leaving for good. Still, this was Yoshi, and I'd imagined a different life with him. The time we'd shared together in Jakarta, the languorous romance and our lives in the river house, calm and interwoven, was the closest I'd ever come to being completely happy, even if things hadn't been so tranquil in Japan. He said once that I was always running away from things, and maybe it was true. Since I'd been here, I'd certainly boxed up all my feelings about Yoshi, plunging into the distractions of Rose's fascinating history and the unfolding drama of the land. And then there was Keegan, and where was I going with that? Moving on, maybe? I'd done it often enough before. Yet now that Yoshi was hesitating about coming to visit, I was surprised by the depth of my sadness.

Andy urged me again to join them and I declined, though I didn't mention my plans for the evening, as if I were still seventeen.

They weren't in a hurry to leave—it was still early. Andy asked what the chapel had been like, and I went inside to get the pictures I'd printed. The rooms were cool, dim after the bright patio; the screen door slammed and the murmur of their voices followed me. The life I remembered in this house was gone, pure and simple, and had been for years.

Back on the patio, I spread the images of the windows across the glass-topped table. While they didn't come close to capturing the splendor of the chapel, they were beautiful nonetheless. Andy and my mother passed them back and forth, commenting on the colors, the artistry, and the remarkable nature of this find. Andy said they ought to open it up for tours, and my mother agreed.

"I suppose it will depend on who ends up with that land," she said pensively, still studying the images. "But maybe even a developer would see the value and keep it intact. Kind of like a centerpiece. I can imagine Art doing something like that, can't you? Is it still a functioning church?"

"It was deconsecrated," I said. The idea of the chapel surrounded by sprawling high-end homes filled me with a kind of helpless rage. It wasn't proprietary, as I'd felt with Oliver, but rather a deep sense that the windows should be set apart, valued for something beyond their monetary worth. "That's what Suzi said, anyway. There's special liturgy, I guess. But apparently a church can be reconsecrated, too. I get the impression the church officials are trying to get it back. I hope they do. Because no, actually, I can't see Art valuing these windows at all. Not in the way they should be valued."

"Well, of course the church wants them back—beauty aside, the land must be worth a fortune," Andy said, ignoring my comment about Art, and missing my point altogether.

"It must," my mother agreed. "The land alone is worth a mint."

My concerns about her plans for the house flared again. I hoped my mother wouldn't use the chapel to justify selling Art the land. I wanted to say something, but with Andy there, I really couldn't. And maybe I couldn't anyway: it wasn't my business, as both she and Blake had so clearly pointed out.

They finished their wine and invited me once more to join them. I waved from the porch as they pulled out. I collected my clothes from the dryer and carried them upstairs, where I spent half an hour putting things in order, lining the note cards about Rose up on the desk like a school project. Then I left, slipping on my jeans and a long-forgotten pair of heeled sandals that I'd found in the back of my closet, glad to get away from the house, the empty e-mail. I rolled the Impala windows down all the way, the rushing air tangling my hair. As I reached the village I had to slow down because the traffic was so thick. I parked behind Dream Master and crossed through the gravel lot to the dock.

Keegan was waiting for me, standing with his hands in the pockets of his cargo shorts, looking down the outlet to the place where it curved and disappeared into the trees. The outlet was calm and clear, the turbulent waters after the rain having receded. I shook off the memory of Max by the foaming water. From this distance, Keegan hardly looked older than he had in high school, though he'd traded his motorcycle for a van with side airbags, and his leather jacket for a windbreaker. I waved, smiling as if I were a teenager again. First with the arguments at the house and then with that kiss on the shore, I'd fallen in, been swept headlong into the dynamics of the past, which I thought I'd left behind.

Keegan gave me his hand to help me into the boat. He sat behind the wheel, engaged the motor, and chugged slowly through the outlet to the lake. People were strolling, holding hands, eating ice cream; some of them waved from the sidewalk. We passed under the bridge and then traveled past the marina. Blake was on the deck of his boat, and I waved as we glided out into the open water, feeling contrite because I'd leaked his secret. I'd been angry with him about the land, angry with my mother, too, and I'd spoken without thinking. He waved back, and Keegan pressed the throttle hard. We took off, bouncing over the waves. He was relaxed, comfortable with the lake and the speed, like athletes so born to their sport that they seem to become other creatures when they swim or leap or run. Keegan in a boat had always been that way.

It was twilight when we started, the wealthy homes and the scars on the land all faded into the same dusk. The sky had deepened into darkness by the time Keegan finally slowed down in the middle of the lake. It was a clear night, the stars vivid, and even out this deep the water was smooth and calm.

"You thirsty?" he asked, opening the cooler stashed at his feet and pulling out a bottle of wine.

"Sounds nice, thanks. It's a pretty night."

"Doesn't get any better," he agreed. He opened the wine and poured some into plastic glasses, and we floated, not speaking, comfortable in the silence, the night growing deeper around us. *On a boat,* Rose had written, *you are no place at all.*

Maybe it was the darkness, or the quiet, but I found myself telling Keegan about my dreams, the things I'd lost in the foliage and the trees and could never piece together once I finally found them, the wallet that had been lost and held for me for so many years, my identity sealed inside.

"I had dreams like those once," he said. "A kind of series, not exactly the same. It was during the time when I was wandering around a lot, after I got out of art school, before I came back here. I was on a ship to Mexico. I'd got on it in California. It was a freighter, and they gave me work, and though I could speak enough Spanish at that point to get the jobs done and even joke around a little with the rest of the crew, I couldn't really join in when they got together in the evening for a drink. There were a couple of other foreigners on the crew, but they didn't speak much English, either. So I was alone a lot. Alone at sea. Not much to do but read the couple of paperbacks I'd thought to bring. Read and think. Work and sleep and dream.

"I started having this recurring dream around that time. It was in a forest, too, like yours, except I was always following a path, the trees getting thicker and denser and the trail more faint, and there was always a moment when I looked down and realized I wasn't human anymore—I'd transformed into some sort of animal, a different one each night. A lynx, a wolf, a panther—something fierce and seeking."

"And what happened? How did they end?"

"We got to Mexico. I got off the boat. There was a bus, and the name of the company was Linea de Los Lobos—Line of the Wolves. So it seemed kind of like a sign, and I got on. I took it to the last stop, which was a beautiful village in the highlands. I stayed there for a year. Fell in love, learned to speak the language. Then I got word that my mother was sick, so I came back."

I nodded, drank a little more. I wondered who Keegan had been in love with. The patterns of his life were largely unknown to me, no matter how familiar he seemed.

"You came back," I repeated. "And how was that, at first?"

Waves lapped at the boat. Keegan finished his wine before he answered.

"Truthfully? I didn't think about it. I didn't think about it as I was coming back. It was just something I was doing for the time being. Then I met Beth. Even then, I kept telling her I wasn't planning to stick around, I didn't want to get serious." He gave a short laugh. "She's a good person, Beth. She didn't deserve a lot of the things I did. Out of sadness, when my mother died. Out of a feeling that I'd taken a wrong turn somewhere and ended up in a life I hadn't really intended to lead. Talk about dreams—toward the end, after Max was born, I kept dreaming that I walked out the front door and found myself transformed into a lynx again, wandering in a city I didn't know."

"So you think they're important, then? Dreams?"

"Oh, yeah. You know, the Iroquois take dreams very seriously. They see them as the secret wishes of the soul—the heart's desire, so to speak. Not all dreams, maybe, but the important ones. And when they recur, I tend to think they're important. I kept dreaming of the lynx when I was in the village, too. Then I'd be rushing through a jungle or swimming a river at night in a dream. This was during a time when I'd stopped doing any creative work, and the lynx kept taking me to fields where things were growing, or rivers where fish were leaping out and piling on the shore. So I knew I had to get back to a creative life again, a life of making things. It wasn't just the bus, the outward journey. It was where it was taking me inwardly, as well. And that was true later, too."

We were drifting near the middle of the lake. Below the water the land fell three hundred, four hundred, five hundred feet deep, a point where even at the height of day no light traveled through to reach the depths. For a second I felt breathless, imagining the vast water below and the vast air above, and myself so small, floating in the midst of all that space. I thought about all my dreams of lost spheres falling into pieces.

"I don't know. My dreams don't make a lot of sense."

"Maybe you haven't dreamed enough," he suggested.

"Maybe not."

I was thinking of Japan then, the faces of all those people floating just beneath the surface of the water, the jolting earth, the way I jerked out of sleep, paralyzed by the responsibility I felt to fix whatever had gone wrong. We drifted for a time, lost in our own thoughts.

"I've never told those dreams to anyone else," Keegan said after a while.

"I guess I haven't, either." This was true. Yoshi had never asked to know what the dreams were about, but had simply turned and held me whenever I woke up from one.

"That's good. You should be careful, sharing dreams."

I thought of Rose, revealing her life's dream in the ruins of the monastery, and of Joseph, his dreams like a net to snare the future.

"You know," Keegan said, "after your father died I used to take the boat out and float in the water near your house, watching people move through the lighted rooms inside, hoping for a glimpse of you."

"You did?"

His face wasn't visible in the darkness, so I couldn't tell what he might be feeling, though I remembered the numbed sense of loss and guilt that spread over everything and made it impossible for me to feel anything else during that time. I thought of the letters, Rose writing of that moment before she stole the chalice from the church, *that night I was so heartsick I could feel nothing else.* Looking back, I'd been that way, too, for years and years, shutting myself off, pressing sadness and loss down beneath my adventurous and busy days so I wouldn't feel overwhelmed. Now grief engulfed me, as if I'd been walking on a thin crust that had formed on its surface and had broken through, falling suddenly and deeply into its darkness.

"I did. Not forever. Just for a couple of weeks."

"I'm so sorry."

"Are you crying? Look, Lucy, I'm not trying to guilt you. I just wanted you to know that I was thinking about you, even then."

"I know," I said, wiping my eyes. "I'm not really crying."

"You really are."

"It's old stuff, that's all. It's still hard to remember that night, what might have happened, and what did. He was in the garden when you dropped me off. That was the last time I ever saw him."

"Lucy." Keegan took my hand then. He didn't say anything else.

After a minute I pulled myself together and wiped my eyes. "I found out all this stuff about Rose," I said, to change the subject.

We talked a little bit about the chapel then, and the windows, luminous and mysterious, how forcefully they'd stayed with us both. We talked about Suzi and Oliver and what might happen with the land. I told him more about Rose, her dreams, how I'd been trying to understand her life, to reconstruct how her story had ended up woven into the story of this chapel full of windows.

"I'm going back to Seneca Falls on Friday," I said. "I don't know what else I'll find. Maybe nothing. But I'm hoping for the end of the story, or at least to find another piece of it."

"And then what?" Keegan asked. "How long will you stay?"

"Well, then Yoshi comes. And then—I don't know."

Water lapped lightly at the edges of the boat. We were sitting in the back, near the diving platform, and I was vividly aware of Keegan next to me, the faint heat of his body in the evening air.

He slid his hand up my arm, let it rest on my shoulder. I was so tempted then to give in to the powerful currents of desire, to slip back into that familiar way of being, that time before, when Keegan and I were still carefree, driving off into the lake-scented darkness as if we'd live that way forever. That was impossible, though. So much time had passed, so many things had happened. And he had his life here, while I did not.

"Let's swim," I said, pulling back, slipping my shirt over my head. I was wearing a bathing suit underneath; I pushed off my shorts. Before he could answer I was poised on the edge of the boat, and then I dived, cutting deep and clean, the water closing over me. I went down and down, feeling the depth by coldness because there was no light.

I wondered what I would find at the bottom if I could dive far enough, what wreckage I would discover scattered along the landscape beneath the weight of water. Boulders and mud and moss, and the swift movement of dark fish brushing my skin, and maybe the long-lost dinner boat that had caught fire before it sank, and maybe the plates and the forks and the glasses those people had been holding in their hands when they saw the flames and leaped. Maybe their crinolines and corsets, their shoes and boots, discarded as they tried to swim to shore. Maybe my father's lost tackle box or the plane that had gone down fifty years ago, knifing through the clear water just after takeoff, the bodies floating upward, drifting with the currents, miles away. Or maybe I'd find ice picks and axes scattered by the midwinter crew that was out cutting thick blocks for the ice houses when the frozen lake began to tremble and crack under the weight of their sleighs and they fell into the icy water, the men in their thick coats, the horses with their harnesses, the sleigh plummeting until it reached the muddy bottom, dragging everyone along.

My lungs began to spark and I caught myself in all that darkness, the world just the same whether my eyes were closed or open. Threads of panic ran through me. I had to force myself not to move, to let myself float for a second to gain my sense of direction, for there was no light to guide me. I kicked harder, rising, I hoped, rising and not falling, my panic growing because I could not see, could not tell how long until I could breathe, and then I was bursting through the surface, tipping my head back to inhale the beautiful clear night air.

"Damn, Lucy," Keegan said. He was in the water, too, and he took several strokes to reach me, pushing an inner tube into my hands. The rubber was still warm from its day in the sun. "You were down so long. I was beginning to think I'd lost you."

"Thanks," I said, breathing more evenly now.

"Hey." He was treading water next to me and he put one hand on the tube, brought his face close to mine. "You sure you're okay?"

"I will be. It was so dark. Hard to know where the surface was."

Kicking, his foot grazed my calf, the fabric of his shorts drifting along my leg.

"Sorry," he said. He was setting off little currents in the water that rippled all around me. I remembered what Yoshi had said, how he felt I was always trying to keep such a tight rein on everything and then closing down when I couldn't. But from what was I running now? From the bloom of the past, from the life Keegan had made, so rich, so solid, so rooted in this place? Or was I running from Yoshi, or even from myself?

"You're swimming in your clothes," was what I said.

"I am. It seemed like an emergency situation."

Sometimes loneliness, I thought, and remembered Yoshi again, his kindness and long patience with the grief I'd been pressing down and carrying around for so long,

Keegan's foot again, this time running lightly along the length of my leg. His eyes were bright with laughter.

"I'm *not* sorry," he said. "Not that time."

I didn't want to think anymore, I just wanted to go back to that time before everything had changed, and so I turned the inner tube to kiss him the way we used to kiss, in the dark fields, on the dark lake, except that now the water was between us, was around us, and every touch set off currents, his hand stroking my arm, my leg, and the little waves moving between us in reply. It wasn't as if we had never done this, back in the days when we used to slip away at every chance. This was a game we'd played on long summer nights, to see how long we could stay below, every touch amplified because we could not see.

I put an arm around his neck and he had an arm around my waist. He let go of the tube and then I did, and we slipped gently beneath the surface, still kissing, drifting slowly down through the darkness. We weren't falling, we weren't floating, we simply were, warm against each other in the dark night lake, his touch as gentle as the touch of water. My thoughts traveled past the sleighs and sunken ships, the detritus of shattered lives, through the images of the women in the windows, the things they carried, the stories they told. They settled on the image of Max, standing so calmly on the edge of the roiling water, a step away from falling. They flitted away and came finally to my father, standing in his boat, barely visible against the dawn, like a silhouette or a figure in a negative print, and then he fell, he struck his head and went down and down through this same water, he had fallen and fallen and never come back.

All my nightmares were at the bottom of this lake, everything I'd ever lost was there. I pulled away from Keegan and swam back to the surface, breaking through, gasping again in the clear night air. This must have been how it felt to be born into the world, to open my mouth and feel the rush of air for the very first time.

Keegan came up a second later, shaking water from his hair.

"Lucy," he said.

And I said, "I can't, Keegan, I can't."

I swam to the edge of the boat and climbed up the narrow metal ladder. Keegan followed and sat across from me, so close our knees touched.

"Are you sure?" he asked.

I nodded. For the first time in years, I was clear. "I didn't want it to end," I said, meaning both that last kiss in the dark lake and all the time we'd spent together being young and wild, thinking we could go on that way forever. "But I think it had to."

"Do you?" He took my hands in his. His shorts and shirt were cling-ing to his skin. He was still wearing his shoes. He must have been frightened, to dive in after me like that. "Because I have always won-dered, if your father hadn't died, if we might have—look, I just always thought we'd end up together."

"I know. I used to think so, too, I really did. But I was leaving, Keegan. That whole spring, I was. If my father hadn't died, I still would have gone."

I remembered the urgent restlessness I'd felt that final spring, when I was riding wild with Keegan and yet heading every moment to a future I knew would not include him, how I'd chosen a college three thousand miles away.

"You have made such a good life," I said, feeling the truth of those words, thinking of the growing glass, the fire, the clean lines of his apartment, built in a space once deserted, full of debris.

He smiled, a little sadly. "It is a good life. A very good life."

"And Max—he is such a wonderful boy. You wouldn't have Max if we'd ended up together."

He nodded. After a minute he slipped his hands from mine and rested them on his thighs.

"No. That's true."

We were silent for a moment, waves lapping against the side of the boat.

"When is he coming?" Keegan asked. "Your boyfriend from Japan."

"Yoshi. He gets here on Saturday."

"All right." He nodded, gazed past me at the dark lake. "Don't bring him by the glassworks, okay?"

"Okay," I said, though my heart hurt at the thought of how many doors had just swung shut, how many possibilities had just fallen away forever. At the thought of Yoshi, who might or might not come now that I'd traveled so far away, who had not called or sent me anything but that brief e-mail in the last two days.

"Okay." Keegan shifted his gaze back to me, then reached up and touched my cheek lightly with the palm of his hand. "Okay, Lucy in the sky. I suppose we ought to get back to shore."

We didn't speak on that long trip. At the dock, Keegan helped me out, and I hugged him, quickly and awkwardly, filled with regret even though I knew I'd done the right things. He turned his attention to the boat and I walked away, past the glassworks, past Dream Master, which rose up against the starry night sky, shadowing everything even in the dark, and slipped into the Impala.

When I got home, I found a note from my mother on the counter. *Yoshi called,* it said. *Call back.*

There was a message on my phone, too, but I didn't listen. Whatever it was would keep until the morning. I was just too drained to call him back. My lungs still ached. I went upstairs instead without turning on the lights, and got into bed without taking off my still-damp clothes, and lay there suspended in the darkness as if in water, drifting until I finally fell asleep.

Chapter 15

I WOKE UP WITH THE SUN FULL IN MY FACE, AND PUSHED OFF the blankets. I'd been dreaming about Rose, and in my dream she'd been walking around wearing the same clear colors of the windows, her hands pale, translucent. The events of the evening before came flooding back as I showered and dressed, leaving me feeling strangely empty, as if I'd finally shed something I'd been carrying with me all these years, in all my travels. I went back into the bedroom and called Yoshi, who picked up on the second ring. I lay back on the narrow bed and closed my eyes, filled with a surprising sense of relief to hear his voice, to remember the sure weave of our days, the sound of his even breathing in the room at night, even when the earth was so unsteady.

"Hi," I said. "What's up? Where have you been?"

"I'm back in the hotel," he said. "I've got an early flight out. Didn't you get my message?"

"I was out. Also, my phone was dead." This was true, but it was also true that I'd been avoiding the Internet and hadn't bothered to charge my phone.

"Ah. I've been on the island. No Internet. Kind of nice. And it was beautiful, let me tell you. Neil and Julie send their best."

"I wish I could have been there," I said. The water in that sea was so clear. Vivid fish darted through the gardens of coral, and the world was silent except for the rush of air in the tanks. I'd learned to dive in college, and I'd convinced Yoshi to come with me when we first met. He didn't think he'd like it, but after that first dive he was hooked. "I'll pick you up tomorrow. At noon, right?"

"That's right. I transit in Tokyo. Then New York. Then Rochester. Is it warm there? Because I didn't bring much, and I packed for the tropics."

"It's not that warm," I said. "But I think you'll be okay. We have stores here, you know."

He laughed, a low, familiar sound, and I laughed, too, though my eyes teared up because I was so glad to be talking to him again.

"I'm glad you're coming," I told him. "I thought you might not. I'm sorry I've been so distracted." I'd have to tell him about Keegan, but I wanted to do it in person.

He was quiet for a minute. "I'm glad I'm coming, too," he said. "I'm ready for a change."

"Right—what's your news?" I asked. "Anything happen in your meetings?"

"Yeah, it's work stuff," he said.

"Did you negotiate the bridge?"

"Well, yes. The bridge is going through. This is what I've heard, anyway."

I waited.

"Well, I was going to tell you in person. But I guess I'll tell you now. I quit, Lucy. I turned in my resignation letter yesterday."

"Really?" I was too stunned to say more.

"Yes. It seemed like the only thing to do. I couldn't support the decision on the bridge. And it was pretty clear that if I kept making waves, I'd eventually be fired."

"But how could they fire you? You're so good."

"I'm good, true, but I disagreed. Which is to say I was disagreeable, at least in the view of management. I was not a team player. I heard this from three different people, who all said I needed to consider my future as I went into these Jakarta discussions. So after I talked with you the last time, I did. I went for a long walk the night before, you know, down that street where the night market is? I walked and I thought, and I couldn't see a future where I had to keep silent all the time about things that really matter to me. In the meeting I spoke up in favor of rerouting the bridge, and after the meeting I offered my resignation letter. I thought they might not accept it, but they did, so I packed my stuff and went snorkeling with Julie and Neil."

"So you're unemployed," I said, feeling the same admiration I'd felt for Yoshi as when we had worked in the orphanage, but also as if I were free-falling through space. "We're both unemployed."

"Well, needless to say, the Indonesians really like me," he said, trying to joke. "I might apply for a position with them."

"Jakarta was a good place for us," I agreed, a little giddy with how quickly everything was changing.

"Don't worry, Lucy," he said. "This is freedom."

"If you say so."

He was so quiet I thought the connection had been lost.

"Come on," he finally said. "I felt I had no choice, Lucy. So I'm trying to be positive. I shouldn't have told you until I saw you face-to-face."

"It's okay," I said, as much to myself as to Yoshi. "It's only a job, right? And soon we'll see each other, face-to-face." I tried to make my voice calm, but I still felt like I was falling through the sky, no earth in sight. If this was freedom, it was also more than a little terrifying. Yoshi's tone was light, but he took his work seriously, and this job in a country he'd felt was his own had mattered to him more than others. He'd kept such long hours and worked so hard, and I knew this must be difficult for him. "Yoshi, I'm really sorry about the job."

"Don't worry. I have some ideas."

"All right. Wow—well. So, I guess I'll see you Saturday."

"Yes. I'll dream my way over the Arctic."

After we hung up, I stood in the patch of sunlight on the floor, the room around me just the same as it had been seconds before, though everything else was shifting, changing. I thought about practical things, wondering if we'd have health insurance, enough savings to finish off the three months on our lease.

The beautiful piece of glass I'd made with Keegan was sitting on the white dresser. A thin shaft of sunlight radiated through it, making the colors glow. I picked it up and held it, warm and heavy in my hand, thinking of Rose a hundred years ago, writing, *I do not know what will become of me.*

I spent the day sitting by the lake, listening to the shifting shale, the steady waves, rereading all of Rose's letters until I nearly knew them by heart. I thought about her life, and compared it with my own, which I'd always thought of as greatly adventurous, but which had in fact been much easier and safer than hers. She'd gone off to a new country with no money and barely the promise of a job, expecting a child. No health insurance for her, no social network, no family except her brother. It must have been terrifying. Yet she was strong and independent, and she had never given up, even though the circumstances and social mores of her time had left her at a great disadvantage. It was inspiring, really, to consider what she'd faced, and with what spirit she'd faced it, and I longed to know more. Taking the kayak out, I looked back at the house, so far away and small and insubstantial from this distance, and wished I could have known her, or known about her, growing up.

On Friday morning I got up before my mother was awake. I left her a note on the counter and drove straight to Seneca Falls. My curator was back, wearing a cotton dress in a dark orange print. She was tan, and had changed all her earrings into citrus-colored studs, bright seeds. She smiled when she saw me, but her eyes were red behind her glasses and she cleared her throat before she spoke.

"Hi. Thought you'd be back today. Just sign in. The boxes are out and ready for you, on the table upstairs. I kept the letter, because the director is coming this afternoon and I think she needs to see it—in case it's important historically, you know."

I nodded, relieved, mostly; I'd been afraid the boxes would already have been locked away, out of bounds. I felt no guilt at all over the letters I had taken, sitting at home in the manila folder marked "Rose."

"Thanks. Can I see that letter, at least? Just for a minute? I did some research over the weekend and I'd like to cross-check it with what I found."

"I made you a copy, actually. I could tell you were serious. Here."

She handed me the pages, Rose Jarrett's sharp handwriting cast into shadowy tones of black and white and gray.

"Thanks." I started to leave, eager to get upstairs, but hesitated, turned back. "You okay?"

She gave a short laugh and waved her hand. "Yeah, I'm fine, I'll be fine. Big fight with the boyfriend, that's all."

"I'm sorry. Hey—at least you got a great tan."

"A great tan and about three thousand mosquito bites. I forgot the bug spray. Mea culpa, to be sure. But would you break up with someone over that?"

"I might not be the best person to ask," I told her, because I had, in fact, over the years broken up with people for reasons every bit as trivial, determined not to assume any complications or emotional baggage, determined—though I could not see it then—not to let anyone too close. That's what I'd finally realized out on the lake with Keegan. It had been easy enough, living the global life I'd led, to keep myself free of any attachments, even to feel noble in my pursuit of the next great job. I hadn't often paused to consider the people—or the possibilities—I'd left behind. I thought of them now, though, all the romantic partners I'd kept at arm's length. Whatever ended up happening with Yoshi, at least I hadn't run away. Though I'd come close.

"It was just bug spray," she said, and sighed.

"You know what? I'm pretty sure you're better off without him."

A phone rang, and as she answered it I went up the curving staircase. The last big box was waiting on the walnut table with the others, as promised. Light filtered in through the lace curtains and made patterns on the polished wood. The air smelled of dust and old paper. Rows and rows of books lined the shelves and I let my eyes linger on the sturdy spines, thinking how human books were, so full of ideas and images, worlds imagined, worlds perceived; full of fingerprints and sudden laughter and the sighs of readers, too. It was humbling to consider all these authors, struggling with this word or that phrase, recording their thoughts for people they'd never meet. In that same way, the detritus of the boxes was humbling—receipts, jotted notes, photos with no inscriptions, all of it once held together by the fabric of lives now finished, gone.

I was methodical this time, not digging aimlessly, but making little stacks according to type. Downstairs the door opened and closed, voices drifting; the phone rang. I sipped my cold coffee, and searched.

I had my eyes open for a binder like the one in which I'd found the other letters, but it wasn't until halfway through the last box that I found several more envelopes, this time held together with two ancient rubber bands that crumbled when I tried to pull them off. The handwriting on the top one was familiar, Rose's sharp and slanted script, and my scientific training was no help to me then; my hands trembled. I scanned through them quickly, not stopping to read, not yet, aware of the time. More notes, ledgers, birthday cards from friends, and, every now and then, another letter. I set these aside as I found them. When the box was finally empty, I settled back in the chair and began to read.

30 April 1915

Dearest Iris,

Today is your 4th birthday. Joseph writes that you are well. He sent me a little drawing you made, the figure of a person with two big eyes and stick legs. There was also a cat, which must be Shadow, because you have drawn him with a black crayon. And you wrote your name, the letters so big, in dark blue, the same color as your eyes. Good for you! I will see you soon, I am saving the money to come and see you. To make a life for you here.

Since it hurts my heart to imagine you there without me, I will write to

*you about this life here, which is so different than any life I have ever lived
or imagined. The people here are not like any I have known. They come
and go, so many. People gather here almost every evening to debate the
issues of the day. They are so passionate, arguing about the plight of workers and the situation of women. They are artists and nurses, teachers and
even some lawyers, musicians, too. Books and ideas fill the rooms. Sometimes the fierce discussions transform into music and singing, or recitations.
A few actors come, and sometimes the baker from next door, and the
woman whose husband oversees a museum. In this company I am often
quiet. I can hardly keep up with the swift wit, the arguments. But no one
minds. People drift over to talk. I feel I have many friends here.*

*I made a new friend last week. Her name is Beatrice. She came to me
during one of the evenings when they were acting out a skit in the living
room. She is petite, the mother of four children, the oldest not much younger
than I am, and she is almost as quiet as I am in a crowded room. Her eyes
are dark and sparkle with life and follow everything. She told me that I
have an interesting face and quite extraordinary eyes, that she had been
observing me for some time. Her husband is an artist and she thinks he
would like very much to paint me. He would pay me to model and it would
not be much work, and I could do it easily even after my long days. Thank-
fully, I am not in the factories. Vivian heard of an elderly woman who
needed a companion, and so I spend my days in her grand house, walking
the miles back here in the evening, glad for any weather after the hours and
hours inside, bent over whatever tasks she gives me.*

*Because I want the money so, because it would bring me closer to you,
I said yes about the modeling. The artist is Frank Westrum. She acted as
if I should have heard of him, but of course I have not.*

*When I asked Vivian if this would be a good and honest thing to do, she
said quite emphatically that it would be, indeed it was an honor.*

*I must tell you of Vivian. I have been in this city for six months now
and she has become my good friend. At least, I hope we are friends,
because I admire her so. I am grateful to her, also. This is her house, you
see, and many people live here, and we share resources and the work.*

Vivian is much younger than Mrs. Elliot, maybe even ten years. Her mother died when she was born and her father died while she was still in school. This is the family home. I think she once lived a very merry life, with parties and gowns and dinners and theater. And yet she was moved by work she had done to help the poor, the women she met who could hardly afford to feed their children. So after a time she began to study nursing, and to hold these salons. She knows everyone. Twice a week she goes out to the poorest of the poor, to their dim homes, crowded and spare yet often immaculate, tending to their illnesses, leaving without pay.

I know, because sometimes I go with her.

It is very difficult to see such suffering. And yet it is a relief in some way, for I see how desperate lives can be, and feel thankful for my own. I feel I was right to leave you in my brother's home, in comfort, in safety, however much it grieves me still.

Now it is late, so late, I am tired. Sleep well, sweet birthday girl, and dream of

> *Your loving mother, Rose.*

I put the letter down on the table. So, I'd been right; she had modeled for him, if not in the studio in Rochester, then earlier, in New York City. I wondered if their relationship had been more than artist and model. Beatrice was her friend, and I didn't want to imagine that Rose had betrayed her. I understood Oliver a little bit better in that moment, the fierce attachment he'd formed to Frank Westrum and his reluctance to have that persona challenged in any way. I found my phone and pulled up the picture I'd kept, the one of the Joseph window in Keegan's studio. The image was so small, but I stared at it, trying to decipher the woman's features, wondering if it was Rose, and if so, what she had been thinking as she stood in his silent studio, letting him draw her image late into the night.

The next was a card, white stock, with the initials CWE in gold script.

2 May 1916

My dear Rose,

I hope this letter finds you as well as I left you after my visit. It gladdens my heart a great deal to see you are happy in your new life, and to know that your brave stand for the rights of women did not end completely badly. I promised to write to you of Iris, and I am happy to report that she is very well. I saw her yesterday, playing in the front yard with dolls made out of fabric, and when I paused and spoke to her she spoke to me so nicely, with fine manners and, I am delighted to say, a lively and curious intellect as well. She is thriving. You would be proud. I will check on her from time to time and write with any news. Meanwhile, rest your heart—she is safe and very well.

> *Yours truly, Nelia*

Another brief letter, in the familiar bold handwriting.

17 May 1916

Dear Sister,

Iris had her 5th birthday in the garden. Cora baked a cake that looked like a flower, gold and white icing and yellow custard in the center. We had lemonade. Iris has a new purple dress and new shoes, too. Cora put away her mourning clothes last month. I work the farm but I am looking into starting a lock business. I have a knack with locks.

Mrs. Elliot told me she saw you. She said you are fine. I have a hard time listening to that woman. She is still causing all sorts of trouble about the vote. I am studying to become a citizen and you should, too.

> *Joseph*

10 September 1916

Dear Sister,

Your letter arrived and I am glad to know Mother and Father are well. Ellen wrote to me, too. I married Cora yesterday. It has been a year since

Jesse died, we have waited. I asked Cora but she doesn't think you should return to this house. I was hoping this was Jesse's view, but it is hers, too. I am sorry. I am sorry I did not see you, too. I did not establish an account with the money you sent because there have been expenses, for clothes and new shoes and also books. I have spent wisely. Iris is happy, she plays in the garden all the time.

> *Joseph*

The next letter in the pile was thick, written by Rose and dated earlier that same summer, written on thin paper with garlands of light blue flowers—forget-me-nots, I realized—framing the corners.

> *June 1916*

Dearest Iris,

I saw you today, playing outside. You are so grown up! Your hair is so long—and you had grown tall. But I knew it was you. I stood beneath the oak tree in Mrs. Elliot's front yard, and I watched you. I can hardly describe how full and happy my heart was in that moment.

It had been almost a year and a half since I had seen you. Finally, I had saved enough money to visit. It was the modeling that made it possible. It was hard to sit in the studio evening after evening, for it was cold in the winter and stifling in the summer, and I had to hold every muscle very still, even when I was about to faint with fatigue. Watch your eyelids, he'd warn, hold your chin a little higher, and I would do my best. He is a kind man, if somewhat gruff and abrupt, and my friend Beatrice is kind, too. Sometimes she teaches me design, for she studied before she married and she is very, very good.

So I sat, and worked, and saved, and I came to see you.

It is June, the first bloom of summer, but it was chilly when I arrived. Like spring, like March, instead. I meant to see Joseph, of course, and to pay a visit to Cora, whose name is Jarrett now, though she does not feel like a sister. It was overcast and you had taken out all your winter things again—the blue coat and the pale blue hat and mittens I had fashioned to send to you at Christmas. I left my suitcase on Mrs. Elliot's porch and walked across the street, so impatient to see you, to touch you. The mittens were falling from your hands, dangling from your wrists on the little strings I had made, and your hat was off, too, bouncing against your back, and your coat swinging open, because it really was not very cold, revealing your sunshine dress. The hollyhocks were blooming, their soft bell shapes hanging from the tall stems, and you picked some and began to shape them into dolls—an unopened bud for the head, the blooming flower for a skirt. We used to do this together, I taught you how. You were intent, and did not look up until I squatted down beside you. Then you pushed your hair from your face and smiled.

"I'm making dolls," you said. "Do you want to help?"

"Yes, I'll help. They're very pretty."

"My mother taught me," she said, and this pierced me with joy, because even though you did not know me right away, you certainly remembered.

"Your mother loves you so much," I said.

"I know. She's pretty and she made me these mittens."

"Those are very nice mittens," I said, and I remembered sitting downstairs, knitting those mittens for your little hands, while conversations swirled around me.

"I got them in my stocking. They were put away. Mama says I may play with them awhile, but I must put them back, I mustn't get them dirty."

I waited for a heartbeat, two, then three, taking in the meaning of your words.

"Who said you must put the mittens away?"

"Mama said. Mama Cora. Did you come to see her? She's in the kitchen, making bread."

"No," I said, and then I could not say more.

You finished your flower doll and handed it to me.

"I made it for you," you said. "You are a pretty lady." And then you stood up and ran off, laughing.

I let you go, your pale blue mittens flashing against the folds of your coat.

I had to pause. I stood up and walked to the window, which overlooked the expansive front lawn, and watched cars travel up and down the street. I was filled with compassion for Rose, squatting on the damp ground with the daughter who did not know her, and there was nothing to do with this emotion because Rose was gone, long dead. I thought of my great-grandfather, whose story had seemed so seamless from our vantage point in history, struggling in his early years to start Dream Master Locks, taking care of a child who was not his own, married to a woman with endless aspirations for their lives. Close-up, their lives were as complex and chaotic as my own, full of mistakes and disappointments and good intentions gone awry. I felt duped, for I'd believed in the clear-cut heroic arc of my great-grandfather's life, and I'd known nothing of Rose, erased from the family lore as surely as if she hadn't existed. I went back to the letters to find out what she'd done next.

When you left I walked and walked, far out of the village and down the rutted country lanes, the flower doll wilting in my hand. I found myself at the edge of the lake. Foam made a lacy trim to the cold gray water. I wept. I had not imagined this. You were always so present that I never imagined I was all the time fading from your mind.

I want you to know how I struggled. I sat down on a large stone, waves lapping near my toes, and tried to think what I should do. I could see two possibilities. I could go back to the house and announce that you were mine and take you with me back to the city. Vivian would make a place and so would the others. No one would ask about your father, they would assume he had died in the war.

But what would you do, while I was at work? And I must work. And how would you feel about my tiny attic room? Would Cora let you go, or would she argue that I was unfit, because I'd been to jail, because of the work I do with Vivian, traveling among the poor?

What life could I give you? A life of the mind, rich with artists, laboring their creations—you would have that. You would be loved, certainly. But there are no other children in this house. And however deep the pleasures are for me in this community, would it be fair to bring you here, to bring you up here? For I have been to jail, it is true. Many others have, too. We are marked with our pasts, and with our present convictions. Almost weekly, I walk through streets of desperate poverty. I climb dark and narrow stairs to flats where so many children linger in the shadows. They do not go to school because there is not enough money to buy them all clothes, and they are afraid, perhaps because their mother is ill and expecting another child whose birth she might not survive, or because their father has been hurt in an accident and cannot work. Whatever slender thread of hope they have is fraying with every second. They work in the factories, these children, girls of 11 or 12 already hunched over machines, boys hauling wheelbarrows full of coal to fuel the furnaces, or they make flowers of cloth until they drop.

Would I have you there, in the midst of this?

Also, though I do not love this work of Vivian's, I know it is important. And when I do it, I feel whole.

The lake was a cold gray-blue. I kept seeing you, running across the lawn, your beautiful mittens flashing. Anger churned within me. I tried to let it go. To still myself, and think what would be best. One thing I knew was this: to act rashly, out of anger, would be wrong. I wanted to be sure that my love for you was something that did not put my own feelings first, but rather looked from the outside, as a stranger might, and considered what would be the best for you, my beautiful and beloved daughter.

For this is what I have learned, in my short life: do not act out of anger. Act from love, or not at all.

I have seen it, how anger makes a space for what I must call evil. This is what I had come to understand, going with Vivian through the turmoiled streets, into the buildings where people suffered, where they died, and where grief and anger infected those who loved them as surely as any illness did, as insidious as any virus. I used to have a simpler idea. I used to think there was good and there was evil, that Geoffrey Wyndham was evil because he left me, left us. I thought his family was evil, too, because they lived carefree in the grand house while others labored on their land and hardly had enough to eat and were nothing in their eyes.

This is what I used to think, that some people were simply good and others were not, and that I, of course, was good. But now I think instead that evil is a force in the world, a force that seeks, and it finds its way into our lives through anger and loss, through sadness and betrayal, like mold on bread, like rot on an apple, it takes hold.

I was angry in the ruins when they laughed, shutting a door on the way I loved God and loved the church. I was blinded by anger when I stole the chalice because it bore the name of people who had hurt me.

And I was possessed by anger to think that Cora had let you forget me, had erased me—your mother—from your life.

I could have picked you up and boarded the train and made a life for you here.

But you were happy, well cared for.

It was my own brother who would raise you.

And Cora, though I do not admire her, though she does not like me, loves you.

I sat on the boulder on the edge of the lake for a long time. My legs were numb when I finally stood. I walked all the way back to town, gravel on the edges of the road crackling beneath my boots. Mrs. Elliot made me sit by the fire, and when I told her the decision I had reached, she did not scold me or try to change my mind, but only put her arm around my shoulders and said, Dear Rose, I am sorry to have brought this terrible sadness into your life. And I replied it was not she who brought it, but my own decisions, every time. And that is true.

I wrote to Joseph. I enclosed all the money I had saved for you. And in the morning I got up and carried my bag to the station. I traveled all day and all night and I did not sleep. The handle of the suitcase cut into my hand as I walked. I welcomed that pain because it was real, it was physical, and I knew it would someday end.

That is all, then, Iris dear. Sweet child of my heart.

My throat was tight by the time I finished reading.

There were several letters left. I still had an hour, but suddenly I wanted to get away, to read the rest of these in a private place, to be sure I had them with me and could keep them safe. For the director, however well intentioned, might lose them. Or, if Oliver ever found these, he would want to display them in a glass case in the Westrum House and add Rose as a footnote to Frank Westrum's story. Whatever their historical value to the world, these letters were personal, first. They'd been written by a woman lost in my family, and though they hadn't been written to me, though I'd been decades from being born when her hand had moved across these pages, I felt quite powerfully that they were somehow meant for me to find, nonetheless.

I put all the other papers back in the box. The letters I folded carefully and put into my bag. I left the historical society, waving to the curator, who was on the phone, and walked down the wide streets with their tall trees. There was a little park that overlooked a small lake that had been engineered when the canal was built to contain the falls. Underneath the tranquil water were whole streets and factories, abandoned, flooded, silent in the currents. A boat glided past, headed for the locks. I sat down on the grass, pulled another letter from my bag, and read.

14 October 1916

Dearest Iris,

Five months have passed since I saw you in the garden, and though the pain of leaving you has not gone away, the days have passed. Lately they have passed in such a way that I have become convinced that I did the right thing to leave you there. For you see, I have gone to jail again.

You know that I go with Vivian when she visits the homes of the poor. More and more, I go. These visits are not joyous. On almost every one the mother will send the children into another room or scatter them outside, and she will beg to know how she might keep from having another child. Perhaps she has seven children already; perhaps she has been told she will die if she has another. Perhaps her husband drinks and loses every job he gets, perhaps he works hard and cannot find a job, perhaps he is sick. Perhaps she is powerless, as I once was. It does not matter. For us to tell her what we know is not legal. The information we possess about the basic physiological facts of life is illegal to convey. Mr. Comstock saw to that. Vivian used to be afraid of this law. She kept silent. Then she watched a woman who had begged for information die in childbirth, and the child died, too. So now when they ask, she speaks. I do, too. There is no kindness in this law, no mercy.

Though we put ourselves at risk, we tell them what we know. When we heard that Mrs. Sanger and her sister Mrs. Byrne would open a family planning clinic, we made up our minds to volunteer. It was a windy day. Before the clinic opened, the line stretched for several city blocks. We helped hand out information. That is all we did—we handed out booklets with facts about the body. I hope, if you should ever read this letter, that you will be astonished that such simple actions should cause such great consternation and uproar. The lines grew and grew each day, but on the 26th of October the police arrived and closed the clinic and arrested us all.

Beatrice and Frank came to get us, she so quick and plump and outraged, he silent as always, standing firm and tall beside her. We walked out with them from the white-tiled cells. Mrs. Sanger will go on trial and Mrs. Byrne is still in jail and has embarked upon a hunger strike. We fear she will die but she says it makes no difference if she dies, when thousands of women die each year in childbirth because they were kept in ignorance, helpless to decide their own fates. Everywhere people speak of her, in the subway crowds, on street corners. I heard one man say "They are imprisoning a woman for teaching physiological facts!" And this is so.

I am glad now, Iris, that you are not here to see your mother arrested and sent to jail. Still, I never stop thinking of you and wondering how you are, what small pleasures fill your days.

> *Your loving mother, Rose*

I checked the date again—1916. This history, told through Rose's eyes, didn't seem very far away, and it made me wonder how my own life would have unfolded if I hadn't been able to study or work or even know the most basic facts about my body. A difficult history was hidden beneath my independence, like the ruins of the factories beneath the tranquil surface of this water. The rights I took for granted seemed suddenly very new, measured against the centuries. I picked up the next letter and began to read.

3 March 1920

Dear Iris,

Today I received a letter from Joseph saying that you were well, that he and Cora were well, that everyone in the household has survived the influenza, though so many have died in the village. For this I am deeply grateful—I trembled to open his letter, fearing it would say otherwise. Today I went to the little church. For many years I did not go at all. I felt I could not, because I was still angry. But I have been to many funerals of late, and after one I stayed when all the people had left. I sat in the silence. I let myself feel all the fear and sadness and anger that had driven me away for so many years. I let myself feel sorry, too, for the mistakes I have made in my life. The silence was great. After a time, I cannot explain it, the silence was a comfort. I felt a little as I used to feel as a young girl. And so I went back. Sometimes I go to the services. And sometimes I go alone and sit in the silence. This morning, when I got the letter saying you were well, this is what I did.

It is hard to express the joy your good health gives to me. Here the epidemic has taken so many. Vivian has been ill for several weeks. I, too, recover slowly. The parties in this house, those fierce, exciting meetings, ended with the war, of course. Now we receive news daily of friends who have been infected with this influenza or who have died. The closest to me, the deepest and saddest loss, is my dear friend Beatrice, who seemed perfectly healthy and who even came to assist when Vivian was so ill, and who may have come to me when I was sick, I can't remember. But then she herself fell so swiftly into a feverish delirium and did not know who I was. I held her hand, but she did not rouse or speak to us. She died within a day.

So it is with this disease. The world changes overnight.

They say the right to vote will finally pass this year. She did not live to see it.

Frank is nearly inconsolable. Quietly so. He sits in the dark house day after day. His work had fallen out favor and he will not adopt the popular artistic fads, and so he was insular even before this loss. Beatrice was his interface with the world, and his buffer to its blows, and she is gone. I bring him cornstarch pudding and keep him company for an hour or two, but there is not much more I can do. I am 24 and he is 48 and I cannot pretend to know his grief.

30 April 1921

Dear Iris,

I cannot believe it—you are ten years old today. I think of that sweet morning when you were born, the flowers blooming outside the window. The moment I held you I felt that I had known you all my life. Mrs. Elliot is here to visit for two weeks. She is helping pack up the house. She told me she had seen you turning cartwheels and had paused to cheer you on. She also brought a photograph of you dressed in lace and pleated cotton. You are so serious. Maybe Cora told you to be still. I wish I could see you smile. Joseph writes very little, occupied with his business. Locks, the sort that clamp onto a door, the sort both he and I could open with a touch.

Mrs. Elliot told me all this amid the packing. These beloved rooms are stripped and filled with boxes, the shapes of absent furniture bright on the faded walls.

Vivian will go to live with Mrs. Elliot in The Lake of Dreams. She promises to watch out for you and write to me of you, too. Poor Vivian has never completely recovered her strength—she who used to be so active—and this house is too big and too empty and simply too much. It has been sold; our days here are numbered, dwindling one by one.

Frank, too, has gone—to Rochester. He finds the city cold, but peaceful. He writes that he is happy. We still miss Beatrice, his beloved wife and my dear friend, and it is a comfort to speak of her. In the wake of her death Frank was disconsolate for so long that I feared he might never regain himself. He seemed disengaged from life, and did not even care about his art. So I stayed sometimes and made him tea. This is how it began. Quietly, with a mutual respect and friendship and the memory of Beatrice, whom we both loved.

And now we love each other. I have agreed to go to Rochester when this house is all packed away. But I will not marry him, or anyone. Nor will I live with him. He has bought a house near the center of the city, and I have taken a room in the house of a woman I knew slightly in the days of our splendid parties. Her name is Lydia Langhammer. She is a nurse. I have already begun to write in search of work.

So I will see Frank every day and have that pleasure, and I will always be able to go to my own room and shut the door and delight in my solitude, too.

Dear girl, may you grow in wisdom and in kindness, always.

> *Love, your mother Rose*

> *1 October 1925*

Dearest Iris,

Oh, my dear, I saw you today. I spoke to you. You do not know who I am, you think only that I am a friend of Mrs. Elliot, and her niece Mrs. Stokley. I gave you a false name, Rose Westrum. True enough in heart. Perhaps you found me too intense, perhaps you noticed that our eyes have such a similar look—the same blue, as changeable as water. I found you utterly beautiful, perfect in every way. When another guest remarked on our resemblance, you were not exactly pleased. You are 14, and I am 30, so to you I am old. There is no one save Mrs. Elliot who knows of our connection, even Mrs. Stokley who took you in does not know.

You were glad to leave The Lake of Dreams. I do not blame you, though I wish you had not run away and put yourself in so much danger. I wish also that you did not have to work, but I am glad that the work is good.

I am glad you can take classes at the college. I always send money to Mrs. Elliot for little things you might like, and I was so happy to see you wearing the blue cardigan with tiny buttons that she had given you. And I feel glad somehow to know that the famous author who once lived down the street was born and died in the same light beneath which I once stood, dreaming that the world would shift and change, or even end.

Love from Rose, your mother

I walked the few blocks to the car, following the wide purple path that had been painted on the sidewalk, mulling over the letters, the complex arc of Rose's life, glad she'd found happiness, gladder still that she'd seen Iris again, even if her presence had remained forever secret. Iris had been born in 1911, which meant she could still be alive, though she'd be in her midnineties by now, and of course I had no way to begin to look for her. I slid inside the sun-hot car. When I put my bag with its stolen letters on the floor, I hit the glove compartment door with my elbow, and it swung open. I hadn't thought to look inside before, and it was empty except for three pencils, never sharpened, their orangey-pink erasers intact and hardened with age, the marina logo my father had designed printed on them in blue. He must have left them here one day long ago, when he'd taken the car out for a Sunday drive. I wondered if anyone did that anymore, drove just for pleasure. How odd, for that matter, that this storage space was still called a glove compartment, left from a time when women wore gloves whenever they went out. I wondered where my father had been going, what he'd been thinking about, that day. I snapped the little door shut, and slipped the pencils into my bag next to the letters Rose had written and received. And then I drove back over roads that were becoming so familiar, through the start-stop traffic in the villages, through the verdant fields rippling in the evening breeze. Tomorrow I'd get up and drive back to pick Yoshi up in Rochester. He'd be somewhere over the Arctic Circle just about now, sleeping a restless, interrupted sleep, flying west with the night.

When I reached The Lake of Dreams I parked downtown, on the

main street, grabbed my bag, and walked to the pier where Blake's boat was moored. I hadn't spoken to him since we'd argued over the boxes of old toys in the living room, and I hadn't talked to him yet about Avery's anger over my lapse. I couldn't blame him for being upset, and the image of him standing on the dock, watching as Keegan and I had driven out into the dusky lake, had lingered. I was full of the letters, too, bursting to talk about Rose and her extraordinary story, which was also ours.

Blake was working on the *Fearful Symmetry,* painting stain onto the wooden trim. It gleamed a clear, glossy brown. He rested the paintbrush across the can and stood up when he saw me coming, wiping his hands on a stained white rag he pulled from his pocket. I stepped over the railing, onto the deck.

"Hey," I said. "That's looking good."

His hair was golden red in the sun. He nodded. "I think so, too."

"You know, I'm sorry, Blake. Mom said Avery is still mad."

"Yeah, well, that would be something of an understatement. Is she overreacting a little? Maybe. But she's really upset, and I can see her point. She wanted to be the one to say something, you know? She wanted to choose the time."

"I didn't think clearly," I said, understanding in that moment how deeply Blake's allegiances had shifted. He had his own family now. "Would it help if I called her?"

Blake shrugged. "Maybe. She's really mad at me. She didn't know I'd told you, Lucy. She didn't know that anyone else knew, and when she found out—well, you can imagine how she felt."

My bag with all the letters was hanging from my arm, and though I'd meant to share everything I'd learned with Blake, it suddenly seemed trivial compared to what was unfolding between us.

"I feel terrible. What can I do?"

He looked past me, over the water, and sighed. "Nothing, at this point. I mean, it would be good if you talked to Avery."

"I will."

"Okay." He managed a small smile. "Just don't expect her to name the baby after you."

"Okay on that, too."

We were quiet for a moment, the boat moving slightly on the gentle waves.

"Yoshi's coming tomorrow," I said.

"Hey, I'm glad to hear that. You guys are good?"

"I hope so," I said.

He nodded, no doubt remembering Keegan and me traveling out on the lake the night before. "I was beginning to wonder."

"Keegan and I were never meant to be."

"You okay with that?"

"I'm okay. Sad a little. I mean, Keegan is great in a lot of ways. I just got disoriented for a while, so far away from home. So close to all the lost past."

Blake smiled. "Yeah, I get that. Well, look—we're doing a July Fourth party on Tuesday," he said, gesturing to the half-stained railing. "Here on the boat. That's what I'm doing, getting ready. I'm inviting everyone, Art, Joey and Zoe, Austen, Mom, a few friends, some people from the restaurant, too. Mom promised not to tell anyone else about the baby, and we're going to formally announce it then. The baby and the wedding, by the way. I'm not telling when we're getting married." He smiled. "You'll have to wait like everyone else. You're invited, by the way."

"Well, thank you. And congratulations." I hugged him, the bag catching between us as he put his arm briefly around my shoulders.

Then I left, walking down the dock and through the village to the Impala, driving up the lake road until the house came into view. The sun was setting by then, and light flashed off the cupola windows in spectacular shades of gold and fuchsia and orange. I parked on the lawn and walked straight to the shore, shedding my shoes as I went, and dived off the end of the dock into the cold clear water of the lake.

Chapter 16

YOSHI'S FLIGHT WAS DUE TO ARRIVE EARLY, SO I WAS UP AT dawn, rough clouds scattering to the east and muting the sunrise, the sky flaring red and gold, as if on fire. My mother had been spending a lot of time upstairs, going through the closets and packing up my father's things. Quietly, without saying anything about it, she had started sleeping there again. Her door was ajar, her breathing soft and even, so I moved quietly, down the stairs, the kitchen tiles cold on my bare feet as I made toast and tea.

Breakfast over, I got into the Impala and took the highway. There was little traffic so I got to the airport with an hour to spare, taking a seat in one of the black Naugahyde-and-metal chairs to wait. At this early hour the regional airport was almost empty. I'd brought my computer to catch up on e-mail. My account was so full it almost shut down, so I spent the first few minutes deleting spam and chain messages. Neil and Julie had sent photos from their recent snorkeling trip, so the screen was suddenly full of a tropical paradise, with Yoshi sitting on the white sand beach, leaning back on his elbows and smiling, his legs crossed at the ankles and his jet-black hair cut very short, looking so relaxed it was hard to believe he'd just quit a job and didn't have another.

I found myself smiling back. I thought of the rain, and I remembered how happy we had been.

While I was working through the inbox, a message popped up from Oliver, of all people, labeled "point of interest." I clicked it open, thinking he'd probably just put me on a mailing list for the Westrum House, but in fact it was a real message from Oliver himself.

Dear Lucy,

First, allow me to apologize for being so terse with you during the visit you and your mother made to the Westrum House. I hope you can understand my concerns about thoroughly investigating any claims regarding Frank Westrum. One cannot be too careful, I find, in this high-tech era. I would not wish for any misinformation to go viral, as they say. Yet I am aware of my own tendency to be a bit overprotective of his legacy, and a recent conversation I had with your Reverend Suzi helped me reach the conclusion that perhaps I had been too abrupt, even rude, when we last met.

So let me apologize. And let me also inform you of a recent discovery I made while going through the studio more thoroughly. I found a piece of paper, shoved in the back of the drawer marked 1938, with a penciled note. It said only this: Iris Jarrett Wyndham Stone. I would not have noted this before, but now of course I assume she is your Iris. I send this news with my best wishes to you and to your family.

Iris Jarrett Wyndham Stone. The note from Oliver was so generous, so unexpected. I read her married name over and over again, and whispered it out loud. I remembered finding her baptismal certificate and that the name Wyndham had meant nothing to me then. Now the sad and complicated history radiated from every letter. I did a quick Internet search but came back with nothing except Wyndham Stone Turf near Batavia and Stone Jar Antiques in Oswego. If Iris was alive, and she could be, she could be anywhere at all.

When I'd worked my way halfway down the screen, I found a message from Serling University, which housed the Vivian Branch archives in its history collection, and had been working all this time on my request.

I'd forgotten all about this. I opened it to find a note from the archivist
saying she had come across two letters of interest, both written by Frank
Westrum to Vivian Branch and her sister Cornelia. She had scanned the
documents into PDF files and these were attached. I clicked on the first.

9 September 1938

My dearest Vivian and Cornelia,

I write to let you know the windows are complete.

*Last evening I left Rose resting in the parlor of the sanatorium, feeling
better. I hope so, at least. I stood outside for a very long time in the dusk.
The light was on, I saw her shadow move behind the curtains. She was able
to see all the windows but the final one before her health deteriorated, but
I hope she will rally enough to come home before I must ship them off to
you. They have meant so much to her. I would like her to see them all together,
just once. People passed me on the street, talking, and some glanced at me
lingering at the bottom of the steps, but I stayed until she went upstairs to
her room and put the lamp out and slept. I hope she slept. Increasingly, she
coughs so much that it is hard for her to rest. This is such a cruel disease,
and I am so helpless in the face of it. I walked for a long time by the river. It
was dawn before I turned home and fell into a restless sleep myself.*

*There is no need for me to go on; I know my suffering will only bring
you grief. But I write to let you know that all the windows are done. I
believe they are beautiful. They hang against the windows in my studio, and
I think you would be pleased to see them, all the women gathered, their feet
resting gently on the border Rose designed. She took it, as you may know,
from an image she saw as a child, a pattern she sketched and remembered
for its beauty. Though I followed your instructions about the women you
wished to depict, I consulted Rose about the images and design and the
choice of colors, as I'm sure you wished me to do. Truly, we were partners
in this creation, and so I think of these as being her windows in some true
sense, born of your generosity and vision, yes, and of my work, true, but
born also of my conversations with Rose, who is a sister to you in your
concerns. You will understand that I made these windows with her in*

mind, thought of her with every piece of glass I cut, and I put them all together as if I could assemble our lives in such a beautiful and accurate way. Which of course, I cannot.

In any case, they are finished and await your inspection.

       Regards, Frank

                         28 September 1938

My Dear Vivian and Cornelia,

May this letter find you well in The Lake of Dreams. I was so pleased to have you visit, and to hear from you so quickly. It is joyous to me that you like the windows. I know that the two of you and Rose have dreamed of such a chapel for decades, and your generosity in funding this project will inspire generations, I feel sure. I find the windows have a life of their own, a resonating beauty apart from anything we did to create them, and I shall be sorry when they do not stand in my studio any longer.

But pack them up, I have. The shipping company will collect them tomorrow, and they will be delivered to you no later than two weeks from now.

Also the last funds have arrived, and I thank you. Do let me know when the installation will be. I cannot wait to see your chapel.

Rose is a little better now. She did come here one afternoon and stood for a long time amid the windows. They say she may be able to return home next week, so we hope.

       Regards, Frank

I read these letters several times, exhilarated at this direct, clear link between Frank Westrum and Rose. And because I felt magnanimous and thankful to Oliver for sharing what he'd found, I forwarded the notes to him, without letting myself consider it too fully. By the time I looked up, the level of activity had risen, people streaming in and scattering throughout the terminal. Yoshi's flight had landed. I closed the computer and stood up to wait, still thinking of Frank's notes, the poignant image of him standing outside the sanatorium, watching her silhouette through the curtains, beyond the layers of glass. Thinking of them working together, Rose drawing with the same sharp lines that comprised her handwriting, sketching the designs Frank would translate into glass, a beautiful symbiosis. His notes were undercut with such sadness, and I wondered what Rose had been suffering from, what cruel disease he meant. Tuberculosis, I guessed, and it made sense that she might have contracted this from the work she'd done with Vivian. Or perhaps her bout with influenza had left her weakened, or damaged her lungs in some way.

People, brisk or languorous or weary, began to stream down the escalator. Yoshi was among the last, looking a little dazed, a bag slung over his shoulder. He was wearing cargo shorts and a blue T-shirt and his hair was short. He was tan and so good-looking that I felt stilled for a moment as I watched him riding down the escalator, considering all that had happened in this brief time, how close I had come, in my pursuit of the past, to canceling this moment altogether. And perhaps Yoshi had considered ending things between us, too; I still didn't know if this was the end of the beginning or the beginning of the end. I felt suddenly shy. When he saw me he smiled, held up one hand to wave. I wove through the current of other passengers and put my arm around him, kissed him quickly.

"You're here," I said.

"I made it," he agreed.

We got his bag and walked out of the terminal, talking too quickly about the most mundane things: his trip, the weather, the history of my father's golden car. I drove out of the city and back over the familiar roads, pointing out landmarks; Yoshi remarked on the wideness of the car seats and the expansive countryside, fields and farms in every direction. The dark green highway signs for one town after another flashed by: Watkins Glen, Corning, Elmira. I told Yoshi about the George Eastman House, which housed the International Museum of Photography and Film, and about Mark Twain, who'd lived in Elmira, his octagonal study with its fireplace and many windows, like a freestanding cupola, now on the campus of Elmira College.

"What do you think?" I asked when we got close to the exit for The Lake of Dreams. "Are you tired? I could take you to the house and you could sleep. Or we could stop and walk around the village for a while."

"I'm tired, but I know I won't sleep," Yoshi said. "Show me around. I'll just walk until I can't anymore."

So I parked. We strolled through the village and stopped at the bank, which was open on Saturday mornings. My mother looked up from the papers on her desk and stood, smiling, to shake Yoshi's hand. She liked him right away, I could tell by the way she lingered in the conversation. She promised to be home early from work. Then we got ice-cream cones and sat in the park, watching sailboats skim across the lake, and Yoshi told me more about his trip to the island, pulling photos up on his camera, carefully skirting the issue of work, of the fact that we were both as adrift in the world as those boats were on the water. Skirting, too, the gaps that had opened up between us in these past two weeks. Yoshi lay back on the grass and dozed a little, and I walked along the seawall. The house Rose had first lived in was across the street, a narrow Victorian with lacy trim. Iris had been born in that house; there was the garden where she'd made her dolls of hollyhocks. I glanced at Yoshi, dozing in the sun with his arms clasped behind his head, so familiar, and yet containing a universe of history and perceptions that I could never know.

When Yoshi woke up, we walked down to the pier, but though the *Fearful Symmetry* was tethered and bobbing on the water, neither Blake nor Avery were there, and so we walked on. I pointed out Dream Master rising from the edge of the outlet, imposing. For me it had always been a symbol of my family history, and even though its cracked cornices and need of tuckpointing were clearly visible, seeing things through Yoshi's eyes did what even my years away had not been able to accomplish: it was a building, nothing more.

"Your grandfather built it?" he asked.

"Great-grandfather. He was Rose's brother. They came to this country together."

"Ah. That must have been hard."

"I think it was. It was hard for Rose, anyway."

Yoshi nodded. "My mother talks about the loneliness she felt when she first moved to California. It wasn't that she didn't like the United States. Just that no matter how long she stayed here, it never truly felt like home. Maybe that's why she and my father have been so willing to move every few years."

"Well, it is lonely, isn't it, being by yourself in a new country? At least your mother had a phone. Rose and Joseph had letters that took three weeks to arrive, and no money."

We walked on, stopping at The Green Bean to have some coffee. It wasn't crowded, so we got a table right by the water. I went to look for Avery, and when I couldn't find her, I left a note of apology in the kitchen, folded and taped to the stainless-steel fridge. A flock of ducks, a mother with her babies, floated by us, traveling down the outlet past the glassworks, where tourists were once again lined up waiting at the door. I didn't let myself think of Keegan handling fire inside, or the glass wavering and growing like a living thing. The ducks went on their way, floating and swimming with the current. They could follow this outlet to the Erie Canal, travel all the way to Buffalo, and beyond. But the place they passed first was the dock of the glassworks, where I'd climbed into Keegan's boat with such a feeling of anticipation just two days before.

"Yoshi," I said. He looked up smiling, and I glanced away. By the time I looked back I could tell from his face—suddenly serious, so braced for bad news—that he knew something was wrong. I told him quickly that Keegan was the person I'd been dating when my father died, that I'd gone out on the boat with him, that I'd kissed him twice since I'd been here and stirred up the unfinished past, but that in the end I couldn't go forward, because it wasn't right.

"You mean morally right?" Yoshi asked. "Are you saying you'd see him if you broke up with me?"

"No. No, I mean it didn't *feel* right. It wasn't the right thing to do. I got confused, that's all, being back here, and seeing him again, and you were so far away. I'm so sorry, Yoshi. I was off balance. I've been off balance for a long time. You know that's true. Maybe since we went to Japan. This was something I had to settle from the past. And now I have."

He didn't answer right away. He folded his arms and looked off across the water, keeping his emotions to himself. I tried to imagine how I would feel if the situation were reversed, and found that I was scared. Always before, I was the one to break things off. I was never the one who got hurt. But it was possible that this could happen now.

"Yoshi? I'm really sorry."

He looked at me then, waved one hand. "I can't talk about it," he said. "I'm so tired. I feel like I'm falling through space."

The water flowed by; we waited for our order. It seemed best not to break the silence. As the waitress brought us coffee and cinnamon bread, I had a flash of insight that seemed, on the surface, to have nothing to do with anything, but went back to the drive we'd made that morning, the green exit signs flashing past: Canandaigua, Seneca Falls, Corning, and Elmira; back to just yesterday, to the letters I still carried in my purse.

And I feel glad to know that the famous author who once lived down the street was born and died in the same light beneath which I once stood, dreaming that the world would shift and change, or even end.

Elmira, home to Mark Twain, who was born as Halley's Comet passed over in 1835, and died in 1910, when it passed over once again.

I took out my phone and did a search for the white pages in Elmira. And there she was, just like anyone else listed in the phone book: *Stone, Iris J.*

"What are you doing?" Yoshi asked.

His tone was normal; maybe we'd just carry on and everything would be okay. I moved my chair over so he could see the screen. "Yoshi, look at this. It's Iris. I found her. She's in Elmira."

And then I explained the essence of the story, how Rose had left her daughter and yet followed her from afar, how I'd found the letters. How Iris might not know about Rose at all, or about the windows, or about her mother's extraordinary life.

"Are you going to call?"

"Do you think I should?"

"Why not?"

"Right, you're right—why not?"

Still, I had to enter the numbers four different times before I could bring myself to press SEND. It might be the wrong person, or if it was the right Iris Stone, she might not want to talk. She'd be ninety-five years old, after all; she might not remember, or it might be such a shock that she'd collapse, or she just might hang up. But all the time I was thinking of Iris, I was also hesitating because of what it might mean for me to find her. It was like standing on a threshold, a door in the world that would open into a place you'd never expected to be, a place from which you couldn't return. Welcome or unwelcome, knowledge was something you could never undo.

"What are you waiting for?" Yoshi asked.

"I don't know. It's just a little unsettling, that's all. I don't know what I'll find."

He shook his head. "Is it at all possible you won't call in the end?" he asked. "Could you imagine finding her like this and never getting in touch?"

I laughed, glad for his calm, pragmatic view. "No. Not really."

"So why wait? What's the worst thing that could happen?"

"I don't know." And I didn't—that was the problem. It wasn't so much about finding Iris as it was about finding out whatever she might reveal about my family. Still, I pressed the final button. I let the phone ring. Six times, then seven. No answering machine, apparently. I was about to hang up, both disappointed and relieved, when a low voice spoke across the wires.

"This better not be a solicitor," she said, severely. "You got me out of the bath."

"Don't you have an answering machine?" I asked, waving my hand at Yoshi's quizzical look.

"Who is this?"

I took a deep breath. "You don't know me," I began.

"Good-bye, then. I'm not buying anything."

"Look, please, don't hang up, okay? It's important. I'm not selling anything, I promise."

"Well? What is it, then?"

"My name is Lucy Jarrett," I said in a great rush. "My father was Martin and his father was Joseph and so was his grandfather. I have an idea that we might be related."

There was a silence so long that I wondered if we'd been disconnected, or if the shock of my call had been so much that she'd collapsed after all.

"Hello?" I said. "Mrs. Stone, are you all right?"

"I'm quite fine," came the crisp reply.

"Good. I'm so sorry to call out of the blue. I know it must be a shock."

"What's your name?"

"Lucy Jarrett."

"And how old are you, Lucy Jarrett?"

"Twenty-nine. Thirty in October."

"I see. Twenty-nine and thirty in October. Well, let me tell you this, Lucy Jarrett. I'm not interested in my roots. I cut my ties, do you understand? Long ago. Long before you were born. It's not personal. But I'm going to hang up now, and I don't want you to be calling me again. Do you understand me? Am I clear?"

"Yes, very clear, but please—let me give you my number. Because I have some information about Rose Jarrett. Maybe you knew her as Rose

Westrum. That's who I want to talk about, when you're ready. If you're ready, I should say. About Rose."

There was a long silence then, and when she spoke I had the sense that her voice was trembling a little, though that might have been the connection.

"What are you talking about?" she asked.

I took a deep breath and glanced at Yoshi, who was watching me intently, as if he didn't know me, his expression so tight and pained that I knew he must be thinking about Keegan. "I found some letters," I said. "They are letters written to you. From Rose, who knew you from the time you were very small."

There was a silence.

"Give me your telephone number," she said.

I did, and after repeating it once she hung up without saying good-bye, leaving me with a vast silence and a pounding heart.

"What happened?" Yoshi asked.

"I don't know." I shrugged, put the phone down on the table. "She's the right person. She recognized Rose's name, and at least she took my number. I'll just have to wait and see if she calls back."

"I think she'll call back," Yoshi said. "She'll want to know what you're talking about."

I nodded. "How are you doing?" I asked.

"I don't know, Lucy. I mean, I never expected to get here and find this."

"I didn't want to tell you on the phone. But actually, I didn't mean that. I meant, are you tired?"

"Not really, no. I started to fade awhile ago, but I think I've got a second wind. I'm good for a few hours."

"There's a place I'd like to take you. A place I love. If you're up for it."

He didn't answer right away, and all my fears rushed into the silence.

"I think I could handle it," he said, finally. "I think it would be okay."

The place I had in mind was the gorge, where I'd spent so much time in my last year of high school, a place I hadn't been since the night my father died. Yet as we were driving by the church a car pulled out of a parking place just in front of the door, and on an impulse I pulled in. I'd heard there were plans to move the Wisdom window back to its place in the chapel in the next few days—Oliver had insisted on this, arguing for the integrity of the complete collection—and I wanted Yoshi to see it.

We went in the side door and I waved to Joanna, the secretary. Then I led Yoshi through the maze of corridors. They had hung the window in the fellowship hall, and it was even more striking than I remembered. Early afternoon light poured intensely through the colors, through the patterns whose style had grown so familiar, the stems and flowers, the interlocking moons making the repeated shape of the vesica piscis, an ancient sacred geometry, the hands of the people all upraised, turning into leaves, into words, rising up.

"In the Japanese creation story there's a moment like this," Yoshi said. "The story tells of a time when the earth was floating on the water, and then a pair of immortals sprouted up from the earth like reeds. Some parallels, anyway—everything interwoven."

"I like that—sprouting up like reeds. I'll take you kayaking in the marshes while you're here. Now that the depot is closed, we can follow the shore for miles."

We paused outside the offices so Yoshi could use the restroom across the hall. As I waited, Suzi hurried out of the office, carrying a briefcase.

"Lucy," she said, pausing. "What brings you here?"

"I was showing the Wisdom window to Yoshi. He just got in from Japan. Thanks, by the way. For whatever you said to Oliver Parrott. He sent me information that helped me find Iris. She's ninety-five. She lives in Elmira."

"That's amazing that she's still alive. Have you talked with her?"

"A little. Not really. She's supposed to call me back. I've learned so much more about Rose. I'll have to stop in sometime and bring you up to speed."

"Anytime—just give me a call. I've got to rush off to a meeting right now."

"Right. And Yoshi's here."

"Yes. You know, Lucy, I was thinking about our last conversation, your concern about Rose. Forgiveness is at the heart of the church, God's forgiveness and love, and whatever mistakes she made—whatever mistakes we all make—they don't cut us off from life, or from a spiritual life, unless we choose to let them."

I felt myself flush, because it seemed that maybe she'd read through my concern about Rose to the story I'd almost told her about the night my father died, the sense that I could have made a different decision and changed everything.

"Well, thanks," I said, sounding flip, I knew, and I was sorry about this even as I spoke. "That's good to know."

She nodded, smiled, started down the stairs. "Okay, then. Be well."

By the time Yoshi emerged, she was gone.

Back in the car, driving along the road that hugged the lake, Yoshi and I didn't speak much. I worried; his silence could hold almost anything. As we neared the end of the lake I left the main highway and drove down the narrow, curving gravel road to the parking area. It had changed over these last years, become less wild. There was now a neat signboard displaying posters of the various sorts of ferns and fossils to be found, along with warnings not to pick anything, and gravel on the path that we followed as it wove and narrowed and finally ended in the stream below the falls.

Water was pouring over the stony riverbed. I waded out into the center, up to my knees, and let it rush past, so clear my bare feet stood out pale against the dark stones below. Soon Yoshi was beside me, staggering a little on the slippery rocks. I caught his hand to steady him.

"Lucy," he said. "If it didn't matter, why did you even tell me?"

"Because I didn't want to have it between us. That secret. That lie."

"Are you sure?" he asked.

"It's over," I told him. "It was over before it began. I'm sure."

He nodded. "Okay. I believe you. I'm glad it didn't feel right," he said.

I smiled, and then he did. "Come on!" I shouted over the rush of the water. Slipping, laughing, we made our way to the falls. I stepped beneath the cascade, water pounding off my face, my shoulders, and lifted my arms high, my hands open like the people in the window, as if I could catch the downpour, let it fill me up. Yoshi stepped in, too, laughing out loud in the wild hard rush of water, and in that moment the uneasiness that had trailed me throughout the day washed away completely. I took a step toward Yoshi, meaning to kiss him like we were in a monsoon, but my foot slipped and I fell trying to catch my balance. I fell through the falls into a calm space behind the wall of water, a wet shale wall to my back and the water like a curtain rushing down before me. The world beyond the water was a blur of green and stone and blue. A moment later Yoshi pushed through, the water pouring down in sheets so smooth it looked like glass, and stepped into the calm. He helped me stand, and pressed his hands against my wet face, and this was the moment from the past that mattered, this was the moment I wanted to continue. We stood there kissing in the little hollow between the water and the stone, a place completely and utterly private, a place I'd never known existed.

We stayed behind the curtain of water until we grew chilled, then stepped out to sit on the warm rocks, our feet dangling in a pool hollowed out by the power of the falls. Yoshi told me the story of how he'd spoken up at the meeting, feeling the room go coldly silent around him. We talked about money, how much we had and how long it would last, and we talked about what we might do next. We both had enough experience to move easily into new jobs, but we decided that this time we'd both look for work, and we'd be more careful about what kinds of jobs we took, and where.

Yoshi made it back to the house and through the early dinner my mother fixed—grilled chicken and a salad—before jet lag hit him like a train. He barely made it up to the cupola, where I'd set up a space for us, hauling up two old futons and putting on clean sheets. I'd left the windows open and the early evening twilight filled the little room.

"Nice," Yoshi said, collapsing on the futon and closing his eyes. Within seconds, he was asleep.

I went back downstairs and chatted with my mother while we cleaned up. When I told her about Iris, she was surprised that I'd called and a little disapproving, concerned I might be stirring up histories better left hidden.

"What's to lose?" I said. "Besides, I'm too curious not to find out what I can. If Oliver hadn't sent the information, I never would have found her."

She laughed. "Well, that's one way to spin it," she said. "By the way, I like Yoshi. He's very charming, isn't he? It's so strange, he almost has a British accent. I didn't expect that, somehow."

"His mother's British," I said. "He spent some time in London, too, though they moved around the world a lot for his father's work. Sometime I'd like to go there with him. I've heard it's a wonderful city."

"Well, I hardly know him. I mean, he just got here. But there's something very easy and comfortable about him. You feel right away like you've known him a long time. Do you think he'll be up for a trip to Niagara Falls tomorrow? Or will his jet lag be too bad?"

I said we'd have to wait and see. Then we discussed what to bring to Blake's Fourth of July party. My phone rang and I went to get it, drying my hands, still debating between potato salad and fresh fruit.

The voice on the phone was low, unfamiliar, and rather clipped.

"I'm Ned Stone," he said. "I'm Iris Stone's son. I understand you called my mother earlier today."

I took a breath, thinking of my mother's concerns. Who knew, really, who these people were? "Yes, hello. My name is Lucy Jarrett."

"That's what my mother said. She wasn't quite clear, though, on what you wanted."

"Oh—well, I don't want anything, really. I've found some information about Rose Jarrett, about your mother's family. Some letters that were written to your mother. So I was calling to see if she could shed some light on them. And to tell her they exist."

He cleared his throat. I tried to imagine how old he might be. If Iris was ninety-five, he could be well into his sixties.

"I have to tell you, my mother was quite upset about your call. Unnerved is a better word. She left home when she was quite young, and it wasn't a happy situation, though I don't know the details. My mother hasn't had a particularly easy life. I don't want her to be unsettled at the end of her years by whatever you think you have to tell her. And frankly, I'm sorry to have to say this, but calling out of the blue like this, with such strange news—it makes me wonder about your intentions, if you don't mind my saying so."

"I understand," I said. "I'll do whatever I can to ease your mind." I repeated the story then, my father and grandfather and great-grandfather, the letters, finding Iris. I did the genealogy in my head, even as I spoke. Ned Stone would be my father's second cousin. When he didn't reply right away, I went on—the church records, the windows, Frank Westrum, the letters I'd discovered in the dusty box of the Lafay-ette Historical Society. "It's just that we never had this part of the story in our family, we never knew Rose or your mother even existed. I was so excited to find her. Plus, I thought she might want to see these letters."

There was a pause then, and I tried to imagine the man on the other end of the line, who sounded careful and tailored and very precise, the sort of person who would have a home office with thick, sound-absorbing carpet and framed diplomas hanging on the wall.

"You've read them?"

"I have."

"Would you find them upsetting if you were my mother?"

I hesitated. The last days had been very exciting, but they had been unsettling, too. The old story, the story I'd learned by heart all my years of growing up, had held a certain comfort, had given the world a weight and stability, and the discoveries I'd made had shaken my sense of who I was even as it altered my understanding of the world. Would I trade this knowledge? No. In fact, I wanted more, I wanted it all. Yet it hadn't been easy knowledge, and I didn't know how it might feel to have your world turned over when you were ninety-five years old.

"Actually, I think they might be upsetting," I said, sitting down on the sofa, looking out the windows at the dark lake. "I guess it would depend on if you wanted to know the truth, or at least another facet of the story, or if you wanted to keep the story you've always believed."

He hesitated.

"All right," he said, finally. "Tell me what you think you know."

So I told him that Rose was his grandmother, that his mother hadn't known her.

There was a long silence.

"That's very shocking," he said. "If I believe you, that's hard to absorb."

"The letters are very beautiful. They tell the story better than I can."

"Why don't you send them?" he suggested at last. "Send copies of the letters to me. I'll have a look, and then I'll get back to you about this."

"I'll scan the first two and send them right now," I offered, groping in my purse for a pen. I wrote his e-mail address on the back of a grocery receipt.

After I sent the letters off with a short note, I drank a glass of wine on the patio with my mother, lingering in the deepening dusk, the night. I wondered if I'd done the right thing and my mother shrugged.

"No taking it back now," she said. "You'll just have to wait and see."

I didn't have to wait long, as it turned out. Within two hours, just before midnight, he called me back.

"All right," he said. "My mother is ninety-five years old, you understand, and I don't want her distressed. If things get distressing for her, or even if she's tired, you'll have to leave. But she lives with me, and I've talked to her, and she'd like to meet you, and you can visit us on Monday afternoon if you'd like."

"I can be there," I said, writing the address on the back of my hand, the ballpoint digging into my skin. "That's fine, then. I'll be there at two o'clock on Monday."

Chapter 17

THE NEXT DAY YOSHI WAS FEELING PRETTY RESTED, SO WE took him to see Niagara Falls. It was about a two-hour drive, so we left early in the morning, and we did it all, standing on the edge of the magnificent, roaring falls, putting on raincoats and taking a boat ride up the river into the clouds of mist at their base. We had a drink in the revolving restaurant at the top of the tower, where Yoshi toasted the day and my mother toasted Yoshi and his visit. We got back to The Lake of Dreams quite late, and my mother had to work early the next day. She was gone by the time I got up, but she left a fresh pot of coffee, and a note wishing us a wonderful day. Her handwriting was so similar to mine, a little cramped and hurried, and I was glad that things between us had eased, that somehow discovering these new facets of the past had brought us closer than we'd been in years.

When Yoshi finally came downstairs, we took our breakfast out to the dock and sat there in the sun, breaking off pieces of the olive bread I'd bought at The Green Bean and spreading them with hummus, tossing crumbs to the ducks that darted in to sweep them from the surface of the lake. The coffee was strong and I poured it over ice. We drank and talked. After a while, I got the canoe out and we paddled in an unhurried way along the shore, admiring the beauty of the undeveloped land, the chapel in the distance, red and white and gray against the greenery. We went far enough that the construction site came into view, the earth stripped down to bedrock in places, piled in bleak, ugly mounds. I thought of the walk I'd taken with Keegan, the mystery and silence of the forest and the land left untouched, a kind of wildness that was growing rarer in the world.

"I'm glad you spoke up about the bridge project," I said. "Even if it means we're broke. It was the right thing to do."

Yoshi rested his paddle across the boat and shook his head. "I don't know. It was exhilarating at the time. But later I wondered. I mean, it's not like me, is it? So rash."

"You thought about it. We talked about it, a little. So it wasn't rash. Besides, I don't care," I said, and the strange thing was, it seemed I didn't anymore. Whatever need to achieve had been driving me to this point in my life seemed to have dissipated, like water easing through the stones on the shore. It had to do with settling things with Keegan, I knew that. And somehow, it had to do with Rose as well, with the way she'd lived her life, so unconcerned with the things that had focused the other part of her family, the descendants of her brother—money and status, the shiny evidence of success. We hadn't known about her, which was telling, but she'd have been considered a failure if we had: unmarried, with no visible accomplishments, a woman who'd left her child in the care of others. Yet I admired her, and knowing about her life had changed the way I thought about my own. Rose had made mistakes, to be sure, but she'd had the strength to live by her own convictions, to know what she wanted and to try to get it, even when her culture put up one obstacle after another. And her love for Iris was so present in all the letters, even though she'd had to leave her. "I don't care about the job," I said again. "I've been thinking maybe it's time for both of us to do something new."

"Like what?"

"I don't know, exactly. I was thinking about that work we did in Jakarta for the orphanage. I was thinking it would be nice to do something good in the world. Even if we have to give up some of the perks."

We drifted, floating. The lake was calm, the water touching the sides of the boat and retreating in clear ripples.

"I guess we could look around," he said. "Surely there must be some good a couple of science geeks could do."

"You'd think so, wouldn't you?"

I pushed the paddle into the reeds, seeking to float into deeper water, and the motion startled two herons, who rose up suddenly from where they'd been hidden in the marsh, lifting on their powerful wings, their legs trailing behind them as they gained purchase on the sky. We watched them soar, and rise above the trees, and float away.

"This is such a beautiful place," Yoshi said.

It was beautiful a few hours later, too, when we got into the Impala and drove through the countryside I knew by heart, down the low ridge between the lakes to the outskirts of Elmira, going to meet Iris. I'd expected a house something like the historical society house: nineteenth century, full of heavy furniture and antimacassars and little glass dishes with stale hard candy. It was Iris's voice, I suppose, its querulous quality, that had me picturing this. So I was shocked, driving up, to find myself traveling down a long gravel driveway toward a contemporary house, full of windows overlooking a wooded lot. I parked beneath an ancient ginkgo tree with its fan-shaped leaves, and admired the clean lines of wood on the patio, the stone walls and endless glass.

The woman who opened the door was about my mother's age, thin, her hair dyed a light, even brown.

"Are you Lucy?" she asked. Her hand was dry, fleeting, in mine. "Come in, please. I'm Carol, Iris's daughter-in-law. And this is my husband, Ned."

Ned was tall, genial, with sparse gray hair and a warm smile and no trace of the family eyes. His were brown, and shadowed.

He shook my hand, too. "I'm the oldest," he said. "My brother, Keith, is in Florida. My mother lives here; she has a separate apartment that's attached to the house. She spends part of the winter down south with Keith. So it works out."

He was talking fast, nervous, I realized, and Carol put one hand on his arm, a gesture that seemed to travel through him like a wave, calming him. He looked at her and smiled.

"This is Yoshitaka Aioki," I said.

To my surprise Ned gave a slight bow and said, *"Konichiwa,"* and Yoshi, after a moment's surprise, replied in Japanese, and then the three of them were conversing in an easy, delighted way, the language moving too quickly for me to follow very well. But I gathered that Ned and Carol had spent many years living just outside of Kyoto.

"Ned was sent there by his company," she said, turning to me, switching to English. "We thought we'd stay four years at most. But we fell in love with the place, and ended up being there for fifteen years, right up until Ned retired. Come on in," she went on, gesturing to the living room, which opened off the stone foyer, a room with a tall ceiling and a sweeping wall of windows overlooking the trees. "As you can see, we brought home a lot of souvenirs."

At first, though, I couldn't see. The room was furnished very simply, with low white couches and wooden tables. Then I noticed the beautiful collections of tea and sake sets on the shelves that flanked the fireplace, and the Hiroshige prints framed and hanging on the far wall.

"Have a seat," Ned said, settling himself on one of the low stuffed chairs as Carol left the room.

Yoshi and I perched on the edge of a white sofa. "Thanks. This room is beautiful. So simple and elegant."

Ned smiled. "Believe it or not, we have a tatami room upstairs."

We talked about Japan for a few more minutes; mostly Ned talked while I watched him, looking in vain for any family resemblance. Like my father, Ned had been drafted, but the war had ended before he was sent to Vietnam. He had stayed on in the army for four years, learning to repair airplane engines, which fascinated him so much he got a degree in engineering once he was discharged. He met Carol the day before his thirtieth birthday when she sat down next to him on a bus. They had three children, all grown; only the youngest, Julie, who was about my age, was still living in the area.

"So these letters," he said, reaching for a file folder he'd left on the table. "They took me by surprise. My mother, too. Her first response was that it was ridiculous, and must be a practical joke. But I gave her one to read, and she recognized Joseph Jarrett from the descriptions.

"Apparently, she knew Cora and Joseph were not her birth parents, though she'd never told any of us about that. Maybe my father knew. In any case, she never knew her father and she didn't remember her real mother very well at all. She went away when my mother was so young, my mother came to think of Cora and Joseph as her parents—which was fine, until my mother hit her teen years and got rebellious, and the little cracks that had been there all along began to deepen. Your grandfather was born when she was fourteen, and that changed things, too."

"In 1925," I said. "The year they moved up to the house on the lake."

"Was it? Yes, I think my mother lived there for a little while. There was a lot of tension. Eventually, she ran away. She moved in with a friend of friends here, and that was the saving grace, I guess. She took a job in one of the glass factories. But that was essentially the end of her connection to the Jarretts. Reading those letters was quite emotional for her, you should know. She stayed up very late last night, going over them again and again. But she wants to meet you. As I said, however, I'd like this to move slowly. And without distress to her."

He was nervous again, talking faster.

"I understand," I said.

A few minutes later, Carol appeared in the doorway, holding the arm of a tall woman whose hair was thin and white on her scalp, like dandelion fluff. I stood up, remembering Rose's very first letter, how she'd described Iris's infant hair in exactly this way. Her eyes, blue and fierce and familiar, met mine.

"Is this her?" she asked.

"This is Lucy, Mother. And her friend Yoshi. Come, let's have a seat." They crossed the room and sat on the opposite sofa.

Once we were all settled there was a silence, which expanded in the room. Even Ned was quiet.

"You look like your great-grandfather," Iris said, at last.

"Do I really?"

She nodded. "It's the eyes."

"I have something for you," I said. "Something that was made for you."

I reached into my bag and pulled out the cloth, wrapped carefully in beautiful sheets of rice paper from Japan, faintly blue, with embossed white cranes. Iris took the package—her hands were long, the fingers pale and bony, slightly trembling. She opened it slowly, folding the paper carefully back. The cloth unfurled, silvery white and delicate, the row of overlapping moons along the border wrapped in the now familiar pattern of vines. It was so finely woven that, lifted and held up, it was translucent, the border along the bottom standing out more darkly than the rest. I told her the story then, as briefly as I could: the cloth with its border of moons, the cryptic letters and pamphlets locked away in the cupola, my search through historical archives, and the windows. I'd made photocopies for myself to keep, and now I handed her the binders, Rose's binders, which held all the original letters.

"These were written to you. Written by your mother, Rose, for you."

She let the blanket fall and smoothed it across her lap, then took the binder.

"You've read them?" she asked, looking up.

"I did." Now that they were not history anymore, but connected to the life of this woman sitting across from me, I understood that it had been a kind of trespass, really, reading these letters not meant for any eyes but hers. "I'm sorry. I didn't know you were alive, you see."

She nodded slowly. "What do you think of her, then?"

"I think she was very brave. She had passionate beliefs, and she fought for them."

"Is that so? I never knew her. She left when I was so small. They said she'd done something wrong and had to go, and that I should call Cora Mama, and so I did. I have one memory, lying on the sunny bed, her fingers doing the itsy-bitsy spider. I can still see them, climbing in the air. That, and a feeling about how it was to have her in the room. But that's all I have, and for a long time I simply didn't think about her."

She paused, and Ned reached over and put a reassuring hand on her arm before she went on.

"It wasn't until you and your brother were born, Ned, that I started to remember and wonder what had happened. You were my children and I was her child, and so of course I wondered. But by then it was too late. I remember the house in town, where we lived before she went away. There was linoleum on the kitchen floor and a woodstove there, and we heated the other rooms by the fireplace. It was very cold in the winter, and my room faced the northwest, so sometimes I woke up to find the light all strange, dim, and I'd realize that the drifts had gone right up over the windows. They said she had done something wrong, but I always felt I must have caused it somehow. That I must have been bad enough to make her leave."

"Oh, no. No," I said, while Iris wiped her eyes. "It wasn't your fault at all. Your mother was sent away because she marched for the right to vote. And got arrested. There was a huge suffrage march in Washington in 1913; others happened all across the country in response, and Rose, your mother, joined the one that happened in The Lake of Dreams. She was warned against it, but she was moved to do it anyway when the parade passed the house. She went to jail, and then they wouldn't take her back. Cora and her first husband, I mean. Your uncle, my great-grandfather, tried to help, but he didn't have much to give then, either. Leaving you was not her choice."

Iris nodded, but still didn't speak. I gestured to the letters on her lap. "She came back for you," I added. "You'll read what happened. She came back a year or so later and met you in the garden of the house in town, and you talked. She wrote about this, in one of her letters." I paused here, because I didn't want to tell Iris that she hadn't recognized her own mother. "You can read them," I said. "There's so much more. She loved you so much."

There was silence before Iris finally spoke, her voice soft and a little tremulous. "It is very hard for me to accept it," she said. "Very hard. I can understand it, now that I am older. I can see that perhaps she had to do it. Sometimes there are circumstances we can't control. And yet. She left. I grew up without her."

I started to speak, but Ned held up his hand to silence me. For a few moments we all sat quietly. Iris's lips trembled, but she didn't cry.

"Not entirely without her," Carol said finally. "You knew Rose Westrum, didn't you? So you see, she came back, even if you didn't know it was her. Probably she thought it best, by then. It seems she watched over you all her life."

Sunlight poured in through the wall of windows and fell through Iris's thin white hair, the wisps like scraps of mist against her pale scalp. Her eyes were just like mine, like Blake's, that vivid blue. The skin was stretched thin over the bones of her hands.

"Yes. I knew Rose Westrum. She was a friend of the people who took me in. She sent me a note just after I was married, saying she had known my family. I never answered her. Why would I? Why would I dredge up all that past?

"I'd run away, you see, when I was fourteen. That's the year that your grandfather was born. My mother—Cora—was not young. She must have been in her forties by then. She must have given up the idea of having children. I remember the kind of surprised silence that settled over the house when we knew she was pregnant. Still, I wasn't paying very much attention. I'd come home from school and bring her tea on a tray, and I had to do the shopping. Everything was quite still and suspenseful all autumn long. But the baby was born healthy. He was a very sweet and docile baby, and I liked taking care of him.

"Cora was a very gentle mother to him. Very loving. She'd been the same to me when I was a child—indulgent, really—but as I grew older we fought. She said I was willful, a blunderer. It's true that I was clumsy, and larger than she liked, and that I outgrew my clothes so quickly. Sometimes she reminded me that she had taken me in when my mother left. So I'd feel beholden and do what she wanted. And I suppose it's true that I was willful, as she claimed. I had ideas about my life, and dreams and wishes, just like any young person does, and she found me forward, too radical in my thinking. She'd press her lips together so hard they nearly disappeared in a little line. I was not good, I made a game of seeing how many times a day I could make her do this.

"I suppose there had been talk of my future before the baby was born, but that was suspended, too. Everything hung still, frozen like vapor in the winter air. I was nearly fifteen, when he was born, and many of my classmates had already left school to take work in the factories along the outlet. It wasn't uncommon in those days, you have to understand, for people to leave school. Almost everyone did. I didn't know a single girl who went to college. They were needed on the farms or to help earn money. Or they fell in love and got married.

"So that summer after Joseph was born I took a job in the knitting factory downtown, partly to get out of the house. It was as if I'd disappeared from the face of the earth, anyway. At least that's how I felt. I was young still, so maybe I was just envious. I tried hard to be useful, certainly, to please them. But when he was born I felt like an old doll, set aside. That factory is long gone now, of course, but it used to sit on the outlet across from the glass insulator factory. I remember because I could look out the big windows, across the water, and see all those people working at their machines like I was working on mine, and I wondered if they were bored, like me, and if they had dreams of other lives, the way I did. I couldn't look long, though. I couldn't be distracted from my own machine. It would be costly to make a mistake and even dangerous. My first day Mrs. Tadley got a finger caught in her knitting machine and there was blood everywhere, and then there was a meeting to warn us not to do the same. She had ruined five sweaters' worth of yarn.

"My machine made socks. It was shaped in a circle and the needles all around it flashed so quickly my eyes couldn't follow them. The sock came out from below and I cut it free, passed it to the right so the next person could sew the toe and send it on. At first it took all my attention to fit my rhythm to the swift pace of the machine, but later my hands moved almost by themselves, so I could look around a little. There was Sally Zimmerman in the next seat, head bent, running one sock after another through the machine to seal the toes, and beyond us were the windows and light filtering in through the clattering noise and the filaments of dust and fabric that filled the air. At night I'd brush my teeth and spit out blue threads. My ears and my nose gathered lint, as well.

"The days were long and I worked every day but Sunday. I'd walk the few blocks home so tired I could barely move my feet, and fall into bed. Later that summer, we moved to the lake house.

"This is what caused all the trouble, in the end.

"I was so tired, you see. Just asleep on my feet, most of the time. But I always got up and tried to help around the house. Sometimes I'd go out and sit by the lake in the sun and listen to the waves and maybe fall asleep.

"One afternoon Cora had to go out, and she came to the dock and told me to listen for the baby and get him up if he cried, she would be home within two hours. The sun was warm and I'd dozed off, I suppose, for I woke up hearing his cries, thin and small, floating over the lawn. He was teething, and fussy, and so I got him a bottle and changed him and brought him outside, where Cora had a play area set up under the willow tree, right near the water. Is it still there, I wonder, that tree? It is? Those low branches swept over the lawn and the leaves were also so beautiful, but such a mess when they fell. He liked to sit there and play, passing toys from one hand to the other, and after half an hour or so he'd slump over and start to cry. So I settled him in the shade with his toys. I was right there. I had my book. I sat down in the lawn chair and read about five sentences. The sun was so warm. I remember the sound of the waves. I closed my eyes.

"I don't know what woke me up, or how much time had passed.

I sat up, feeling groggy, and looked over at the blanket beneath the tree. It was empty. I kept looking at it, panic so great it froze me in place, but then I heard a sound and turned. He was ten months old and he'd figured out how to crawl. I didn't know, I'd been away, working. I hadn't been paying attention. While I'd slept he'd crawled to the edge of the water, crawled in. The waves were touching his chin. He was laughing, but then he slipped and fell face-first. I jumped up and ran to him. It was probably the longest minute of my life. He wasn't crying or anything, just moving his hands in the water, floating, but his face was down. I swept him up in my arms, I was shaking.

"I didn't see Cora right away. She was standing by the barn, shading her eyes, a terrible look on her face. She'd seen it all. So. That was the beginning of the end for me. She never forgave me, or believed it was an accident. Eventually, I ran away."

"It wasn't your fault," Ned said. "It *was* an accident. And he wasn't hurt."

"No. He was laughing. He was so little he didn't understand danger."

I was thinking of Max, standing over the rushing water, turning back to smile at me as if nothing were the matter at all.

"What did you do?" Yoshi asked. "After you left, what did you do? Where did you go? It must have been hard, you were so young."

"Yes. It was hard. Though when you're young you don't think about that so much. You don't realize you're setting a pattern for your life. They found me—I was staying with a friend—and when I said I didn't want to come back to the house, they sent me here, to Elmira, to a Mrs. Stokley, who needed a boarder. So I went. I took a job in one of the glass factories. I wanted to be a teacher, but of course I didn't have the training. When I was twenty-one, I met John Stone at a company picnic. He was an engineer, like Ned. He was flying a kite that day."

"My father," Ned said. "They were married for fifty-seven years."

"And you never saw Joseph again? Neither your uncle or your cousin?"

She shook her head. "My cousin, no. My uncle did come to visit. Just once. It must have been near the end of his life, goodness knows—I was in my fifties. He brought a photo from his childhood, and he took me to lunch, and he indicated that I'd be remembered when he died. I didn't put much faith in it, of course. And of course, since I never heard another thing about it, I knew I'd been right."

While we'd been talking, the door in the foyer had opened and shut again, softly, and a young woman dressed in shorts and a white tank top had taken a seat on the step down into the living room, resting her chin on her hand and listening intently. She had long hair pulled back in a ponytail. As the conversation paused, Carol introduced her as Julie, their youngest daughter.

Julie smiled and said hello. I replied, taking her in. Since Ned and my father were second cousins, Julie and I must be third cousins, if there were such a thing. Even if there were, did it matter? That was the sort of cousin you might not know about even if you grew up in the same town. She was tall, not quite as tall as me, but nearly so. I stood and she shook my hand.

"So you're a hydrologist," she said. "That's so interesting."

"I like it."

"And you work in Japan?"

"Well, not exactly." I glanced at Yoshi. "We were living in Japan, but we're on leave right now. Thinking about the next thing, whatever it might be."

"I know what you mean. I've done my share of that."

"Julie is a teacher," her father said. "But she has a passion for animals. She rescues them. That's her real love."

I didn't know what to say—in this way we were not at all alike. I wondered if her apartment was full of stray cats.

"Exotics," Julie said, as if reading my mind. "I rescue exotic animals whose owners didn't know what they were getting into and finally abandoned them. So far I've adopted a boa constrictor, two monkeys, and three iguanas. The monkeys aren't at home, of course—there's a great facility in Kentucky that takes them."

"Julie," Carol said. "Grandma Iris asked to get the papers out of the house safe earlier. The old photos and so forth? But we couldn't seem to get it open. Your father has forgotten the combination, and we can't find the place where we wrote it down. I wonder, do you think you could help?"

"I can try."

Julie opened a door in the built-in cabinets and sat down at the safe, her ear pressed to the metal, her fingers resting on the dial. She closed her eyes, and my own heart quickened. The patterns of the internal mechanism flashed into my mind like a vision, the pins moving in their quiet patterns. Slowly, slowly, she turned the dial, listening to the voice of the metal. I knew how smooth and hard the safe felt against her cheek, how softly the tumblers shifted and clicked, each one like a breath released. She held herself still, listening, and then her face relaxed, breaking open with satisfaction. The feeling of success, of completion, welled up in me, too. She opened the little metal door and reached inside.

"Look at that," Ned said, chuckling.

"It's a gift," Carol agreed. "She's been able to do that since she was five years old. I don't know where she gets it."

"My uncle used to do that," Iris said, her voice far away, her eyes not quite focused on the here and now, as if she were seeing the world through the dual lenses of the present and the past—like trying to navigate the world in 3-D glasses.

"Me, too," I said, spreading my fingers. "I can do it, too."

They looked at me, my outstretched hands, in surprise. Then Julie pulled out a stack of papers and handed them to her father, who sorted through what looked like bonds and wills and deeds until he came to a single yellowed photograph, which my great-grandfather had given Iris on his single visit. It was a family portrait, dated August 22, 1909— the year Geoffrey Wyndham drove into the village in his Silver Ghost, a year before the comet. There were notes in pencil on the back. Rose was in the center, wearing a dark dress with a pale collar and cuffs. The other family members, also dressed in formal black, flanked her: a stern patriarch with his white beard, the older brother and three older girls who might have been cousins, their faces serious in the presence of the photographer. Rose's mother and an aunt and a grandmother sat stiffly on chairs in front of the others.

"What was the occasion?" I wondered.

"No one knows," Ned said. "A wedding, or a funeral, or maybe just a photographer passing through the village."

"Here's Joseph," Iris added, her finger tapping beneath the boy standing next to Rose, squinting into the camera as if trying to discern the future. She paused, her voice softer. "And that girl must be Rose, I suppose. My mother."

I looked more closely, thinking of Rose's letters, the girl who had stood at the ship railing watching her country recede into mist. She was so young in this photograph, just fourteen, her hair still down, falling around her shoulders. She wore a ribbon around her neck and she was half-smiling, as if about to turn and make a joke; she alone of all the family—the serious older girls, standing in a row, and the careworn parents and aunts, and the grandmother, as old in the photograph as Iris was now, wearing a black bonnet and a visage like a withered plum—Rose alone looked happy.

What was she was thinking in that moment? What did she dream, and how did she imagine her life? On a summer morning, surrounded by her family, she turned, about to laugh, unaware of Edmund Halley or his comet, a chunk of ice traveling through the coldness of space, whose arrival would cast such a strange light across her life. She did not know that a door was about to open in the world and she would walk through it, terrified and hopeful, into a future she could never have imagined.

"I'm tired," Iris said. She'd put the folder full of letters on the sofa, and her hands were resting on the blanket in her lap, her fingers working the edge of the silky fabric. "I'd like to have a rest, I think."

Ned was on his feet at once, reaching down to help Iris stand. She took his arm. I stood, too, and clasped her hand for a second. Her fingers were cold. I told her that I had something I'd like to show her, once she'd had a chance to read the letters and digest them. I explained about Frank Westrum and the windows and Rose, though I wasn't sure how much she was taking in. Ned was interested, though, and he paused with Iris in the hallway.

"You say there's a whole museum, full of stained-glass windows."

"Yes. Rose helped design them. She knew the artist. They were very close, in fact. She modeled for him."

"I see. Well, I think we'd all be very interested in knowing more, when my mother feels up to it."

"Yes," Iris said, and they started moving slowly back down the hall-way to her room. "I would like to see them." Yoshi and I stood for a few minutes longer, talking with Carol and Julie. I gave them the brochure I'd brought about the Westrum House, along with a description of the chapel.

"It's just overwhelming, I think," Carol said, as she opened the door. "I know I'm overwhelmed, so I can only imagine how Iris feels. She has to reconsider her whole life."

She walked with us to the car, admired the Impala's sleek golden lines, and promised they would be in touch. From the end of the long driveway, she watched us disappear into the leaves.

"I'm worn out, too," I told Yoshi as we drove. "I'm emotionally wiped out. How about you?"

"Not so much. It's not my family, so it's just interesting from afar. Though, you know, my mother's family is from southwest England, near Bristol, I think. So maybe we're related, too."

"Oh, don't start."

He laughed. "It's incredible, though. The whole story is. And that you found her, after all these decades."

"It really is."

We talked about this as I drove, leaving Elmira for the blooming fields, daylilies running through the ditches like fire, the fields alive with butterflies and insects, the lakes deep blue and shimmering as we drove along their shores.

Halfway back we'd settled into a companionable sort of silence when the car began to shake and fill with a steady thump-thump-thump. I eased the Impala onto the side of the road and checked—sure enough, the front passenger tire was completely flat. Yoshi rummaged in the trunk—there was no spare—while I called my mother to see if she had a road service. She did, and I put in a call for help.

We were on the edge of a field high between the lakes, water visible in the distance. It was warm, and I was so worn out that I walked a few feet into the field and lay down, trying to ignore the buzz of insects, the cloud of dragonflies that lifted, translucent, from the edge of a nearby puddle and flew away. After a minute Yoshi came and sat down beside me; I shifted so that my head was resting on his leg. He stroked my hair, letting his fingers linger on the soft skin below my ear. Beneath me the earth felt alive, rich with growing things, and beneath his touch I felt alive as well, alive and sleepy and nearly content. I ran my hand along Yoshi's calf, hard and muscled, thinking how good it was to be here in this sunny field with him, the deep blue lake set like a bowl into the green fields of the earth. Then we heard the truck arrive, the door slam, and we both stood up, shaking seeds and bits of grass from our clothes.

A man in a white cap had left his tow truck and was rummaging in the Impala's huge trunk, which Yoshi had left ajar. He'd pulled out an empty red plastic gas can, a bag of tools, a folded blanket, and my father's tackle box, and placed them carefully on the gravel shoulder. "They don't make trunks this big anymore," he said, looking up and smiling at us when we drew near. "Just thought I'd take a look-see, maybe there's a compartment for the spare." Yoshi stood close to me, his hand warm on the small of my back, as the man searched and came up empty. He cheerfully and deftly unbolted the Impala's whitewall, leaned it against the bumper, and replaced it with a temporary spare. The lake in the distance was blue, sheened with silver. He put everything back inside the trunk and slammed it shut, and we drove off once more.

Chapter 18

WHEN WE GOT HOME IT WAS EARLY EVENING AND THE kitchen counters were covered with green cardboard quart containers filled with just-picked strawberries. My mother and Andy were standing side by side near the sink, their silver heads bent over the task, working and laughing. A pile of discarded stems grew high between them, and several earthenware bowls were mounded with wet berries. The air was thick with the scent of strawberries and sugar; by the stove, placed carefully on a dish towel, eight jars of jam, ruby red, were resting. One of the lids sealed with a click as Yoshi and I came inside. My mother turned, smiling and holding up one hand to quiet us. Her hair was damp, clinging to her scalp, and her cheeks were flushed with heat. There was a streak of red below her elbow and her fingers were stained red, too. We stood still, and a second later another jar clicked, and then a third. My mother laughed and let her hand fall.

"There—I've been counting the seals, and now they're all done. Aren't they beautiful? I always love this part, the jars like jewels on the counter. We'll be so happy to have these when the snow is six feet high."

"They look good right now," Yoshi said, slipping off his shoes at the door.

"Sorry we're so late. The road service took a while."

I crossed the room and took a strawberry from a bowl, biting through the red to its soft white heart, and offered one to Yoshi. We'd gone out early in the morning so many times when I was little, picking strawberries from their low bushes, or cherries from the trees, Blake and I eating as many as we picked. We'd come home with a car full of fruit, the kitchen growing warm and full of sweetness as the day unfolded and the jars of plump gold or red spheres or the pale sliced moons of pears lined up in rows, filling all the counters.

"Have a taste," Andy said. He wiped his hands on a towel and offered us a bowl of dark red jam, swirled with foam. "We got some of that fresh bread of Avery's, and some of her organic butter, too, and let me tell you, it's out of this world."

Yoshi and I sat down at the table, suddenly ravenous, and ate, telling the story of our day in Elmira: the beautiful drive, Yoshi's conversations in Japanese, Julie's familiar gift with the combination safe, and Iris's amazing story. My mother looked up from her work, her hands resting on the berry-stained counter, when I started describing Iris, how temperamental she'd been, how deeply it had affected her to learn the truth.

"It was very moving and very sad," I finished. "That's what I've been thinking about all the way home. Ninety-five years old, and she still felt abandoned. I hope it helps her to know what really happened."

"I hope so, too," my mother said. "I have to tell you, I'm relieved it went well. I mean, she could have been crazy, or mean, or dishonest, couldn't she? Or just someone you'd rather not know."

"It's true. You can't choose your relatives, can you? Your mother's been kind of worried all day," Andy said. He stepped past her, carrying a bowl of smashed berries to the pot, and kissed her cheek as he passed. My mother glanced up at him and smiled.

"Everything was fine," I said. "We were fine."

While my mother and Andy finished preparing the berries, Yoshi and I made a salad and rice. We grilled salmon on the patio. It was late when we all sat down to dinner, the sky darkening to pale blue, then indigo, as we passed the food and poured wine. Distantly, boats hummed on the lake. Yoshi rested his hand on my thigh as we finished, and it seemed to contain all the heat of the field where we'd waited for the road service to arrive, the sunshine and the buzz of insects, and the scent of earth and sweat. We carried the plates back inside, admired once more the gleaming ruby jars. Then my mother and Andy left for a late movie. We watched their headlights recede, Yoshi standing behind me, pushing my hair aside, kissing my neck. He took my hand when I turned, as if we were dancing, and when we climbed up to the cupola it was like walking underwater, slow and graceful, full of forceful currents.

When I woke up hours later, I'd been dreaming. From the floor of the cupola the night sky was visible in all directions, struck with stars, as if the sky were a dark canvas flecked with holes, beyond which shone some clear white light. It was easy to understand how ancient people had imagined another world beyond, the myths of trees that would somehow grow past the limits of the sky and take them there. Easy to understand why they had not wished to name such power, too. I thought of the Wisdom window, all the people growing from the earth, being filled with breath and life, and of the Iroquois creation story Keegan had told me, how a woman, pregnant with the breath of a god, fell through a hole at the root of a great tree into the night, fell far to the sea below, where a turtle rose to catch her and the animals dived to the depths to bring back bits of mud and to make the world. *You live here,* the stories all said, *but you are filled with the breath of the Divine, and the world in your care is full of amazements.*

Yoshi slept. I turned to look at him. His mouth was slightly open and his breath faintly stale, his chest rising and falling in such a steady, gentle rhythm. I ran my hand along his arm and he twitched, then turned in his sleep and reached for me, his arm slipping around my waist. I curved against him, and we lay there at the top of the house, floating together in the night.

My dream, the one that had woken me, gradually surfaced again— not frightening, but intense, full of seeking and a sadness that lingered.

I'd been fishing with my father, floating in the hour before dawn. It was still dark and he was hardly visible next to me. We cast our lines and floated, cast again. We needed better lures, he said, and I pulled the tackle box from beneath the seat and opened it. Gray-green metal, it caught the faint moonlight. Opened, it revealed rows of lures, each in their own compartment. Iridescent, made of greens and blues and deep oranges that seemed to have been drawn from the depth of a prism, richly hued, yet also somehow luminous. They were like gemstones, smooth and spherical and trailing feathers, streamers, bits of lace. Some were tiny perfect images of the earth, blue-green and wondrous, each turning slowly in a mist of white. I wanted so much to hold them, yet when I touched them they broke into pieces, and the dream energy turned urgent and frustrating as I struggled to hold the broken halves and fragments together, to wrap the beautiful lures in twine or thread them on tiny metal dowels. Something was wrong, terribly wrong, and then my father showed me another box with lures that were whole, smooth and gleaming, and I despaired at those in my hands, so makeshift, seamed, and broken, held desperately together by thread and metal rods and wishing.

I stared up at the stars, concentrated on my breath and Yoshi's in the little room. Surely this dream was connected with the windows full of women and with finding Iris, the piece of the family story that had been broken away a century ago, broken away and obscured. Yet it was connected also to the dreams I'd been having since the night I arrived, dreams that seemed to go deeper than the ripples on the surface of life, deeper even than memory. Dreams born out of the restless searching I'd been doing since I left this place so many years ago. I thought about those dreams, all the seeking of round things, hidden in leaves, spilling like mercury, and now here, spheres falling into pieces, caught in a metal box. Yoshi's hand brushed my thigh, and I thought of how we'd sat at the edge of the sunny field while we waited for the road service, the pulse of his thigh beneath my cheek. I wanted to be there again, in the sunny field with Yoshi, the deep blue lake set like a bowl into the green fields of the earth, wanted that moment of peace before we heard the truck arrive, the door slam, and we sat up.

We had walked through the grass to meet the man in the white cap. The trunk of the Impala was still open and he pulled out a bag full of tools, an empty red plastic gas can, a folded blanket, and my father's tackle box, placing them carefully on the gravel shoulder, looking in vain for a spare. "They don't make trunks this big anymore," he'd said. Yoshi stood close to me, his hand warm on the small of my back. We watched him work. The lake in the distance was blue, silvery, and the fields were alive with dragonflies. He put my father's things back inside the trunk and closed it.

I sat up, the bright, broken lures of my dream spilling their pieces everywhere. The air was cool and still, and the stars hadn't moved. After my father drowned, the searchers had gone out, diving for hours, bringing back a lake-filled boot, his sodden hat, his fishing pole.

His tackle box, however, they'd never found.

His tackle box, hidden all this time in the trunk of his car.

I knew as surely as I knew my name or the rush of breath in my lungs that my father hadn't been going out to fish the night he died. He'd gone out onto the lake to think, to float on the water in the darkness and grapple with whatever had woken him or kept him from sleep, whatever had weighed so heavily on his mind.

I slipped from beneath the sheet, careful not to wake Yoshi, and pulled my shorts and T-shirt from the tangle of clothes on the floor. We'd carried the heat of that field with us all day, brushing against each other like sun against grass, like stems pushing through the soil, and the clothes we'd discarded so quickly as we'd kissed at the top of the cupola stairs still held something of that warmth and sunshine. I went down the stairs gingerly, trying to stay at the edges so the steps wouldn't creak, and stopped in the kitchen to collect the car keys from inside the cupboard door. Then I went out through the porch and across the lawn and driveway to the barn.

I was barefoot, the grass wet and the gravel harsh against the soles of my feet. The barn doors swung open quietly. The Impala was a shadow in the dim light. After my eyes adjusted, I groped my way to my father's workshop, stumbling against the lawn mower and knocking over a rake with a clatter. The flashlight hanging on the wall didn't work, the batteries long dead, but the old lantern still had an inch of kerosene at the bottom, and the matches were where they had always been, to the right of the jars of nails, above the shelf of planes. I lit the wick, and the glass globe filled up with light, casting objects back into their shapes, their shadows.

The car trunk opened easily, swinging upward. I moved the lantern forward, light flickering into the darkened spaces. The tackle box, dull green, was pushed far back in the corner, and I had to put the lamp down before I could lift it out all the way. It was locked. I found a wire on the workbench and then I sat down right on the floor, the concrete cold and gritty against my legs. The wire was thin and warm in my hand. The night fell softly around my shoulders and I still felt halfway in a dream, as if my father were present, watching me slip the wire into the keyhole and press my ear against the box, listening, listening, with an ear that knew how to hear.

Silence, and then the subtle rush of metal on metal. The click, soft, almost imperceptible, when one of the pins fell into place. One, and then another, and then the final sound in the sequence, one, two, and then *three*. I sat up. The lid was ajar, and I opened it.

The lures were as they always had been, dull, feathered with wire, plastic worms, each one different than all the others, none of them luminous, none of them a sphere. No little moons and planets, floating in their own misty atmospheres, filled the compartments. I'd seen these lures hundreds of times as a child, had helped my father make them, spreading the wires and bits of plastic or shining metal on his workbench, coaxing them into shapes we imagined fish might dream of, and strike. I was filled with nostalgia, remembering the sharp, final sound of scissors on metal, the hiss of wire, the laughter of my father as he held the lure up, bright or dull, spinning or trailing, so we could admire our imaginations, our handiwork, the artifacts of pleasure.

I lifted out the insert with its bounty of lures. Everything was so ordinary, so much as it had always been, that I half expected to see the space below filled with rolls of wire and twine, small pliers, extra fishing line. Maybe my father had simply forgotten the tackle box, left it in the car after a trip to another lake, and found himself out that night on the still, dark waters with his pole and no lures. It was possible. However, when I saw the bottom, I knew my intuition had been right. The space, usually orderly but cluttered with equipment, was empty except for a bundle of papers, several sheets together, folded in thirds, bound with a dark red rubber band that disintegrated when I tried to slip it off.

The page on top was unlined, with a single sentence in my father's handwriting: *Found in kitchen, west wall.*

I closed my eyes and focused on my breathing, in and out, a pulse like the sea, waiting until I calmed down. Remembering the night I'd come in from the gorge, rushed with wind and guilt and anger, to find my father standing in the garden, smoking and thinking. Remembering that last spring, the kitchen torn apart for several weeks, walls stripped down to their studs, the air tasting of dust and metal, the new appliances sitting in their boxes on the porch, my father in his work clothes, pulling a bandana from his pocket to wipe the gritty sweat from his forehead and glancing through the broken plaster and dust to find these pages. I opened them, as he must have done, slowly, because I both wanted to know and did not want to know, and my hands trembled as I moved the cover page to the back and started reading.

It was a formal document, the last will and testament of my great-grandfather, Joseph Arthur Jarrett. The boy with his comet dreams had grown into a man who built a lock factory and restored this house, and who wrote, at the end of his life, in a firm, slanted script not so different from his sister's. I moved closer to the quivering golden light of the lantern, its faint hiss, the scent of kerosene, everything falling away into shadows except this paper, these words. There was a tribute to Cora, and a memorial bequest to the flower guild she had enjoyed. There were several other small bequests, to the library, to the church, to the hardware association. The bulk of his estate, however, was to be divided between his son, Joseph Arthur Jarrett Jr., and his niece, Iris Jarrett Wyndham Stone, who had last resided in Elmira.

To amend for the things I denied her. To remind my son that the world does not owe him a living by any reckoning.

It was dated May 1972, about six months before he died.

There were bats in the barn; one swooped low as I sat back, the papers in my hand, trying to assimilate all the dates, all that these pages meant and implied. In 1972 Rose had been dead for thirty years and Cora for more than a decade, so when my great-grandfather died there had been no one left alive in the family who remembered Rose directly or knew her story, no one to testify to the envelopes that had arrived every month in the early years, money that was spent on Iris, yes, for the new dresses and shoes or the books and tea sets, but that may have gone for other purposes as well—to help pay the expenses on the new business, to buy the grand falling-apart house on the lake and ensure its restoration. It was impossible, from this distance in time, or maybe ever, to separate good intentions and mistakes from calculated moves, impossible to know exactly what had transpired all those years ago, but it was vividly clear from this will that he'd carried regret with him always. At the end of his life, he had wanted to make amends, and it seemed he died believing he had done so.

Another bat swooped low and floated back into the rafters. The concrete was cold, but still I sat for a long time with the will in my hands, watching the pattern of flickering light and shadows on the ceiling and the wall, thinking of Rose, whom I had never known but had nonetheless come to love. Finally I stood up, brushing dust and grit from the backs of my legs. I put the tackle box back in the trunk and closed it, extinguished the flame on the lantern and returned it to the workbench. Then I went outside and stood in the driveway, looking at the house, its eaves and porches, the cupola where Yoshi slept, the peeling paint, the unkempt garden, overgrown and heavy with wild roses. We'd grown up here, Blake and I, running across the lawn, diving off the dock into the lake, believing that the world had a certain order, an inevitable pattern, as fixed as constellations in the sky. And all the time these papers saying otherwise had been sealed up in the kitchen wall.

The air smelled of roses, and waves shushed against the invisible shore. I tried to imagine my father's thoughts on that last night, as he smoked one cigarette, then two, then walked across the lawn and took the boat out, grabbing his pole but not his tackle box. Had he even known who Iris was? Had he been trying to find the story of her life in those weeks before he died? And who had sealed these papers away in the kitchen wall all those decades ago? Sealed them but not burned them, hidden them where they might never be found, or would surface only after so much time had passed that any memories of Rose and Iris would have faded into dust. It might have been Joseph Arthur Jarrett himself, having changed his mind. Or it might have been my grandfather, who must have felt blistered with the anger radiating from these pages if he'd read them.

On the patio, the iron chairs were cold and damp with night condensation. I sat down, so agitated I wasn't thinking clearly, and pressed Blake's number on my speed dial. It rang ten times, twelve, fifteen, but finally he picked up, his voice gravelly with sleep.

"What is it?" he wanted to know.

"You were asleep. I'm sorry. Is Avery there?"

"Yeah, trying to sleep. Look, Lucy, what the heck's going on? What difference does it make if Avery's here?"

I stood up and walked to the edge of the patio, looking out across the lawn to the lake, the soft shuffling of shale beneath its waves against the beach.

"It's about Rose. I didn't want to wake you both."

"Well, thanks for that." I heard his footsteps, and then a space opened up around his voice as he stepped out on the deck.

"Lucy, this is all ancient history, okay? Whoever this Rose person was, whatever sort of scandal she caused a hundred years ago, it just doesn't matter anymore. Can't you let it go? Get some sleep, and let me get some, too."

"Look, that's just it, I found her daughter," I said. "I found Rose's daughter, Iris. Yoshi and I met her today. She's ninety-five, and she lives in Elmira. We met her family, too."

There was a silence, a rustling, and I imagined Blake sitting down on one of the deck chairs, looking up at the very same sky.

"Okay," he said, finally. "Tell me why it's so important. Why you're calling now, at one o'clock in the morning. You didn't just get back?"

I thought of the trip home through the blooming fields, daylilies running through the ditches like fire, the fields alive with butterflies and insects, the lakes vivid blue as we drove on the ridges between them, how after that meeting I'd seen the world the way you do when you've been a long time under water, everything luminous and vibrant, strange and new, charged with life. I couldn't tell Blake about any of this, or about the dream of lures that had woken me, brought me to the barn and the tackle box and finally to this moment. And suddenly, remembering the rolls of drafting paper at Dream Master, their penciled plans—secret plans, unshared—I hesitated to tell Blake about the will.

"I know it's late. I'm sorry, I couldn't sleep. But doesn't it seem astonishing to you that there's this whole branch of the family we've never known existed?"

"It does." He sighed. "Of course it does, it's interesting. But honestly— it's not life-or-death interesting. It's not wake-me-up-in-the-middle-of-the-night interesting. Lucy, don't you think maybe you're dwelling on this a little too much? Why not just relax and enjoy showing Yoshi around. Maybe if you weren't between jobs and here on vacation, this might not seem quite as important as it does right now."

Despite what I'd told Yoshi earlier, Blake's comment touched a nerve.

Maybe this was one of the reasons I'd never let myself be between jobs before, had never paused, going from scholarship to scholarship, good jobs to better ones, so I could always come back and run into Art or Joey or even Zoe and think to myself: *So there.*

"What do you mean? It changes everything."

"They're, like, third cousins once removed. It doesn't change anything at all."

"Blake, the story changes everything."

He laughed, exasperated. "Okay, okay. I'm not going to argue with you at one o'clock in the morning, Lucy. I'll see you tomorrow at the party. Meanwhile, good night, okay?"

Then the phone went dead.

I sat on the patio for a few minutes longer. There were bats here, too. Winged shadows, I had always liked them, their small intelligent eyes, their fondness for insects and the night. There were caves on the depot land and perhaps the bats lived there, clustered silently along the walls, aware of the voice of the land, the susurrations of the water and the swift growing of the plants, listening to the strange new sounds of metal against rock as the bulldozers scraped away the earth.

If my grandfather had found this will, had he looked for Rose and Iris and never found them? It was possible. I'd had a hard time tracking Iris down, even with the letters from Rose and a great deal of luck. Or perhaps he'd never looked for her—that was possible, too. I tried to imagine how it must have felt for my grandfather to read that will—if indeed he had seen it—his father's words, so harsh, like blows: *To amend for the things I denied her. To remind my son that the world does not owe him a living by any reckoning.* Bitter words, and perhaps the writing of them had been enough; perhaps my great-grandfather had put this will into the wall so no one would ever see it, the flashing anger of a moment.

Or, if my grandfather had read this will in the silence of the house after Joseph Arthur Jarrett died, he might have shoved the papers in the wall and smoothed the plaster over with even strokes, as if to erase those words, though his father's disappointment was already engraved forever on his heart.

I thought of my father and Art, growing up in this house, those words buried in the wall, all that bitterness sealed away but present, shaping everything that followed, like water shaping rock. Like it or not, it had shaped me, too.

Lights flashed across the lawn and over the surface of the lake, then went off abruptly; gravel crunched in the driveway, and my mother's laughter carried through the night, and voices, softer, floated through the darkness. Then silence, the thud of the car door falling shut and more laughter, and the flash of lights again as the car backed out. My mother came in through the porch. I called out hello.

"Lucy?" she asked, coming to the screen door, then pushing it open and stepping out onto the patio. She was dressed in white and silver, like one of the flowers in her discarded night garden, her perfume drifting through the air. "What are you doing up? Where's Yoshi?"

"Oh, he's sleeping. I couldn't. How was the movie?"

She smiled, but it was a private smile, and despite the jam-filled jars and Andy's kindness and my own best intentions, I felt a surge of anger at everything she was leaving so willingly behind. So easily, too, it seemed from outside, though I knew that wasn't fair. Maybe it was because I had been thinking so much about my father, about his last restless days. Or maybe it was the scent of strawberries still lingering in the house. "It was terrible, actually, but we had fun. You know, it's been years since I laughed so much with anyone. We stopped at his place for pie when it was over."

"He's quite the cook."

If she heard my tone, she ignored it. "Yes, he really is. The pie was incredible, deep-dish, with clotted cream. He says he finds it relaxing to cook."

"Well, that's lovely."

"Lucy. Honey. Just be happy for me. For heaven's sake, just be happy, period."

"You know," I said, not deciding to tell her, the words just coming out in a rush. "The night Dad died, I ran into him here, in your garden. In the middle of the night, before he went fishing. He asked me to go with him. And I said no."

My mother seemed startled. "The night he drowned?" she asked slowly.

"Yes. That night. I mean, if I'd gone, everything would be different. He'd probably still be alive, and everything, everything, would be different."

"Oh, honey," she said. She came and put her arms around me. "Is that what you think? What you've thought all these years? Oh, honey, no. No. What happened to your father was not your fault, or anyone's fault, and you can't fix it."

"If I'd gone fishing with him," I insisted, "everything would be different now."

"Yes, maybe. And if he hadn't gone fishing at all everything would be different, too. If it had been raining, if and if and if. You can't do this, Lucy. You just can't. Believe me, I tortured myself for a long time, too. Your father had had something on his mind for days. After the accident—and at first I wasn't even sure it was an accident—I couldn't stop wondering: why hadn't I pressed him harder to find out what was wrong? I woke up when he got out of bed that night. I caught his hand as he was leaving the room and asked him what was wrong and he said nothing. He kissed me, and he said not to worry. Those were his last words to me. I couldn't sleep, though, so I went up to the cupola. I heard you come in, Lucy. I heard the motorcycle come and go, I heard you talking in the garden with your father. It was fine, everything you said. It was not your fault, what happened."

I didn't speak for a moment. Bats rushed above us, like leaves drifting, like scraps breaking free from the sky. The relief I felt at having told her was physical.

"I know that. It's just—"

"Your father is gone, honey. He's been gone a long time. He would want you to live your life."

"I know. I know that. But Mom, you said he was preoccupied. Do you happen to know why? What was on his mind?"

She sat down, shaking her head. "Oh, Lucy, do we have to? I don't want to talk about the past anymore. You've found Iris, right? So your quest is over. The past is the past, Lucy," she added gently. "It doesn't help you to dwell there. You miss too much of what's going on right in front of you. Believe me, I speak from experience on this. Don't get stuck."

The will, those pages with their slanted handwriting, was burning in my hands. I imagined telling her about it, but as with Blake, something held me back. This will left half of everything to Iris, and all these decades later, I had found her. Would the will still be valid? Would Iris even care? Would my mother? I didn't know, and that was just the trouble. I felt like I was walking on sand.

She looked at me—puzzled, irritated, concerned. I knew she wanted more than anything to walk away and go to bed, to drift into sleep, the scent of pine and strawberries permeating everything, the memory of Andy's laugh, the touch of his large, capable hands, all of this easing her into pleasure, sleep, dreams. Still, after a moment she sighed and pulled her chair closer to the table. I thought of the morning we'd sat here looking at Rose Jarrett's cryptic notes—just over two weeks ago, though it seemed a lifetime away. I turned the pages in my hands.

"I don't know," my mother said. "I don't know the answer to your question. As I said, I thought about it night and day for months after your father died. Trying to understand what had happened. We weren't old, you know—your father only forty-five that summer, and I was forty-three, and for a long time after, I'd wake up in the morning believing it hadn't happened. I think that's why I closed off the rooms. I wanted a wall between then and now, between what we'd dreamed for our lives and what had really happened.

"Anyway, all I can tell you is that he had something on his mind. He was preoccupied. Not worried so much as distracted. It was like he was listening to music I couldn't hear. Sometimes I'd have to ask him a question three or four times to get an answer. He was finishing the kitchen renovation, and he kept having problems with the subcontractors. I didn't want to add to his stress. I figured he'd tell me eventually, once he'd had time to work it out, whatever it was."

She stared at the table, then looked up and spoke again. Her eyes were dry, but her words were rough with emotion.

"Does it matter, Lucy? Because I think we're still in different places with all this. In the beginning I kept searching for reasons, too. I tortured myself with the idea that I might have changed the outcome. If I'd only done this, or said that, a different set of events would have followed. Maybe so. But *this* is what happened, and nothing changes that. It was an accident, and over the years it's become a comfort for me to think of it that way."

We'd never spoken so directly of my father's death before; we'd driven grief underground, like water pressed beneath shale, threatening to emerge without warning. I didn't want to cause her any further pain, but I put the will, those angry pages, on the table. I explained what it was and how I'd found it. I told her what it said.

She sat back in the chair, then picked up the papers and shuffled through them, though it was too dark to see.

"Really? He left half of everything to Iris?"

"He did. If he meant for this will to be seen, that is. He might have put it in the wall himself. Changed his mind, sealed it away instead of burning it."

She nodded slowly. "Either that, or someone else did. Your grandfather or grandmother. It's hard for me to imagine it was your grandfather, though. You never knew him, of course."

"No, I only heard stories."

"He was genial, he liked the good life and was happy to float along on what his father had accomplished. Art's a lot like that, when you get down to it. He feels entitled to everything, somehow. He was the sort of person who went along to get along—though, who knows, he might have bottled up enough anger to do this. Your grandmother, though—especially after your grandfather had that stroke—was very protective of her boys, especially of Arthur. I can see her doing this. Of course, I never knew your great-grandfather, so I can't really say what he might have done."

"Well, someone didn't want it to be found."

"Yes."

"That seems awfully mercenary, if it was all about the money."

"It might have been money. Or it might have been anger or embarrassment. They were very proper, both of your grandparents. Very concerned with appearances, with the family name. It's a small town, and word would have gotten around. It might have been a sense of shame as much as anything, if either one of them did this.

"That's your father's handwriting," she said, picking up the first page and reading it again. *Found in kitchen, west wall.* "He must have come across it during the renovation that last spring." She sighed. "He never mentioned it. He wouldn't have, though. Still, I knew something was off."

"So maybe this was what was on his mind."

"Yes," she said slowly. "I can see that. It might have been."

"If it's true, it could change everything."

In the silence we listened to the soft voice of the lake, whispering and whispering to the stony shore where they had pulled my father from the water.

"Well, not everything," she said.

She stood up and slid the papers back across the table. The radiant happiness that had surrounded her when she'd come in had disappeared.

"Let's just think about this," she said. "Let's not mention it to anyone. We can talk to lawyers and so forth, but for the time being, I don't see the need to discuss it with others."

"It's been such a strange day," I said, because I didn't want to consider too deeply why she might wish to keep this quiet.

My mother reached over and put her arm around my shoulders. She smelled unfamiliar, of strawberries and sweat.

"Go to bed, Lucy," she said. "Get some sleep."

I went upstairs, climbed into the room at the top of the house where Yoshi was sleeping in the middle of the futon. He moved away as I slipped in beside him. I lay there for a long time, the events of the day and discoveries of the night coming around and around, as if circling on a conveyor belt I could not switch off. I tried relaxation exercises and reciting lines of poetry and, remembering how I had felt in the chapel, for the first time in years I even tried self-consciously to pray, but the cupola was filling with the grainy gray light of sunrise before I finally slipped into a fitful, dreamless sleep.

Chapter 19

WHEN THE LAND AROUND THE LAKES WAS HOME TO THE
Iroquois, they celebrated each harvest season by setting bonfires along
the shore to make a ring of fire. This tradition was still celebrated every
autumn after the leaves had scattered across the surface of the lake and
the fields were stripped bare of their splendor, brown and dormant. Over
the years people had begun to light a ring of fire on the Fourth of July
as well. Boy Scouts sold flares and people plunged them into their lawns
or deep into the pebbles of their beaches; Yoshi and I bought four from
a stand outside the grocery store, and I explained what would happen:
as the post-solstice twilight faded into darkness, the flames and flares
would be lit up along the shore, making a necklace of light.

This was what we were waiting for when we gathered in the park
by the marina. Blake had docked in the slip closest to the shore, and he
and Avery had set up coolers of drinks, along with baskets full of delicate
turkey and watercress sandwiches from The Green Bean. Family and
friends sat with drinks on the edge of the seawall, or gathered in groups
on the boat or the dock or the lawn. There was a band concert going
on in the gazebo and children ran out to dance barefoot in the grass,
parents chasing after them when they ran too close to the water. I found
Avery on the boat deck, wearing a close-fitting T-shirt that made her
pregnancy clearly visible.

"I'm so sorry," I said. "It was my fault completely."

She met my gaze. "Not entirely," she said. "Blake didn't have to tell."

"I was giving him a hard time," I said. "About sticking around here and taking a job at Dream Master. He was just giving me a context, that's all. I'm the one who let it slip for no reason."

She sighed, looked off over the lake, sipped at her sparkling water.

"All right," she said at last, and looked back at me again.

"We're good, then?"

She shrugged. "Not exactly. Not quite yet. But there's no undoing it, so we might as well move on."

I nodded. That seemed a little harsh, but fair enough. Honest, anyway.

"Besides," she said, relenting a little, "we're telling everyone tonight. No formal announcement, we're just telling people one by one."

"Okay. Congratulations, by the way. I'm really glad for you both."

At this she smiled a little, and gave a quick nod, and then one of her friends was coming over, hugging her, and I stepped aside and took my drink back to the park, where Yoshi was waiting. I slipped my arm through his, resting my head for a second on his shoulder, and he glanced at me, smiling, before he went back to the conversation. He was talking to Joey, who was with the same long-limbed, long-haired woman I'd seen him with at Dream Master. Zoe and Austen were there, too, standing on the boat with Art. Across the expanse of lawn I glimpsed Max, dancing with wild abandon to a Sousa march, and Keegan, dancing with him for a few beats, before he laughed and swooped down, lifting Max and putting him up on his shoulders. I felt a pang of affection and the slightest bit of regret, but it was gone as quickly as it came, and I turned my attention back to the conversation.

They were talking about The Landing. They had the land and a zoning change was making its slow way through committees and would be announced within a day or so; Joey was optimistic that they'd get permission to build. I thought of the beautiful chapel, which stood in the center of the parcel they wanted, and of my mother, telling me not to mention the will I'd found, and felt a rush of paranoia: why *not* say anything? Was she planning to sell her property to Art, after all? Was she changing her mind about Dream Master? I wondered suddenly, too, what had been happening with Oliver and Suzi and the chapel.

"You're pretty far from building anything, though," I said, sipping at my wine.

Joey shrugged, nonchalant, full of the smug, unearned confidence that had always driven me crazy. "Yes and no. We're almost good to go. I've already had calls from a dozen people interested in owning a piece of this. It could potentially be the biggest thing we've done."

I thought of the marshes, and the herons rising when I disturbed their reedy home, rising and floating high, huge and graceful, above the trees. I looked across the water at Blake, standing on the boat and laughing with Andy and Art and two other people I didn't know, and my mother, talking with Avery now, who was looking very happy. "New Year's Eve," I heard her say. "We're getting married New Year's Eve."

The band played, and finished, the last notes floating out over the water. We ate and drank and talked as the sun went down and the darkness deepened. Fires began to appear, first just a few and then more and more, flaring here and there around the rim of the lake. It was such a lovely, familiar evening, the air as soft and warm as breath, but the secret of the will was like a transparent wall between me and everything else. I kept moving from group to group, drifting in and out of conversations.

Finally, Yoshi and I sat by ourselves on the seawall, dangling our legs into the lake. I told him about the will and all it implied.

"Well, it's not necessarily sinister. Maybe your mother just doesn't want to take any dramatic action until she knows what it means," he suggested. The lake had turned a misty gray that blurred into the deepening sky. "After all, the will may not be valid. And if it is, then it would probably be pretty complicated to figure out who got what all these years later."

"You think I'm overreacting?"

"A little bit," he said, nodding.

"Maybe I am," I said, remembering my conversation with my mother about Oliver's intentions. She'd been completely right. "It's always like this after a few days here. I start to lose my bearings. The surface is one way, but then there are all these other things going on, sometimes going back decades, swirling undercurrents that I just don't understand."

"This time is different, though," he said. "You have Rose's story now, which must put a new light on everything."

It was true, I did. Her story, and the radiant windows of the chapel and the Westrum House, had stretched and changed the way I saw the world. Everything was connected in a way I had not understood before. Her dreams, as well as my great-grandfather's, had brought us to this dusky evening, to this moment in time when everything might shift and change again.

Blake walked down the dock, his boat shoes echoing faintly against the wooden slats. He'd strung tiny white lights on the railings.

"Hey there, you two," he said. "I'm going to run Mom up to the house. Want to come and check out the fires along the way?"

"Sounds nice," I said, splashing my foot in the water, "but I've got the Impala. So I can't."

"Yoshi? Want to come?"

"You should," I said, knowing how Yoshi loved to sail, realizing this might be his only chance, given how busy Blake always was, how our time here was already beginning to dwindle.

"You wouldn't mind?" Yoshi wanted to know.

"I wouldn't, really. I'll meet you at the house. I might take a walk first."

I waited until everyone had boarded and the boat had glided out onto the dark water, becoming nothing more visible than a net of moving lights. Then I finished my glass of wine and walked through the park, through the streets crowded with summer tourists.

I'd left the car behind Dream Master, where I knew I wouldn't get towed. As I walked along the outlet, the building turned a dark, blank-eyed, and impassive face to the world, but when I cut around to the parking lot, a light was visible in Art's window. He had left the party before I had a chance to say hello. I wondered if he was inside at his desk, or if he'd just left the light on. I wondered what, if anything, he knew about Iris, or the will, or Rose. So I went in.

I walked through those corridors where I had played as a child, running over the dusty linoleum, thrilled with the scents of metal and sawdust. This place had defined so many generations, and it looked caught in time. A row of safes for sale stood against the wall, made by some other company now, their little doors ajar. I walked up and down the aisles, studying the displays of locks and the bins of nails, the racks of paint chips and brushes.

When I finally made it to the door of Art's office, I found him staring at a computer screen. An old-fashioned adding machine sat on the desk, cascading paper onto the dusty tile floor.

He didn't hear me right away, and so there was a moment when I stood and watched him, concentrating hard, traces of my father in the shape of his hands and forearms, in the way his sideburns tapered into his graying hair. When he glanced up and saw me he was startled, and his face opened and went slightly slack with surprise; then he laughed, relaxing back into the chair.

"Lucy," he said. "What a surprise."

"Big leap?" I asked. "From hardware to software, I mean?"

He chuckled. "Sure is. You any good with spreadsheets?"

"I am, actually."

"Ah. Want to have a look?"

"No, not really."

He looked at me then, taking me in for the first time, and the uneasy expression that moved across his face echoed his look when he'd first seen me.

"No?" He folded his arms across his chest. "Then, what can I do for you?"

I felt sorry for him then, because he suddenly looked old and vulnerable behind that desk.

"I was just passing by and saw the light was on," I said, gesturing to the window. "I parked here and went to the party. I saw you, but didn't get to say hello."

"I stopped in. It was fun. I always like the ring of fire, and the concert—I like that, too. Your father and I used to light flares as kids. It doesn't seem that long ago."

"I've been driving his car," I said. "You know, the one he fixed up?"

"I know. I went out to look at it earlier. He sure loved that car."

"Yes, he did. My mother hasn't had the heart to touch it all these years, so it's mostly just been sitting in the barn."

He nodded and looked out the window at the gravel parking lot, where the Impala sat at the edge of light from the streetlamp, the silver arrows glinting.

"He'd be glad, I think." Art said. "Glad to know you were enjoying it, Lucy."

I leaned against the chair. "I am enjoying it. Though it drives like a boat. And the other day I had a flat tire, coming back from Elmira. I had to call the car service, you know, and the guy who came pulled everything out of the trunk. You'll never guess what I found."

"I can't imagine—a tire iron?"

"Yes, actually. And my father's tackle box."

Art sat up straighter then, leaning a little forward. He folded his hands carefully on the desk.

"Yes? Are you sure? We looked and looked for that the night he died."

"I know. He used to take me fishing. All the lures I remember were there."

"I see."

"Did you fish with him a lot when you were younger?" I asked, sliding into the chair, its leather smooth against the backs of my legs.

"Yes, as a matter of fact. We did. Summers, we were out on the water every morning. Me and Marty. We'd catch a whole string of fish some-times. Other times we'd come back empty-handed."

I nodded, thinking with nostalgia of all the mornings I'd spent with my father in just this same way.

"It's funny, though," I said. "The lures were in the tackle box, just like you'd expect, but none of his tools were in the bottom. No tools, no wire, nothing. It made me sad, somehow, all that empty space. Then I found the papers."

"Really?" Art said. "What papers were those?"

"A will. Your grandfather's will, in fact."

Briefly then, without pausing to weigh the possible consequences, I told the story—Rose and her daughter, and the will written by my great-grandfather, which included Iris.

His expression didn't change. After a minute, he sighed and leaned back in his chair, clasping his hands behind his head.

"So, do you have this will?" he asked. "Could I see it?"

I'd left it in the Impala, locked back in the tackle box.

"It's at the house," I said. "My mother put it away somewhere, I'm not sure where."

He nodded.

"Not that it matters," he said. "Such a will would hardly be valid, all these years later. Rose is long gone, and probably her daughter, too. What difference could any of it make?"

He had no idea, I realized. Not about the chapel or the windows, the fascinating life Rose had led, the other branch of the family, living not very far away.

"Well, actually, she's still alive. Iris, I mean. I met her recently. She has two grown sons, and grandchildren about my age."

"Are you serious? You say you met her?"

"Yes. It was really kind of amazing. She's ninety-five years old. Very together. She has the family eyes."

"Does she know about the will?"

I thought this was a strange first question to ask. "Not yet," I said. "I found it after I met her. But I think she should know, don't you? I mean, it might not be valid, but emotionally it might matter to her. To know she wasn't excluded."

Art's voice got lower then, not warm exactly, but inviting me to hear a confidence. I thought of Iris, and of Rose, of all the things I knew about the family that he did not know, and leaned a little forward, so I could listen. Listen, gather more, collect another piece of the puzzle that might let all the others fall into place.

"Lucy," he said softly. "Surely you understand that the marshland is worth a great deal of money at this moment. It hasn't always been valuable, and it may not be again. This is a golden moment, is what I'm saying. Probably this will you're talking about is null and void. I'm not all that concerned about it. But even so, if you contact this person, this long-lost relative, you open up the door to competing claims, even litigation. And I warn you, the moment will pass, and anything you might have had—anything your family might have had—will be gone."

"It isn't about money," I said, but even I could hear the uncertainty in my voice. I was thinking of Blake, and the falling-apart house, even as I was remembering floating in the marshes with my father.

"It's always about money," Art said. "Make no mistake, Lucy."

Art waited a moment. When he spoke again, his voice was wistful. "I loved your father," he said. "He was always such a sunny kid, the one everyone was drawn to, growing up. That was hard, and I did some things I regret, and so did he, but I loved him. I like to think that if he'd lived, we'd eventually have made things right between us."

I took a deep breath, the air full of the scent of cut wood and iron. "It seems to me you had plenty of chances to make that happen."

He shook his head, gazing beyond me to the doorway, to some distant point in the past. "Your father was a very stubborn man. He had his ways. He wouldn't listen."

There was something in his tone, so nostalgic, yet so laced with sorrow and regret. And I didn't think that sounded true about my father, who had the gift of listening, who had taught it to me. I held still, feeling the quality of the air change in the room. I even blinked slowly, as if Art were a wild animal I didn't want to frighten away.

"When?" I asked softly. "When didn't he listen to what you had to say?"

Art didn't look at me or even seem to hear me.

"I tried everything," he said. "Everything I could to get him to listen to reason."

"And he wouldn't?"

He shook his head, passed his hand over his eyes as if wiping away sleep.

"No. He would not. I tried three, four, five times. He wouldn't even speak to me by the end. When I found him that night he just kept casting his line into the water as if I wasn't even there. That's how it always was with Marty. Like I wasn't even there."

Now I could hardly breathe. "He was casting out his line," I murmured.

"Yes. Into the reeds."

"The night he died."

"Yes."

He looked across the desk then and we stared at each other, not speaking, as if his words had torn open the very air and all the oxygen was fading from the room.

"I was trying to do the right thing," he said, as if I would surely see the reasoning and understand this. "I was trying to help him. Help you all."

I closed my eyes for a second. "And he wouldn't listen."

"No." He looked away again, out the window this time, into the back parking lot, where the gravel was a dim gray beneath the streetlamp. "Marty would never listen to me. He'd showed me those same papers. The ones you found, I bet. Showed them to me and told me what he was going to do, didn't want to hear anything I had to say about it. And it was his land, sure, like he said." Art made a gesture of frustration, a swift cut of his hand, as if reliving the argument with my father.

"His to throw away if he wanted. Foolish. Not my business, though. But this was. Dream Master was *my* business. And I told him, again and again, if he found this person, if she laid claim to one piece, then what was to keep her from getting it all? Your father, he didn't know what he was opening up, what he was getting into."

Or maybe he did, I thought. Maybe he'd been enjoying a quiet kind of revenge. I didn't say this, though. I only nodded. I'd gone very still as Arthur talked, anchored by a strange calm, as if I'd stepped outside myself and was watching the conversation unfold from far away. In the silence, Art spoke again.

"I couldn't sleep for thinking about what he might do with those papers. Days, this went on. Then I woke up one night in the middle of the night. Was rudely awakened, I should say. Joey was always on the wild side, but usually he had the good sense to sneak in when he broke curfew. That night, though, he came home spitting mad. He was throwing things around, a car was waiting for him in the driveway. Before I could get up and ask what was going on, he'd found what he needed and left again, slamming the door hard on his way out. Damned if I could get back to sleep. Beautiful clear night it was, the kind we used to wait for as boys. I had a feeling Marty would be out there. In the marsh, where he always went—I had a hunch he'd be there. It's where we always used to go. So I drove to the lake and took the boat out. I just wanted to talk to him if he was there. And he was. He wasn't hard to find. It was a very still night."

I nodded, remembering how I'd stood talking with my father in my mother's moon garden on that same night, surrounded by such quiet it seemed I could hear the flowers in their delicate unfurling.

"He must have heard me coming, but he didn't even look up. I pulled the boat up near him, cut the motor. Then we just drifted. He kept casting his line, reeling it in. Wouldn't speak. We drifted, two boats, dark fish swimming beneath us."

Dark fish swimming everywhere, I thought.

"Finally, I grabbed hold of his boat. The metal was cold, and I was so frustrated; I told him he was being a fool. He turned around, maybe he only meant to knock my hand away, but his hand hit me in the face. I stood up, and he did, too. I don't think I hit him first, but maybe I did. Who knows, I might have. I just kept saying Marty, stop it, damn it, stop, but he wouldn't, and so I pushed him away. Hard. Hard as I could. He lost his balance, fell. I did, too, on the recoil. I fell into the bottom of my boat, almost capsized it. Went skidding away, careening. It was dark. I didn't see anything as much I felt it, heard it. It was a terrible sound, his head cracking against the side of the boat. It must have been his head. He didn't cry out, shout, anything."

Art paused and looked at me and it was all anguish on his face. I couldn't speak, caught in that still place, that airless vacuum, the dark fish swimming all around.

"I tried to find him," Art said. "I looked and I couldn't see him. It was so dark. It seemed like such a long time I was there, after he fell. But I don't know. I wanted to get help. I remember thinking I would get help. So I left. I left him."

I still didn't speak, remembering the voices traveling across the lawn in the beautiful dawn, my father lifeless on the stones, his skin swollen and iridescent, like a fish, the way my mother knelt beside him and touched his cheek so gently, and how he did not turn to kiss her palm.

"It wouldn't have made any difference," Art said. He was looking at his hands now, speaking to them. "It wouldn't have mattered, by the time I got to shore. Even by the time I left, nothing would have made a difference."

He wasn't looking at me, but I knew what he wanted, what he was waiting for in that dusty room with its fluorescent lights—he wanted me not just to hear him but to agree with him. To say it was okay, what he'd done, reasonable under the circumstances, and thus to become complicit in my father's death. Art looked so old now, sitting behind the desk, as if the telling had deflated him, leaving his skin to sag and cling more closely to his bones.

"Lucy," he insisted, meeting my eye at last, pleading now. "Talk to me, please. It would not have mattered one bit if I had stayed."

I stood up without a word, shaking, and walked out into the night.

He followed me, a shadow in the darkened door of the building. "Lucy," he called after me, speaking softly, his voice carrying across the grass. "Don't forget that you and your brother have a great deal at stake in this, too."

I stopped at the edge of the outlet, so filled up with pain and rage and outrage that I could barely breathe. Art stayed on the stoop outside Dream Master for a moment longer, the building dark behind him, looking in my direction. Then he turned and went inside, the door falling shut behind him, clicking as it locked.

How long I stood there, I couldn't say. The evening was mild and the streets were still full of tourists. Bursts of laughter floated out over the water from The Green Bean, and people strolled along the path, holding hands, eating ice cream, passing me, sometimes stepping around me, as if I were a pillar or a bench or a statue. I stood that still, caught in the airless, breathless pain of that long ago morning when they carried my father from the lake.

The windows above the glassworks were all dark—maybe Keegan was already asleep, Max breathing lightly, the rooms filled up with calm. I started walking hard and fast along the outlet into town, my thoughts so wild and scattered. It was a beautiful night, clear and warm, and so many people were lingering outside restaurants or strolling along the lake. Twice, people passing cast odd glances in my direction, and I realized I'd spoken out loud—a word, a phrase, agitated, nonsensical.

I walked in that state for a long time, past all the cozy homes with their lights on, people moving inside, reading or watching television or washing the dishes. Doing ordinary, untroubled things. They couldn't see me striding past their houses, tears flowing down my face at some moments, possessed by an anger so fierce I was almost doubled up at others. I walked to the edge of town and then back, past the church with its arched red doors. I thought of the Reverend Suzi, but it was too late to call her. The streets were quieter by the time I found myself in the parking lot again, standing with one hand on my father's Impala, the car he had loved so much, the place he had hidden his last secret.

The papers were still inside—I'd put them back in the tackle box because it seemed the safest place—reminding me of why I'd gone to see Art in the first place: to tell him about Iris, to talk with him about the ownership of the land. Not to hear this confession, words like lightning, transforming my known world like sand melting into glass.

Dream Master was dark. I went inside through the back door, which, oddly, was unlocked, as if Art had left in a hurry. I went into the storefront and, without deciding to do it, started pulling things off the shelves: gallons and quarts of paint crashing onto the linoleum, bucket after bucket of nails, a whole shelf full of doorknobs. I tipped the barrel full of marbles and they bounced and scattered across the store, shards of light glinting through the window onto their moving edges. It felt so good to hear things crash, to see the display of light fixtures teeter and go down. I made my way down one aisle, then another, the floor beneath my feet growing sticky with spilled paint, treacherous with marbles. The safes crashed one by one, each making a satisfying thud against the floor.

As the last one fell, a car drove down the street perpendicular to the store, lights flashing in the plate-glass windows. I froze, holding still until the car had turned and driven away. But the moment was broken. I didn't have the will to destroy anything else. Instead, I picked my way through the ruins and went down to the office, turned on the light.

There, I went through the files, pulling them out and stacking them on the floor. I don't know what I was looking for exactly, and I didn't find anything of much interest. Receipts and records of sales and shipments, going back decades. Maybe because of the flames on the beaches all around the lake, maybe because of the painful leaping in my heart, I had fire in my mind as I searched. I kept thinking how easily these papers would ignite, how they'd go up in smoke, how the flames would lick at the walls until they caught on the rafters hidden beneath and traveled upward into the attic, dry as kindling, where nothing would stop them. There was an old gas tank buried beneath the parking lot, and I thought of that, too, how a spark might travel there and ignite a vast explosion.

I went so far as to take a sheaf of old invoices and light the corner, letting them burn out over the metal trash can. Ash formed and fell. My fingers were stained black.

Would I have set fire to this building, imagined by my great-grand-father, created from his industry and imagination, so full of the artifacts of the past? I don't know. It was possible, alive in my mind, that I might do so. I opened the cupboards where we used to hide as children and started pulling papers out of there, too, letting them fall into a heap on the floor, the heap that could become a bonfire. The pile grew to my ankles, my calves, my knees. One match, I kept thinking. There was lighter fluid on the shelves, and paint thinner. One match and the place could go up in smoke, and fire, and ash.

Then I saw the handwriting. My father's, neat and slanted to the left, different from Rose's script, the letters long but more rounded, more fluid, unmistakably his. They spelled out the date January 1972 on a pale blue ledger with a cardboard cover. That was the year he met my mother. The year he was sent to Vietnam. I sat down at the desk and ran my fingers across the rough paper cover, imagining my father sitting at this same desk, reaching for a pen. January, snow as high as the windows, maybe falling through the cones of the streetlights in the early dusk, maybe swirling in eddies across the drifts in pale late afternoon light. And my father, so young, so full of dreams for his life, standing on the cusp of change, though he did not know it. It could break your heart to think of it too closely, to imagine all that might have happened, to know all that did.

I sat at the wide desk where a long line of ancestors had sat before me, and I opened the ledger. There were my father's careful notes on the neatly ruled pages, with their pale blue and red lines and the columns, all the numbers my father had written down so precisely. I was taken back then, to the Sunday evenings when he sat doing the accounts at the dining room table, a pencil tucked over his ear and his fingers flying over the adding machine. I ran my fingers over the numbers, flipped the pages. Number after number in his neat handwriting. Numbers and dates and more numbers, tallied into precise columns at the bottom of each page. There was such a precision to this work, such an order, that even looking at it brought me a deep sense of comfort. All the pages were full. At some point the dates switched to February, and then to March, and then they ended.

When I looked up again, all the wild anger that had driven me had drained away. I was left with only a weariness so strong I felt I might not be able to get up. But eventually, I did. I skirted the pile of papers and turned out the light, making my way through the hall and back out into the empty parking lot. The door had been unlocked; anyone could have caused the damage. That's what I told myself anyway as I drove up the lake road. The house was all lit up, and when I came in, my mother and Yoshi and Andy were gathered in the kitchen by the phone.

"There you are," my mother said.

Yoshi put his arm around me.

"Where were you?" my mother asked. "Why didn't you answer your phone?"

"I was just walking."

"For four hours? Lucy, it's after midnight."

"No, it's not!"

"Look."

I squinted at the clock on the stove. It was.

"I'm sorry," I said. "I walked for a while and sat by the lake, and I just lost track of time. I'm so sorry you were worried."

"Are you sure you're okay?"

"I'm fine." I took Yoshi's hand, laced my fingers through his. "I'm fine, just tired." I kissed him on the cheek in a showy way, eager to get away. "Come on," I said. "Let's go upstairs. I'm beat."

Chapter 20

WHEN WE REACHED THE CUPOLA I WALKED ACROSS TO THE futon with its rumpled sheets and sat down on the window seat overlooking the lake and the wild garden where I'd last spoken to my father. All the time he'd been holding this secret so close that even my mother hadn't known.

Yoshi sat down next to me and took both my hands in his. He waited, steady, until I could take a deep breath and tell him the story. I remembered how comforting it had always been, in the midst of the unsettled earth beneath us, to have Yoshi there. Once I started talking, there was a relief in the telling that I hadn't expected, and some of the pressure in my chest began to ease.

"He really said that?" Yoshi asked, his voice low and even. "He actually admitted that to you?"

I pressed my lips together for a second, then took a breath.

"He did. He said it was an accident. But that's not the thing—the thing is that he left my father there. He couldn't find him, and he just left. And he never said a word."

Yoshi kept holding my hands. He left the silence open so I could speak.

"He came to the funeral," I said, remembering. "And all these years he's been so damned nice to everyone, helping my mother, giving Blake a job, trying to hire me—all so we'd think he was wonderful, when all this time he did this, and he knew."

"He said it was an accident?"

"He did."

"Well, maybe it was. Maybe he was trying to make amends, Lucy. This must have been eating him alive," Yoshi observed.

I pulled my hands away, pressed them against my cheeks. "Don't defend him. It's not defensible, what he's done."

"Hey," Yoshi said. "Is it me you're mad at here?"

"No." I took another deep breath. "No, I'm sorry. It's not."

"All right."

"Right." I closed my eyes for a second. "All right. I don't know what to do. I certainly can't tell my mother."

Yoshi shook his head and gave a little disbelieving laugh. "Why not?"

I considered that. His family wasn't geographically close, but they were open in a way my family had never been. Why couldn't I say anything? Because I didn't know how my mother felt about Art and about the land; I didn't know what she was planning to do. And because I wanted to protect her from this knowledge.

"That's not your job," Yoshi pointed out when I tried to explain. "Lucy, you can't carry this with you, not saying a word. It will eat you alive, too, if you do."

"And then there's Blake," I went on, aware that I was not really responding to Yoshi. "Blake is right in the middle of this. Even if he doesn't know what happened, he's been woven into everything. Art is right, he has a deep stake in what happens."

"So do you."

"No, I don't."

"I'm not talking about money, or property, or this house."

I couldn't see Yoshi well in the darkness, but his voice was a little heated. I tried to search his face in the shadows, but his eyes were as dark as the night, unreadable. "What I mean, Lucy, is that you have a stake in the truth. It's not like anyone is going to put your uncle in hand-cuffs. He says it was an accident, and it probably was. It's a moral problem, not a legal one."

"If what he says about it being an accident is true."

"What? Do you think he's lying?"

"I don't know what I think. Maybe. He asked where I put the papers. I mean, I think he's genuinely unnerved by the will."

"Where are they?"

"In the car. I didn't tell him."

But then I thought of what I *had* told Art about the papers—that I had given them to my mother, that she had put them somewhere in this house. It wasn't rational, but I was seized with an urgent sense of panic, as if I might glance out the window and find Art striding across the lawn to search the house.

I sighed. "I guess you're right. I guess I have to tell her," I said.

We sat quietly for a while, side by side, the night air soft around us. Yoshi reached over and slipped his hand into my hair, gently massaging my scalp.

"You're so tense," he said. "Lie down for a minute." And so I did, sliding down to the futon and stretching out on my stomach. Yoshi ran his hands lightly over my back, drawing faint lines across my skin. "Relax," he said, and then his hands were on my shoulders, pressing away the tension I hadn't known I was carrying. My shoulders, arms, back, all relaxed, releasing anxiety like water. Waves lapped in the near distance, splashed against the dock, and I concentrated on that steady sound, imagining I was floating on water, being carried gently away.

Yoshi lay down next to me, resting one hand on the small of my back. I drifted, and drifted, his breath and my breath mingling with the sound of the waves, until at last I fell asleep.

When I woke it was still dark. I checked the time, but only an hour had passed. It was the deep middle of the night, hours before dawn. Next to me Yoshi slept, and below me, in another layer of the house, my mother slept, too. I stood up carefully, so Yoshi wouldn't wake, and made my way downstairs. I got a glass of water and stood on the porch steps, too restless to sit, too tired to swim or walk. Out here, the voices of the frogs were loud and low, floating through the trees from the direction of the marshland, and I thought of the herons sleeping there amid the rustling weeds, or standing on their reedy legs. I thought of the silence of the forest I'd walked through with Keegan, the sense of enchantment I'd had in that wild place, as if we'd stepped outside of time. I thought of all the people who had walked this land, and the traces they'd left, the stone grinding bowls and shards of pottery, the remnants of houses and barns, the patterns of underground bunkers. I thought of Iris, who had spent the last summer of her childhood in this house, had perhaps even stood in this same spot on a night not unlike this one, listening to the voices of the water and the frogs, searching the sky for a sliver of moon. And I thought of Rose, the traces she had left, even though she had never, to my knowledge, stepped foot in this house, or even in the beautiful chapel she herself had helped design.

So then I knew what I wanted to do. I went back and slipped the car keys off the hook. I got into the Impala, and I drove.

It wasn't far, less than five miles away. I pulled off the road onto the wide grassy shoulder and walked to the chain-link gates. Now that it was no longer officially a base, now that there was no equipment stored inside and no weapons were buried in the earth, the security, which had been so intense when I was growing up, was almost nonexistent. The single padlock on the gate opened beneath my hands; I slipped inside. Behind me, streetlights glared into the darkness. Where I stood, however, the night was complete, covering everything in its soft embrace. I started walking through the tall grass to the chapel as I had just a few days before. I didn't understand time, how so much could have happened so very quickly, how I could have known so little the last time I was here.

Opening the chapel door was easy. The lock was old-fashioned and gave way quickly. I stepped inside and stood still for a few minutes, letting my eyes adjust to the darkness. Gradually, shapes began to emerge:

the rows of empty pews, the pulpit and the lectern, the altar behind the communion rail, where empty candleholders glinted faintly in the scarce light. I slipped off my sandals, a habit from Asia, and walked to the front of the church, the tiles gritty against my bare feet. The Wisdom window had been returned to its place. The other windows would be removed soon for cleaning and restoration, but for now the chapel was intact, as it had been originally designed, and if I couldn't see any of the images, I knew from the glimpses of pale glass, of lead lines, that they were there. The vine-laced moons stood in pale relief across the bottom of each one. Rose, a century ago, had seen this pattern and carried it with her through love and disappointment, across the wide ocean and into the lonely winter nights. She had fashioned it into a blanket for her child and, years later, into the borders for these windows. This was the trace she'd left in the world, a piece of her story that had lodged itself in my imagination all these decades later.

I slid into a wooden pew, the wood smooth, the silence and the darkness sifting down. I sat still; moment by moment, my breathing grew calmer. I made myself inhale deeply, relax. *Ruah,* breath. Spirit. Wisdom. I imagined the Wisdom window, the clear glass indicating the rush of the Divine presence, creating and shaping everything. Not pictured, never named, but the source of all. I sat still in this place where so many had sat before me, trying to listen past my grief and confusion, thinking of Rose Jarrett a century before, in another country and another church, listening, too.

When, I wondered, had this story really begun? Was it in the moment when Rose, having lost everything she'd loved, had slipped the heavy silver chalice into her pocket? Or had it begun much earlier, when Geoffrey Wyndham laughed in the ruins, dismissing her dreams, or later, on the dark staircase, when he forced her to make a choice she didn't really have? Had it begun with the comet, that strange light, or had it begun long before, in events and social structures that caught my ancestors like a net the moment they were born?

Whatever its beginning, the story had unfolded, one event leading to the next, beauty and loss surfacing in every generation, until I sat here, a hundred years away from that comet, woven into the story in ways no one could ever have imagined.

In the darkness of the silent church I finally felt safe enough to let myself imagine the lake at the quiet hour before dawn; my father in his soft blue fishing hat, floating on the tranquil water, wondering what to do with knowledge he had not sought but could not discard. The sound of an approaching boat was faint at first, like a shadow in the mist, a shadow in his heart. In the gray, grainy light of almost dawn, Art's voice floated to my father, and he answered, and at first their argument was civil, reasonable, calm. But then the voices were less reasonable, rising like smoke in an angry upward spiral, until they were both standing, shouting, truly fighting, and both were falling, Arthur into the bed of his boat, ricocheting into the reeds, and my father slamming his head against the metal edge and slipping into the cold, clear darkness of the lake, too stunned to move.

I pressed my face into my hands.

Something about that night was still loose, untethered, flitting through my thoughts. In this stillness I could sense it, like the brush of air from a wing.

Around me the beautiful windows, connecting me to other lives and other times, to things done and also deliberately left undone, stood dark. Rose, I was sure, had acted out of love, yet for Iris her mother's absence had remained an unresolved sadness at the center of her life. I thought of what Rose had written about anger, about its power to corrupt, to make a space for evil. Maybe she was right. Maybe evil, that old-fashioned word, could be called other things, disharmony or dysfunction. Maybe Rose was right and evil wasn't attached to an individual as much as it was a force in the world, a seeking force, one that worked like a self-replicating virus, seeking to entangle, to ensnare, to undo beauty.

The thing I needed to see had been flitting around and around in the darkness, like something winged, and now it settled.

All these years, I'd been asking the wrong question altogether. The question was not what might have happened if I'd gone out fishing with my father. The question was what might have happened if I'd never gone out that night at all.

That night, I'd flown on the back of Keegan's motorcycle through the cool dark air to the gorge, where I'd run into Joey. He had taunted me my whole life long, the sort of contempt of indifference that wears a deeper scar every time it happens, and the anger of generations was coiled around my heart. So I had felt justified, even thrilled, stealing Joey's clothes and casting them into the trees, throwing his keys so deeply into the bushes that they were most likely there still, rusting into the earth. My remorse for all that had come much later, and had never been great, a mild uneasiness at most. And yet, in the deep silence of the sanctuary, I heard Art say what I had not been able to take in before: Joey had come in that night making a lot of commotion, much more than usual. He had banged drawers, searching noisily in the dark for clothes, for another set of car keys. I imagined Art, woken from a sound sleep, swinging his legs over the side of the bed. Art, swearing under his breath and getting up, going downstairs to drink a glass of water, knowing he wouldn't sleep again. The night had been mild, like the nights of his youth, and he found himself thinking of the fishing place, of taking the boat out for a little while. Why not? He put his glass in the sink and headed for the lake. My father was already there.

What had happened to my father was not my fault. I was not responsible for his death. I did not push him, or leave him alone in the water.

Yet it was not only others, in another country or on a dark lake, who had been ensnared in this pattern, repeating itself through the generations.

It was also me. I was woven into the story like everyone else.

I sat there for a long time, until the windows began to gather the light and distinguish themselves from the cold stone walls. The women in each frame began to emerge, carrying jars or bowls or stories, going about their lives. It gave me comfort to see them. The vibrant figures of the Wisdom window took shape, too, animals and plants and people with their arms uplifted, their hands becoming leaves, becoming words amid the healing rush and weave of Wisdom, encircling, creating, playful, and delighting. I thought of Rose, and all her letters. I thought of her sitting on the edge of the lake, struggling against anger, making the hardest decision of her life.

When the sun was fully up, I left. I took care to lock the church behind me and walked slowly back through the fields, the long weeds alive with wind. I wondered if I could call my experience in the chapel prayer—not a long list of asking, after all, or a rote string of words, but rather a kind of sacred listening. The Impala stood at the entrance, a remnant of a lost time. I drove it back to the house.

No one was up, so I made coffee. When it was late enough I called Blake and told him I needed to see him right away. He was groggy and puzzled and hardly pleased, but he agreed to come. In fact he arrived even before my mother came downstairs, tying her robe tightly at the waist.

"What's going on?" she asked, joining us at the table on the patio. The breeze had picked up, but it was warm. I'd placed smooth stones on my folder of images and letters to hold them in place.

"Beats me," Blake said. He sat back and clasped his hands behind his head. "Lucy made it sound like life or death, though."

"Lucy?" my mother said. "What is it? Are you okay?"

"I'm okay," I said, and finished pouring coffee for us all. It steadied me, doing that ordinary thing. I put the pot down and held the warm cup in my hands. Gray clouds scuttled across the edges of sky, threatening, but still far away.

Then I told them what Art had said in the office at Dream Master. I watched them both as I talked, speaking out of some calm that went so deep it seemed as if I contained a bottomless spring from which it welled up.

They listened. My mother made a teepee of her fingers and pressed them against her lips. I didn't leave anything out. When I got to the part where Art pushed my father, my mother closed her eyes. She didn't move, but tears slid down her face. Blake looked away, gazing out to the lake, choppy and gray in the early morning light.

"Why are you doing this?" he said at last, turning to me, his face unsettled by anger. "Damn it, Lucy, why can't you just leave things alone. You blast in here and you think you know everything. Well, I don't believe for a minute that any of this is true."

My mother wiped her fingertips across her eyes and looked at me.

"Is it?" she said. "Lucy, is it true?"

"It's what Art told me," I said, too stunned to reply to Blake. Whatever I'd expected, it hadn't been their disbelief. I'd never thought to question what Art had said, because his suffering had seemed so real. "Why would I make it up?"

"Big mystery there," Blake said. "Because you don't want to see the land developed. This serves your interests."

"Well, it serves yours to ignore what's right in front of you."

Blake's face tightened, but he didn't reply. I forced myself to take a deep breath, because now I was angry, too, and yet I kept thinking of Rose's words: *Do not act out of anger. Act from love, or not at all.*

"You saw the will," I said to my mother. "You saw the will and asked me not to mention it, I don't know why. But when I did mention it to Art, this is what happened."

I handed the envelope containing the will to Blake, who opened it and read. For several minutes the waves rushing against the shore made the only sound.

"I just wanted to think about it," my mother said. "About what it might mean. Lucy—you don't imagine I knew anything about this?"

She got up and went into the house and came back a moment later with a file.

"Mom," Blake said, looking up from the will. "What are you doing? Look, we still don't know all the facts. We haven't heard anything from Art himself. We only have Lucy's version. Maybe she misheard."

"I did not mishear."

My mother held up her hand to quiet us. She opened the folder.

"This is the contract," she said, pulling out a document. "Art and I have been talking back and forth for years about this house, the land. I've known that he's wanted this, and I've known why. At first I was pretty resistant to the idea, but over the years it came to make more sense to me. I guess as the weight of the house grew and got heavier I started thinking about what it might be like to live in town and not have to listen to its complaints all the time. Then, too, Art has been kind all these years. A real help. I've come to rely on him. Whatever he's done, that's all true."

She flipped to the last page, and I saw that she had signed the contract, and dated it June 25, the day after we'd gone to see the Westrum archives and stopped at Joan Lowry's packed and lonely apartment. Now she ripped this page off and tore it in half, and then again, until it was in tiny pieces. When she opened her hand, the shreds flew across the lawn, some catching against the bushes, others swept by the breeze to the shore, where they were caught and carried off by waves.

"Mom," Blake said.

"I believe Lucy," she said. "Because I remember how things were, and I remember things the two of you will never know. I can see it happening. What Art described—I can see it all. Your father meant to come home that night. He'd had something on his mind for days and he couldn't sleep. The last thing he did was kiss me and say he'd be back soon, and not to worry. But I did."

"What if I don't believe it?" Blake asked.

"Well," my mother said. "You're a grown man. Believe what you like, Blake."

"The will is real," I pointed out. "Even if you don't believe the rest, the will in your hands is real."

"Why don't you talk to Art yourself," my mother suggested. "See what he says."

"He'll just deny it," I said, certain suddenly that this was true. And what proof did I have of all he'd said—nothing but his words in the silence of Dream Master late at night. Nothing at all.

"Maybe."

"Or he'll just say it was an accident."

"If the story is true, it had to be an accident," Blake countered. "Art has his flaws, like anyone, but he's not cold-blooded."

I thought of Yoshi saying, *It's a moral problem, not a legal one.*

"I'm going to tell Iris," I said, folding the will and putting it back into its yellowed envelope. "You do what you have to, but that's what I need to do."

"She'll have to know," my mother agreed.

Blake sat back in the chair and gazed out across the water toward his boat, a muscle working in his cheek.

"This is unbelievable," he said, finally. "Sell or don't sell, Mom. Sell it to Art or to someone else. But this business with the will is just crazy. It's probably invalid, being so old and stuck in a wall, but if it's not, why bring it up? Why should a bunch of strangers end up with the things we've worked for all our lives?"

I left my mother and Blake on the patio. Yoshi was in the kitchen, reading an article on strip-mining in a copy of *Harper's* that he'd bought at the airport, a cup of coffee on the counter.

"How's it going out there?"

"It's okay."

"Really?"

"No, actually. It's terribly tense."

Yoshi nodded. "I'm sorry. Can I help?"

"Not really."

"Okay. Then can I change the subject?"

"Please."

He pulled the laptop across the counter and flipped it open.

"I sent out a bunch of inquiries after we talked about jobs. A few people sent listings in reply. Mostly I don't think they're very interesting, but there are a couple that caught my eye. One in Papua New Guinea, and one in Cambodia."

I scanned through the job descriptions, which were with aid agencies and NGOs.

"They sound interesting," I said. "Hard, but good."

"Different than we're used to. The pay is okay, but they don't have the same benefits, not by a long shot."

"Right now we don't have any benefits at all," I pointed out.

After a second, Yoshi laughed. "True enough," he said. "I wrote back, asking for more information, asking if there were other positions that might be interesting for you."

"Okay. That's good. I'll send some queries, too."

On the patio, my mother and Blake were still deep in conversation. I sighed, and found my phone, not sure if I was doing the right thing but knowing I was doing the only thing I could. Ned answered on the second ring, and seemed surprised to hear from me.

"Is your mother okay?" I asked.

"I think so, yes. She's been absorbed by the letters. We haven't really spoken of them in much detail. She hasn't let anyone else read them, either."

"I wanted to invite her to see the Westrum collection. When she's ready. To invite all of you. And there is a chapel full of windows she ought to see as well."

"Yes. Didn't we discuss all that?"

"We did. I just wanted to confirm." I hesitated. "And something else has come up since," I went on, touching the envelope that held the will. And then I told him, carefully and concisely, everything I knew.

Chapter 21

IN THE TRANQUIL LIGHT OF THE WESTRUM HOUSE, IRIS looked less pale than she had at home, her eyes quick and vibrant. She was wearing a pale blue suit with a dark scarf tucked around her throat, and little pearl clip-on earrings. Her hair had been carefully styled. Ned hovered, helping her down the sidewalk and up the steps, but when we were inside she stepped away from him and went to speak with Oliver, who offered his arm to her in a way that seemed courtly, allowing her to accept his help without feeling dependent. It was thoughtful, and I admired his gesture from across the room. Iris curved her fingers around his elbow as they moved from one window to another, Oliver telling her all about Frank Westrum and the history of the house, his voice booming, using his free hand to gesture. Iris listened, studying the windows. Stuart Minter stood behind the desk; he'd flashed a smile and waved when he saw me come inside, and I took Yoshi over to say hello.

When my mother arrived with Andy a few minutes later, Yoshi and I introduced them to Ned and Carol, and then we stood together in a friendly but uneasy cluster. I'd sent a copy of the will to Ned, who'd told me he intended to consult a lawyer to see what they might do. I'd gone with my mother to a lawyer, too, a friend of Andy's who did estate work and who'd suggested things could potentially be complicated. Still, it wasn't clear what would happen, and we hadn't spoken of the matter to the Stones since I'd made that initial call.

When we finished touring the first floor of the Westrum House, admiring all the windows, Oliver led the way to the stairwell, where the woman in her golden-green dress stood with her arms full of flowers. I hadn't seen the window since I'd discovered the letters Rose had written, since I'd entered into her story and understood my connection to her, and I'd forgotten how captivating the window was, six feet high, the cascading irises in her arms life-sized and vibrant. I stood staring at her image, her familiar eyes. I imagined her posing in a light-filled studio, Frank Westrum sketching the curve of her ear, the elegant line of her neck, pausing for a moment as he was swept through with his love for her, which he could never translate exactly onto paper, or into glass.

"It's beautiful, is it not?" Oliver said when we paused on the landing to admire it. I'd given him copies of some of Rose's letters, finally, and he'd shared some correspondence from Frank to Cornelia that he'd found in his archives. "*She* is beautiful. Mrs. Stone, I think your mother was the model for this portrait. Look at her eyes. And look at what she's holding in her arms—they are irises, Mrs. Stone."

Iris didn't speak, and though we all looked at her, it was impossible to read her expression. She didn't take her gaze from the window for a long time. Finally, she released Oliver's arm and sat down right on the stairs, in the middle of the third step from the bottom.

"Mom?" Ned said.

"I'm all right." She pushed back the sleeve of her suit jacket and held up her wrist. "Ned, Carol. Look at that pendant she's wearing. It matches this bracelet. Ned, you gave this to me a few years ago, do you remember? You told me you'd found it. Where?"

"In the boxes I was going through. I didn't tell you exactly, because they were in a box of things that had been sent to you from Rose when she died. From Frank Westrum, actually, that name is on some of the envelopes, though of course it never meant anything to us, not until now. Dad showed me where it all was. He said you'd wanted to throw it out, but he'd put it away because he thought it might be important someday. You know how he was."

"Yes," she said. "That's the way he was. Did you save the rest?"

Ned nodded. "There are some drawings. There's a piece of stained glass, a field full of blue irises."

"Ned," she said, after a long moment. "Mr. Parrott. I wonder if I could sit here for a while, just by myself. I'd like to do that, if the rest of you don't mind."

So we left her, following Oliver upstairs to a corner room with tall windows on two walls. Oliver had gathered all the stained-glass windows he'd had in storage that contained images related to Rose, and these hung against the clear glass.

The first window I'd seen, the window that had started me on this whole adventurous search, was hanging on the closest wall, backlit. It had been cleaned since I'd seen it in Keegan's studio, then still coated in grime from its years sitting uncovered in the closed-off chapel. It hadn't been included in the original receipt to the church, I'd realized, and I could only conjecture that Frank had made it for Rose, or perhaps at her request, and then couldn't bear to keep it when she'd become so ill. Now its colors were so deep and true and dazzling; the image of the chalice in the bag of grain, the crowded figures of the men and women in the background, were all infused with light.

The interwoven spheres and vines ran along the bottom. I'd done some research, and I'd found this motif everywhere. These overlapping circles were ancient, tracing back to Pythagorean geometry—geometry, a measure of the world. In more mystical terms, the shape had always evoked the place where worlds overlap: dreaming with waking, death with life, the visible with the unseen. Rose had probably glimpsed this pattern in a medieval church and woven it into the blanket for her child.

"What are you thinking about so seriously?" Yoshi asked. He'd gone around the room from window to window, and now he came and stood close.

"Rose," I said. "My great-grandfather's dream. It was always his dream we knew about and not hers, and that's the problem. I think that's what she's saying somehow, in this window. I mean, in a personal sense, not as an interpretation of the text. But in this story, Joseph always has these dreams, right? I looked it up. That's what puts a wall up between him and his brothers to begin with. His arrogance, their envy; that's why they throw him in the pit and sell him into slavery. This cup in the grain, it's the cup he uses later for divination. For dreams. And it's not until he sends that cup off with his brothers—even though it's a trick to get them to come back—that balance is finally restored."

. "Maybe," Yoshi said. "It sounds plausible enough to me."

I thought of Rose, packing the soft blanket to send to a daughter who would never know her, and the chalice slipped beneath her skirt and carried through the night. I looked again at the women in the crowd around the sack of grain. This cup, buried in the grain as surely as Rose's story had been buried in the family narrative, spoke to me.

"There was some good news earlier," Yoshi said after a few minutes, when he judged that I'd finished looking at the windows. "Want to come and see?"

We retreated back down the stairs to the lobby, where we sat side by side on a low bench, going through the e-mails that had come in that morning. Yoshi's contacts in both Papua New Guinea and Cambodia were cautiously optimistic about finding a position for me; they were talking with other agencies to see what was available. I'd sent out queries of my own, and as we waited I checked, shading the screen of my phone against the flickering light that fell in through the trees.

"My friend Alice thinks there might be a position opening in Mali, but it sounds a little too corporate. She gave me the contact name, though."

"That's good. Worth looking into."

"It is. I'll write when we get back."

"I guess we just have to keep looking hard. It may take a while to find what we want."

We sat for half an hour longer, talking quietly about what we hoped would happen, how we might see to the closing up of our place in Japan. I kept thinking of a line from a Mary Oliver poem I'd read: "What is it you plan to do / With your one wild and precious life?" What indeed?

I hadn't seen Iris leave the stairs and go to view the windows upstairs, but she must have, because eventually she came down with Ned, trailed by Oliver and Carol, and my mother and Andy.

"They're going home," my mother said, coming up to talk while Iris paused at the desk to sign the book Stuart was holding out to her. "I think she's very tired. It must just be emotionally exhausting to take all this in."

"It must. Have they said anything about the will?"

My mother glanced across the room. "Actually, yes. They were very nice. They suggest a meeting tomorrow afternoon, in The Lake of Dreams. Their lawyer, my lawyer, Art, and his lawyer. Apparently, secretaries are calling each other even as we speak. They want to move quickly, before the town board meets to issue any zoning changes. I don't know what to expect at all. But it seems they have something to propose." She glanced at her watch, and sighed. "I really need to get back to the bank before lunch. They've been so good to me, I don't want to push my luck."

They were all crossing the room now, Ned on one side of Iris and Carol on the other. When they reached us they paused to say good-bye. Iris touched my hand.

"Thank you," she said. "For finding her. And me."

Since the afternoon was so fine, Yoshi and I didn't go directly back to The Lake of Dreams. I was acutely aware that our days here were beginning to dwindle, and that most of his vacation had been spent dealing with my family issues, past and present, or trying to find another job. Yoshi wasn't the sort of person to complain, or inflict his stress on other people, but I could tell from the way he was sometimes distant and reflective that he had a lot on his mind. So instead of going back to the house, we picked up some sandwiches and drove to a state park near Ithaca that I'd always loved. We hiked along a cascading stream through the gorge, then swam in the pool at its base. It was too cold to swim for long, but we jumped in for as long as we could stand it, then sat on the rocks by the water in the sun.

When we got back to the house that evening, my mother was just getting home from work. Blake was there, too. We saw his truck first, parked at an odd angle in the gravel driveway. I expected to find him in the kitchen, but he wasn't there, and after we called to him a few times, he answered from upstairs, his voice muffled, floating down from his old room, where he was standing amid the dark blue walls with a pile of books in his hands, looking at his posters of the moon, of the beautiful image of the earth from space.

"It's like a cave in here," he noted. "What was I thinking?"

Our mother, walking up behind me, laughed. "You were a teenager," she said. "That's where your mind was. Growing into some new state of being. Look at Zoe. That should remind you."

He shook his head. "I was growing in the dark, I guess. How was the trip?" he asked, putting his books on the desk—even as a teenager, he'd been reading about boats.

"Good," I said.

My mother added, "Yes. It was moving."

Blake nodded but didn't comment. At first I worried that he was still upset about the decision to tell the Stones what we'd discovered, but when he spoke again, he changed the subject. "Well, I stopped by because I have some news."

We went downstairs to the dining room and sat at the big round oak table. I'd polished the wood with lemon oil before Yoshi came, so it gleamed softly in the light from the two high leaded windows.

"So," Blake said. "I talked to Art. It was pretty tense. He didn't confirm or deny, at the end of the day. But I've had some time to think about things. I want you to know that I quit. I left this morning. I cleaned out my desk and left."

"He let you go?" my mother asked. "Just like that?"

"He tried to talk me out of it, but his heart wasn't in it. There was some vandalism on the Fourth of July. I don't know if you heard that. Some damage, things knocked off the shelves, mostly just a dumping of papers. He's still trying to put things in order." Yoshi had discreetly taken a seat in the living room, where he was looking at a magazine; he glanced up at this, our eyes met, and he gave a slight shrug. Blake continued. "He's been going through a lot of old papers and things as a result. I think he's been pretty weighed down by the past, and by worry over how this Landing business is going to turn out. Long story short, no—he didn't have much to say."

"Well, I don't know whether to laugh or cry," my mother, said, holding up her hands. "Both of my grown children are now unemployed."

"What about Avery?" I asked. "Is she okay with this?"

Blake laughed. "Yeah, she's much more okay than I am, actually. She's always been a risk taker, and she figures things will work out. Anyway, I still have my pilot's job," he added. "You know, running the cruises."

"I think Avery's right," I said. Though Yoshi and I were no closer to jobs and had no idea where we'd end up living next, I'd started seeing that the change could be a good one for us both. Plus, not looking to the future so much had made the present moment all the more vivid.

"Glad you've got such a great attitude," Blake said.

I smiled. "Well, both Yoshi and I are unemployed, so to keep myself sane I've decided that worry is a waste of energy. Yoshi's going to make curried noodles for dinner. Want to stay?"

"Sounds good."

We pulled out the Chinese checkers and played until the sun began to set.

The meeting with the lawyers had been set for four o'clock the next afternoon. It didn't end until close to six. My mother pulled into the driveway, gravel popping under her tires. I met her on the back steps.

"Well?" I said. "Blake must have called three times already. What happened?"

"Let's go sit on the patio," she said.

So we did. Yoshi stayed upstairs, working on the job search, while my mother explained what had happened. It seemed the will was valid, and Iris did indeed have a claim on the estate. But so much time had passed that her claim could be challenged, and though the will had been properly signed and notarized, no one knew for certain how it had ended up in the wall. If my grandfather had put it there, it was fraud. If my great-grandfather had done it, it was a change of heart. Iris was aware of all of this. Ned had also done enough research to understand the complexities of what was going on with the depot land, and with Art's desire to buy my mother out and annex this property to lots along the marsh with his upscale development in mind. He knew about the temporary stays on the sales initiated by the Iroquois and by the conservation groups.

"So they came up with a rather amazing plan," my mother said. "They asked that the land remain ours, but that a legal document be drawn up so that it can never be developed. Something like the Forever Farms program—have you heard of that? Their whole family has been involved for years with the Nature Conservancy, and so they know all about this process. If everyone agrees, I can keep this land and this house as long as I want, and then sell it to the conservancy if I ever desire to leave. But I can't sell to anyone else, and I can't develop it myself. Art would have to agree to contribute the adjacent acres he's purchased as well. Essentially, what they're suggesting would preserve the marshes. Your father would have loved that. The white deer would be protected, and all the wildlife, because this would involve quite a lot of acreage. Plus, this plan would allow for Oliver and the church to keep the chapel intact, which they've been lobbying hard to do. The idea is that it would be used for services and weddings and so forth again. It would be preserved and maintained as an artistic heritage site under the auspices of the Westrum Foundation, but independent of both the Westrum House and the conservancy."

"So—that's quite a plan. What's not to like?"

She shook her head. "I don't know. It seems like there must be a catch, but I can't see one, and neither could the lawyer. We're all going to think it over. But I think this deal was offered in goodwill. I think they have no desire to end up in court."

"But why would they do this? I mean, the land is worth a lot of money. I just don't understand why they'd let it go."

My mother shook her head. "I don't know, of course. But Iris is ninety-five years old. She doesn't need the money. Her sons have done very well, and they're both pushing seventy. And after that it starts to become a lot of arguing in court about money that's going to people who have almost no connection to the events that set all this in motion. They'd have made a different decision fifty years ago, I'm sure. But now—now they'd rather have this land given in their name, and ours. It's a beautiful thing to do, if it's real."

It was real, it turned out, and in the end they hammered out a deal. Art was the last to agree, but knowing that he'd lost my mother's land changed his sense of urgency about the remaining lots along the marshes. Plus, though he never acknowledged what he'd told me about the night my father died, I remembered his expression as I left, and I knew it must haunt him still. Perhaps his desire to develop that land in the first place had been an attempt to erase what had happened there. Though he never spoke of it again, I will always believe he signed the papers to assuage his sense of guilt.

In any case, they made the deal. My mother negotiated a sale of her house and land that would allow her a final year to clear things out. The conservancy started talking about converting the house into a nature center. My mother started talking about buying a condo in town.

As for Art and Joey, they made a bid on some of the other, smaller parcels along the lake. I watched, expecting, I suppose, that something would break, and change. That Art would show up one day full of remorse and confess what he'd done. That some kind of great justice would have to prevail, with Dream Master suffering a reversal of fortune, going out of business, or bursting into flames from spontaneous combustion.

None of this happened, of course. Instead, Art started the zoning process right away. His artist's renditions were scaled down and posted on a billboard near the gravel entrance to The Landing. Over the summer, lots sold swiftly for his asking price. By October, his garish machines were stripping topsoil from the earth, tearing out the groves of trees by the shore—oaks and pine, maples and elms, all falling, strewn across the land like the bones of dinosaurs. I glimpsed Art overseeing the construction, his baseball cap pushed back on his head, his large hands planted on his hips, as if nothing had ever happened or gotten in his way.

Other things changed, too. Restorers came and took the stained-glass windows from the chapel for cleaning and repair. We saw the trucks parked in the field, and we went to watch. It was such a delicate operation to remove the windows, which turned out to have been installed in panels. The crew stood on ladders, tapping with their chisels and hammers at the seals between the glass and stone. It made me hold my breath to watch, but they were very good, and one by one the windows came out and were packed carefully away. Oliver estimated that they'd be gone for three months, long enough for him to do enough fund-raising for the grand opening he planned to have. He showed us the mock-up of his brochure, which featured the Wisdom window on the front and included descriptions of all the other windows, too. He'd added a biography of Rose, and he told us that he'd changed all the literature at the Westrum House to reflect her contributions as well.

A few days before we were to leave The Lake of Dreams, Yoshi and I went downtown for one final stroll, and we walked down to the *Fearful Symmetry,* which was docked at the very last slot in the pier. Avery came up right away when I called hello, holding on to the railing with one hand to keep herself steady, carrying a bag full of books in the other. She looked just the same, slender and fit, except for the round swell of the baby.

"Hi there," she said, offering the bag as she reached the deck. "Want any of these? We're cleaning out. Clearing out. I can't wait."

"You're moving?"

"We are. It's so exciting. We just signed a lease for a little house on Orchard Street. It has two bedrooms and a bathroom with retro pink and black tile. It has a little garden in the back. Best of all, it doesn't sway!" She laughed.

"What about the boat?"

"Sold. Signed, sealed, and to be delivered this afternoon. Blake!" she added, turning to shout down the stairs. "Blake, your sister's here. With Yoshi." She waited until he appeared and then looked back at us. "He should tell you himself."

"Tell us what?" I asked, as Blake emerged from the stairwell. "Tell us what?"

"It's sold," he affirmed, running his hand along a railing in a way that let me know the decision hadn't come easily. "We'll be all off-loaded in a couple of hours. Landlubbers," he added, and tried to smile.

"Not exactly," Avery said. "Tell the rest."

"Well, I'm starting a new venture," he said. He gestured across the water to where the cruise boat was docked, people filing on for the early afternoon tour of the lake. "I've been having these conversations off and on for years with Mike Simms—you know he owns that business, right? He's wanted me to come in as a partner, with the thought of buying him out eventually, and I haven't wanted to do it. Didn't want to be tied down at first; didn't want the daily hassles, either. But after I quit at Dream Master, I went to talk to him again. I think we've worked out a deal. It's not just going to be tour cruises anymore. We're going to expand and add a lunch and dinner cruise as well. They do that on some of the other lakes, and it's a good seasonal business. Avery's doing the food," he added, and smiled.

"I needed something a little less twenty-four–seven," she said, ignoring his compliment. "With the baby coming, I've hired a manager for The Green Bean, and another chef, but I didn't want to stop cooking altogether. This seemed like it could work."

Yoshi and I helped them for a while, carrying several boxes down the dock to Blake's truck, driving over to see the new place. It was small and ramshackle, with a 1950s kitchen, but very charming, too, with a wide front porch. When we were done, we walked back downtown to pick up the car and drive back along the lake road.

"Well," Yoshi said, stretching his arms out across the wide front seat. "We have six days left before our flight back to Japan. We have no jobs and limited savings—nothing but our dreams."

"That's right," I said. "Whatever else, we're free."

Epilogue

ON THE NIGHT BEFORE YOSHI AND I LEFT THE LAKE OF Dreams, our last night in the airy darkness of the cupola, I lay awake for a very long time, searching for constellations. Scorpio and Sagittarius were visible; I traced the lines between the stars and wondered, as I often had before, how these intricately imagined characters had ever been assigned to such sketchy patterns in the sky. I wondered how these same stars might look from another perspective—say, from the moon. Next to me, Yoshi slept, his hair dark against the sheets, his breathing steady, and a comfort, like the sound of the waves against the shore. We'd woken weeks ago to the uneasy shifting of the earth, and now we were here, our known universe having altered in ways we never could have imagined.

I watched the stars, fixed and burning in the night.

Was it a dream, what happened next, or a kind of waking vision? Did I sleep? The same patterns of stars were visible, the same curved edge of the moon, but I was standing in the shallow water on the shore, my feet sunk deep into the smooth shale beach, waves splashing my knees and small fish swimming around my ankles. My toes dug deep into the stones, flowing out like roots, and my arms reached like branches to embrace the sky with its scuttling clouds, its beautiful pale round moon. My fingers, far above, fluttered into leaves.

I sat up, exhilarated. The air was soft, and Yoshi's legs were tangled with mine; I eased myself free and climbed across the futon to the window. There was the moon, full and tranquil in the sky, making a path of light across the black expanse of water.

The wind stirred softly. I thought of Rose, of the chalice she'd taken, lost from her things or stolen again or sold and melted for the silver, of her stained-glass windows, her rows of vine-woven moons, and of the people in the Wisdom window, their arms lifted to the sky. I remembered my mother's tulips, radiant, emerging from their leaves, delicate cups swaying on their stems. The singing bowls by my bed in Japan, and a goblet forming, flowerlike, at the end of a fragile glass stem.

I lifted my arms like the people in the window, my legs and torso like a stem, my arms a crescent curve. Male or female, it didn't matter. Then or now, no difference.

I was a tulip, a cup, a calyx.

I was, in that moonlight pouring down, a chalice.

My dream stayed with me in the weeks and months that followed, but I didn't share it with anyone except Yoshi. It seemed best left in metaphor, akin to the herons rising at the edge of the pond. Best left unnamed. I didn't want anyone to laugh at me or raise their skeptical eyebrows or to simply not pay attention. I thought about it, though, every time I saw a flower blooming, a person dancing, or hands cupped to lift water.

Yoshi and I flew back to Japan, taking one train and then another and finally walking down the cobblestone street to our apartment, which was just as we had left it so many weeks before. We cleaned it out entirely, selling our appliances and giving away everything we couldn't ship to our next life in Cambodia. For those were the jobs, finally, that had appealed to us, the jobs we'd been offered and had taken. My father had fought in Vietnam and he'd written about Cambodia in the letters my mother had saved, bound together with a piece of green ribbon. My mother had a photo of him standing in front of the Royal Palace. I didn't know much more than that, but the connection, however tenuous, made the decision to go there feel right. So we packed and cleaned. The earthquakes had eased—the underwater island had finally formed. On our last day there, Mrs. Fujimoro gave me a beautiful silk scarf, and in return I gave her a kaleidoscope made of brass with hundreds of shifting pieces of glass. We bowed to each other in the street.

By mid-October, we'd returned to The Lake of Dreams for a final visit. We sat on the patio, the leaves edged with gold or orange or flaming red against the vivid blue sky, while I unwrapped a box that had arrived, searching through the thick layers of tissue paper to find two small stemmed glasses made of delicate green glass, the sides paper-thin, translucent. Inside the box, a card said, simply: *For Your Wedding, from Keegan and Max.* I handed one to Yoshi, imagining how it had taken form, the glass growing liquid and the cup emerging on the green glass stem—its delicate, human shape.

When Yoshi and I were married, we exchanged these cups in the Japanese tradition. We had the ceremony in the Wisdom chapel, with the Reverend Suzi Wells presiding, our friends and family filling the pews, and the women in the windows all around us, Rose and Frank somehow present, too. Ned read from the Song of Songs, and I asked Zoe, who was staying with my mother while her parents were on a cruise, to read a poem she'd written for us. Zoe had cut her hair short and gotten a tattoo of a little butterfly on her collarbone, all of which made her look younger and more vulnerable than she would ever have intended. Yoshi's parents flew in from Helsinki, and sat next to my mother and Andy. Iris came with Carol and Ned, and Julie brought her boyfriend. Oliver came with his wife, and Stuart Minter brought his partner, Alex. Blake and Avery were there, too, though they sat at the back and didn't stay for the reception; their son had been born just the week before and they were still dazed, still tired, reluctant to leave him. They named him Martin, after our father.

Art and Austen sent a gift—a set of white plates—which I gave to Goodwill, unopened.

After the wedding we lingered outside, the leaves vibrant reds and yellows against the blue autumn sky.

Three days later, we flew to Phnom Penh.

The beauty and the poverty here engulfed us like the heat; we wandered down the sunstruck streets, through market stalls with baskets of bright carrots or greens or whole fish, past the restored colonial buildings and shacks built from thatch and tarps. The scars of the past are visible everywhere, especially on the outskirts of the city—here a blackened stairway that ends in the sky, there a pond, perfectly round, which began as the crater of a bomb. I glimpse this in the faces of people, too, the past jutting like sharp stones into the swift currents of the present, and I am humbled every day by the suffering and the resiliency that I witness.

Yoshi took a job with an NGO that monitors the development of water resources along the Mekong River as it flows from China through Laos, Vietnam, and Cambodia. What happens with these dams will matter to the future of this river and the people who live here for generations, and Yoshi comes home every day full of energy and ideas. My work, too, is good, though my own job came, surprisingly enough, not through any of my former contacts but through Suzi, who knew of an ecumenical group here working to improve the lives of rural women. I travel into the countryside and help set up foot-powered treadle pumps. They are made of bamboo and metal pistons and families take turns running them to collect fresh water from their wells. Everything begins with water. It helps the gardens, and when the families sell their surplus vegetables, they use the money to buy chickens for eggs or a cow for milk or to send their children to school. The program has grown so much that lately my focus is shifting to training others to demonstrate the pumps and travel to the provinces.

We live at the edge of the Mekong, one of the world's great rivers. Every year when the monsoons come, the river fills and presses so hard against the sea that it changes its direction and flows north to flood the Tonle Sap, the great lake that the Cambodians call Creator Lake for its profusion of life. Graceful boats travel across the surface of the water and men lean to cast their nets, fishing. I think of my father, of course, but without the sadness I carried with me for so many years.

The boats are vessels, carrying the fishermen out each dawn. Long and narrow, they curve at the ends, arced like crescent moons. The heart is a vessel, too, pulsing blood in its orbit through the body, and in English the word *to bless* comes from the Old English *blestian,* or "blood." The challenges in this place are real and sometimes very difficult, but I've learned to slow down and look for beauty in my days, for the mysteries and blessings woven into everything, into the very words we speak. I stand each morning at the edge of the balcony and watch the boats skim across the water. I feel the blood beating through my veins— vessels, too.

I listen. Not to locks anymore, but past the stillness to the deepest longings of what the mystics would call my true self, something I have come to understand as prayer. This is Rose's greatest legacy to me. Her cloth hangs in our house, against the painted concrete wall; Iris gave it to us as a wedding present. Last year, during the slow, hot season and then the sudden time of rains, as I grew as round as one of Rose Jarrett's interlocking moons, as I swelled like the river beyond our little house, I thought of Rose so often. When our daughter was born at the end of the cool season, we named her Hannah, after no one at all, though it's true that we got the idea from the Japanese word *hanashobu,* which is a kind of iris that grows in marshy land. It's true, also, that we sometimes call her Hannah Rose.

A few months after she was born, we had a lunar eclipse. Yoshi and I sat all evening on the balcony to watch the great pale moon rising over the river, a shadow falling over its edge, slowly eroding its light. I thought of Joseph Jarrett, waking from his dream to the light of the comet, and of Rose, walking home alone through the vineyards on that same night, more alive and terrified than she had ever felt before.

Near the end of the eclipse Hannah stirred from her sleep. Yoshi went inside to get her, moving through the rooms, talking to her softly. Then he brought her out to the balcony. "Look," we said to her that night. "Sweet girl, look, the moon." She saw it, emerging slowly from the mouth of the shadow, and laughed, reaching for the sky as babies will, as if she could grasp the moon in one small hand and slip it into her mouth like a wafer.

She laughed again when she couldn't catch it, and reached higher, and we held her up. This would not last, of course. Soon, she'd be frustrated or hungry and we'd go inside, leaving the night sky with its burning stars. But for that moment the river flowed like black glass and we stood gazing at the wild, pale beauty of the moon, waiting to see how the world would shift, and change.

THE JARRETT FAMILY

Joseph Arthur Jarrett   m.   Cora Evanston
(1894–1970)   (1887–1958)

Joseph Arthur Jarrett II   m.   Rachel
(1925–1972)   1951

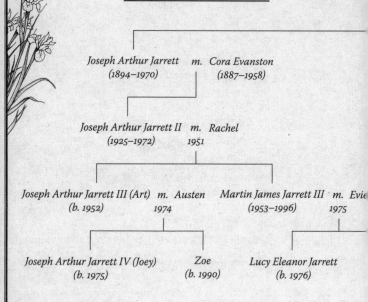

Joseph Arthur Jarrett III (Art)   m.   Austen   Martin James Jarrett III   m.   Evie
(b. 1952)   1974   (1953–1996)   1975

Joseph Arthur Jarrett IV (Joey)   Zoe   Lucy Eleanor Jarrett
(b. 1975)   (b. 1990)   (b. 1976)

THE WESTRUM FAMILY

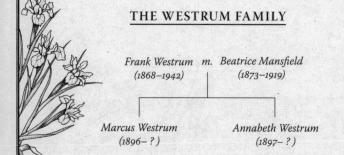

Frank Westrum   m.   Beatrice Mansfield
(1868–1942)   (1873–1919)

Marcus Westrum   Annabeth Westrum
(1896– ?)   (1897– ?)

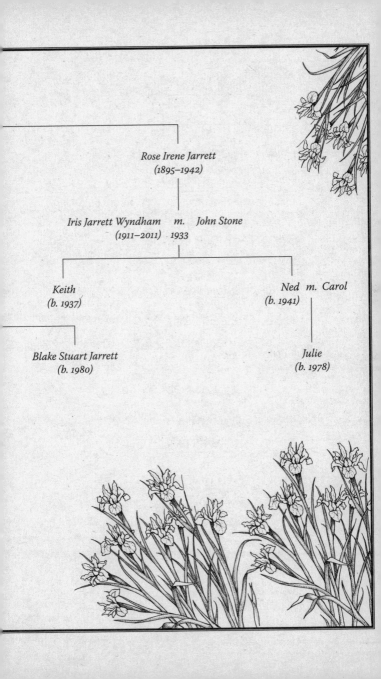

Rose Irene Jarrett
(1895–1942)

Iris Jarrett Wyndham   *m.*   John Stone
(1911–2011)   1933

Keith
(b. 1937)

Ned   *m.*   Carol
(b. 1941)

Blake Stuart Jarrett
(b. 1980)

Julie
(b. 1978)

Acknowledgments

THE LAKE OF DREAMS IS FICTIONAL, AS ARE ITS INHABITANTS, and exists only in the realm of the imagination. However, in writing this novel I drew deeply on my extensive experiences in the spectacular Finger Lakes region of upstate New York, an area rich in history and beauty. The Women's Rights National Historical Park in Seneca Falls is real, of course, and I am grateful to the archivists there who spoke with me at length about their work.

Writing is such a solitary pursuit, and I am forever thankful for the patience and support of friends, colleagues, and family as I secluded myself with this book. Special thanks to Tom for so generously sharing his many gifts and talents, and for being so steady in chaotic times; warm thanks also to Abby and Naomi. My thanks to Edna Gordon for kind hospitality and fascinating insights on the Somerset Levels, and to my friends at the University of Kentucky, especially to Gurney Norman for his long support of writers and writing.

Geri Thoma is insightful, warm, and wise, and no one could have a better agent. My thanks to her, and to everyone at the Markson Thoma Agency.

The people at Viking Penguin bring terrific expertise and talent to every facet of publishing, and I am grateful to them all, especially to

Kathryn Court and Clare Ferraro. First and last, I thank Pamela Dorman, a gifted editor, whose belief in my work made this book possible. Molly Stern's smart, insightful editorial suggestions strengthened this story in ways large and small. Beena Kamlani brought a very keen and sensitive eye to the editing. Liz Van Hoose gave the final draft a crucial reading, and Kendra Harpster nurtured this book as it grew to completion. Thanks also to Stephen Morrison, as well as to Dick Heffernan and Norman Lidofsky and their fantastic sales teams. Paul Buckley and Carla Bolte created the beautiful jacket and book design. Shannon Twomey, Nancy Sheppard, Rachelle Andujar, Andrew Duncan, Leigh Butler, Valentina Price, Hal Fessenden, John Fagan, Maureen Donnelly, and Julie Miesionczek all gave their talents to help bring this book into the world, and I thank them.

I extend my thanks to the community at The Lexington Theological Seminary, where I've taken several classes, as well as to the clergy at Good Shepherd Episcopal Church, who generously answered many questions. Thanks also to my spiritual direction group for thought-provoking discussions, candor, and much laughter. Finally, I am grateful to many authors over many years for their brilliant, perspective-shifting books, especially *The Dream of the Earth* by Thomas Berry, *In Memory of Her* by Elisabeth Fiorenza, *Women, Earth, and Creator Spirit* by Elizabeth A. Johnson, and *The Silent Cry: Mysticism and Resistance* by Dorothy Soelle.

KIM EDWARDS

THE MEMORY KEEPER'S DAUGHTER

'Crafted with language so lovely you have to reread the passages just to be captivated all over again' Jodi Picoult

It should have been an ordinary birth, the start of an ordinary happy family. But the night Dr David Henry delivers his wife's twins is a night that will haunt five lives for ever.

For though David's son is a healthy boy, his daughter has Down's syndrome. And, in a shocking act of betrayal whose consequences only time will reveal, he tells his wife their daughter died while secretly entrusting her care to a nurse.

As grief quietly tears apart David's family, so a little girl must make her own way in the world as best she can.

'*The Memory Keeper's Daughter* is an enthralling novel about the deepest secrets that can never stay hidden' *Easy Living*

'Deeply moving. Kim Edward's intricate descriptions and beautiful use of language make this a mesmerising read' *Woman*

'An enthralling tale that will keep you page-turning until well past bedtime. A truly riveting read' *She*

He just wanted a decent book to read ...

Not too much to ask, is it? It was in 1935 when Allen Lane, Managing Director of Bodley Head Publishers, stood on a platform at Exeter railway station looking for something good to read on his journey back to London. His choice was limited to popular magazines and poor-quality paperbacks – the same choice faced every day by the vast majority of readers, few of whom could afford hardbacks. Lane's disappointment and subsequent anger at the range of books generally available led him to found a company – and change the world.

'We believed in the existence in this country of a vast reading public for intelligent books at a low price, and staked everything on it'
Sir Allen Lane, 1902–1970, founder of Penguin Books

The quality paperback had arrived – and not just in bookshops. Lane was adamant that his Penguins should appear in chain stores and tobacconists, and should cost no more than a packet of cigarettes.

Reading habits (and cigarette prices) have changed since 1935, but Penguin still believes in publishing the best books for everybody to enjoy. We still believe that good design costs no more than bad design, and we still believe that quality books published passionately and responsibly make the world a better place.

So wherever you see the little bird – whether it's on a piece of prize-winning literary fiction or a celebrity autobiography, political tour de force or historical masterpiece, a serial-killer thriller, reference book, world classic or a piece of pure escapism – you can bet that it represents the very best that the genre has to offer.

Whatever you like to read – trust Penguin.